Lizzie

Lizzie

Dorothy Shawhan

LONGSTREET PRESS, INC.
Atlanta, Georgia

For Jessie and Judge Lucy

Published by
LONGSTREET PRESS, INC.
A subsidiary of Cox Newspapers,
A subsidiary of Cox Enterprises, Inc.
2140 Newmarket Parkway
Suite 118
Marietta, GA 30067

Printed in the United States of America

1st printing 1995

Library of Congress Catalog Card Number: 95-77241

ISBN 1-56352-227- 6

Book design by Gary G. Pulliam
Jacket design and illustration by Honi Werner, with illustration derived from a detail of "Lady in White" (c. 1913), by Thomas Dewing

The writing of this book was supported by a grant from the Mississippi Arts Commission and by Delta State University.

Lizzie

BOLIVAR LANDING — Graveside services were held at Memorial Cemetery today for Elizabeth Marshall Dunbar, 66. She was a resident of Whitfield.

Born in Holly Springs, MS, in 1902, Dunbar lived in Bolivar Landing from 1920 to 1939. From 1922 to 1928, she edited and published a newspaper for women.

Dunbar was preceded in death by her father, former governor Stephen A. Dunbar, and her mother, Miranda Marshall Dunbar. She leaves no survivors.

The Antique Shop

Cavanaugh Antiques is in one of Bolivar Landing's oldest buildings, a cavernous brick building with a tin roof that extends out over the sidewalk. It had once housed cotton brokers in the first half of the century when gins stood at either end of Main Street and ran all day and all night during the fall picking and white gold floated in the air so thickly that it was hard to breathe. Even now Mr. Cavanaugh on an occasional trip into the bowels of the building will find a forgotten cotton sample, the fibers black with dirt, the brown paper around it honeycombed with tracks of silverfish. What lives turned on the price this brought per pound, he wonders. What fates hung?

Mr. Cavanaugh's mind works like that, and so the antique business is ideal for him. If only that chifferobe could talk, he thinks, we'd hear some stories. But since it can't, he makes them up. That is, he makes some of them up and the rest he actually hears as truth from people who sell him things. He has reached the place where he doesn't know the difference in fact and his own fancy, but he doesn't think that matters. What matters is that people hear a story. On that he can oblige. He has lived all his seventy years in this place, seen with a keen eye the coming and the going, the living and the dying, heard with sharp ears the talking and the silences, too. He is a living chronicle, a free trip to the past for anybody with time to spare.

Now at the sound of the tin cowbell on the front door, he looks around from behind his roll-top desk to see who's there. He has his desk positioned like this on purpose, far in the back of the store, so he can see customers, size them up, before they see him. His line of vision cuts across the tops of walnut tables crowded with cut glass and odd pieces of Haviland china. He knows the young woman standing tentatively at the door in jeans and tennis shoes and a blues festival T-shirt, though she doesn't know him. He wonders that she's gone out shopping dressed like that. He knows she and her husband, Charles Able, a native of Bolivar Landing, have moved here from Indiana and that her husband is taking over the family's plantation after his father died. He knows that she wants to furnish the Victorian gingerbread cottage they're restoring on Main Street. He watches her silently over the tops of his half-lenses, always perched on the tip of his nose.

"Anybody here?" she calls in a crisp Yankee way, accustoming her eyes to the gloom and getting her bearings. Then she sees a brass candlestick that attracts her, and she walks briskly toward it, picks it up, feels the heft, checks the bottom for a price. "Reasonable," she says aloud and puts it down. Then to her right she sees the Dunbar desk. She catches her breath slightly and moves slowly toward it. Mr. Cavanaugh watches her face through the massive gilt-framed mirror that hangs near the desk. He admires the way her sun-streaked hair sweeps behind her near-perfect ears, the way tiny gold rings pierce them.

"Gorgeous," she whispers and strokes the silky cherry wood with a smooth, young hand. Her wedding band reflects golden in the shiny wood, her eyes shine. Mr. Cavanaugh knows she is imagining it in her living room, herself writing invitations to dinner parties. It is an old plantation desk, with glass doors for bookshelves at the top and a writing surface that folds up and locks with a brass key. She turns the key and slowly lowers the desk top to reveal a series of pigeon holes and tiny drawers and secret compartments. "Lovely," she says. Mr. Cavanaugh decides it is time to make his move.

"Young lady," he booms, starting toward her, "I see you have an eye for quality."

Startled, she turns quickly in his direction, then smiles when she sees him. "This is a wonderful desk," she says, her hand still caressing the desk top.

"Yes," he says. "Governor Dunbar's desk. His second wife died two months ago, and I bought this at the estate sale."

"Who was Governor Dunbar?" she asks, not up on her Mississippi history.

"A famous son," he said. "Governor, lawyer, cotton speculator, one of the wealthiest men in the state before the crash." Even without the history, he knows she is hooked.

She raises the desk top back up and turns the key. Then her eyes travel down the row of small drawers at the bottom half of the desk, and her face registers dismay. A gaping hole like a missing tooth in an otherwise perfect smile glares at her. "Oh, no!" she says. "A drawer missing. I didn't see that."

Mr. Cavanaugh had anticipated that the missing drawer would be a problem. It enabled him to get the desk at half its market value, but now the flaw is his.

"Actually," he says, "the story of that missing drawer should increase the value of the desk, if anything."

She looks at him skeptically. "Oh?" she says.

"Yes. Actually, it's a very sad story."

"Well?" she says, a little impatiently, looking at her watch.

"Governor Dunbar had a mad, loose daughter," Mr. Cavanaugh says, coming to the point quicker than he would have liked. "One day she was angry at him about something, probably because he had lost his money and couldn't give her all she wanted anymore. Wellsir, whatever it was, Lizzie, that was her name, Lizzie jerked that drawer out of his desk and threw it across the room so hard that it splintered. Cherry wood and all, it didn't make any difference, it just collapsed like a handful of pick-up-sticks."

"My goodness," she says, putting her hand in the empty space, "a mad, loose daughter."

"I remember her, " Mr. Cavanaugh says. "I could tell stories that'd make your hair stand on end." He pauses, expectantly. She is running her hands over the desk as possessively as a lover, opening each drawer. If she thinks he is letting this desk go without a word, she is sadly mistaken. "When I was a boy, she had a dress shop in town, and the teenagers gathered there after school. She laughed and joked with us. She treated us like we were grown up and gave us Coca-Cola. She was fun to be around. She was a little chunky by then and had dyed her hair red, but she had the prettiest eyes and hands, I'll never forget."

"Hmmm," Mrs. Able said, preoccupied with her exploration of the desk.

"She had been a belle in her day," Mr. Cavanaugh went on, "though wilder than most, probably. The old folks always said she knew how to have a good time."

"Nothing wrong with that, is there?"

"Oh, of course not," Mr. Cavanaugh answers, feeling somehow attacked. "But she had a reputation. After the dress shop closed, she ran a boarding house for the levee men, here in the thirties, you know, building the levee. A single woman that way, taking in a dozen men or so—people talked about her. A lot of them thought she wasn't exactly what she ought to be. It was like a honky-tonk there at the governor's fine house. Governor Dunbar had moved to Jackson by then and left her with it. Always loud music and carrying on over there at night." He couldn't tell if Mrs. Able was paying any attention or not. She was going over every inch of the desk again, opening each drawer like she was looking for something.

"Then, of course, after the fire they sent her away."

"What?" the young woman says sharply, looking up into his face.

"Oh, yes," Mr. Cavanaugh replies, relishing the moment. "Some said she set it on purpose for the insurance, but I doubt it, because why would you go crazy afterward if you did it on purpose? Anyway, after the governor's house burned, she was quite mad, they said. They had to take her to Whitfield."

"Convenient, I suppose, to be rid of such a woman."

Mr. Cavanaugh stares at his customer blankly. He doesn't know what she was implying, but he doesn't like it. He continues as if she hasn't spoken. "This desk escaped because Governor Dunbar had taken it to Jackson with him, but many family heirlooms went up in smoke."

"Did she have property?" the young woman asks him.

Mr. Cavanaugh is happy for her interest, but he can't tell what she is driving at. "Some land, I believe, yes, I think maybe some cotton land. At one time her father was the wealthiest man in the state, before the Great Depression. . . .

"Well, I don't really know," Mr. Cavanaugh says finally, puzzled by this line of questioning and unsettled by a faint memory of some talk from the past when he was a young man and Lizzie Dunbar was freshly sent away. A question had floated around town then for a time, a question never answered. How had Millard Trapp wound up with Lizzie Dunbar's property? Wasn't there some protection for the property of one sent off to the asylum? Of course, Trapp had been the governor's law partner, so it must be all right. But some had wondered.

"As Peter Farb says, sometimes when people are declared insane or evil, especially minority people like women, it's just a sign that their property is up for grabs."

Who in the hell is Peter Farb, Mr. Cavanaugh wonders. And what is the woman getting at? He does not like the turn this conversation is taking.

"My dear, clearly you are not from the South," Mr. Cavanaugh says. "We take care of our own down here."

The young woman smiles, wickedly, Mr. Cavanaugh thinks. "I'm sure you do," she says. Then turning her attention back to the desk, she asks, "Do you think my computer would fit here?" Mr. Cavanaugh freezes. The idea!

"If that's what you want, you'd do better at Wal-Mart," he says frostily.

Mrs. Able knows she has said the wrong thing. "It's just

that I'm a historian, and this desk makes me feel like writing somehow." Mr. Cavanaugh's jaw muscles relax at this. He has a soft spot for historians, being something of an amateur one himself. He almost knows what she means. But she would do better to get herself a fountain pen and some high-quality paper.

Suddenly Mrs. Able opens her purse and takes out her checkbook. "I'll give you $1,500," she says. Mr. Cavanaugh is so surprised at her decisiveness that he almost forgets to play his game, but he recovers in time.

"My dear young lady," he says, "for the very desk of Governor Dunbar?"

"Take it or leave it," she says briskly, already putting the checkbook back. "No denying that missing drawer."

"Well, since I know your husband and his family, have known the Ables for years, I guess I'll let you have it."

She smiles in a knowing way as she writes out her check and hands it to him. The name on the check says Jane MacAuley, no Able to it. Mr. Cavanaugh is confused. "I thought you were Charles Able's wife."

"I am," she says lightly, "but I'm Jane MacAuley, too."

This is going to be hell on genealogists someday, Mr. Cavanaugh thinks. He does not approve of this at all. What will they call the children, poor little things?

Now that the desk is hers, Jane MacAuley seems much more relaxed. She continues to poke around the shelves and is almost chatty, telling Mr. Cavanaugh that she will be teaching at the college in the fall, that she misses southern Indiana with its rolling hills, that the Delta is the flattest place she thinks she ever saw.

Then as she is pressing on the back of one of the bookshelves, a panel of wood slides slightly to the right. She pushes it and it continues to slide, revealing a small compartment. On the secret shelf sits a perfect row of little red books. In harmony, she and Mr. Cavanaugh sigh an "Oh," and stand in awe. Then she reaches in and pulls one out. It has

"Lizzie Dunbar" on the flyleaf in a child's large round hand. The year is 1909.

"Her diaries," Jane says, breathless with discovery. Mr. Cavanaugh is sick at heart. He stares at the check in his hand and wishes more than anything that he could turn back the clock on this deal. He knew the whole thing happened too fast. What he wouldn't give to add those little books to his personal stash of papers gleaned from old desks.

"Primary sources," Jane says, carefully turning the brown pages. "These may tell us a great deal about child-rearing practices and social constructs in Mississippi at that time."

Mr. Cavanaugh doesn't know about all that. What he's thinking is that here are some early stories straight from the pen of the mad, loose daughter, stories he will never read. He is so obviously dejected that Jane, even in her excitement, notices. "I'll turn them over to the state Archives, of course; I won't keep them." This information is no comfort to Mr. Cavanaugh, who makes it his business to keep papers away from the Archives. Once they disappear down in Jackson, it takes an act of God to get at them again.

"Listen to this—'Miss Meems let me help her sort pamphlets for her suffrage meeting in Greenville. They were all different colors. Kate and I worked all afternoon. We couldn't make out some of the hard words in the titles, but we could put them together by the colors.' Isn't that remarkable?"

Mr. Cavanaugh wants to tear up that check, run Jane MacAuley out of the store, and retreat to the back with those little books. Instead he calls Booker to come and work out the details of delivering the desk to the Able place on Main. He is gloomy the rest of the day. Rather than being happy to have doubled his money, he feels bested and like he has suffered a loss.

Miranda Dunbar
1902

I could hear the doctor and Stephen talking in the next room. They thought I was unconscious, but my mind was lucid, clear enough to know that blood was gushing, my body drained and light as a reed on the bed. I focused my eyes on the window where red streaks bled across the morning sky. No one had thought to pull the curtains through the hard night.

I concentrated on the light, and then on a bird, an ordinary gray bird, that soared and dipped back and forth across my vision in an ecstasy of life. I envied the bird, and then unaccountably I became her, diving down to peck a worm from his cold earthen house. The worm struggled, his body stretched taut before he snapped out of the ground. My babies are dead in the nest, and so I swallowed the worm myself. Then refreshed, I flew back to the dogwood tree by the window, cocked my head, looked inside with my right eye. A large woman crouched at the end of the bed, head down, crying. She was holding the feet of a pale young woman, scarcely twenty, covered with a white sheet.

Two men entered the room. One was young and harried, the other gray and kindly. The young one carried a newborn baby wrapped like a large caterpillar in cotton flannel. He held it awkwardly, not cradled, but with stiff arms held out from his body.

"Genesis," called the young man, and the large woman raised her head. The face was black and streaked with water. "This is Elizabeth Dunbar." He laid the caterpillar in her lap as if offering a sacrifice. "Find a woman to nurse her. Miranda is too sick."

"Where the other?" the black woman said.

"There was no other," the young man said sharply. He clenched his hands around the bedpost to stop their trembling. His face was pale and sweating. The one he called Genesis looked up at him, startled. "Do you hear me?" he said angrily, reading her look. *"No other."*

"Stephen," said the gray man gently, taking his arm. "Don't."

"Miranda mustn't know," the young man pleaded, his anger gone. "She couldn't bear it." He took the young woman's limp hand. "Oh, God, she's so cold."

The gray man pushed Stephen aside and took her wrist. Then he reached for the other wrist and then he felt her throat.

I wanted to fly into the sunrise. I had lost interest in this scene. I spread my wings to test my strength.

"Quick, Genesis," the young man said, frantic now. "Give me the baby." He seized the cocoon and placed it face down on the woman's breast.

A soft weight pressed my heart, a sweet stirring at my neck. My daughter yawned and sighed, and I could not leave her. The miracle of it—a yawn, a perfect pink tongue that will someday repeat words I teach her and tell me her secrets. She opened her eyes, blue and smooth as a robin's eggs, and looked at me with interest. I wasn't lonely now. I would stay.

"Miranda!" Stephen was speaking loudly and crying. "Darling, this is your daughter. This is Lizzie."

I smiled and asked no questions.

Stephen Dunbar
1902

Nothing, nothing I have done deserves this. If it is a message from God, then he has failed because I will not accept it, I did nothing to deserve it, a just God would not send this upon his children. Unspeakable, grotesque beyond imagining, even the doctor—who has seen everything, must have seen the worst that nature can do in forty years of practice—even he gasps, but recovers, quickly recovers, and says, "A boy." Then, "Dead. I'm sorry, Stephen."

Dead. I am weak with relief. Then the rest is up to me, and I will cancel it out. I can do that, thankfully, I can do that and I will. Nothingness, return to nothing, this body will return to water and then to nothing, nothing that has to do with me, this has nothing to do with me.

"Stephen!" The doctor's arm is around me. "Sit and put your head between your knees. Your second baby is coming now. Don't faint on me, Stephen."

I tremble with disgust and nausea. What God could imagine this process, the blood and pain, the horror, the death of it, death, this is worse than, death is sleep and nothingness but this is filth, humiliation, grief. Generation from the place of excretion perverse God who designed this. Woman, the essence of, after Eden, sin must be sin only sin could manifest in such a shape, but not mine not my sin, I did nothing. I must not faint, I will not, blood I could never stand the sight of I will concentrate, focus, I must move quickly I will act I will not be defeated I can act quickly I must while the doctor is while

Genesis is before Miranda is conscious then it will be over. It
will be over then as if Never as if Before cancelled out and past
time, time will be before.

Quickly in a torn sheet as if a dead dog that must be
disposed of before it rots and stinks before Miranda knows I
wrap it shroud it wind it tightly. They do not notice me they
are too busy with Miranda. "Jesus, oh, Jesus," Genesis is praying
she is mouthing empty words to an absent God. Anger now
fury at her praying at the idiocy. No God will make this right
can right this only I only I can and I will I will do this.

I am out of the house now the body is warm still but not a
body really not human just cells a hideous mistake a cosmic
joke somewhere a god is laughing thinks he will humiliate stop
me but No. I am running now down the path to the pond.
Roosters crow as if the day is any day a normal day crowing as
if it is yesterday before the birth when we were fools
anticipating, eager for the babies twins magical twins Miranda
said they are special a special gift our gift. I stop in the ring of
pines that surround the pond the cows are here they are here
before me knee deep in water drinking the cows are watching
silent they chew and watch stoic and silent in the pond to drink.
They must not see I wade into the water and shout at them
they are startled, but do not go far they watch amused, chewing
their cuds, amused at the wild man with the swaddled bundle,
which is not my son, this is not my son. I run at them and they
move then they back onto the bank still watching. I imagine
they find It and drag It to the house a trophy and everyone
would know then how deep is the pond is it deep enough to
hold this nothing is deep enough bricks bricks would do a stone
large stone yes a stone I see a stone on the bank half buried in
the dirt I wade from the water freezing cold. The rock is solid
and smooth heavy as a tombstone fit for a burial but not really
burial but cancellation, correction. I tie the stone to the bundle
with the ends of the sheet. I walk into the water until it reaches
my neck and then I want to keep walking I want to hold to the

stone and keep walking until first mouth then nose then eyes are under and then nothing and peace and death and I have feared death above everything but now so easy but No not defeat not death but baptism yes a baptismal a new life after this life I am changed I can never again I let go the burden sinks easily in the muddy water down out of sight gone now all traces gone.

I am trembling violently I cannot control I stumble to the bank and fall the sun then blood red the sun is rising. I exult and shake my fist at the sky.

Miranda
1903

A year and a half since Lizzie's birth and still Stephen and I are not together again as man and wife. I think there is something wrong with this, but I don't know. I don't know if this is normal or not, and I don't know whom to ask. It is not a subject I can discuss, especially not with Stephen.

When Lizzie was born, he moved into the bedroom next to mine, and he has stayed there. I have wanted many nights to go in and lie down beside him, but wouldn't he ask me if he wanted me to? What if he asked me to leave? I couldn't bear that. Better to live like a nun forever. But then what if he hesitates because Lizzie is in my room, and he thinks he can't come to me there, or that I won't leave Lizzie? Maybe I am not warm enough. Maybe he thinks I rather not. Many women are that way, so I've heard. Maybe he has someone else, as many men do, they say. But that's intolerable to think. I don't know, I don't know. All I know is my own heart and that I miss him. He is distant since Lizzie came, not just physically but in other ways, too.

I would like another child, and I did tell him that, though it took me days to find the courage, and I blushed and stammered like a schoolgirl. He said the doctor said I shouldn't, that I am not strong enough, but I feel fine. He wants me to go to Jackson and see a specialist. He says I must concentrate on taking care of Lizzie and not think of another one. Maybe I am ill and don't recognize it. Maybe the doctor in Jackson can tell me.

One Sunday afternoon when I was more depressed than

usual, I decided to go down to the little house and see if I could talk to Mother. I didn't really imagine that I could because we had never discussed such subjects before. Some subjects don't bear discussion, she says, and this, undoubtedly, is one of them, but I felt desperate this particular day. Stephen was closed up in his study, and Genesis had Lizzie with her picking up pecans in the grove. We had been to church together as usual, Stephen, Lizzie, and I. Mother does not go. Ever since Daddy died she does not go.

I was in my room alone where I had been reading since Sunday dinner. Late afternoon shadows filled the room, and the clock downstairs in the hall struck four. I looked up from my book and around at the room I had had since I was born with the pink roses on the wallpaper and the oak mantelpiece filled with photographs of generations, and I thought how I love this house and how in all my lifetime here I have never felt such loneliness and misery as now. I closed my book, stood up, and looked in the mirror of my dressing table. Dark circles hung under my eyes, and I looked older by a good ten years than I remembered from the last time I looked.

I walked out my door and down the hall to Stephen's study. The door was closed. I raised my hand to knock, but couldn't. He would look at me in the new way, as if I were a stranger, he would hold me at bay with his eyes, with the way he held his body, and I could not face him now. I turned and walked to the stairway, the bannister smooth and cool beneath my hand, where Leroy and I slid the curving way to the bottom every morning at breakfast time. At the window on the landing, I stopped and looked out over the pasture to Mother's house, the little dogtrot house with a tin roof where her people built when they came to Mississippi in 1842. They had prospered and before the War built the big house. The little one had been used for the tenants until Daddy died, and Mother moved down there. We assured her there was plenty of room with us, this house has sixteen rooms, but she said she prefers solitude.

I walked down the rest of the stairs and through the wide hall to the front door. As I opened it, bright yellow leaves from the maple tree blew in and swirled around me, and they were so beautiful scattered on the hardwood floor that for a moment the heaviness lifted and I forgot. I wanted to write a poem, for a brief minute, a poem about the fall and leaves on the hardwood floor. But the moment passed, and I walked on, past the front-porch swing, down the brick steps, and around the east side of the house to the path that cuts through the apple orchard to Mother's house and on through the pasture to Genesis'. The branches were heavy with fruit, and the cidery smell of fermenting apples hung in the air.

When I was down the hill, I looked back at the big old house I loved, the brick chimneys at either end of it, the solidness and stability of it, the long shadows it cast in the last rays of the October sun, and I wondered if any of the generations of women who had lived there had been as miserable as I. I stood and looked at it long and hard as if I might see a sign from one of them as to how to go on, but I saw nothing.

A thin blue curl of smoke came from Mother's chimney, and I found her in front of the first fire of fall knitting a Christmas sweater for Lizzie. We sat, not saying much, her needles clicking, the fire crackling, the mantel clock ticking the melancholy afternoon away. Finally the weight on my heart seemed to push words out. "How long after I was born did you and Daddy . . . come together again?" I blurted.

Mother looked up startled and dropped a stitch. "Good heavens, Miranda, what a personal question."

"I'm sorry," I said. I could feel my face burning. "Stephen hasn't . . . not since Lizzie. Is that normal?"

"Who knows what's normal," she said. "But you had better be glad of it. You almost died with Lizzie."

"But isn't the first one like that? Doesn't it get easier?"

"It's never easy. It's always a walk through the shadow. Let me tell you a story that I've told you before, but now that you've had a child you will hear it in a new way.

"My people came here from the Carolinas in the 1840s, came in a wagon, my Grandmother and Grandfather Monts with two little ones and a third on the way. My grandmother was twenty years old. They tied up the horses to that oak tree you can see turning gold outside the window and camped here until they got this house built. Their third child, my mother, was born in the wagon with no doctor in sight. Nine more children were born after that, roughly one a year, the births stopped only by my grandmother's death at the age of thirty-two. She was used up, an old woman, teeth gone and hair white."

She picked up her knitting and began again as if the question were answered.

"But this is the twentieth century," I said. "Aren't there ways, I've read of ways . . ."

"The only sure way is the one Stephen's chosen," she said. "It's to his credit that he's protecting you."

"I don't feel protected. I feel rejected."

"You shouldn't, dear. You should feel honored."

"Honored? He hardly looks at me anymore."

"Men are weak that way," she said. "He knows if he gets close things will happen."

"Surely you don't mean he'll live the rest of his life celibate."

She stopped knitting and looked at me. "Of course not," she said, "you couldn't expect that, but that will not affect your happiness if you're sensible. You have Lizzie, a good living, the house, the servants. Be thankful that he's a considerate man."

"What you suggest is intolerable," I said, in tears.

"The alternative is worse," she said. "A husband who won't let you alone. You'll see I'm right. Give it time. You'll become friends, companions, spiritual partners. You'll be free, darling."

"Free?"

"From a most unpleasant duty. Think of it as one less thing you have to do."

Genesis
1903

"Do it for Miranda," he say, hands tight around my throat. Whiskey breath hot in my face. Teeth and eyes shining in the dark like a cat. Nightmare, I think, heart racing, racing that's all. Wake up in a minute, be all right. Wake up, see Jessie Lee home beside me. This ain't really happen, ain't really happen, Lord, Lord.

"She can't," he say.

I try to move out from under him. "No."

"Yes," he say, wrap his legs around me, move one hand up my gown.

"Keep it in the family," he says. Can't breathe, can't breathe, can't think where we, why, wake up now, wake up be home.

Then Lizzie cry out from the crib, and I remember I awake now know Miranda gone to the doctor in Jackson I awake now I know know why I on the pallet sleeping know why now take care the baby while Miranda gone.

"She wants you to wants you to, what difference, how can it hurt, she can't, she's sick, she can't, she doesn't want to either, she doesn't like it, hear, she said get Genesis to, get her to do it no one will know. I rather Genesis do it with you she said that would be good get Genesis to do it."

I crying now, moaning no no no no.

"Hold still, you got to hold still, wait, wait, you're moving too much, damn you, I can't, wait, you'll like it, it's the idea you don't like, the idea of you instead of Miranda, but in the overall scheme it's all the same, it's your job, part of your job you'll like it I promise, if you don't we won't ever again but try and see just this once."

Miranda didn't say it I'm thinking no, Miranda doesn't want this. I heard of this happen in other houses but not me never thought me not Mr. Stephen so stiff so distant never look my way.

"You read the Bible," he say, "don't you read the Bible? They do it all the time in the Bible, the maids and the masters, God told them. Sarah wanted Abraham to wanted him to do it with Hagar, don't you remember, God wanted them to, why not you? You don't mean no, you don't really, you want this too, I can tell you do."

Lizzie scream out now, and I throw him off me I'm strong I throw him over on his back on the floor. He drunk and stunned lay there on his back in his drawers and undershirt. I jump up grab Lizzie. I run out the door down the stairs to the front hall and walk the floor singing walk the floor singing to Lizzie he won't touch me holding Lizzie singing to Lizzie till the sun come up. Feel safe when the sun stream in those little windows all around the front door.

Hear him upstairs moving around, hear him in the bathroom running water. Lizzie sleeping and I'm holding her still walking up and down the hall. Then after while here he come down the stairs, shirt, tie, vest, coat, hair slicked back, he look through me like I'm a thing, like last night never was, he say cold, "I want my breakfast right away."

"Yessir," I say. "Yessir, I'm coming."

Stephen
1905

Sometimes I think the child is bewitched, maybe by the bizarre circumstances of her birth, maybe by the fact that she spent her first few months with the servants so the women could nurse her. Miranda was too sick to nurse her and was quite unreasonable and cried because she could not have the baby. Before long her milk dried up, and she never mentioned it again. But it may have been at this point that Miranda lost control of Lizzie.

Lizzie is a sprite-like creature who moves quicker than the eye. One minute she is riding the horsey on your knee, but the next she has vanished. If she doesn't get her way, she holds her breath until she falls over unconscious. I was sure Miranda was exaggerating when she first told me of this. But a few minutes ago, I saw for myself. I was here at my desk, opening the morning's mail with a heavy, daggerlike letter opener, a wedding present from Spain. Lizzie was at my feet, playing with her doll, alternately kissing it and beating it with her hairbrush. When the sun caught the gold of the letter opener, she raised her head suddenly, then flew into my lap reaching for it. Of course I refused, explaining how dangerous it was, how she could put her eye out with it, or fall on it and run herself through. I might as well have been speaking to a stone. She began to scream and sob inconsolably, fighting like a she-bear to get possession of the dagger. Then when she saw it was no use, she folded like a rag doll and lay lifeless on my chest. I screamed for Miranda and ran with the child to the kitchen and ran cold water on her.

"This will not do, Miranda," I told my wife, once the child was conscious and looking at me strangely with those smokey blue unchildlike eyes. "Lizzie is completely undisciplined. She is out of control."

Miranda looked away from me, an annoying habit she has developed when I try to speak to her. "Come to Mama, Liz," she said, holding out her arms.

"No!" she cried, holding to me with a death grip. "No. I want my daddy."

Miranda stepped back, flinching as if she had been slapped, her empty arms falling to her sides. Lizzie gave me a look that in someone older could be interpreted as conspiratorial. I felt angry with them both, at Miranda for being so passive, for letting this headstrong child get the better of her, and at Lizzie for her willfulness.

"Take her to her room," I said to Miranda, prying Lizzie's arms from around my neck and handing her over. As Miranda left with her, the child was reaching toward me and shrieking as if she were being offered up as a human sacrifice.

I have no idea how to be both mother and father to a daughter, but it is clear that I had better learn. Miranda is not the woman I married. Doctors can find nothing physically wrong with her, but she has changed. Since Lizzie's birth, she has shown no interest in me whatsoever, in my career, my hopes and dreams for the future. Instead of being grateful to me for sparing her the pain of more children, and I'm sure she understands that, I believe she despises me for it. Lizzie is her only joy now; she looks only at Lizzie with eyes of love.

I had thought to leave Lizzie's instruction primarily to my wife, as is natural in most families, but now I think I must take charge of my child's education.

Genesis
1906

I don't know what we gonna do with Lizzie. Trouble follow her around. She don't miss nothing with them bright little eyes, reading already and trying to write. Sit up at the table drawing and putting words in these little red books Miranda bought her in Jackson. Say she gonna write me in there. I was finishing up the dinner today when she come down to the kitchen. She was climbing around on the kitchen stool, sitting astraddle it, laying on her stomach on it, watching me.

"Why you getting so fat, Genesis?" she say. Four years old and talking as plain as a grown person.

"I eats my greens and cornbread," I say. "If you would you'd grow slick and fat, too."

"Greens are nasty," she say. "They're just weeds cooked up."

"They good for you," I say. "Make you tough."

"Is that greens in there?" she say, patting my stomach, seven months gone.

"Chile, you better get out of my kitchen," I say. "Get on in the dining room."

"I asked Mama what you had in there."

"What she say?"

"Said she hadn't noticed, but maybe you swallowed a watermelon seed. Is that what happened to you, Genesis?"

"I ain't studying you."

"How you'll get it out is what I wonder," she say. "It's a big one."

"See can you take these biscuits to the table without

dropping 'em," I say, trying not to laugh. She run with the biscuits and in a minute here she come back, busting through the swinging door.

"I swallowed one," she say.

"Biscuit?" I say. "Ruin your dinner."

"A watermelon seed, silly," she say. "Yesterday. I love watermelon. I want to grow one, too."

That tickle me so bad I don't know what to do, but I don't want her to see me laughing. "Get my spitting can out the pantry," I say. "I gots to spit." I turn my back laughing fit to kill, and she run for the can. Come back and hands it to me. I don't look her in the face. Had I would have noticed and stopped what come next. Miss Miranda come through the door about that time and say Mr. Stephen coming up the walk.

"Everything about ready, Genesis?" she say. "He said he'd be in a hurry today to get back to the office." Lizzie run out to meet him, and me and Miss Miranda get ice in the glasses for the tea and take up the rice and gravy and chicken and put it all on the table. Then we hear him coming through the house fast, calling me and Miranda. Sound mad enough to die. We runs to the hall, and here he come carrying Lizzie.

"Two grown women in the house," he say. "Two goddamned adults and look at this child." Lizzie look down at us like she can't wait to see what gonna happen. She have a big dip of snuff under her lower lip. She must have got it when I sent her to the pantry. Brown juice running out the corners of her mouth and all down the front of her white smock. Tears starting out her eyes, too, because the tobacco must of burned her, but she too hardheaded to let on.

"I can't be two places at once," Mr. Stephen say. "Either I make the living, or I stay home and raise the child. What will it be?"

"Lizzie, what on earth?" Miss Miranda say.

"You, Genesis," he say. "Snuff is a filthy habit, and I don't want to see it in my house again. Miranda, clean her up. We'll talk about this later." He set Lizzie down, and Miranda take her hand and lead her off to the bathroom.

He good and stirred up, red in the face and breathing fast, but he go on in the dining room and sit down, not saying a word. I pour the tea, and pass him what he can't reach. Then I stand there to see if he need anything else.

"Biscuits are cold," he say finally.

"Some more on the stove," I say. "I'll get 'em."

"Don't bother," he say. "They're no better hot." I don't say nothing. I know my biscuits good.

"Well," he say finally. "What are you staring at? Why don't you get back to the kitchen?" I start to go, but then he look at me like it the first time he seen me in years. "Who's the father?" he say.

That ain't none of his business, but I don't say that. Don't say nothing.

"Answer me," he say. "Whose is it?" Still I don't say nothing. Then he fold up his napkin careful and tuck it in under his plate. He stand up. His face is sweating now. Veins standing out in his neck. He talk like he having to strain to keep from screaming. "I asked you a question, you black bitch," he say.

"I don't know," I say, scared now. I wouldn't tell him now if he beat me.

"Whore," he say. "Morals of a goat. And you're raising my daughter. Isn't that a good one?" Then he start in making a sound that I guess you would call a laugh, but ain't like no laugh I ever heard. No joy in it.

Miss Miranda and Lizzie come back then. Lizzie shining like a little angel, like she couldn't cause no trouble if she wanted to. They sit down to the table, and I go back to the kitchen, thanking God I don't have to stay in that room.

Miranda
1906

The winter is the coldest on record in Holly Springs. Ice crystals make patterns on the insides of the windows during the night when the fires smolder low in the fireplaces. Outside the snow transforms our town into another world. Icicles grow from the eaves of the houses almost to the ground. Snow-quiet holds us timeless. Nothing stirs but the moon.

I woke last night suddenly, alarmed, and threw back the quilts and down comforter. At first I thought I was frightened by a dream, but the cold of the hardwood floor against my bare feet shocked me awake, and I knew a force more powerful than dream had pulled me from my warm bed. Lizzie. Lizzie. Something wrong. My heart pounded her name in my ears as I fumbled for my robe and slippers. I did not want to wake Stephen in the next room, he does so hate to be awakened, and so I slipped past his door to Lizzie's room. Her door stood open. The moonlight shown through the icy window onto her little white canopy bed—empty.

She often walks in her sleep, but usually comes to my room. She climbs in bed with me and doesn't remember how she got there the next day. I began calling her softly, "Lizzie, Lizzie." I quietly opened the door to Stephen's room, but she was not there. I ran through the house like a shadow calling, but she was nowhere. When I reached the kitchen, I stepped into snow. The back door stood open and snow had drifted all the way in to the stove. I ran out into the yard and whirled around like a madwoman in the moonlight, too terrified to scream for my lost child. Then I saw a tiny footprint in the snow, and another and another. I followed them past the henhouse and past the stable where the horses huddled.

I felt alive in every nerve as though I could see through the snowdrifts and would know if Lizzie were there. I felt I could hear the horses breathing in their stalls, the feathers of the chickens settling on their roosts, the spiders in the eaves of the henhouse spinning webs of ice.

I walked down through the orchard, past Mother's house, quiet and dark, and across the pasture. I was almost to Genesis' house when I saw her. She stood in her long white nightgown like a snow child in a circle of light that fell from a coal oil lamp in Genesis' window. Her breath hung in white clouds around her. She was intent on the lighted window. I ran toward her calling, shivering now with the bitter cold, close enough to see frost forming on her black curly hair. She turned and looked at me, her eyes glittering, and turned back to the window.

Then an unearthly scream split the air and made the hair on the back of my neck rise and freeze there. Lizzie flew to me, and I caught her in my arms. "Genesis," she said. "Something is happening to her."

The baby. Of course. I ran around to the door, carrying Lizzie, not stopping to think about the effects on one so young and impressionable. My only thought then was for Genesis. The door was unlocked and so we walked in and saw Clytee, the midwife, and several other women, neighbors. As the warmth of the room surrounded us, we began to shake, realizing how cold we had been. Our toes and fingers hurt so much as they warmed that Lizzie began to cry. "Hold your hands over the fire," I told her, positioning her by the fireplace. "How is Genesis?" I asked as I joined the circle around the bed. Genesis lay like a figure on a sarcophagus. Her long, still body dwarfed the narrow bed.

"Baby don't want to come," Clytee said. "Don't come soon, she can't last."

"Oh, God," I said. "We ought to have the doctor. Why didn't you come for me?"

"She say not to," Roberta said.

I took Genesis' hand. It was ice. Her mouth was bloody where she had bitten her tongue and lips. Her face was swollen and distorted. "Genesis, can you hear me?" Her eyelids fluttered.

"It almost here," Clytee said. "Another push or two. But she wore out."

"Genesis," I said bending down over her. "Listen. You can't quit now. Please. I'm going for the doctor."

"Won't do no good, but go ahead if you want to," Clytee said.

I turned to go, but in that lightning way of Lizzie's, she had vanished from the fire and materialized across the room, perched at the head of the bed. She put her mouth close to Genesis' ear and said, "Can I have the watermelon? I want to cut it in the snow." Genesis opened her eyes and looked at Lizzie. Then she *laughed*, a deep belly laugh as only Genesis can give. In a rush of blood and water, the laugh flung the baby into the world, straight into Clytee's capable hands. In their circle around the bed, the women linked their arms together, swaying and singing a welcome to the girl child. Clytee cut the cord and washed the baby and put her in Genesis' arms.

"Sistine," Genesis said. "Her name Sistine."

Lizzie watched in a spell, stiller than I have ever seen her. She took the baby's hand and counted on its fingers, "Five," she said in wonder. "So tiny."

"You were once that small," I told her. "Genesis gave you your first bath."

"Did I come out of Daddy's tummy?" she asked.

"No," I said.

"Genesis'?"

"No, mine. I'm your mother, Lizzie. That's what being a mother means."

"Oh," she said, almost as if she were disappointed.

She was quiet as we hurried home through the cold moonlight, but as we reached our kitchen door she said, "That was not a watermelon. You and Genesis lied."

This morning the weather inside the house is as severe as that outside. The town is closed down, and Stephen is not going to the office. We are trapped here together in a cage of ice. Lizzie explained the whole birth scene in lurid detail at the breakfast table. Stephen told her that was not a nice subject for little girls and that she should forget about it and never talk of it again. He has a weak stomach and couldn't eat his fried eggs. He is furious at me for allowing her to be there, and of course I shouldn't have. She has asked me a million questions about that night and even drew pictures of it in her diary, which I hid for fear Stephen would see it. I can never seem to do anything right where Lizzie is concerned.

Stephen
1906

"We always locked the doors at night," I told Miranda.

"We never did," she said.

"This is the twentieth century," I said. "You have got to start locking the doors."

"The keys are lost," she said.

"It is possible to buy new locks and keys," I said. "People do it every day."

"Daddy always said in case of fire we could get out quicker without locks."

"With all due respect," I said, "how long can it take to turn a key?"

"I never liked a locked door," she said. "Locked doors are so . . . cold. They're insulting to the neighbors."

"That's crazy," I said. "Suppose thieves come."

"They never have," she said. "My people have lived in this house over fifty years and no thieves have come yet."

"Luck," I said. "Your folks had it and mine didn't. You like to remind me of that, don't you?"

"I didn't mean that," she said.

"Probably not," I said. "You meant to remind me that this is not my house."

"Stephen, *no*," she said. "Why do our conversations always turn out this way?"

"What way?"

"Wrong."

"You tell me why," I said. "I would like to know."

"I don't know. We can't talk anymore."

"I can talk," I said. "And I can tell you that if the door had been locked, Lizzie could not have gotten out. What if she had frozen to death? Doesn't that matter to you?"

"I wish her bed were still in my room," she said. "I would hear her if she got up."

"She's too old to be sleeping with her mother. I thought we had been through all that. You would keep her an infant forever if it were up to you, Miranda." She said nothing. She looked far off into the distance as if I weren't even there. "And the psychological damage, too, did you not think of that?"

"What?" she said.

"A child as young as Lizzie watching a baby born. That's enough to traumatize her the rest of her life." This seemed to get through to Miranda. Her face was stricken.

"Do you think so?"

"I think it's quite possible," I said. "Freud believes, and so do I, that the experiences of childhood form the direction for the rest of one's life."

"But children used to see such things, didn't they? Pioneer children? I mean, it is a natural process, a part of life. My great-grandfather delivered his little sister because the others had gone to—"

"I don't want to hear that," I said. "It's a bloody mess. Nothing to expose a young child to, especially a girl."

"Of course you're right," she said, and started up the stairs. "I'll see about new locks," she called back. "I'll do it when the ice melts."

The smallest change requires a struggle. If Miranda had her way, we would be frozen forever in some lost past that never existed except in her imagination.

Meems Clark
1907

Today I had to send her home. I have never had that experience before, a child I couldn't control. With five children of my own and their playmates coming and going, I am used to a house and yard full of children, but not like this one. She is both precocious and reckless, a spoiled only child with a dreamy mother and an ambitious father, and the mix is not good.

For Katie's sake I have tried to put up with her. Katie loves her more than she does her own brothers, I do believe. She thinks Lizzie is the cleverest, funniest creature alive. Poor Kate has always been so sickly that I've kept her with me all the time, taken her to my suffrage meetings and temperance meetings until she's like a little old woman in many ways. She can sit for hours in her starched pinafores listening to speeches, her thin hands clasped in her lap. While this pleases me on the one hand, because I see a bright future for her and because I have such a sense of having shaped her, yet on the other I worry that she is missing an important part of childhood. At first I thought a friendship with a child like Lizzie would do her worlds of good.

When they were as young as two years old, Miranda and I would sometimes meet on the sidewalk, strolling the little girls. The children would look at each other with pure delight, laugh and crow and without language clearly communicate in some basic way. Their natural affinity has continued, and I have encouraged it. I had hoped that their friendship could temper the extremes in each other. That Kate could soak up some of

Lizzie's high spirits and funlovingness; that Lizzie in turn could learn some of Kate's thoughtfulness and love of order. Instead, they seem to exaggerate the opposite qualities in each other. As Kate becomes more serious, Lizzie pushes her recklessness to the limits.

We have had scrapes before, times when I have had to lecture the girls. Once I had worked all morning on a chocolate cake for the literary circle. It stood three layers high, with the rich chocolate frosting swirled around it. I left the house to cut roses for the table, and when I got back and glanced in the pantry, there sat the poor cake, naked as it had been two hours before. Every bit of the icing was stripped from it, so skillfully that hardly a crumb of the cake was disturbed. The guilty knife was resting on the cake stand. What seems funny now was not at the time. Furious, I went to look for the boys, but they were not to be found. Then I climbed the stairs, fuming, and found the little girls in Kate's room playing with the cat. Lizzie had a chocolate smudge on the end of her nose, Kate had chocolate-frosted bangs, and even Koca, our white cat, was happily smeared with evidence.

Kate immediately burst into tears, but Lizzie looked at me boldly. "My beautiful cake is ruined, girls," I said. "I could cry. You knew I was making it for my meeting."

"Ladies don't like icing anyway," Lizzie said, tossing her long braids of hair back over her shoulders. "They mostly eat the cake part."

"Is that right?" I said. "That is new information to me."

"We're sorry, Mama," Kate sobbed.

"I don't know what to do with you girls," I said.

"You could make more icing," Lizzie said. "We didn't lick the cake. We used the knife." She said this as if she were offering reasonable options to an unreasonable child.

"I will decide what to do with the cake," I said sharply, wanting to see more remorse instead of a legalistic defense. "My question is how to punish you."

"Punish?" Lizzie said in amazement. "I skin the cakes at home all the time and nobody cares."

"Indeed," I said. "Well, you had better not skin any more here, young lady, or I will skin you. Now wash that chocolate off yourselves and come downstairs with me. I have a chore for you."

So I put them on the back porch to crack pecans and pick the meat from the shells, but of course that was more of a mess and trouble for me than it was a punishment for them. The cake episode was one of many creative and irritating disturbances that Lizzie has brought to our house, but the case today was dangerous and so of a different nature altogether.

My only material legacy from my father is locked in a desk drawer in the library. Nestled in an ebony box are two dueling pistols with long brutal barrels and cherry-wood handles inlaid with mother-of-pearl. My father was the editor of a small weekly paper. He was a man of courage and principle, but he was also a man of his place and time—the South and Reconstruction and the code duello. The life of a country editor as Mark Twain pictures it is not much exaggerated. We lived with death threats, cross burnings, hate mail, a wide variety of harassments. He never left the house without a gun, and we lost track of the number of times he fought in duels, except for the last fatal one. The fact that duels are outlawed now, that men go to the courts for satisfaction instead of to the dueling grounds, gives me hope for the human race's ability to progress. I refuse to accept that wars are inevitable. I have to believe, as a woman with sons, that differences on a global scale can be settled in ways other than killing.

At any rate, I kept the guns. I hardly know why. I had not even thought about them in years. They were securely locked away from the children, or so I thought. But today Kate and Lizzie with their insatiable curiosity found the necessary keys, unlocked the desk, unlocked the wooden box, and aged me a good twenty years. John was a part of their scheme, too. The older boys, who tease him unmercifully, had slipped away without him, and he was home with the girls.

I was in my study, really a large closet with a window on the second floor, writing out an agenda for a meeting later in the week, when I heard Kate racing up the stairs calling me. Her cry was almost hysterical, quite unlike her ordinarily, and I got up at once to see what was the matter. I met her at the door of the study. Her little face was paler than usual. "Don't tell Lizzie and John I came," she cried. "They'll say I'm a big baby. But go quick, Mama. They're in the orchard."

"What are they doing?" I asked.

"Just go see about them, " Kate said, not wanting to be a tattletale. She was literally wringing her hands and hopping first on one foot, then the other. "Please, Mama. Go in a hurry."

I was halfway down the stairs when I heard a gunshot, but still I didn't make any connection with it and the children. Kate gave a piercing yell behind me, though, and began to cry and scream, "They're dead. They're dead, and it's my fault." She sank down on the stairs with her face in her hands. I ran then as fast as I could, down the stairs and out the back door, tripping, holding up my skirts, not able to imagine what was happening but sick with dread.

"Lizzie! John!" I was screaming. When I reached the orchard, I saw Lizzie under an apple tree, picking herself up off the ground. The exquisite hand-smocked pinafore that Miranda had made was torn and grass stained. Her left hand seemed to be bleeding. John ran toward her and was trying to help her brush the dirt away. Relief and anger hit me full force at the same time.

"Elizabeth Dunbar, John Clark, what are you doing?" I called as I started toward them. Getting nearer, I saw the dueling pistol, slightly blackened, lying a few feet away. "Are you hurt?"

She looked up at me defiantly as I came closer. "Those guns are no good," she said. "You ought not to have them around."

"I don't have them around for five-year-old girls, you

ridiculous child," I said.

"I wanted to shoot an apple," she said. "I could do it, too, with a good gun that didn't knock me down." Whether the target apple was on John's head or still on the tree, I didn't have the heart to ask.

"You could kill yourself," I said, wanting to shake her teeth out. "Or Kate or John. What were you thinking?" She stood there looking at me silently, cradling her bleeding hand. Her curly hair had escaped from her braids and made a dark halo around her face. She can be the most angelic-looking child when she needs to. "Let me see your hand," I said, and she put it out for me. A powder burn had taken a bit of skin off, but the wound did not appear serious.

John stood with his head hanging, scuffing his bare toe on a tree root, trying to be invisible. "You, John," I said turning to him. "You were the oldest one here and should have stopped this nonsense. I am disappointed in you, John."

"The guns was Lizzie's idea," he said.

"I don't want to hear it," I said. "You are all responsible."

So I took them to the house to clean Lizzie up and put a bandage on her hand. I lectured them severely and knew I had to do something to make them realize the seriousness of what they had done. When Lizzie was at last washed and bandaged and in one of Kate's clean pinafores, I told her I was sending her home and that she and Kate would not be able to play together for a long, long time.

"Oh, please don't do that, Miss Meems," she said, bursting into tears and throwing her arms around my knees, her round rosy cheek pressed to me fiercely. "I love you and Kate. Please don't send me away." This was the first time I had ever seen her cry.

Kate cried, too, but John said, "Good. Girls don't do nothing but cause trouble."

"Double negative," I said. "Furthermore, in my experience, boys and girls share equally in the trouble-causing department."

I stood firm in sending her home, but I'm sure her banishment won't last long. I talked to Stephen and Miranda, too, for all the good that did. Stephen, though he didn't admit it, was secretly pleased I believe at Lizzie's "spunk." He doesn't like me either and probably thought I exaggerated. Miranda was upset but didn't know what to do about it. "I can't do anything with the child," she kept murmuring. "Not a thing."

I don't know who deserves the most sympathy in this situation.

Genesis
1908

Prayer meeting. He look like prayer meeting. Couldn't imagine when he come down to the kitchen, told me that. "Bring the child, too," he say, "every morning at seven, right before breakfast."

How's I'm supposed to be setting there praying and getting hot biscuits out the oven at the same time? He can't stand no cold biscuit, have to be hot enough to melt the butter fast. So he start off the day mad about them biscuits when it's his own doing only he ain't figured that out.

Take more than praying to raise that Lizzie, if that what he have in mind. I don't know what gonna become of that child. She ain't afraid of the Old Scratch. Yesterday I found her clean up in the top of the big sycamore tree behind the woodshed. "What you doing up there girl?" I holler.

"Planning a treehouse," she call down. "I'm going to build one up here so me and Sissy can play."

"Ain't taking my baby up no tree," I say. "You better come down from there before you break your neck."

"You worry too much, Genesis," she say. I can't hardly see her, she so high up, swaying in the tip top. Make me feel weak in the knees to look up.

"Come down from there right now," I say, "don't I'm gonna call your mama."

"She can't do anything with me," she say. She right about that, too, but I can't say so to her.

"Come down," I say, "and we'll see can we find some

teacakes." That usually work and this time it do, too. She come swinging down the tree like a monkey.

When she gets both her little bare feets on the ground I say, "If you's mine I'd take a switch to you."

"But I'm not, Genesis," she say. "So you have to feed me teacakes like you promised."

This morning Mr. Stephen he have her reading the Scripture and saying a prayer. Reads good and ain't been to school yet. And when she set in to praying she tickled me so bad I didn't know what to do. "Lord, God," she start out, like a preacher, and then she pray for everything on the place from Mr. Stephen clean down to the stray cat that hangs around the woodshed. Pray that her mama won't be scared of snakes no more and that I will get patience. Bless the breakfast and all the plants and animals that had to die so we could eat them. I thought she wasn't never gonna stop, and Mr. Stephen thought so, too. I looked up once and seen him frowning. Biscuits sho weren't fit to eat this morning.

Don't know what's back of this prayer business. Maybe he feeling guilty about some certain things, which he ought to. But why he have to drag all us into it? He could git up, pray hisself, see would it do any good. Stead of that he have to make everybody miserable. Guess he want people saying, "Sho a good man. Have a prayer ever morning with the whole house."

The Antique Shop

Mr. Cavanaugh was reading the *Bolivar Herald-Tocsin* after supper when he saw the article. "Hot damn!" he said aloud, though nobody was around to hear. Mrs. Cavanaugh had gone to a baby shower at the church. "What in the hell . . . ?"

The young woman who had bought Governor Dunbar's desk had gotten her picture in the paper. She was nicely dressed in a skirt and blouse, not like when she came into the antique shop. She was teaching a new course at the college, and the picture showed her at a table with two students. She was holding what looked like one of Lizzie Dunbar's little books, and the students had their notebooks open and pens ready. The thought of the hidden books caused Mr. Cavanaugh to suffer loss all over again. Students and teacher seemed to be having a discussion in the picture, but Mr. Cavanaugh knew how that went. The photographer from the paper had said, "Try to look natural like you're having a class," and so they had posed like this. No telling what they were really saying.

What stopped Mr. Cavanaugh, though, was the course she was teaching: Women's Studies. He had never heard of such a thing. Who thought that up? In the history department, too. He couldn't imagine that Dr. Frye would put up with it.

Professor Frye's chairmanship dated back to the time when Mr. Cavanaugh had been a student, and Professor Frye brooked no nonsense. He was steeped in the classics; he manned the canons of Western Civilization ferociously. Mr. Cavanaugh had majored in business himself, being of a practical turn of mind and knowing he had to make a living, but history was his love, and he had taken every history course he could as electives.

Now he took pride in being thought of as the local historian. He gave Professor Frye a lot of credit; he knew firsthand the rigors of a Frye course. For one test he learned ten pages of important dates about the Civil War and Reconstruction from memory. He wouldn't have dared not. In those days, students worked for grades. You knew you had had a course after one of Professor Frye's. Students who survived remembered his terror tactics with a mixture of admiration and pride.

Mr. Cavanaugh sighed deeply over the erosion of education today. Professor Frye must have lost his bite. That's all Mr. Cavanaugh could figure. If he were at himself, a course like Women's Studies with a HIS prefix would be unthinkable.

What would they read in there? Or do? They can study women until the cows come home and won't know any more than when they started. Nobody can figure out women. He read the accompanying article, but it was annoyingly unenlightening. A quotation from Dr. Jane MacAuley about "uncovering the history of half the human race" and taking an "interdisciplinary" approach, but nothing Mr. Cavanaugh could get sense out of.

Mrs. Cavanaugh came through the door at 9:45 P.M. "I'm back," she called and hung her coat in the hall closet. She walked into the living room rubbing her hands together. "Cold," she said, stepping onto the floor furnace, the heat billowing her skirt with warm air around her so that she looked like a little setting hen. "What's it supposed to do tonight?"

Mr. Cavanaugh turned to the weather page. "Possible heavy frost," he read. "Low 20s in the North, 30 South."

"Oh, no!" said Mrs. Cavanaugh, rushing back to the closet for her coat. "We've got to cover that camellia on the north side. It's in full bud."

Mr. Cavanaugh groaned. "I've already got my shoes off," he said. "Call Andy." Andy was their grandson who lived across the street.

"Clovis Cavanaugh, would you call that child out in this cold to do your work?"

"Yes," he said. "He owes me $10."

"I think it's terrible to teach him to bet," she said. "You never give him decent odds either. You set him up."

Mr. Cavanaugh chuckled. "Better learn from me than somebody else." Then he had a sudden fit of coughing. "Damn bronchitis. Can't shake it."

"Come on, Clovis," Mrs. Cavanaugh said, unimpressed. "Move."

He began pulling on his shoes and grumbling. How would Dr. MacAuley suggest dealing with a wife who values her bushes over the health of her husband?

After they had wrestled the blue plastic tarp over the camellia bush and were settled back in the living room, Mr. Cavanaugh in his armchair with the paper and Mrs. Cavanaugh on the couch watching the ten o'clock news, Mr. Cavanaugh had an idea. Ever since the youngest child left, Mrs. Cavanaugh had been threatening to go back out to the college and take something. Maybe he could get her to take HIS274 Introductory Women's Studies. He watched her watch the news and thought about it. Attractive woman, Mrs. Cavanaugh, pleasingly plump, well groomed, hair not even completely gray yet, skin rosy, the same dimple in her chin as when she was a teenager. An excellent cook and homemaker. Not extravagant. Tolerant of his eccentricities. Fanatical only on the subject of camellias. Only bad habit—bridge. In short, a good wife. Did he really want to send this excellent woman off to study God knows what kind of propaganda? On the other hand, the course was offered by the history department. How subversive could it be?

"A course out at the college you might want to take," he said during the commercial. "Little Yankee woman teaching it, one that bought the Dunbar desk."

"What's the name of it?"

"Well, let's see. Hmmm. Introductory Women's Studies."

"Good Lord," Mrs. Cavanaugh said. "If there's one thing I know about it's women. Three sisters, three daughters. Why do you think I'd be interested in that?"

"Oh, I dunno. New history course."

"No thank you. I want to take something fun. Ceramics maybe. I think I'd like to make pretty pots."

"I'm curious about this course."

"I'm not taking a course to satisfy your curiosity."

"Please," he said.

"Clovis," she said in surprise, "are you serious?"

"Yes," he said. "I want you to."

"When does it meet?"

"At 1:40 Tuesdays and Thursdays."

"Thursday is bridge."

"Oh, that's right." Mr. Cavanaugh's disappointment was visible.

The weather came on, and so they stopped talking to watch. Mrs. Cavanaugh cast a sidewise glance at Mr. Cavanaugh's unmistakably cloudy face. She couldn't think what had gotten into him. Clovis seldom asked her outright to do anything. She did plenty, waited on him hand and foot in fact, but not because he asked her to. They had a pretty good understanding all in all. But this was new.

"Thursday's been bridge for thirty years," she said.

"I know."

"Why don't you take the course yourself?"

"You know I can't leave the shop that much," he said.

They sat in glum silence. The sports were over, and *The Tonight Show* had come on. Mrs. Cavanaugh felt guilty and didn't know why. Mr. Cavanaugh felt disappointed. She got up finally to go to bed.

"Maybe I can work something out," she said. "I'll see." She kissed him lightly on the top of the head and left him smiling in his chair.

Lizzie Dunbar
1909

I wish Kate could come to school. Miss Meems says maybe next year. She says Kate's health is not good enough now. She says school might make her sick. School makes me sick. I told Daddy that, and he laughed. Then I asked him if Miss Meems could teach me, too. His face frowned all over. He said absolutely not. He said he would teach me anything I didn't learn in school. He said we would have lessons every night after supper.

School would be much funner with Kate in it. The girls are silly. They giggle and won't do anything. At recess they sit under a tree and make chains out of clover. Why would they want to do that? Clover withers up in no time. I rather play ball, and sometimes the boys will let me. I play better than most of them, though. When I do something good they get mad and won't let me play anymore.

The two things I hate most about school are sitting still and Stuffy Flannigan who is a bully. He is fat and he has long, stringy hair and he stinks. Every day he pulls my pigtails hard. Today the teacher, Miss Reed, saw him. She told me I could pull his hair back. I didn't want to touch his hair, though. I took my handkerchief and put it over my hand and pulled his hair with that. Everybody in the class laughed, and Stuffy turned real red. He said, "You think you're smart, don't you? I'm gon teach you a lesson you ain't gon never fergit."

"Don't say 'ain't,'" I said. "That's not a word."

Then he made a fist and probably would have hit me, except

Miss Reed was watching. "Smart aleck," he whispered. "Spoiled rich brat. I'll show you ain't."

After school he tried to catch me, but I ran all the way home. He will never catch me. I can run much faster than Stuffy Flannigan.

"Are we rich?" I asked them at supper.

"Precious, did you wash your hands?" Mama said.

"Miranda, you're interrupting a conversation," Daddy said. "I wish you wouldn't do that."

I went to the bathroom and washed my hands because I had forgotten to. Then I went back to the table and said, "Stuffy Flannigan called me rich."

"Compared to white trash like the Flannigans, I suppose we are," Daddy said.

"So we're rich?" I asked him.

"I didn't say that," Daddy said. "Don't ever say that to anybody. It's nobody's business what we have."

"We're rich or we're not," I said. "If we're rich, I'd like to know it."

"We are not rich," Mama said very softly from her side of the table.

"And you think that's my fault, don't you?" Daddy said, putting down his fork and pushing back his plate. "As hard as I work."

"I never meant—" Mama started.

"Oh, no," Daddy said. "You never do." Then he got up from the table. His plate was still full. "This food is not fit to eat," he said. "Lizzie, when you finish, come into the library." Then he walked out.

Mama watched him go. A tear ran over her nose and dripped into her mashed potatoes. Mama cries a lot since Grandmama died, and so I thought she must be feeling sad about that. I don't like to see her cry. Besides, my stomach was hurting real bad, and so I left the table, too, and followed Daddy for my lessons.

Meems

1909

John is a nervous child at best, but the combined effect of the train ride to Meridian, his birthday, and anticipation of the carousel was almost more than any of us could bear. His nails were bitten to the quick and bleeding, and he talked nonstop from the minute he awoke. Even Lizzie seemed docile by comparison.

Once we reached Highland Park, he relaxed a bit. He didn't bicker nearly so much with Kate and Lizzie. In fact, the three of them were on quite friendly terms, certainly a change from the usual. He and Lizzie have always had a natural affinity, but that's been strained by the conviction of the ten-year-old male that friendliness toward a member of the opposite sex is disgraceful.

The children were enthralled by the merry-go-round, as they call it. Even the older boys couldn't mask their interest. Hard to remain detached in the presence of such color and fancy. Like a lifesize music box, the carousel sits in the middle of a large domed barnlike building painted white with large windows and a circle of small windows around the circumference of the dome's base. Gay calliope tunes invite one inside the airy, light hall where those who are not riding on the carousel eat ice cream at marble-topped tables with delicate wrought-iron chairs placed among potted palms. Quite exotic for Mississippi folk.

The carousel itself was made by Dentzel and Company of Philadelphia. Twenty-eight animals hand-carved from apple or poplar and painted the brightest colors travel up and down and round and round simultaneously to tunes that speak of Old World county fairs. In the center are mirrors surrounded by lights alternating with large romantic paintings of Europe, conceived no doubt by homesick immigrant artisans—a peasant cottage, the Danube, a street scene of Venice.

The horses were the children's favorite of all the animals, and a time or two they skirmished about who would get to ride which horse. A fierce black horse with green and red harness, gold bells, and flags was favored above the brown or white or bay ones. I liked the pair of giraffes that towered above the others with their kindly faces and ornate gold saddles and fringed harness. A pair of mountain goats in full gallop, their beards waving beneath their chins, were the funniest, but the ones the children definitely did not want to ride. Nobody wanted to be the goat. More acceptable was the stately King of the Jungle, his mouth wide open in a ferocious roar, a green and red parrot perched on his shoulder, or the tiger burning with red and black stripes and showing his terrible teeth.

One would think such a thoroughly frivolous contraption could bring nothing but joy to the heart of a child, but this was not completely true, at least in our party, because of the brass ring. Ah, the brass ring. The boys competed to grasp it so fiercely that they could think of nothing else—not the lovely animals or the gay music or the bright young faces wheeling in the magic circle. I watched them strain for the ring and felt a kind of sadness for human nature, poor human nature unable to enjoy pure pleasure. I was reminded of the original of this machine, the contraption used to train apprentice knights in the art of jousting. The young cavalier would sit on a wooden horse and be pulled in a circle by a man on horseback. As he went round and round, he aimed his lance at a ring that dangled from a rope. *Carozello*, the brochure said, an Italian word that means "little war," is the word from which the modern word *carousel* is derived.

The girls, on the other hand, did not try for it, but possibly wanted it, too, the glory of reaching the gold, the honor of a free ride. None of the girls tried to reach the ring, with the exception of Lizzie, that is. She tried desperately for it, but she was too small, her arms not quite long enough, even when she stood on the back of her horse and brought the attendant to his feet and the whole carousel to an abrupt halt.

When all the boys but John had grasped the ring at least once, and all the nickels saved for months had been spent on rides, Quilla and I began to try to head the children toward home. John had long before spent all his money, even his birthday money, and came to me in despair. He had not got the ring, and it was his birthday, he said. Please, please, just one more nickel, one more ride. While I was sympathetic, I knew that this could go on all evening. John is slight, nonathletic, not apt to grasp the ring if we stayed here two weeks. I told him firmly no, and he fought to keep back the tears. One of those terrible moments for a mother, when she wants to intervene and make things work out for her child, but knows she cannot.

Kate and Lizzie were preparing to ride one more time, having spread their rides out more than the boys. But Lizzie saw the exchange between John and me. As John backed away and started toward a bench at the edge of the hall, I saw Lizzie slip him her nickel. I was surprised and touched. In my observation, that kind of unselfishness is not common among children of that age; particularly has that not been the case between Lizzie and John.

I would like to remember that poor little John grasped the ring after the ride Lizzie offered, but he didn't. Once again he missed it, but he seemed better able to accept the fact. He left the pavilion smiling. I believe the gift heartened him.

After supper we walked downtown to see a parade and hear political speeches. The most remarkable, but at the same time alarming, aspect of the parade was James K. Vardaman's appearance. He is a tall and striking man with shoulder-length black hair. He was dressed all in white, even a white hat, and he stood in the back of an ox-drawn wagon. His supporters surrounded him carrying torches that lit the night and made him appear almost luminous. His oratory, full of emotionalism and geared to the masses, worked the crowd into such a frenzy that they were screaming and struggling to touch him.

In the midst of the furor, I lost Lizzie and in a panic started through the crowd calling for her. Then I saw her scrambling onto the wagon, saw Vardaman lift her up above the crowd and hold her in his arms. "For our children," he said, kissing her cheek, "we will make a better life for our sons and daughters." The irony of Vardaman's making a point holding Stephen Dunbar's daughter was too delicious. I had to laugh despite my consternation.

Kate Clark
1910

Lizzie stopped by to get me on her way to school, like she promised. I felt like I was going to throw up when we walked out onto the front porch, but Mama said that was just being nervous about school and that when I got in class I would feel better.

"Don't worry," Lizzie said. "I'll be there."

"Yes, help her out, Lizzie," Mama said. "Everything will be new to her." Then Mama stood inside the screen door and waved. I wished more than anything that I could stay home. Why couldn't I be sitting at the kitchen table reading to her and Minnie while they shelled peas? When the clock in the hall struck ten we would have lemonade and teacakes. I wanted to cry, but I didn't because I am much too old for that.

"You look real sad," Lizzie said. "School's not so awful."

"That's not what you said last year," I said. "You said it was terrible and that you hated it."

"It will be better with you there, though," Lizzie said, sort of dancing sideways and looking at me. "We'll have some fun."

"I hope so," I said. "But I doubt it. I won't know what to do, and all the other children will."

"I'll tell you what to do," Lizzie said. "You can count on me." Then she made such a funny face that I forgot all about crying, and by the time we got to school I was laughing.

We put our lunch buckets in the cloakroom like the other boys and girls were doing. It was very hot, too hot for coats. "Where is that Stuffy boy?" I whispered to Lizzie. She had told me all about him. I wanted to see him, but I was scared.

"He won't be here for a long time," she said. "Maybe about Christmas."

"Why? Is he sick?"

"He's poor," Lizzie said. "The poor children have to pick cotton. Let's try to get desks by the window." So we got a double desk by the window, and we were sitting there waiting when Miss Reed rang the bell on her desk. Everybody had to stand up and say their name. When my turn came, I felt like my legs would not hold me up, but they did and after I said "Kate Clark" and sat back down I felt better.

Dinnertime was like a picnic out under the trees, with yellow butterflies all around and some of the leaves already brown and falling. I learned a game that goes "Red Rover, Red Rover, send Katie right over." Lizzie called out for me, and I ran and broke through the line. I was so glad because I didn't want Lizzie to be ashamed of me.

I can read better than most of them, even some of the big children. Lizzie and I can both read good. "I'll bet we could read anything," Lizzie said on the way home. "We could read the hardest book in the world." Her sashes had come untied and were trailing in the dust in the road. She picked up a rock and threw it as hard as she could toward the top of a tree.

I'm not sure what happened next except that a wagon with two horses was going past us in the road, going fast. I looked up in time to see a face. It was an angry face. It was round and big and yellow like a jack-o'-lantern or a full moon. The mouth opened wide and words floated down. "Smarty pants. Think you're so smart, don't you?" Then an arm came up over the head and threw something hard, and the wagon was gone. Lizzie turned around and then her face was covered with blood. She put her hands up to her face and then looked at them, and they were bloody. She looked surprised. I couldn't move or say anything. The blood was pouring off her chin and ears and soaking into her pinafore.

Then I began to scream. I ran toward our house screaming for Mama. She came out on the porch. "What in the world, Katherine?" Lizzie was coming slowly like a little bloody ghost. She was making a trail of blood behind her.

Mama ran out and took her by the arm. "Run, get Dr. Charlie," she said to me. I ran as fast as I could go. Dr. Charlie brought me back in his buggy, except his horse is old and fat, and I think it would have been quicker to walk. When we got to the house, Mama had Lizzie washed off and lying on the couch. We could tell that the cut was not so bad. "Lots of blood vessels in the scalp," Dr. Charlie said. "Leas' little nick makes you bleed like a stuck hog."

I began to shiver, hot as it was.

"We'll take a little stitch or two," Dr. Charlie said, getting out a needle and thread. Lizzie didn't cry or anything, but I felt light and funny. "Put your head between your knees, child," he said to me. "You're white as a sheet." So I sat there with my head hanging, afraid to look.

"How did this happen?" Mama asked.

"Stuffy Flannigan," Lizzie said. "Damn his eyes."

"Elizabeth Dunbar!" Mama said.

Dr. Charlie chuckled. "Them Flannigans are a tough lot," he said. "I wouldn't get in a row with them."

"Ow," Lizzie said when he took the stitch, "that hurt."

"Now then," Dr. Charlie said, "I sewed a fine seam. You stay in the bed the rest of the day and don't tangle with no more Flannigans." Then he packed up his black bag and left.

"Stay here with Lizzie," Mama said to me. "I'm going to call her mother."

"Call Daddy," Lizzie said. "He'll do something awful to Stuffy Flannigan."

Lizzie
1913

Today I went with Kate to the Freeman place to see her Cousin Kate, who is home from New York for a visit. Cousin Kate's father and my Kate's father were brothers. I think that's how it was. Kate introduced me to them all, and it seemed like everybody in the room was named Kate except me and the one they call Uncle Russ. Cousin Kate's father died when she was just a little baby. That would be a terrible thing to happen to somebody. Now Cousin Kate and her mother and her grandmother all live in New York most of the time so that she can study art with some famous man up there that they call "Mr. Chase" and sometimes call "The Master."

I expected a cousin to be about our age, but Cousin Kate is at least as old as Mama and Daddy, even though her family call her Katie and treat her like a little girl. One of the neighbors came over while we were there and said, "When are you all going to come back home where you belong? You ought to be ashamed, Kate, to keep your grandmother off up there when you know she'd be happier to live her last days here in the Hollies."

Uncle Russ chimed in and said, "I've told them the same thing. They've been living like gypsies for years. I worry about their health."

Then the grandmother—they call her Mama Kate—said, "You all talk like I'm on the way out. Kate's talent is important, and it's only right that her mother and I see that she has every opportunity." Cousin Kate looked very uncomfortable and stared at her hands clasped tightly together in her lap. I started to say that I didn't see why, since Kate is a grown woman, she couldn't stay in New York by herself, but I kept quiet because I didn't want to get Kate in trouble for having an impertinent friend.

Cousin Kate has brown hair pinned on top of her head, and a nice smile. She wore a blue dress in the latest fashion with a beautiful, long white silk scarf wrapped high around her throat and flowing down the front in a fancy way that you never see around here. She looked like the city. She was very nice to us and showed us her photograph album. One of the first pictures was of her as a little girl with a cap and gloves on and her doll and carriage. Then there was one of her as a young girl about our age with one of those funny fur pieces that still has the heads on it so that she looked like she had two foxes sitting on her shoulder. The picture I liked best was one I had seen before. It was of the eighth-grade class at Holly Springs school, and Mama was in it, too.

"How is she?" Cousin Kate asked. "She was so smart and talented. Does she still write poetry?" I was surprised by this because I never knew she wrote poetry at all.

"She's not well," I said.

"Oh, I'm sorry. I should go by to see her." But I knew she wouldn't.

We looked at some of the rest of the photographs then, some of their elegant apartment in New York, right near Central Park and the Metropolitan Museum of Art. In one picture, made many years before, Cousin Kate stood in between two handsome cadets at West Point. Kate and I wanted to know more about that one, but Cousin Kate turned the page quickly. Many of the photographs had been taken at the seashore place where the art class met for the summer and painted. Cousin Kate's mother seemed to be in every picture and her grandmother, too. I liked to see the ladies outside in their long dresses and hats and smocks painting at their easels. They had their bicycles and umbrellas all around them, and it looked more like a picnic than work. I began to feel like I wanted to be a painter.

Finally we came to a picture of Mr. Chase, her teacher. He had a long, pointy white beard and a mustache that swooped out on either side of his face. Little round eyeglasses sat on the end of his nose. He looked distinguished. Cousin Kate's face was soft and smiling when she looked at this picture. "He is the most wonderful teacher," she said, "and the best painter in the world."

"Could we see something you've painted?" I asked her.

"They're in New York," she said, "and they're nothing extraordinary."

Uncle Russ was standing near and heard that. "Show the children, Kate. Don't be modest."

"I'm realistic, Uncle," she said. But she stood up and said, "Follow me, girls; one is hanging on the sunporch." The sunporch is a large room of mostly windows at the back of the house. It is full of plants and light and white wicker furniture with pink flowery cushions. Over the mantel hung a painting that made me stop in the doorway in surprise because it looked so familiar somehow and yet mysterious and far away. Sunny fields are in the background, and up closer is a grove of tall, dark trees and a small garden, or the corner of a field, it's not clear. Bending in the field is the figure of a black woman in a white cap. The painting reminds me of Genesis when she works in the garden out behind her house.

"I call it *Work Out in Mississippi Grove,*" she said. We stood in front of it and stared.

"It's beautiful," I said finally, "but sad."

She looked surprised. "Why do you say that?"

"The woman is so small, and so alone."

"Yes," she said, looking back at the painting as if she had never seen it before. "Yes, that's quite true."

Then I noticed that the artist's signature at the bottom didn't say *Kate Clark* at all, but another name that I couldn't quite read, a word that started with an *F.* I started to ask about it, but something told me not to.

I didn't want to leave the painting because I kept seeing things in it, like a little gold bush that was splashed against the dark, but finally Kate said it was getting late, and that we had to go before we wore out our welcome.

"Maybe you girls can come to New York and see us sometime," Cousin Kate said when she walked us to the door. "It's a big exciting city, and we would have lots of fun." We said how we'd love to do that, and on the way to Kate's house we talked about the Statue of Liberty and got excited.

Miss Meems was sitting in the front-porch swing drinking lemonade and fanning when we got back to Kate's. I was glad she was there because I was full of questions about Cousin Kate. "It's too hot to live, girls," she said. She had been working in her rose bushes. Kate and I got us some lemonade and sat down in the rocking chairs to talk to her. "So how was Cousin K?" she asked.

"Fine," Kate said. "Will you take us to New York to visit? She invited us."

"We should do that," she said. "I've never been to one of Kate's shows and neither has Henry."

"She has *shows*?" I asked in wonder.

"Exhibits. Her work has been in art shows all over the country. She's marvelously talented."

"She acts like her painting is nothing much," Kate said.

"Oh, I know it," Miss Meems said, pushing some stray hair back up on her head and fanning harder. "She doesn't take herself seriously."

"They all moved off to New York so she could paint," I said. "That sounds serious."

"They were bored," Miss Meems said. "And they have enough money to live anywhere. Sometimes I suspect them of using Kate as an excuse. But I'm not being completely fair. They do know she's talented, and they're proud of her in their way, but she'll never have a real career in art."

"Why not?" Kate and I said together.

"She won't sell any paintings for one thing. She thinks that's inappropriate for a lady, or Mama Kate and Uncle Russell do. Russell, whom she adores, fills her with ideas about women remaining in their 'natural place' and not meddling in the man's world. He's well meaning, but he does provoke me so."

"In the painting we saw in the sunroom, the artist's signature didn't say *Kate*. The name was something else." As soon as I said it, Miss Meems began to laugh.

"You don't miss a thing, do you? You beat all, Lizzie. You're right. Kate signs her paintings with her middle name—Freeman Clark."

"Free-man," I said. "Is she ashamed to put *Kate* on them?"

"I'm afraid she may be somewhat, sad to say. I think the signature shows her struggle—the artist and the aristocratic lady. She says she thinks her work would be more widely accepted with a male-sounding name, and that may be part of it, but I wonder."

"If I could paint like that, nothing would stop me," I said, rocking back and forth. "I would write *Lizzie Dunbar* in big letters all across the bottom."

"Good," Miss Meems said, smiling. "I hope you will. I hope you will write your name very large someday, Lizzie. You and Kate both."

"Why didn't she marry?" Kate asked.

"Ah, who knows?" Miss Meems said. "Probably she couldn't find anybody to suit her, or to suit her mother and grandmother and Russell, I should say. I think not even the rich young ruler would do."

I felt sad for Cousin Kate then, and for Mama so quiet and alone. When they were my age, they didn't know what would happen to them. You never know. The sun was almost down and a dove in the cedar tree by the porch called its lonesome way. "Did my mama write poems in the old days?" I asked Miss Meems.

"Oh, yes," Miss Meems said. "Beautiful poems. You should ask her to let you read them, Lizzie."

"I will," I said. "I better go now because Daddy will be home for supper." I walked down the street to our house then. All the way I saw things I would paint if I could, like the way the yellow roses climb the columns at the Shurfords or the way the lightning bugs make Mrs. Walthall's gardenia bush shine.

The Antique Shop

Mr. Cavanaugh has a secret. He stumbled onto it by accident. He was not even looking that day. Accidently is best, as far as he is concerned. He badly needed this discovery, too, since he had not yet gotten over the Dunbar desk episode. Every time he thought of that his spirits fell, and he was sure he was losing his edge. But this find almost made up for it.

What he's bought is an oak four-drawer filing cabinet, with crazed black varnish and drawers glued shut with dirt and time. A water mark about five inches up from the bottom indicates it has been in one or more of the overflows of the Mississippi, "floods" people call them now. The piece is not attractive and wouldn't be even if it were stripped down and refinished. The oak is brittle, and its large deep pores have soaked up grime for so many years that wood and dirt have become inseparable. The piece is old office furniture, downright ugly. Lucky thing, too, Mr. Cavanaugh thinks, uglier the better.

He was driving home to lunch yesterday when he spotted the file on the sidewalk out in front of Sammy's Pawns. Sammy has a theory that merchandise moves better from the open air. He says people will buy things off the sidewalk that they would never dream of coming into the store for. He keeps telling Mr. Cavanaugh that he should set a few choice items outside and see what happens. Mr. Cavanaugh listens to him politely, but he scorns the idea. Durn fool, Mr. Cavanaugh thinks while Sammy talks. I'm not running a damn bargain basement. I deal in quality.

When he saw the oak cabinet there between a cane-bottomed rocker and a rusty metal lawn chair, Mr.

Cavanaugh almost had a wreck. He slammed on the brakes of the Falcon, and the jeep behind him filled with fraternity boys from out at the college nearly wound up in his backseat. They squealed their tires and sat on the horn and yelled, but he didn't even hear them. He sat in the street a long minute looking at the filing cabinet, then pulled slowly over, taking his time like he always does. When the jeep screamed disapproval and raced off down the street, he finally noticed. Mrs. Cavanaugh would say, "I'll be a widow before my time, wait and see, from you stopping in the road over some old piece of junk." But fortunately Mrs. Cavanaugh was not here. Now he had to plan his strategy. Under no circumstances could he let Sammy know he wanted that file.

The cabinet itself was not what interested him, of course, but the prospect of what might be inside. People don't like old papers nearly as much as they do old furniture, and he was glad they don't. The trouble is, they often throw the papers out before the furniture ever gets to him. They are big on burning papers. This provokes Mr. Cavanaugh to no end. The past is hard enough to get at without people running around destroying the evidence. And how future generations will ever know anything is beyond him. Nobody writes letters anymore. They pick up the phone and emit a few sound waves and that's it. Electric impulses travel through a cable to an ear in the distance leaving the future absolutely nothing, unless some waves get trapped in a microchip or on a piece of plastic tape which won't last ten years anyway. First hot day and the tape melts. So much for modern technology.

In this frame of mind Mr. Cavanaugh got out of the car, the prospect of trying to preserve the past single-handedly weighing on him. He stopped at the cane-bottomed rocker, but his eyes veered toward the right to the filing cabinet. He thought he could see a little piece of paper sticking out from the top drawer, but he resisted the impulse to rush to the file and tear the drawer open. He stood there looking over his glasses, arms folded across his chest, calculating.

"Yo, Mr. C.," said Sammy, coming out of the shop and starting toward him, snapping his fingers and moving his head like a duck to the loud music blaring from the speaker over the door. Another one of Sammy's marketing theories is that people buy more if they are accompanied by deafening music. His gold chain glittered from the dark hairs escaping over the neck of his T-shirt, which probably said something vulgar. Mr. Cavanaugh couldn't make out the words. "Nice chair. Picked it up out in the country from Alligator. Old woman told me it was her granddaddy's. Said he used to rock her to sleep in it, and she must of been eighty herself."

"Hmmm," said Mr. Cavanaugh, giving the chair a little push and sending it back on its heels.

"I'd put that chair at a hundred if it's a day," Sam said.

Mr. Cavanaugh knew the chair had been manufactured at a furniture factory in Tupelo that specialized in reproductions, but he admired Sammy's creativity. "Interesting," he said and examined it so carefully and so long that Sammy was already figuring the tax in his head. It wasn't the money that excited Sammy, though. He lived for the day when he could beat Mr. Cavanaugh in a deal. This had become such a challenge that he looked for old things to buy up as a sideline to the usual new junk pawn business, things he thought would tempt Mr. Cavanaugh.

"Rocks good," said Mr. Cavanaugh sitting down in the heat of the day and rocking like he was on some shady front porch. Then he glanced over at the filing cabinet. "That's a ugly piece of junk there," he said. "Somebody bring it in to pawn?"

"I bought a whole houseful of stuff last week and that was on the back porch. Old black woman died and the kids come down from Chicago, sold it all."

"Anything inside?" Mr. Cavanaugh asked casually.

"Let's see," said Sammy, stepping over and taking hold of the handle on the top drawer. Mr. Cavanaugh stopped rocking and almost stopped breathing with anticipation. He kept himself in the chair with the greatest difficulty. The drawer was stuck, but after a few kicks and blows to the cabinet Sammy yanked it open. Dust and fragments from dry old papers drifted from the drawer and yellowed the ground around the cabinet. Sammy grabbed a handful of the papers, and the top one broke half in two.

"Wait!" Mr. Cavanaugh shouted, jumping to his feet. *Idiot!* he almost added, but stopped himself in time.

"What?" Sammy yelled, jumping back.

"Nothing," said Mr. Cavanaugh recovering, "just that brown recluses love old papers."

Sammy slammed the drawer shut in a cloud and distanced himself. Sammy couldn't stand a spider. A real handicap for a man who deals in people's junk.

"Tell you what I'll do, Sam," said Mr. Cavanaugh, sitting back down and rocking again. "I'll give you $150, tax included, for this old chair, not that it's worth it, but my grandpa had one just like it."

"Man," said Sammy, "I give more than that for it. I got to have $200 to make a dime." He was inching toward the door of his shop.

"Can't offer more money," said Mr. Cavanaugh, shouting to be heard over the loudspeaker that was sending shock waves into his chest, "but I can take them spiders off your hands. When I send Booker with the truck, I'll tell him to haul this file off and dump it. Booker's not scared of spiders like me and you are."

Sammy feared there was something terribly wrong with this proposal, but he couldn't figure what. He just knew he couldn't deal with that cabinet on his own.

"Well, O.K.," he said. "Look like you done beat me again."

"How you figure?" Mr. Cavanaugh said. "I'm paying $150 for an old chair that won't half rock and a truckload of spiders."

Put like that, the deal sounded better. Sammy consoled

himself by thinking he had tricked the old man good on the age of the rocker. Mr. Cavanaugh handed him three fifties, looking awfully happy for a man who was getting beat in a trade. Sammy would have liked a clearer victory.

Mr. Cavanaugh left the pawn shop driving faster than usual, speeding in fact, through town. He whipped into his driveway on two wheels and ran straight for the phone to dispatch Booker.

"Where have you been?" Mrs. Cavanaugh said when he came into the kitchen. "The cornbread's not fit to eat."

"Irma," said Mr. Cavanaugh, "your cornbread is eternally ambrosial. Time cannot diminish it." Then he practically swallowed his dinner whole, so eager he was to get back to the shop and get into that filing cabinet.

Miranda
1914

Every evening they read in the library. Lizzie reads aloud to Stephen. I am not much interested in the books Stephen chooses, histories and biographies of political figures, but Lizzie seems to like them, though she does have an interest in fiction and poetry, too, and likes to write verse in her diary. She asked the other day to see some of my poetry, but when I looked I couldn't find any of it anywhere. Maybe I threw it out in some spring cleaning, but I don't remember doing that. Anyway, it doesn't matter because it was not very good.

I am making a large needlepoint version of the Dunbar family crest because Stephen asked me to, so while he and Lizzie read, I sit by the fire and stitch. My mind at these times is generally out the window somewhere, in the orchard or in the garden or remembering some incident from childhood. On the evening when Stephen told us the decision that would change our lives forever, I didn't even hear it. The first I heard was Lizzie's shriek. Then she hurled herself into her father's arms and said, "That's wonderful, Daddy, oh, how exciting!"

I looked up startled. "What do you think of the idea, Miranda?" Stephen asked. Confused and apologetic, I put my handwork down. He becomes so angry when I don't listen to him, and it seems increasingly hard to do so.

"Fine," I said blankly, attempting a smile. I could feel the weather change.

"You didn't hear me, did you?" he asked, a chilly edge around his words.

"I'm sorry. I was—"

"Woolgathering," he said. "What I said was that I am running for governor."

I jumped to my feet, spilling the needlepoint canvas onto the hearth. "Oh! How horrible."

The two of them looked at me across the room as if I were an alien being. "Mama," Lizzie said reproachfully.

Stephen's mouth was frozen in that way that makes me feel I have failed him, his eyes hard. His words cut across the room. "If only once I could feel you supported me," he said.

"I had no idea," I stammered. "When did you . . . Why?"

"Because I was asked. Because I have a lot to offer the state. Because I can win."

I sat back down abruptly and tried to gather my thoughts, tangled and unraveling. Since Lizzie's birth my life has been unhappy, but through the years the edges have worn off my discontent until it is comfortable like an old dress. Life is by its nature flawed, I tell myself. Look at the good parts—I am healthy and so are Stephen and Lizzie. We want for nothing because Stephen has a gift for making money. We live where generations of my family have been born, lived, and died. Their presences fill the house and sometimes I catch glimpses, Father filling his pipe in front of the mantel, Mother kneading bread, her sleeves above her elbows.

"Move? Would we have to?"

"The governor lives in Jackson still, I believe. I could hardly run the state from Holly Springs."

"Oh," I said.

The smell of burning wool filled the room, but I was oblivious. I sat staring at the pattern in the rug, worn and familiar, woven by some nomad across the sea. Then Stephen rushed across the room to the hearth. He jerked the crest, charred and darkened from the tongues of fire, and cursed. "You've ruined it," he said, his teeth clenched. "Am I nothing to you? Me or the Dunbar name?"

Stephen
1915

You would have thought somebody had died, the way Miranda carried on. Most women would be happy to have a husband with ambition. They would pitch in and help win the election instead of whining about moving to Jackson. She has a way of draining the joy out of everything I do. When I remember how she was when I met her, I can hardly believe she's the same woman.

I had just gone to work as a clerk in her father's law office the first time I saw her. She had walked into town to shop and stopped in to say hello to Mr. Marshall. She was a pale blonde beauty, so shy she blushed at a simple hello. She wore a light blue dress with ruffles and carried a matching parasol to protect her white skin from the sun. Her youth hung on her like dew, and there was a softness about her, a pliableness, as if she was not yet a fully grown woman.

I took her hand and looked directly into her blue eyes, and she dropped her eyes and stammered in confusion. I resolved then to marry her. I set about to accomplish the goal like I do any other, slowly and methodically. I listened to her silly poetry in the porch swing for hours, and I enthralled her with stories from my past experiences, so much wider and more varied than her own. I never even kissed her mouth until the wedding night.

I was not the rich young ruler that the Marshalls had envisioned for their daughter. I was dirt poor with no past, no legacy but a sound mind and strong body. But I won their darling without a struggle, much to her parents' discomfort. I beat out a front porch full of suitors without resorting to seduction and in a year was enjoying my prize in this house. She liked me then. She listened when I talked to her and paid attention to my comfort. Then Lizzie was born, and she began to withdraw. What I had thought was malleability in her character was mere weak-mindedness and passivity. Now she doesn't care if I come home or not.

Sometimes I try to imagine what it would be like to have a true partner in the life I've chosen, the kind of partnership that God intended when he created male and female, the kind I was sure that I could have with Miranda. She would be attractive, of course, not a woman who has let herself go like Miranda has. She would understand my need to accomplish something. She would be at ease in social situations. She would be politically informed and able to hold her own in conversation. She would be active in the church—sing in the choir or play the organ. She would be the manager of the house, not putty in the hands of the Negroes like Miranda is. She would be attentive to me so that I didn't have to ask for everything I wanted done. And I in turn would be her guide and protector.

But that is not my lot. All I have accomplished I have done alone. I have read of women whose minds are permanently unsettled by the traumas of sex and childbirth, especially those who lived sheltered lives like Miranda, and so I have sacrificed my own needs for intimacy for her protection. I protected her, too, from knowing of Lizzie's hideous twin and of the horrors that lurk in our genes. And I have been mostly faithful to her, too, at least as far as she knows, except that a male's drives are altogether different from a woman's and that to leave them unattended is unhealthy for a normal man.

Thank God for Lizzie. She is the only one in the family who understands how hard I work and what it means to me to run this race. If only she were a little older she could take on the public role of political wife, and Miranda could be left alone where she clearly prefers to be. But Lizzie's still a child, only

13, though her perceptions are those of a woman, or maybe I should say, a man. Any encouragement, any bolstering when things are rough, any support from home will have to come from Lizzie if it comes at all.

Their reactions tonight when I told them I am running were completely predictable. Lizzie was thrilled for me, she understands the drive to achieve. She danced me around the room and then began to plan ways she could help in the campaign. She could make speeches, she said. We could go to the Neshoba County Fair to campaign, and she would astonish everybody by being the youngest speaker.

The more Lizzie talked, the more Miranda faded into the wallpaper, except for her declaration that she would not move to Jackson. She will, of course. But I hope she is not unpleasant about it. I despise a scene.

Genesis
1915

I been with Miss Miranda since the beginning. My people come here with hers, slaves, from Carolina. Lived and died alongside each other through the war and the mancipation and reconstruction. All that didn't seem to make much difference in how we was.

We about the same age, I think. Mama use to tell how we played round her feet when we was babies, tripping her up in the kitchen. I was always bigger and stronger and felt more like Miranda's mother than anything. She dreamylike and couldn't never take up for herself. Leroy, he'd pinch her under the table until she cry, but she wouldn't tell on him. Then they'd send her from the table for being a crybaby, and I'd have to sneak her supper up there to her.

Folks like her that's always trying to please everybody, seem like they can't please anybody. Seem like stronger people can smell weakness on them, like the scent of blood, and they can't help going in for the kill. But it ain't weakness exactly either. May be strength. May be she so content down within herself, or wherever it is she go, that people can't stand it, they won't have it, they got to bring her back here no matter what.

She don't deserve her lot. Anytime I get to thinking mine is hard, I turn around and look at hers. You keep house for people, do their wash, change their beds, cook their food, you know things. Know more than you want to. I'm sure as I am of anything Mr. Stephen ain't touched her since Lizzie was born. And I'm just as sure ain't a word passed between them about it and won't.

He gonna suffer yet for how he done when them twins was born. It was a disgrace for Christian people was what it was. The little boy come out first, and he was terrible to see, he didn't hardly even look human, covered with long black hair all over. Mr. Stephen he took it as a reflection on his manhood I guess. He said "abomination" and commenced to vomit. When the little thing died right straightaway, thank God, he quick wrapped it in a sheet and left the room. Come back in and the whole thing was erased, like it never happened. I don't know what he done with the body, throwed it in the pond probably, like a dog, his own son, without a song or a prayer.

He ain't lacked for pleasure since then, as everybody in town know except probably Miranda. She get paler and thinner, further away from this world. She starting to hunch over like a old dog that's been whipped.

That Lizzie ain't no comfort for her neither. She too much like her daddy. I could shake her the way she team up with him to put her own mama down. All they talks about anymore is the election. Election this, election that. Miranda try to take part, but every time she make any kind of suggestion, they give each other them looks, smile, and roll they eyes. Wonder do they think she don't see them? Course I don't guess they care if she see them or not.

Lord knows what'll happen to us if he win, and we has to move to Jackson. She attached to this house, this land. She attached in a way most people don't get attached anymore, down deep, with her heart.

Lizzie
1915

When Mama called me at four o'clock the morning of the state fair, I was already up and dressed. It was cold and I was shivering so hard I couldn't hardly get my stockings on. Mama said the shivers were probably part excitement. "Why don't you come with us?" I asked her.

"I don't like crowds," Mama said.

"Miss Meems and Kate are going," I said. "Miss Meems goes lots of places."

"We're different," Mama said. "Turn around and I'll button you up. Besides somebody needs to stay here and see about things."

"What things?" I said. "Genesis sees about everything."

"Hold your braids up so I can reach the top button," Mama said. "You and Daddy will have fun."

"Looks like you would want to hear his speech and see the ones he'll have to run against."

"Take it all in for me, Lizzie."

"Did they have state fairs when you were little?"

She laughed and said, "I'm not *that* old. Of course."

"Did you ever go?"

"Once," she said, "with your grandmother and grandfather Marshall and your Uncle Leroy. We rode the train to Jackson, like you and Daddy will. I had cotton candy for the first time, and your grandfather bought me a pretty handkerchief with 'Mississippi State Fair' on it. It was a lovely trip." She finished buttoning my dress and then patted my shoulders.

"Where is it?" I asked.

"The handkerchief? Oh, goodness, that was years and years ago."

"Seems like you would have kept it."

She looked off out the window for a minute, then she looked back at me real sadly.

"I had forgotten until you brought it up," she said, "but Leroy threw my handkerchief out the train window as soon as we left Jackson."

"That was mean," I said. "Did Grandpa whip him?"

"I don't think so," she said. "I cried and cried."

"I would have socked him if I had been there."

"Young ladies don't sock people, Lizzie," Mama said. "Now come on and eat your breakfast."

So she stayed home like she always does, and Daddy and I caught the 6:00 A.M. train and came all the way to Jackson. The towns along the way were red and gold with fall leaves, and everybody on the train was happy because they were going to the fair. My favorite part of the ride was the dining car where we ate roast beef and ice cream, and Daddy let me drink coffee.

We spent the night at the Hotel Royal because it's halfway between Union Station and the fairground. It's the most beautiful place I ever saw. Crystal lights and floors that shine. I felt like I didn't sleep at all, but Daddy said I probably slept more than I thought. Then the next morning we went to North State Street to watch the parade. So much to see I didn't know where to look first. Bands, men on horses, motorcars, wagons full of children who had come in from the country for the day, floats with all kinds of characters like Uncle Remus and the Old Woman in the Shoe. I was waving at the Old Woman and her children and didn't see the next group until they were almost even with us. Six women in white dresses were marching, and they were carrying a big blue banner with words on it. The banner said "Mississippi Woman Suffrage Association." One of the women was Miss Meems.

"Miss Meems," I called out. "Hey there!"

She looked around and smiled. She couldn't wave because she was holding the banner, but I could see her lips say, "Hello, Lizzie, Stephen."

I was so excited to see somebody I knew in the state-fair parade that I was dancing around and waving and saying to the people around me, "She's our neighbor back in Holly Springs."

"Hush, Lizzie, you're embarrassing me," Daddy said and so I stopped.

"Miss Meems's club got to be in the parade," I said. "Isn't that wonderful?"

"Meems Clark is more of a crank than I thought," Daddy said, "out here making a public spectacle of herself." This surprised me. I had been imagining myself and Kate next year in white dresses carrying a banner.

"Her club is good," I said. "Kate told me about it. Woman suffrage is about women getting to vote and straightening out the government."

"I know what it's about," Daddy said. "And it's about a lot more than women voting."

"What?" I said.

"It's about values, the family, our way of life, but this is no time to explain the complexities of suffrage." So we watched the rest of the parade, then we went into the fairground. I got a candy apple on a stick, and we started down the fairway to see the exhibits.

I told Daddy I wanted to bring Mama something from the fair and to be on the lookout for handkerchiefs. "Why handkerchiefs?" he asked.

"Because Uncle Leroy threw hers out the train window a long time ago when they came to the fair."

"Oh," he said. "I never heard that tale."

"Why doesn't she ever come with us anywhere?" I asked. "She never has any fun."

"She'd rather stay home with a book," he said. "She could come with us if she wanted to."

Up ahead, I couldn't believe the good luck, I saw Kate standing at a booth with a lot of ladies. She was handing out little pamphlets to everyone who came by. The sign on the booth said "Votes for Women." Miss Meems was standing on a bale of cotton making a speech to a crowd of people gathered around. "Look, there's Kate," I said and started to run toward her. But Daddy caught my arm and turned me around in the other direction.

"I don't have time to get mixed up with them," Daddy said.

"I just want to say hello."

"My speech is in exactly an hour, Lizzie. I want to get to the grandstand in plenty of time."

"Maybe I could go see Kate, then we could both come down and hear your speech."

"Absolutely not," he said. "I won't let you out of my sight in a crowd like this."

I would have nagged some more, but he seemed grouchy, and I guess he was worried about his own speech. Over my shoulder I could see Miss Meems talking to the crowd and making gestures with her hands. I wished I could hear what she was saying.

We went by the animals next, and I liked seeing the pigs and cows, except the barns smelled bad. I tried to figure out why the judges had thought the ones with blue ribbons were the best, but I never could. The Fain Seed Company had a cage on display that a lot of people were gathered around. We stopped to see what was in it, but even when I saw I didn't understand. In the cage was what looked like a rooster, but he was taking care of some baby chicks. He was gathering them under his wings just like a hen would do. A sign on the cage said "Votes for Women." Everyone was laughing.

"What's so funny?" I asked Daddy. He was laughing, too.

"He looks like a rooster, but he's not really. Something's been done to him."

"What?"

"Never mind," Daddy said.

"Is it a joke?"

"The whole suffrage business is a very bad joke," Daddy said. "Don't waste your time worrying about it."

So we went on to the platform for Daddy's speech, and he was the best one by far and got the most applause. After that he had to shake hands with a lot of people, which you have to do if you run for an office. I shook a lot of hands, too. Then we saw exhibits of everything in the world—canned tomatoes and jellies, and pumpkins and corn and apples and peaches and cakes and pies and embroidery and crochet and on and on like that.

We were halfway back to Holly Springs before I realized I had forgotten all about buying Mama a present.

The Antique Shop

"Worst old junk I ever saw," Booker muttered as he heaved the oak filing cabinet from Sammy's Pawns into the back room that Mr. Cavanaugh calls his "clearinghouse." Mr. Cavanaugh was fussing around like this monster was Louis Quatorze. Then he sent Booker to the front to watch the store while he investigated. The delicious moment had finally come when he could open the drawers and read the papers inside. He thought they might be records from a dairy company that once prospered in Bolivar Landing, or maybe one of the general stores on Main Street. He lifted the first folder from the drawer with as much care as if he were a neurosurgeon slicing a brain. He was not prepared for what he saw.

The first folder was labeled "Addresses — public — governor's race." Inside were scores of newspaper clippings about Stephen Dunbar's speeches in the governor's campaign. Disappointing, until at the bottom of the stack Mr. Cavanaugh found a manuscript written in pencil on tablet paper. The handwriting was round and deliberate, like a child's. At the top was "Neshoba County Fair 1915." Here is what it said:

> Mr. Speaker, Candidates, Voters of Mississippi, Future Governor Dunbar:
>
> I believe I am well qualified to speak in favor of one of our candidates for governor of our fair state. I have known Stephen Dunbar for thirteen years. He was there when I took my first step and when I said my first word. He was there when I learned to read. He was there when I learned to pray. He was there to teach me right from wrong. He has always been

with me as head of our household, for, you see, I am his daughter.

My father, Stephen Dunbar, grew up in the country out from Pontotoc. His family was honest but poor. He worked in the fields all day, and at night he studied his lessons with a coal oil lamp. He understands the problems of the common man and is just who we need as our governor.

By the sweat of his brow Stephen Dunbar worked his way up to be the best lawyer in the state. He will be able to get things done with the legislators because he understands the legal system.

Mr. Cavanaugh wondered why this next paragraph had a large, black X through it.

Some of the things my father will try to get done are child labor laws, school attendance laws, and more money for education. In some parts of our state girls and boys no older than I work as much as 60 hours a week with no chance to go to school. We need a law that will raise the age when young people can go to work. We also need laws requiring children to go to school until they have a good, solid education to go out into the world with. And our school system needs enough money so that all the children in our state have an equal opportunity to an education. A literate public is the key to the survival of democracy.

REMEMBER—"Get It Done with Dunbar!" And when you go to the polls, tell them Lizzie sent you. I thank you.

The idea that he had happened upon Dunbar family papers dawned slowly and was incredible to Mr. Cavanaugh. Once, as he continued to read, the irrational notion crossed his head that Sammy had performed a masterful forgery and was now down at the pawn shop telling everybody and making a fool out of him.

Clearly, though, these papers were beyond Sammy's powers to deceive. These were the real thing if ever anything was. Mr. Cavanaugh read until closing time and would have read on into the night, oblivious, except that Booker came back to see if he had had a heart attack.

"Keep it quiet about these files, Booker. They are most remarkable."

"Is?" Booker's eyes twinkled. He was used to Mr. Cavanaugh's ways.

"Those archives people will get them sooner or later, but for now they're mine."

"Better get on home to supper," Booker said. "Miz Cavanaugh done called once." Reluctantly Mr. Cavanaugh pulled the string on the bulb hanging from the ceiling and followed Booker to the front to lock up. He arrived home only an hour late for supper, but his mind was almost a century behind.

Meems
1915

"The bottom rung has got on top." I can hear Mother say it now if she knew Stephen Dunbar were running for governor.

She never liked him, and I don't either. All his talk about log cabins, humble beginnings, following a plow over red clay hills. I don't have any hard facts about his background, but I don't believe for a minute the past he has created for himself. You can look at his hands and tell he's never hit a lick at a snake. You can look in his eyes and see nothing at all. Those two things alone are enough to make me suspicious.

To this day we know no more about where he came from than Father did when he took him into the newspaper. Stephen learned quickly. He did his work. Father was not one to judge, not even when he heard from one of his former Tulane classmates that Stephen had washed up here from a scandal in New Orleans, something involving his whole family and precipitated by greed and bad faith. "People can change," Father said.

"At least keep him away from the money," Mother said.

One evening Father brought him home to dinner. I was returning from a suffrage meeting, though Stephen didn't know that, didn't know my politics. My spirits were high. I wanted to test him. "What do you think about all the suffrage talk, Mr. Dunbar?" I asked, trying to keep my convictions out of my voice.

He considered the question carefully, polite to the letter. "Perhaps," he said, stirring sugar into his iced tea, "a higher law is at work in that case."

"Oh," I said. "And what law might that be?"

"Natural law," he said. "Law that ordains women as mothers to the children and angels in the home, that created woman's spirit purer and truer than man's."

"Nonsense," I said, "in other words, women are too good to vote?"

He laughed at that, but it was a strained, humorless laugh, his upper lip taut above his perfect white teeth. He was clearly startled to find a country girl with political opinions.

"Stephen may have a point, Mimi," Father said. "Biological differences have determined the roles, and maybe Nature's way is not all wrong."

"Oh, for goodness sake, Father," I said in amazement, not realizing then that your own father may turn against you in the company of other men, "am I forever to be disenfranchised because I have the capacity to bear children? That biological fact has not affected my brain."

"Something clearly has," Mother said. "Can't you see our guest is in need of a biscuit?" I passed the biscuits, wondering at the skill with which Mother invariably diverted attention from any issue that can cause conflict. "Now tell me, Mr. Dunbar," she went on, "what is your general impression of Holly Springs?"

This question was more down Stephen's alley, giving him the chance to tell my parents exactly what they wanted to hear, that it is a lovely town, a model progressive community, one that anyone should be proud to live in, that when he followed the mule those years on the family farm, he dreamed always of a better life in Holly Springs, et cetera.

Not long after that, Stephen left newspaper work to read law in the offices of Marshall & Lamar. And in the true American tradition, he set his sights on the boss's daughter. Miranda and I were best friends then, though she never shared my political interests. She was, is, as apolitical as anyone I've ever known.

In regard to the relationship between Miranda and Stephen, I made a mistake that I have regretted ever since. I told her I thought Stephen Dunbar was an opportunist and that I didn't trust him. This was not the first or last time that forthrightness cost. Miranda, in love, cooled toward me, and Stephen, sensing my dislike and no doubt threatened by my views, worked to cut her off from her old friends, including me.

From little hints she dropped, I gathered he convinced her that I disliked him on the basis of class, held against him his poverty and alleged rural beginnings. So although as girls we shared every secret, now I know almost nothing as to how her life is.

Lizzie is my only connection to her now, and a live wire she is. Lizzie is thrilled with the idea of the governor's race. She came over today for help in writing a campaign speech to give at the Neshoba County Fair. Ironic, since I don't think I can support Stephen in this race. That depends on his position on suffrage, but my guess is that he will neatly sidestep the issue, unless having a daughter has changed his mind. I agreed to help her with the speech anyway, not for Stephen's sake but for her own.

She brought a draft with her, and I was amazed at how politic it was for a child. She has listened well to the rhetoric swirling around us. She understands the conventions of the political speech and what her audience wants to hear. My criticism was that her speech had nothing of substance about the issues. I made some suggestions along those lines—nothing about suffrage, knowing Stephen would veto that, but compulsory school attendance, increased funds for education, and child-labor laws.

Lizzie plans to surprise Stephen with the draft. She left here in high spirits. The campaign will be good practice for her. And if justice is possible in our political system, someday she will be a candidate for office herself.

Stephen
1915

Meems Clark thought I wasn't good enough for Miranda, and now she's trying to get at me through Lizzie. How Henry Clark lives with her or why I will never understand. I guess he's given up the fight, lets her wear the pants without question.

I had settled into my study with the newspaper late this afternoon after a hard day in court when Lizzie burst in with a speech she wants to give for me at the Neshoba County fair. I was touched by the idea. She's the only one in this house who's given me a word of support or encouragement. Certainly it won't hurt to have a pretty child like Lizzie speak in my behalf.

"Want to hear?" she asked.

"Fine," I said, folding the newspaper and settling back. She stood in front of the fireplace, straight as a poker, lifted her chin, and began to speak. She had the speech essentially memorized already. Her clear young voice rang through the room with such feeling that tears came into my eyes. Then she came to a part about child-labor laws.

"Wait," I said, "hold on a minute. Go through that part again."

She repeated the paragraph, and I said, "Who told you that?"

She looked at the floor and didn't answer.

"Come on. I know you didn't think that up on your own."

"Miss Meems helped me, but just a little."

"You can't make promises like that, Lizzie. Not if you want me to win."

"But you're for those things, aren't you? Better schools and more children in them?" She walked over to my desk and sat down at it with the manuscript of her speech in front of her. She cupped her chin with her hands and stared at it. The glass doors to the shelves above the desk reflected her forlorn little shape.

"Meems Clark oversimplifies because she doesn't understand the whole picture. For one thing this is a very poor state, and more money in education means more taxes.

"Miss Meems says we need to raise taxes."

"That's the reason she'll never be elected to anything, thank God."

"It doesn't cost money to keep little children from having to work so hard, does it?"

"Lizzie, this is a rural state. Farm families depend on all the members pitching in, and besides, hard work never hurt anybody. When I was a boy—"

"Miss Meems says—"

"Meems would have the government meddling in everything and to hell with individual freedom."

Lizzie gave a deep sigh and came over to me, sat down on the arm of my chair. "I wanted you to like it," she said, putting her arm around me and resting her head on my shoulder.

"Honey, I do, I do," I said, patting her hand. "It's fine. Just take out the campaign promises, and the rest is good."

"But then it won't have anything about the issues."

"Trust the issues to me, Lizzie. Don't worry your head about them. Look, here's all we have to do." I got up and walked to the desk, took my pen, and made an X through the part Meems had prescribed. "Now, I'll be honored to have you make this speech for me." She brightened up and hugged me and ran off down the hall to practice on somebody else.

I manage not to ever think about Lizzie's birth, but I can't help wishing sometimes that a healthy male body could have had Lizzie's mind and spirit. As it's turned out, with Miranda so helpless, I've been the only parent, and I'm not sure I've been the best one for a girl. If she were a boy, I would know what to teach her, how to direct her. As it is, the best I can do is try to leave her some property and hope to heaven she makes a decent match.

John Clark
1916

He did it. He won and soon he'll be Governor Dunbar, and Lizzie is moving to Jackson. I stayed gone all day on purpose because I knew she would come to the house to say good-bye, and Kate would cry and Mama would cry, too, and I absolutely can't stand it when they cry. I don't see why Mr. Stephen had to run for governor anyway. Politics is dumb. I would never get mixed up in politics. Everybody is sad that they're moving except Mr. Stephen, I guess. And me, of course. I'll be glad to get rid of Lizzie.

So first I went hunting, but I didn't see any birds, and I kept thinking about Lizzie Dunbar for some reason, how she's different from lots of the girls, she's meaner or something, I don't know how to explain it. Thinking about her moving away makes me feel funny inside. I used to hate to see her running up the walk to the house. She had a home, too, but she always had to be at ours. She and Kate drive me crazy, so why am I thinking about her and wishing things could keep being like they were?

Hunting wasn't any fun, so I found Joel and we got some boys together for a football game, but nobody was playing right, and I kept getting mad, and finally Joel and me got into a big fight, and we rolled in a ditch and fought like dogs for the longest. "What's wrong with you today, John?" Joel kept saying. "You're just crazy is what."

Finally Mr. Burdine, he's the school principal, he came walking by and saw us. He stepped in the ditch and grabbed us up, me in one hand and Joel in the other. My nose was bleeding, and Joel's eye was swole up. "What in thunder you boys doing?" he asked, shaking us hard. "Can't you find a more productive activity for Christmas vacation? I'll just have to see about you." So he made us shake hands and then come up to the school and scrub down the walls, scrub the rest of the day with no lunch and no heat. "Idle hands are the devil's workshop," he'd say every time he stuck his head in the door till me and Joel wanted to kill him, and our hands were blue with the cold, and we couldn't remember why we were fighting even, because we're best friends.

About dark Mr. Burdine bounced in and said he guessed we better go home since our folks would be getting worried about us. "I hope you've learned your lesson," he said. "Pretty is as pretty does," whatever that's supposed to mean. So Joel started toward his house, and I started toward mine, and when I got about even with the Shurford's big oak tree, here comes Lizzie crying her eyes out.

I was about to duck behind the tree, but she looked up and saw me and right quick started choking back the sobs and wiping off her eyes with her hands.

"What's wrong with you?" I said.

"Nothing," she said. "What's wrong with you? You've got blood all over your shirt."

"Do not," I said.

"I can see it," she said. "I've got eyes. You been fighting?"

"You been crying. Your eyes are all red."

"Are not."

"Are too."

"Are not."

Then we both started to laugh at the same time. And we whooped and laughed until we had to lean up against the tree. Finally she said, "Six in the morning we leave for Jackson."

"Reckon we'll ever see you again?"

"Oh, sure," she said, shrugging her shoulders. "We'll be back up here lots."

"Not to live, though."

"Yes, we will. When Daddy gets through being governor."

"Well, O.K.," I said. "I better get on."

"Me too," she said. Then she looked up at me, and the moon hit her face and the tears were shining on the rim of her eyes, right ready to spill over, and I thought *oh, please don't cry, I'll do anything to keep you from crying*, and I don't know what happened to me then but something, something strange, and before I knew it I took one of her hands and I leaned down and my lips touched her cheek and she drew in her breath fast and I thought *maybe she will slap me* and I turned then and ran home as fast as I could and she ran home, too. When I got to our porch I could see her disappearing down the walk toward her house, still running.

Lizzie
1916

Daddy is mad at me, I think, but I don't know why. I can't figure out what I've done.

"We'll call you Elizabeth from now on," he said at supper, from up at the head of the long table. "You're becoming a young lady."

"No, I'm not," I said. "I'm still Lizzie inside."

"*Elizabeth* sounds more like the governor's daughter, don't you think, first daughter of the state?"

"The state can call me that," I said. "But I rather you would call me Lizzie."

He frowned and said, "You're not a little girl any longer; you have to face that." The big hall clock struck seven, dong, dong, and the sound echoed around the room. When we moved here I thought the room was beautiful with the long, shiny table and the crystal chandelier and all the silver, but now I think it's lonesome. It doesn't get warm and cozy like our dining room in Holly Springs. It's always cold in here. We sit far away from each other at meal times, too far away to pass the food, and the servants, who are convicts from Parchman, serve us. I like the convicts better than anybody I've met in Jackson. I like to imagine what crimes they've done.

"School better today?" Daddy asked.

"I hate school," I said. "It's stupid."

"What do you mean?" he said, frowning again.

"Holly Springs was much better. I learned a lot more."

"Coming in the middle of the term is hard," Daddy said.

"And you miss your friends."

"The boys and girls here don't like me," I said. "They think I'm stuck up because I'm the governor's daughter." My stomach hurt every time I thought about school. I pushed my plate away still full of food.

"Lizzie, how was school?" Mama said, and Daddy gave her such a look. Poor Mama, she can't keep up. Ever since we moved from Holly Springs, she's been in another world more than ever. She wanted to stay in Holly Springs, in that house where Grandmother Marshall was born, and she and Uncle Leroy were born, and I was born. But Daddy said that wouldn't do. What would people say? The governor's wife couldn't live somewhere else and that was that. Then she said, please keep the house so we can go back there, but he said we couldn't afford that luxury. He said you can't go back in this life, and he sold the Hollies house. He said when we leave the governor's mansion we're moving to the Delta where he's bought land, and we're building a new house with modern conveniences. That's where the future is, he said. I feel sorry for Mama, but she does live in the past.

"They're jealous of you at school," Daddy said. "You're the cleverest and the prettiest *and* the governor's daughter."

"I wouldn't tell her that, Stephen," Mama said. "You'll fill her with pride."

"Couldn't I stay here?" I said. "I could read books with Mama."

"That would be lovely, dear." Mama smiled.

"Absolutely not," Daddy said. "I don't need two hermits on my hands. Finish your dinner, Elizabeth."

I tried to choke down a few more bites and then excused myself to go upstairs. I had homework, but it was boring, and I didn't want to do it, and so I sat in the window seat in my gown for a long time and looked out at the capitol, frozen in the January winter, and wondered what they were doing back in Holly Springs. I imagined it was spring and that I could hear the crickets and the locusts and the frogs instead of the horses and buggies going by on State Street and the icicles growing from the eaves.

When it was time for bed, I stuck my head into Mama's room and said goodnight. She looked up from her book and said, "Yes, goodnight," but she didn't even see me I know. Then I went to Daddy's study like I always do. I sat down in his lap and snuggled up against him, his chin resting on the top of my head. I like the way he smells, pipe smoke and shaving soap, and I like to put my ear against his heart and hear it beat. He used to tell me a story or sing a song, but now we just sit quietly for awhile. He put his arms around me and held me close to him, and I forgot about school and everything seemed better. I felt like a little girl again, safe and at home. We sat that way until the clock struck ten, and I put my arms around his neck and kissed him under the chin. Then something happened I don't know. He stiffened up and took my face between his hands, he was breathing hard and his eyes were dark, he held me that way hard, hurting me, staring at my face. "Oh, God," he said very low, his mouth almost on mine. Then he stood up all of a sudden, throwing me off his warm lap onto the cold floor. His face was red as the coals in the fireplace. He leaned against the chair and looked at me like he was furious. "Go to your room," he said. "Right now."

"Daddy," I said, jumping up and going toward him, shivering now. "What's the matter?"

"Get out of here, Elizabeth," he said, and his voice choked like he was crying. "Go!"

I went then. I ran up the stairs to my room and got into bed and covered my head with the quilt. I am still shivering. I feel like I won't ever be warm again.

Miranda
1916

Father, Mother, Holly Springs, the homeplace, and now Lizzie. And Stephen really. I should add Stephen to the list. If I dwelt on my losses I would grow quite mad. I don't dwell. I don't think often, except about what I can see in black and white on a page. But here it is, and I can think of nothing else. Lizzie is going away, far away to a Virginia girls' school.

Stephen is standing in my room telling me. I had been reading, already in my gown. He startled me, and I felt embarrassed about myself and tried to sink down under the covers. He is standing outside the circle of light from my lamp, a dark shadow in the room, his face not distinguishable. "I haven't told her yet, so don't say anything."

"She's still a baby," I say.

"If you paid any attention to her, you'd know that's not true," he says. He can always find the words that hurt. Some days I think that surely I have buried my heart so deep that nothing can reach it, and for weeks at a time nothing does, but then his words cut through and make a wound as fresh and raw as when I realized the extent of his rejection.

"Attention? Stephen, she's my life."

"You pick a funny way to show it. Anyway, the point here is not your relationship to Elizabeth. The point is she's growing up. She needs finishing, needs the rough edges smoothed."

"Finishing?"

"You know what I mean. A finishing school, to make a lady out of her." The lines of his silhouette grow fuzzy, and I think if

I stare at him hard enough he will disappear, he will merge into the shadows completely and be gone and I will wake up and not a trace of these words will be in the air.

"A lady?"

"Will you quit parroting? It is impossible to have a conversation with you."

This is true. I don't know if we have ever been able to have a conversation. I once thought so. I thought, when we sat together for hours on the front porch swing, that our words reached a soul depth. But when I look back on that courtship, I realize that he talked and I listened. What felt like communication to me then was really monologue. Whose fault is that? I should have spoken up, but listening was so sweet. I should speak up now, but I am frozen, trapped. My mind is blank. If I had had the right words, I could have stopped the sale of my house, and I could keep Lizzie home where she belongs, but my words are always wrong. They bring shouts, anger, slammed doors, and then longer and longer silences.

I realize that the shadow is still talking, the mouth is moving faster and faster, coming toward me, no shadow any longer, but a man with a red face and flashing eyes, and bristling mustache, bending over me, staring in my face, shouting now.

"For God's sake, woman, look at yourself! You're no wife, no mother. You've given up. Why would a woman give up who has everything?"

He is angry enough to kill me, this is how murders happen, but I am not afraid. Let him, I don't care. Then I can rest. I won't have to try to figure things out. I can quit reading and looking for clues. I can sleep without the dreams. I close my eyes and rise, away from the lies and pain and misunderstanding to a vantage point where I can watch. I am floating, suspended in the cold air above the bed. How interesting to watch one's murder, like a play, how few have the power of detachment.

He murderous, above her, she weak shrinking desdemona and her pillow nancy my last duchess iphegenia. Then abruptly the curtain. He straightens up and raises his arm as if to strike but strikes the air instead a gesture of disgust, futility, rejection, dismissal. A sound like sobbing in his throat, he exits. She lies rigid as marble, arms folded across her breast, waiting.

Lizzie
1916

When the blood came I cried and cried. I don't know why. I went and got Genesis and she came in the bathroom with me. "Why you crying, girl? Genesis said. "Just mean you a woman now is all."

"I know what it means, Genesis. I'm not an idiot."

"Ain't stopped your sass, anyway," Genesis said. "Take more than a little blood to stop that."

The tears were coming and coming. "It's so messy," I said. "There're going to be years and years of this mess."

"You ain't the first it happened to and you ain't the last. Hand me them drawers. Always soak 'em in cold water to take the blood stains out."

"Boys don't have to fool with this," I said. "This is not fair."

"Have to ask God about that," Genesis said.

"What if you're in school and this happens? You're sitting there in class and then you stand up and there's blood all over your skirt and everybody sees it. Then what?"

"Then you come home, change clothes, go back. Lots worse things could happen to you."

"I can't think of a one." I was sitting on the toilet with my face in my hands, tears running down my elbows. Genesis left and came back with some rags folded up and pinned in a clean pair of pants.

"I thought maybe I would be an exception," I said. "I thought I might be a girl this didn't happen to."

"Child, you are a sight," Genesis said. "Ain't no exceptions to this here. Rich and poor, black and white, it all the same."

"Don't tell anybody," I said. "I don't want a soul to know, not Mama or Daddy or Sissy or anybody."

"Lord have mercy," Genesis said.

"My breasts feel funny. They itch and hurt."

"Growing."

"I'm probably going to look like a milk cow. People will moo when I come in the room. Mooooo, moooooo." Then I got tickled and was laughing in the middle of crying.

"Go to bed," Genesis said. "I ain't studying your old silly self." Then she went back down the stairs laughing and saying, "Milk cow my foot. That girl tickles me so bad I don't know what to do."

I'm lying in bed now, and the tears are coming again, running out the sides of my eyes and down my neck. I'm going to have to get up and find a handkerchief, but I don't want to because I'm afraid the blood will run down my legs. I feel like a baby must feel in a wet diaper except that nobody comes to help me when I cry.

When I shut my eyes tight, my body feels like I'm back in my old room in Holly Springs. I can see everything—my rocker, my chest, my little vanity with the mirror, the canopy bed with all my dolls, the bookcase. I can see the wallpaper that was supposed to be bouquets of roses but that had elves hidden in little towns that only I could see. I miss home. I miss the gardenia bush and the climbing tree behind the woodshed and the front porch and the big black kitchen stove. Most of all I miss Kate. I want to be little again, walking to school with Kate and John. I'd be happy to see anybody from my old school. I'd even be happy to see Stuffy Flannigan.

I think this is what they call homesick.

Lizzie
1916

Dear Kate,

Today was the funniest coincidence. I was walking through the capitol on my way from school when I saw some women at a little table in the rotunda. They were handing out pamphlets to some of the representatives. You know the legislature is in session now. Anyway, when I got closer who should I see but Miss Meems! I'll tell you I have never been so glad to see anybody. A face from home right there in the capitol so suddenly! I ran and hugged her neck. Then we had a nice talk about Holly Springs and you and your brothers and everything.

Miss Meems has worked so hard on the suffrage business, hasn't she? She told me I should put in a good word for the women with Daddy, but I don't think it would help any. He is sending me away to Virginia to school. I feel like this is not fair at all, since I worked so hard to get us elected, remember I made speeches everywhere and gave out flyers? Now that we're here, I have to leave. One night he got real mad at me for no reason that I could tell, and the next day he said I was going, and he has been different to me ever since.

I have thought and thought about this and tried to figure it out. I think it is because he thinks I act like a child and it is time to grow up, but how boring. He does not like it when I run to school (I can still run faster than most anybody, Kate), and he says I must learn to walk like a lady. He says the governor cannot have a daughter running around like a wild thing through the streets.

I guess now I'll be double homesick—for Daddy and Mama and here and for Holly Springs. I have to go next week, even though it's the middle of the term. I was so hoping that you could come down here on the train and spend a weekend, but that will have to wait until later, Mama says.

School here is not fun. People whisper about me behind my back. I try to ignore it, but that is hard to do. I don't have any real friends and so I sit around and read and write in my diary and miss my friends from home all the time. Some days after school I go down to the capitol to the senate or the house chambers and sit in the balconies and listen to them talk. Some of them speak well, but some are not too smart, I think. The other day the fourth-grade children from Davis school had a spelling bee with the legislators, and the children won!

Mama's health is much worse since we left the Hollies. She stays in bed most of the time, except at supper she usually gets dressed and comes down to the dining room with Daddy and me. I am hoping that being in Jackson close to the good doctors will help her.

How are Sally and Shelby and Alice and Nancy? Does Christine still like Keith? What about Thomas and Mary Jane? Do you still go to Kincannon's after school for chocolate sodas? What is on at the picture show? Do you like boys yet? Does John have a girlfriend yet? I think he kissed me good-bye, but I'm not sure, it happened so fast. Anyway, don't breathe a word about that to a living soul, especially John. Please write me ALL the NEWS.

If I don't see you before, remember our pledge to meet on the courthouse steps of Holly Springs in 25 years—9:00 A.M., June 19, 1942! Wonder what we will be doing? Do you think we will still be alive? Maybe you will be the first woman president and will come from Washington. Miss Meems would love that, wouldn't she? I don't know what I would like to be. Maybe a famous writer coming across the waters from Paris. Or maybe the wife of a European prince who lives in a castle with a moat. Wherever I am, I will come to Holly Springs in 25 years, Kate. Don't you worry.

Stay your same sweet self and don't change a bit!

Love from your best friend,
Lizzie

P.S. I just had a wild, wonderful idea, and I'm so excited I know I won't sleep a wink. Do you think Miss Meems and Mr. Henry would let you come to Virginia, too? The name of the place is Hawthorne College, and Daddy says that lots of nice Mississippi girls go there. If you came too, that would be so wonderful, I can't even imagine. Do ask them, please, please. We could have such a time. XXXXX L.

The Registrar
1916

Highly irregular to enroll a girl in the middle of the term like this, but when the governor of a Southern state requests it, the president complies, or asks me to, rather, and so I am here bending all the rules and procedures to join Miss Elizabeth Dunbar to our rolls. I do not approve of this kind of disorder.

The entrance interview was extraordinary in several ways. The governor himself came to enroll the girl. He is a tall, distinguished man in his prime with blond hair and mustache and piercing blue eyes. Most often it is the mothers who come for this duty, but the mother in this case is an invalid, they say. Father and daughter came into my office at 9:00 A.M. sharp, he holding the child by the elbow. Something about the postures of both, the rigidity of his body, the way she hung back, I don't know exactly, brought to mind a sacrificial animal being led to the block. Not a lamb, because the girl is not passive and yielding, but a colt maybe, a fine thoroughbred but skittish and badly in need of training. Silly, of course, to think of this child of privilege in those terms. Hardly a sacrifice to come to a school such as Hawthorne. More than likely she is a spoiled brat who needs the discipline we at Hawthorne can provide.

She is a lovely little thing, cascades of curly dark hair caught in a heavy gold clasp at the nape of her neck, luminous skin, large, smoky-blue eyes. Her clothes were expensive—navy traveling suit tailored perfectly to her developing figure, soft leather shoes and purse. If I had such a daughter, I too would want to put her away in a safe place. She sat at the edge of her chair, her small, gloved hands held together tightly in her lap. She kept her eyes focused on the ink well on my desk and opened unnaturally wide. From time to time she blinked them hard. I realized finally that she was fighting to keep back tears.

We agreed that she would take a modified curriculum and be classified as an "irregular" student. She didn't speak until we came to discussing what her favorite subjects are. I asked her directly, and she tossed her head back and said with a clear note of defiance, "I like to write and that's all I like in school."

Her father frowned and put in quickly, "She's quite good in all her subjects. Her grades are excellent."

"I notice you were enrolled in biology in Jackson," I said, examining her records. "We could fit you into a section of that."

"No," she said distinctly. "I'm as smart as I want to be about frogs."

I smiled at that, but her father's jaw tightened, and he said in a carefully controlled voice, "Biology will be good."

She swallowed hard and her eyes returned to the ink well. She said no more as her father and I planned her course of study. As we finished, I turned to her again and said, "We're happy to have you at Hawthorne, Miss Dunbar, and if I can help you in any way . . . " when the tears spilled, and she turned to her father with a look that would have melted stone and said, "Please don't leave me here."

He laughed apologetically and rose to go. "You'll be fine," he said with false bravado.

"Why are you doing this to me?" she asked, a touch of anger replacing supplication.

I had the uneasy feeling of being the third party, the detached observer from whom she was drawing courage to say things she wouldn't otherwise. I was being used, regardless of my own opinion in the matter. I did not like being in this position.

"Come along, Elizabeth," he said taking her arm and pulling her to her feet. "We must let Mr. Daily get on with his work."

"I can't breathe," she said, looking quite desperate. "I feel like something terrible will happen if you leave me here." Her cheeks were scarlet, and I fancied I could see her heart pounding under her navy suit.

I was beginning to worry, thinking the admission of this student meant bad news for Hawthorne, that she had behavioral problems not revealed on the application. Her father was embarrassed and felt both the need to explain to me and to chastise his daughter. "The first time she's been away from home," he said to me, and then he lowered his head and said in a strained whisper to the child, "Elizabeth, *please*."

"You didn't even ask me," she blurted on. "I think I should have some say-so."

The father's face was a mask, the eyes cold. "I know what's best for you," he said. He put an arm around the girl's waist and practically dragged her to the door, the tension between them fairly making sparks rise from the carpet. I walked out from behind my desk and followed them. He turned to me at the doorway and held out his hand, the other one fast to the back of his daughter's neck, as if to keep her in check until they were safely out of my office. His tone was all cordiality.

"Mr. Daily, a pleasure. Thank you for your time and help. I know my little girl will be in good hands."

She looked me straight in the eye before he hurried her away; it was the look of one bested for the moment, betrayed even, but far from broken.

Reining in the spirited Miss Dunbar will be a challenge for Hawthorne. I will watch with interest. One of the rewards of this job is to meet the students when they come to us as girls— awkward, selfish, willful, passionate to have their own way—and then to see them leave as women—poised, charming, capable of handling any social situation, able to converse on an intelligent level with their future husbands, equipped to begin the education of children, well trained for their crucial roles as wives and mothers. Education for women at its best. It's hard to imagine why our society was so long in realizing the necessity of it.

Maude Temple
1916

The new girl is as wild as a March hare and wouldn't you know she is rooming with me. A tower room of my own was too good to be true, a circle room on the fourth floor where I could be by myself. "We need an older girl to show her the ropes," Dean Powers said. Lizzie is sitting in the window in her nightgown now, smoking. It is four o'clock in the morning, and I have a huge history test at eight.

"I want to get some sleep," I say to her.

"So, sleep," she says.

"The smoke bothers me," I say.

She doesn't answer. She takes a long draw on the cigarette, and I see the tip of it glow red in the dark. I am getting angry. I turn over and bury my head under the pillow, but I am wide awake. I can still smell the smoke, too, and it is making me cough. I lie there fuming for what seems like an hour, and then I sit up again. She is still in the window seat that curves with the tower, her knees pulled up under her chin, her long hair practically to the floor. She lights another cigarette from the one she is smoking.

"If you get caught, you'll be expelled," I say.

"Good," she says. "That would suit me fine. Anything to get out of this hell hole."

Now I am furious that she's talking this way about Hawthorne. "Why did you come here, anyway?" I ask.

"My Daddy made me. Why would anybody come unless they were made to?"

"I've always wanted to," I say. "My great-grandmother was one of the first students in 1842, and then my grandmother, my mother, and two sisters."

"Isn't that nice?" she says sarcastically. "Miss Legacy." She grinds her cigarette right into the new white paint on the window seat.

"Now you listen here," I say, louder than I mean to. I spring out of bed and sit on the window seat so we are face to face. "This is a wonderful school, and we are lucky to be here. Look out there, how beautiful." The gas lamps along College Street are diffused into patches of light in the mist and the dogwood trees are glowing white with bloom in the moonlight. The brick classroom buildings stand solidly like old friends, waiting for morning when all the girls in their blue and white uniforms will come down the tree-lined paths and fill up the classrooms. I feel tears come to my eyes because I love this place, it has opened up a new world to me, and in two more months I'll have to leave it forever.

She looks out the window and then back at me. "I don't see what's so great about it. To me it looks like a prison."

I want to slap her as hard as I can. I am surprised at my anger. I clinch my fists and remind myself that she's only fourteen and also from Mississippi and so what can I expect? She shivers as if she has just realized that it is cold in the room. She hugs her arms to her chest.

"I want to do something bad," she says, "but I can't think of anything bad enough."

"Smoking and being up after lights-out is a good start."

She laughs as if I've made a joke. "That's nothing," she says. "I mean something big, like jumping out of this window maybe." I look down at the sidewalk four stories below where a person would hit, and I feel dizzy and lose my stomach.

"You're crazy," I say.

"Or running away to New York City. I've thought about that, too."

"Why?"

She shrugs. "I don't know. I think those thoughts all the time."

"Well, don't."

"He'd be sorry then, I bet."

"Who?"

"Daddy. For sending me here. He'd wish he hadn't of done it."

"That's immature. Being here is an opportunity."

"Easy for you to say. You're graduating. Lucky."

"You'll get to like it. I know you will."

"Six years," she said in a kind of wail. "If I stay until I finish college, that's six years." She looks so lonely that I begin to feel sorry for her.

"Don't think like that. Think one day at a time. That's what I did when my father died, and that helped."

"Your daddy is *dead*?" she says, like the possibility that a father could die has never occurred to her. "That's terrible."

"Yes, it is, but you have to go on living."

"I couldn't. I couldn't live if anything happened to Daddy." The way the moon is striking her face makes dark shadows under her eyes, and she reminds me of pictures I have seen of orphan children. I reach and pat her hand.

"Nothing will happen to him. Work hard and make him proud of you."

"He doesn't care what I do, just so I don't get in his way."

"What about your mother?"

"She's got bad health and that takes up most of her time so she can't think a lot about me."

"Grandparents, brothers, sisters?"

"No. Just Uncle Leroy and Aunt Inez and three cousins, and they don't like me."

I pat her hand again. The sky is lighter now, a pearly white with a pink glow around the edges. A bird begins to sing in the pale-green ginkgo tree outside the window. "Look, it's morning.

Things always seem better in the daylight, don't you think so?"

"They will never be better for me," she says. "Never ever." She has her head down on her knees. Her voice is muffled, and her words trail off. She is asleep. I help her into the bed and cover her with her quilt. I will stop by Dean Powers' office on my way to history and tell her that Lizzie will probably not be in classes today.

Lizzie
1916

Maude is nice, but a little dull. She reminds me some of Kate, so serious and hard working, except that Kate is more fun, but then Maude is old, too, and that makes a difference I guess. She already looks exactly like a teacher should, with her hair on top of her head except for that one wisp in the back that won't stay put and a pencil behind her ear and those funny little wire-rim glasses. She's going home to Richmond after graduation and teach school from now on. That's all she wants to do. She tries to help me, but she doesn't understand how someone might not love Hawthorne like she does. She gets mad at me when I get into trouble and asks me why I cut class and skip dinner, and I don't know really, except at the time it seems like a good idea.

Maude thinks Cynthia Stone and Lady Margaret Keifer are wild girls and that I should stay away from them, but they're fun to be around. Cynthia can do this perfect imitation of Maude, the way she tries to read walking across the campus and runs into things, and squinches her eyes up to see at a distance. I laugh and laugh and tell them silly things she does. Like the way she washes out her underwear in the sink and hangs it up to dry under a towel because she's too modest to have even me see it. Or how she gets down on her knees by her bed at night to say her prayers, like a little child. But then after we have such a good time laughing about Maude, she'll save me her chocolate cake from dinner because she knows how I love it or she'll help me with my algebra, and I'll feel bad that

I laughed at her. But the next time I'm with Cynthia I can't help it. I do the same thing all over again.

Cynthia and Lady Margaret keep me from feeling sad like I do in my room alone or scared like I feel in class. They are both so beautiful and popular, I can't believe they want me for a friend. They have the room next to mine and Maude's. Cynthia looks exactly like one of my china dolls at home—pale gold hair, blue blue eyes, and skin that looks like it has a light under it shining through. Lady Margaret has black hair and green eyes, and she is the best dancer in the world. They're sixteen, and they know boys at the University of Virginia. One of these boys, Douglas, is engaged to Cynthia. He is tall and handsome as a prince and has an automobile. It's the most beautiful automobile in the world, shiny red outside and soft seats that you sink into. The top is open and when we ride out in the country and the trees and the cows sort of fly by, I feel better, freer or something, and can't believe my good luck to have friends like this. I just wish my friends from home could see me.

Every Wednesday afternoon when the weather is nice, we sign out to walk to town, but as soon as we're outside the gates of Hawthorne, safely out of sight, the boys pick us up in the car, and we go for a ride. They bring cigarettes, too. One day they brought a picnic, and we found a place to eat it on the banks of a stream. Douglas usually brings two or three other boys with him—Albert Percy, who Lady Margaret likes because he is a good dancer and plays the piano, and Hogarth Adams, who talks about golf all the time and constantly takes imaginary swings at an imaginary ball. Sometimes Newt Finley comes along and reads funny poems he's written. I like the cowlick at the back of Newt's head that makes his hair stand straight up like a tiny blond geyser.

Yesterday I wrote a poem, too, a funny one with all of us in it, a verse about each person. And they clapped and said how good it was. Douglas especially liked it, and kept quoting parts of it and saying, "You're a clever one, Lizzie." That made me feel happier than I've felt since I've been here. Douglas is very, very nice. Cynthia is lucky to have a boyfriend like that. Laughing and having fun with my friends, I can forget about home.

This morning in biology class the strangest thing happened to me. I felt like any minute I was going to scream and run out of the room. My heart was beating like I had been running hard, and all I could think was, *I'm going to scream, I'm going to scream.* It was still thirty minutes until the bell, and so I sat with my hands held together as tight as I could, digging my nails into my hands, and trying not to scream. I wonder if I am losing my mind. I can't very well ask anybody, but I am worried. Maybe I will stop going to biology class. Maybe they would not miss me.

The Antique Shop

"Where is he?"

Mrs. Cavanaugh sailed down the aisle between banks of cut glass, startling Booker, who was sitting at the desk reading *Black Betty*. She had an arm full of books, and a pencil behind her ear. "I hate you, Clovis," she said to Mr. Cavanaugh. He emerged at that moment from the back.

Booker was flabbergasted. He had never heard Mrs. Cavanaugh say a harsh word to anybody.

"Hello, Booker, has Yahnah had her baby yet?" she said to him in a friendly tone.

"No'm, be any day probably."

"I'm crocheting a crib blanket for it," she said, "and if CLOVIS hadn't gotten me into that COURSE at the college, I'd be done. Clovis, I knew I should have audited, but oh, no, you said, 'You won't get near as much out of it if you audit.'"

"You wouldn't of," Mr. Cavanaugh said.

"I'll tell you what we're going to get out of this course, Clovis. A divorce."

Booker got up from the desk at this and made his way discreetly out the door, but he couldn't help lingering in the shadows to hear the outcome.

"You know your problem, Clovis? You were jealous of my Thursday bridge. You couldn't rest until you deprived me of it, could you? You were threatened by my women friends. I see it all now."

"Now that's crazy there," Mr. Cavanaugh said. "If that's true, why would I want you to take a course in women's studies?"

"I don't know, but it was a sad mistake on your part because I am on to you now. I know all about the patriarchy, and I'm not going to put up with it. To tell the truth, some days I think I hate all men."

Booker nodded in the hallway. He could understand that. Some days, especially if he had been reading Yahnah's black history books, he felt like he hated all white people, too.

Mr. Cavanaugh felt alarmed. He saw his comforts drifting away. He remembered he had not had hot cornbread in two weeks because Mrs. Cavanaugh had had to study; in fact, almost every evening when he got home from the shop, he had to go back to town for carry-outs. He had been reading the assignments, too—Gerder Lerner, Anne Firor Scott, Adrienne Rich. They made him nervous.

"Furthermore," Mrs. Cavanaugh said, practically throwing her books on his desk, "I'm probably going to make an F anyway."

"Now, now, you aren't going to make an F," said Mr. Cavanaugh in what he thought was a comforting way.

"Don't patronize me," she snapped. "I know more about what grade I'm going to make than you do. How can I do an original research paper in Mississippi women's history if the library doesn't have the sources and can't get them? You'd think Dr. MacAuley would know it's an unreasonable assignment. I am frustrated to the nth degree.

"Original?"

"Unpublished stuff. Old papers like letters and diaries and the Dunbar files that you won't let me near."

"Oh." Mr. Cavanaugh was suddenly a man under siege. "They're not much, actually."

"If I want an A, that is," Mrs. Cavanaugh went on. "And I don't see any use in doing it if I'm not trying for an A."

Ah, so that was it. Mr. Cavanaugh began to see. Would he give up the Lizzie papers for his wife's project and thereby indirectly turn them over to the Yankee woman, who would be down here in a whipstitch and take them over? Or would he keep them for himself and try to persuade his wife to muddle through with a lesser project, regurgitated from some book?

Booker saw the problem, too. He chuckled softly in the shadows. "Brought it all on hisself," he whispered. "Every bit of it."

Cynthia Stone
1916

Wednesday night after lights-out I say to Lady Margaret, "Did you see how Douglas looked at Lizzie?"

"No," she says, "you're imagining things again. She's just a child."

"Child, nothing," I say. "You can't tell me. She knows what she's doing. Smiling so that dimple comes in her chin. Making up that silly poem. She's trying to get him. Why did you ever ask her to come with us anyway?"

"Me? Me ask her? I beg your pardon?"

"O.K., O.K. I guess it was my idea, too, but now what can we do about it?"

"For heaven's sake, Cynthia, you can't go through life being jealous of every woman who looks at Douglas."

"You really didn't feel it?" I say. "That something was starting up between them?"

"I didn't feel anything," she says. "Douglas is just a friendly person. He's nice to everybody."

"And Lizzie is a flirt."

"She doesn't know what she's doing, though. I really don't believe she does. She's been sheltered or something."

"Am I prettier than her?"

"No comparison. Lizzie is cute, but you're gorgeous. You know that." Then she turns over in her bed with her back to my side of the room. She yawns and says, "Go to sleep."

I lie here for a long time with a sick feeling that I have destroyed my happiness by introducing my fiancé to the new girl. I worship Douglas. He is everything to me. The Tidewater house we will live in has forty rooms, fresh flowers in every one. "Your sisters did well," Mama said, "but you, darling, have done brilliantly. My littlest chick has outdone them all."

From the moment I looked into the heart of this diamond as he put it on my finger, I have been his in every way but one. "Your trump card, darling," Mama said. "You must save that for the wedding night." But what if we never get there? Whatever it takes to keep him I will do it.

Douglas Trumble
1916

This is crazy and I know it, but something about that little Lizzie girl I can't get out of my mind. She's always herself, no matter what, she's natural. Life vibrating in every cell of her. She treats all of us the same, like friends. She doesn't get her feelings hurt if I talk to another girl, and she doesn't analyze every word I say. I'm not engaged to her either, and that's probably the difference. But this is crazy to be thinking about. She's just turned fifteen, and I'm twenty and about to graduate and marry. I am the envy of every man at the university. I like to watch their faces when I am with Cynthia. I draw strength from her beauty, and I know I am too weak not to marry her.

Today is Lizzie's birthday, and I've brought champagne and real crystal glasses pillaged from home to celebrate. We have picked the girls up as usual and driven out to McCarty's Lake. The lake sits in the middle of an apple orchard, white with bloom. We take off our shoes, put down our quilts, and spread the fruit and cheese the girls have smuggled from the dining hall. I pour the champagne and propose a toast: "To the birthday of our newest friend, Lizzie Dunbar, the poet—may love follow her through a long and fruitful life."

Hear, hear! We touch our glasses and drink to it. Her face is radiant, like a flower on the end of a white starched stem, and when she looks at me and says, "That is the sweetest toast, Douglas," I shiver, even though the sun is beating on my back.

Cynthia picks up the current. I know she does, but I can't stop. I can't and I don't want to. I want to stay here forever and look at Lizzie Dunbar with the apple blossoms around her and the sound of her laugh singing in my veins and the champagne bubbling in the afternoon sun. I am in an altered state of consciousness. I know other people are here, I can vaguely hear the murmurs of their talk, but all my attention, all my energy is focused on that one small girl. I fill her glass and my own again and again. She is telling me her life, and I am drinking it, thirstily, can't get enough of it, my whole body at attention. I move close to her, I'm drawn rather, unconsciously, so that her stockinged foot touches my leg, and I am shocked by the touch, I feel it in my gut, my mind is concentrated there at that point where we touch. When she speaks I look again at her face, at her neck, and with the greatest effort I keep from touching the hollow in her throat where the life beats. I am a single-cell life form who can engulf her, absorb her into myself so that she can live as a part of me.

Cynthia squeezes in between us. I feel regret and disappointment and embarrassment and a pain that is physical. "How's my ole darling," she says, rubbing my thigh and kissing me on the mouth.

Lizzie crosses her legs like an Indian maiden, her eyes and cheeks bright from the champagne, and she says, "Have you all got the date figured out yet?" and I feel sick because she is so matter-of-fact about it, I feel angry at her for saying that, for bringing that up, but that's crazy—I'm the one marrying, not Lizzie, I'm the one engaged and I am thinking maybe all this I'm feeling is just me, Lizzie doesn't feel anything, any more than she does with Newt or Hogarth, we're all the same to her and that really is crazy then, if I made it all up that's really crazy.

Then I can't sit there I am burning I have to move I have to do something and I want to swim so I stand up and say but they all say we can't we didn't bring our suits. "That won't stop me," I say, and I take off my coat and tie and belt and untie my shoes.

Cynthia says, "You bad boy, you better stop, right now."
She is giggling and blushing and hiding her face in her hands.

Lizzie looks at me straight and says, "Are you going to swim
naked?" She does not mean to be personal I can tell, she just
wants to know, she is interested to know. My head swims I guess
it's the champagne I don't know her face is moving toward me
and then away. "Yes," I say. "Yes, oh, yes."

"Doug-las," Cynthia is squealing like a little pig. "You are
awful, Douglas."

Newt and Hogarth get up then and say they will too, and
we strip down to our drawers and the girls are saying they will
walk back to campus, but they are laughing. Then we ask them
to swim too, we dare them, but they shake their heads and hide
their faces. Then we walk down to the water and take off our
drawers and leave them there and walk into the water not
turning to look at the girls until we are up to our necks in the
water. "Feels good," I say. "Come on in."

"We won't look," Newt says.

"Yeah," Hogarth says, "We'll turn our backs until you get in."

Then the girls begin to whisper to each other, and then they
disappear, Lizzie behind a bush, and Cynthia and Lady
Margaret behind the car. "Ready," Cynthia shouts in a few
minutes, and she and Lady Margaret come out from behind
the car in their underwear, satin and pink ribbons all over them,
they are giggling and holding their arms crossed in front of
them, but Lizzie walks out from behind the tree as unadorned
as the day she was born, fifteen years ago today, she walks
straight through the grass and down to the water with no
shame. Oh, God, she is beautiful. "Jesus God," I whisper and
my eyes swim with water, tears or lake water, I don't know, but
she's blurry and then she's an arc and slices into the water
without a sound. I know that I will never forget how she looked
then, that whatever happens from now on she is etched in my
memory. I watch her swimming toward me, the sun making
rainbows with every stroke, and I think that my body will

disappear out here in the water that I will melt into the water I will become it and then she will swim through me, I will be all around her, hold her up, flow into her and she will flow into me and we will be one with the water and with the grass trees birds sky sun moon stars.

We swim together a long way out and then we turn and float on our backs and I don't look at her but I want to but she wouldn't care she is still the same no different she is herself, just as if she had all her clothes on and was sitting still on the pallet and talking to me. "This is the best birthday I ever had," she says. "Thank you, Douglas. This is a grown-up birthday."

We swim back then and all the way I'm wondering what this means, not just lust it's more complicated I don't know, not just the champagne, what is it, crazy, she's a baby, a girl child, not Cynthia, I lust for Cynthia so beautiful, expensive, so well born Cynthia is well born Mother says so important for your wife Cynthia silver and distant like the new moon but Lizzie is the sun warm sunny Lizzie.

Cynthia and Lady Margaret are ice, staring. They are dressed and drinking more champagne. I am ashamed suddenly. I call for Hogarth to bring my clothes, but Lizzie walks out of the water and behind the bush for her clothes. When we are on the pallet again with the others, hair dripping, Lizzie says to the girls, "I thought you were coming in."

"Some people have more modesty than that," Lady Margaret said.

"But you said . . . " Lizzie looks confused. "We're all such good friends." Her cheeks are burning.

"Have some more champagne, birthday girl," Cynthia says, and her voice is high and brittle. She fills Lizzie's glass again and again. In between she sits in my lap and kisses me, her mouth cold and dry. Ordinarily I would be frantic with wanting her, but now I want her to stop. We drink until the sun dips below the tree line. We are shadows in slow motion. Cynthia holds my hand as the full moon rises, my ring on her finger flashes ice in the moonlight.

Hogarth looks at Lizzie in a new way he has his arm around her she throws her head back and laughs she has never had champagne her laughter bubbles out of her throat, her mouth and teeth are perfect, they are ivory and red wine in the moonlight but then they are eclipsed gone covered with Hogarth he puts his head down and kisses her mouth and then her throat the life spot in her throat where her life beats my life beats there life beats a fire a quick igniting I spring I will smash break kill him kill him my hands around his neck my fist in his face son of a bitch son of a bitch glass shatters shards of crystal in the moonlight, the girls high-pitched glass-shattering screams stop him Cynthia shrieks he is drunk stop him Newt he doesn't know what he's doing blood runs down my arm and down my face. I have stopped Hogarth's greedy mouth not kissing now cannot kiss now his ugly slug mouth cannot kiss Lizzie now. I am happy and then everything is dark.

Dean Powers
1916

Elizabeth Dunbar has been a problem since she waltzed through Hawthorne's gates, and had it been up to me she would have been sent back to Mississippi the day she arrived. The last thing we need at Hawthorne are idle, spoiled debutantes who cannot get on with their families and so are sent here to be made ladies of and to catch a rich husband from the university. If I had some say-so in the choices here, the important decisions, we could make real progress in the business of educating women, but I have none. All policy is left to the men, and my role is to clean up the messes they make.

On my way to breakfast this morning, I passed as usual through the parlor of Main, enjoying the rich elegance of the room, the peacefulness of it as the morning sun lights the chandelier, an island of quiet before the noisy dining room. I stopped in front of the tall mirror as I have each morning for twenty years to see if I am presentable, petticoat not showing, collar straight, et cetera, when in the lower corner of the mirror I saw a reflection of something not quite right on the love seat by the French doors that lead into the garden. I turned and started in that direction, and as I drew closer I realized that a body lay there, knees drawn up almost to the chin, hair tumbling over the edge of the sofa. The shoulders and face were covered with a man's suit coat. I held my breath as I pulled the coat back to look at the face.

It was Elizabeth Dunbar, reeking of liquor.

I took her by the shoulder and shook her awake. She looked

at me with no sign of recognition. She shut her eyes against the morning sun, then moaned and began to retch violently all over herself, the sofa, the carpet. Furious and disgusted, I left her there and went to the kitchen for help. One of the maids came with me, and when we got back to her she had the dry heaves and her eyes and nose were streaming. "Ooooooooo," she moaned. "I am so sick. Why am I so sick?"

"Because you have been drinking liquor," I snapped.

"Not liquor," she said, "Champagne. For my birthday."

I was shocked at her brazenness in admitting her folly. "That is grounds for expulsion," I told her. "We will send you straight home, young lady."

"Really?" she said hopefully, and her face lightened.

"What do you think your mother and father will say? How do you feel about disgracing them?" She looked extremely ill again at that thought, her lips white as her blouse. "Since you are the governor's daughter, your expulsion will be in the newspapers." Her hands began to shake, and she laid her head on the arm of the love seat and sobbed. "Clean her up and put her to bed," I said to the maid. "I can't stand the sight of her."

Oh, God, that men (and now women, girls, children) should put an enemy in their mouths to steal away their brains. To me it's all the same, the bubbling champagne at a wedding reception or the cheap gin of the drunk in the gutter, the same potential for disaster. We have enough suffering and tragedy in the world without purposefully ingesting more of it.

I know of what I speak, having grown up in the house of a man who drank himself unconscious every night and watched while his rich Pennsylvania land, livestock, house, the legacies of five generations, slipped away unnoticed, at least by his pickled brain. He conveniently drank himself to death about the time everything was gone. And then the struggle my mother had to keep a roof over our heads, feed us, patch us up sufficiently for school. Don't talk to me about liquor.

My home wasn't the only one destroyed by drink.

Thousands of others, too. Alcoholism spreads like a cancer throughout the country, yet the president of this institution, whose mission is shaping the lives of young women, drinks brandy with certain faculty members in his office. His wife serves sherry at her little bridge parties. Not to me. I am still the outsider, the "Yankee," though I have lived here now twenty years and the Civil War has been over for fifty, a fact of history that seems to have eluded my colleagues. The "wah" they call it, as if it were yesterday. I am sick of refighting the "wah."

And the women of this country are sick of beatings from drunken husbands, wide-open saloons, shootings in the street, neighborhoods that aren't safe for children, all because of liquor. Oh, I know they call me fanatical behind my back. I see their smirks when I go into town for my WCTU meetings. I know how unfashionable my point of view is among the gentry of old Virginia. But for the first time women are speaking out publicly in large numbers, and they are being heard. And through the efforts of women we are on the verge of national prohibition legislation that will curb our great national disease and make a better place to live for all our people.

So let them call me a frustrated old maid. I am beyond being hurt by name calling. I am engaged in a righteous cause, and in that knowledge I take strength. They laugh and poke fun, but when a problem arises that requires a cool head and disciplinary measures, whom do they call? Who will have to untangle this Lizzie Dunbar mess and reestablish order? And even though I vigorously opposed the rule change that allows girls to sign out for town unchaperoned, now my lot will be to sweep up. Well, sweep I will, each girl who had a part in this escapade, sweep her out of Hawthorne and right back to where she came from.

The Registrar
1916

"Why did you admit her in the middle of the term anyway?" the president said. "This better goddamn well not get in the newspapers or I'll have your ass." He was in a foul mood. His poker club met last night, and he lost money as usual.

"Dean Powers wants to expel her," I said. "Make her an example for the others."

"Damn old tee-totaler," he said. "She'd expel us all if she got the chance." His face and scalp grew so red that his hair seemed to get whiter and thinner, the network of veins on his forehead bluer. "I hate that woman, Daily. Have I told you that?"

"Yes sir."

"She ruins everything." He put his face in his hands as if he were going to cry. "Of all the deans I could have inherited with this office, I had to get an ax-wielding harpy with the charm of a Hottentot." He lifted his head and looked at me through half-closed eyes. "She does not present the right image for Hawthorne."

"Sir, what do you suggest with the Dunbar girl?"

"I don't suggest anything. Discipline is not my problem." He yanked the decanter from under his desk and poured himself a shot. "Drink?"

"No, sir, thank you. I have to meet with Dean Powers in half an hour."

He grimaced and tossed back the brandy. That seemed to cheer him up. "We both know what Powers needs, don't we, Daily?" He laughed until his lungs collapsed into a coughing fit, and then he poured himself some more. "Who was with Miss Dunbar on her little outing?"

"She won't say, just that it was her birthday, and she drank champagne and took a swim."

"Swim, eh? Then an automobile and a boy were involved. She could be pregnant, too, for all we know. Damn! Isn't that wonderful for Hawthorne? Goddamn it all! If Powers would stay on campus and watch these girls instead of roaming around the countryside busting up saloons and preaching nonsense, this would never have happened." The president's face smoldered, and I wondered if heart disease runs in his family.

"I think I'll fire Powers," he boomed. "*She's* the dean of students. This is *her* responsibility, not ours. She drops the ball, and we have to recover." Then his voice grew soft, "I think I'll get rid of that Yankee bitch. I've wanted to for years." He slammed his fist on his desk as if it were Dean Powers.

"The alumnae love her, sir. She's been here longer than either of us. We'd have an outcry. We'll work this out."

"You sure as hell will, you better."

"So you think expulsion is not a good idea?"

"I don't care what you do. You can send Lizzie Dunbar home to Daddy or sell her on the white slavery market or put her in a gunnysack with rocks and throw her in the Shenandoah. I'm just saying the whole business has got to be kept quiet. Not a whisper of this can get out, do you understand that, Daily? My job is to uphold the reputation of this institution, and I intend to do that. One wayward girl and an idiot dean are not going to destroy the good name I've worked to build here."

"Yes sir." Feeling battered and weary, I left the president scowling and picking his nails and walked down the hall to the dean's office. She had the girl with her. Miss Dunbar sat in the chair facing the dean's desk. The dean was standing behind her desk, holding some papers in her hand. Miss Dunbar did not have on her Hawthorne blue and white, but a dark, high-necked dress. Her face was pale, a little drawn, but not very remorseful, or so it seemed to me.

"Miss Dunbar refuses to cooperate," Dean Powers said. Her back was straighter than ever. Dean Powers has perfect posture. "Have a chair, Mr. Daily."

"I'm not going to tattle," Miss Dunbar said, "if that's what you mean."

"Believe me, whoever you're protecting is not worth sacrificing yourself for," Dean Powers said. "Besides, you'd be doing them a service to bring this out in the open before something tragic happens."

"No."

"You were with Cynthia and Lady Margaret, weren't you?"

The girl said nothing.

"I see from your records that you've missed several classes in the past month. Particularly biology."

"Biology makes me nervous," Miss Dunbar said, quite seriously. "I don't go anymore."

"Indeed," Dean Powers said, glaring at the girl over the top of her spectacles. The clock striking on the mantel was clamorous compared to the quiet of the room. We were three stones while the dean stared at the girl until she finally lowered her head and looked at her small hands twisting and plucking at her skirt. Then—this was difficult to see clearly because the sun through the window was reflecting on the dean's glasses— but it seemed to me that the dean's eyes filled with tears, and she said in a husky voice, "Such potential, you have such potential, Miss Dunbar." Then she sat down abruptly and said sharply, "Go to your room. I've asked Maude to wait with you there until we decide." The girl rose and slipped like a shadow from the room.

"As far as I'm concerned, we have no choice," the dean said. "Shall I call Governor Dunbar to come get his daughter or will you?"

"The president is concerned about adverse publicity."

"So am I. But rules are rules. We can't start making

exceptions because a child happens to be from a prominent family."

"True, but—"

"Remember the Strawbridge girl last year? Her offense was far less serious, and we sent her home."

"I know, however—"

"Above all we must be consistent and fair. And we must consider the other girls. One rotten apple—"

A sharp pounding at the door interrupted her. "Come in," she called. The president followed his stomach into the room, the buttons on his gray vest straining, his belt slightly below the equator. His body bears the brunt of a cavalier spirit and years of fleshly pleasure. The dean was hard pressed to hide her disdain. I'm sure with a nose like a foxhound, she could smell the 9:00 A.M. liquor, too.

"I've been thinking," he said, "about this Dunbar matter."

"That's settled."

"Oh?"

"She'll go as soon as her father can come for her."

"You've called him? Before you consulted me?"

"No, but expulsion is the only decision."

"I have an alternate suggestion, Dean." From the minute he crossed the dean's threshold, the president had been in his elder statesman role, the one in which he woos the trustees, the parents, the alumnae. He is much more a politician than a scholar, which explains his success as a college president. At the poker table he is crude and rough as an old cob, but when the need arises, the president can assume impeccable manners and diplomacy like a cloak. Regardless of his dislike for the dean, he has never been anything but courtly in her presence. "May I sit down?" he asked.

The dean flushed. "Please, certainly."

The president settled himself in the chair vacated by Miss Dunbar. He crossed his legs and then folded his hands on his thigh. His brow was creased with concern. "I know all three of us want what's best for Hawthorne," he said, looking from one of us to the other. "The question is to arrive at what *is* best—for Hawthorne and for each student." The dean, if this is possible, stiffened even more.

"Now I was awake last night worrying about this thing," the president continued, "and the conclusion I reached is that we have a lot more at stake than the fate of one student."

"But—" Dean Powers tried to get in a word.

"Dean, I know we have to be fair, and we have to maintain discipline, and I think you are the best in that area of any administrator I have worked with. However—wait, just let me finish—however, this is a case where the greatest good for the greatest number has got to take precedence. I believe. Do you agree, Daily?"

I could kill him when he drags me in this way. "We want to do what's best for Hawthorne, of course, sir."

"In other words, because this girl is a governor's daughter and you're afraid of a public ruckus, you want to let her off scot-free?" the dean asked.

"Dean!" the president said in his best wronged tone. "Did I say scot-free? No, no, no, my dear woman, no indeed. You know that I'm as much in favor of discipline as a college president can be. No, hear me out. I propose that instead of washing our hands of Miss Dunbar and sending her away, that we take a truly disciplinary stance. That like genuine educators, we persevere in the charge that her father issued us by bringing her here and that we make this an experience whereby she can grow and mature."

The dean looked slightly nauseous. "And how, pray, are we to do that?"

"Since the girl slipped away through a network of rules that you helped develop, Dean, I thought perhaps you could tighten the noose just for her, require more of her, keep a closer check."

"I have no intention of becoming a warden," Dean Powers

said. "This is a college, not a penal institution."

"Absolutely," the president said. "I couldn't agree more. I'm just talking about special arrangements for Miss Dunbar between now and the end of the session, only a month away, after all."

I couldn't imagine what he was driving at. Was he seriously proposing locking the child in her room?

"Dean, am I correct that there is a small student bedroom joining your apartment?" The dean stared in disbelief, and the president stretched his arm toward her in a placating gesture. "Wait. Think of the wholesome influence on the girl. Just for a month. For Hawthorne?"

For the first time since I met her, the dean was speechless.

Lizzie
1916

How could such a lovely time turn out so awful? The happiest
birthday I had ever had with friends and the lake and the sky
and trees and sun all around. Then it was ruined. Probably
because I had too much champagne. I remember feeling warm
and melty and safe and then all of a sudden glasses were
breaking, people were shouting, I tried to stand up, but when I
did my head went spinning, up to the moon and down to the
bottom of the lake and after that I don't know.

The next thing I remember, or at least think I remember, is
being carried like a baby in someone's arms and put down
gently, and a boy's voice whispering, "Get her to her room.
Promise? Get her to her room." Then Dean Powers and all the
trouble. The worst of it is not knowing what I did that was so
bad. Oh, I know the rules I broke and all of that, but I don't
know why my friends are not my friends any more. I've gone
over it so many times in my mind that the thoughts have made
ruts through my brain, like wagon tracks, and I can't get the
thoughts out of those ruts for anything.

Whenever I met Cynthia and Lady Margaret on the campus,
their eyes would not look my way. The first time I was allowed
to go to the dining room with the others after the trouble, I was
so happy to be out of my room and to see them again, that I ran
toward them smiling, and they were moving toward me smiling,
but then they walked right past me, not even looking at me,
and met a group of the girls in their sorority to eat with. I
thought they didn't see me, and I followed them to the table

where they were going to sit. Lady Margaret turned to me and said, "We already have eight here. You'll have to find another place."

I stumbled away and would have left dinner, but Maude caught me and made me sit with her. I couldn't eat at all. "You better eat your chicken, Lizzie," Maude kept saying. "You look pale. You will be sick if you don't eat." She is so bossy. I don't know who is worse, Maude or Dean Powers.

"How's your new roomie?" the girls at the table asked me, and then laughed and joked about my rooming with the dean all through dinner. I think it's cruel to laugh at me that way. That was the longest meal I have ever sat through.

All I could think of was that I wanted to make it up with Cynthia and Lady Margaret for drinking too much and making a scene and almost getting them into trouble. The next day I wrote them a letter and apologized, but neither one of them ever spoke to me again.

Now they're gone for good. In June Cynthia and Douglas had the biggest wedding in the history of Virginia and Cynthia was the most beautiful bride. I read about it in the newspaper. The wedding was held in the oldest Episcopal church in Charlottesville, and then the guests went in carriages to Monticello for the reception. Hundreds and hundreds of people came and filled the house and gardens. You have to be very important to have a reception at Monticello. I had so much wanted to be invited. I wonder if I will ever have a wedding. I would like to, but I can't imagine how it would be.

I showed the write-up about the wedding to Dean Powers, thinking that she would be excited about a Hawthorne girl being famous, but she said it made her sick. That's just like Dean Powers to take the fun out of anything. She said Cynthia was much too young to get married, that she hadn't developed her own identity and now she probably never would. I don't see what difference that makes if she's happy and has found the right man. She has a wonderful husband and a nice house and soon she'll probably have children. I rather have that than identity, whatever that is. I think Dean Powers is just mad because she's an old maid. She never has a minute of fun that I can tell. Oh, I hope I don't turn out like her, but I probably will because it looks like I will be stuck here from now on.

Daddy wrote that I couldn't come home for a visit until the end of the summer session. The letter made me desperate. I seriously thought about running away, but where? They don't want me at home, and there's nowhere else I want to go.

At least Dean Powers has let up a little bit. At first she watched me every minute and grilled me with questions. She wanted to know who was with me for my birthday party, what we did—she especially wanted to know about the man's coat that I was covered with when she found me. The coat is Douglas's, but I will never tell her. I'll keep it to remember him by.

I told her all about the party, except for the names of the others who were there. "You had your swimming suit?" she asked.

"My birthday suit," I said, trying to make a little joke.

She caught her breath and said, "You swam naked with boys?" And the way she said it made it sound terrible. Then she said, "Did they do anything to you?"

"What do you mean?"

"Don't play dumb," she said. "You know what I mean." I did know some, but not all the technical details. Nobody had ever told me anything, but I have known where babies come from since Sissy was born. It's how babies get started that is hard to get definite information about. When I asked Mama she said God planted the seed, and you had to be married for the seed to grow, but I knew there was more to it than that. Once a girl from Holly Springs had to go away all of a sudden, and I overheard Mama say to Daddy that she was going to have a baby and her life was ruined. She wasn't married I know, so somehow the baby got there anyway. I had watched cows and dogs mate at home, but it is hard to transfer that to people. The way Dean Powers was acting I got scared I had done something and didn't know it and now I would have to worry about a baby on top of everything else.

"One of them kissed me, I think," I said. "Something was soft and warm on my mouth, but I had my clothes on then, but after the kiss I don't remember."

She groaned and said, "If you were my daughter I would break your neck." Then she said, "Sit down. There is no excuse for such ignorance. I am going to tell you the facts." And she did. When she was through, I felt like I never wanted to see a boy again.

"That is disgusting," I said. "I don't believe it."

"You had better believe it," she said, "if you're going to make a practice of swimming naked with boys."

"Do you think it's already happened, and I don't know it?"

"You'll know it," she said.

"*I* won't ever do it," I said. "I never will. Have you?"

"That comes under the head of personal affairs," she said. "That is none of your business."

The Antique Shop

In the back of the first drawer in the Dunbar file, Mr. Cavanaugh found a college yearbook from a place named Hawthorne in Virginia. The title of it was *The Spinster*. Mr. Cavanaugh thought that name was very odd indeed. He understood that the mission of those girls' schools was to polish up the young women for marriage. He didn't think the word *spinster* would be one they would relish. He looked up Lizzie Dunbar first thing and found her sweet young face still shining there after all these years. The contrast between his memory of the woman and this image threw him into a melancholy mood. He left work early, taking the annual home with him to show Mrs. Cavanaugh.

He still had not been able to bring himself to share the file with his wife, and she was increasingly anxious about her final project for the Women's Studies course. She'll just have to make a B, he thought. I can't give up these papers right now. Booker looked at him reproachfully every time he went back to the clearinghouse. Booker knew.

He had hoped to salve his conscience with the yearbook, and, sure enough, Mrs. Cavanaugh was tickled to death over it—though she didn't really see how she could make it into a research paper. What pleased her most was the title and the epithet "Where singleness is bliss, 'tis folly to be wives." "You see, Clovis," she explained, "this was an interesting time for women. The New Woman was coming into her own, pressing for the vote and for social change. We're mistaken to think all they thought about was catching some man."

"Hmmm," he said, already lost in the newspaper.

Dean Powers
1916

At first I was so angry at having Elizabeth Dunbar thrust into my life, depriving me of my privacy which is absolutely vital to me, that I could hardly stand to be in the room with her. She sulked like a spoiled brat and glared at me as if it were my idea to have her here. When I questioned her about her birthday episode, trying to determine just how much trouble she was in, I was appalled at her ignorance of basic biological information. Then when I gave her a lecture on the facts of life, she seemed to blame me for the way creation is set up.

Attempts at communication failed, and eventually whenever she came out of her bedroom, which opens into my sitting room, I would retire to my bedroom immediately and leave her there alone. I was more angry at the president than at Elizabeth, but he was not around to be the target. Riding after the fox, playing golf, cards, et cetera. Men are never around for the grubby details of daily living. They are gone somewhere. That is the great common denominator of all men I have ever known; they are somewhere else either physically or mentally. They are *in absentia*.

Last Saturday afternoon I was at my desk in the sitting room putting final touches on a speech for the state WCTU convention, when Elizabeth came out of her room and flounced onto my daybed.

"I will die if I have to be in that room another minute," she said. "I will jump out the window."

"Don't ever jest about such a horrible thing," I said.

"I'm not joking," she said. "I mean it."

"I would give anything for time to be in my room alone."

"There's nothing to do," she said. "I've written everyone I know and read every book in the library."

"You would do well to meditate on your wickedness," I said, "and ask forgiveness. That should keep you busy for the rest of the year."

"God is bored with my sins. He told me." You never know what this child is going to say. She dances cheerfully at the edge of sacrilege all the time.

"At least you are communicating with Him," I said. "What else has He told you?"

"He said, 'Go out there and try the dean's patience; she needs the practice.'"

I chuckled in spite of myself and said, "My patience is tried to the limit every day of my life, thank you. I don't need the efforts of you and God."

"What are you doing?" she asked.

"Writing a speech." Then I explained a little about the work of the WCTU. To my surprise, she listened attentively to this and was quite interested, particularly in the campaign for prohibition legislation.

"I made speeches for Daddy," she said. "I like politics."

"Where does your father stand on prohibition?" I asked.

"I don't know," she said. "He doesn't drink because we're Presbyterian, but he does sometimes because the governor has to. Uncle Leroy is a drunkard, but the family is the only one who knows it, so don't tell anybody that."

"If I were you and had an alcoholic in the family, I would think twice before I took another drink."

"Is it contagious?" she asked.

"The tendency runs in families," I said. "Sometimes one drink is all it takes." She looked alarmed at this.

"Do you think I'm an alcoholic now?"

"I think you should never take another drink."

"Daddy says Uncle Leroy would die without his liquor."

"He'll die quicker with it. That's certain."

Then a cloud passed over her face, and she said, "I miss them all so. Even Uncle Leroy. Sometimes I feel like they're all dead back home, and I'll never see any of them again."

"Nonsense," I said, but I felt her sorrow. The sun had disappeared, and a soft breeze was blowing the curtains at the open window. Twilight, the melancholy time of day, the time when memory turns to old losses, dead dreams. The time to keep busy. I lit the lamp on my desk and was about to resume work, when an impulse changed my mind.

"Lizzie," I said, "would you like to have them bring our supper here? The dining room is lonely with the girls gone. Later we could walk to town for ice cream."

She looked as though I had offered her a trip to Paris. "That would be wonderful," she said, jumping to her feet and spinning around the room, her long hair flying. "Daddy sends all this money, but I have nowhere to spend it. I'll treat you to the biggest sundae Brookshire's makes."

Maude
1916

When Lizzie moved out of my tower and in with Dean Powers, I was as happy as I could be. I had my room to myself again and could enjoy my last month at Hawthorne. Or so I thought. But what really happened was that I missed Lizzie, all the coming and going and laughing and talking that she did once she got over her homesickness. I even missed the way she teased me and pulled pranks like short-sheeting the bed and putting a frog in the sink. And so I felt lonely when Lizzie moved out, instead of peacefully alone like I thought I would. I also felt guilty, like I should have kept her from getting in trouble. I knew that Wednesday night when she wasn't back by sign-in time something bad would happen, and I waited up listening until the tower clock above me chimed one, but then I fell asleep, and the next thing I knew it was morning, and they were bringing Lizzie to bed.

Then graduation came. I left Hawthorne, envying Lizzie for being a prisoner there, and went home to Richmond and started applying for a teaching job. By July I was very anxious because I hadn't been offered a place yet. Then I had a letter from Dean Powers. She was coming to Richmond for a WCTU rally. She wanted me to go to it with her, and I wrote that I would love to. I admire Dean Powers greatly. Some of the girls think she is too strict, but I know she has a kind heart. Everything she says sounds wise and true to me, and I want to be like her.

When I got to the station to meet her, I had the surprise of my life. Who should be with her, carrying her briefcase, but Lizzie Dunbar. She looked like a lady with her hair up and wearing a traveling suit, a hat, and gloves. Looking at her, you'd never know how crazy she is. Such a wonderful surprise. The truth is, I'm a little bit scared of Dean Powers, but Lizzie's being there made all the difference. She was laughing and joking with the dean in a way that I never could. I envy her that ease.

We went to the hotel and had a lovely lunch that the dean paid for, thank goodness, since Mama and I are barely scraping by. Most people don't know how generous the dean is and that she has paid the way of many girls through Hawthorne, just as she did for me. She gives those scholarships anonymously, and only by accident did I find out where my money really came from. I was embarrassed that I couldn't invite them home, but Mama said she would never expose our poverty to strangers.

Lizzie and I went to the powder room while the dean settled our bill. Standing at the mirror trying to catch some stray curls back up under her hat, Lizzie said, "I know a secret that is going to set you wild, Maude Temple."

"What?" I said. I couldn't imagine.

"I can't tell. I promised. But just you wait."

"Is it good?" I asked

"You'll think so," she said. "I can't say anymore or I'll let it out. Shoot, I wish I hadn't promised not to tell."

"Just a little hint?"

"Something about Hawthorne," she said. "Now I'm absolutely not saying another word. Straighten your hat up. You look like you're about to take off and fly." She helped me straighten my hat, and I decided that the secret was probably that a rich benefactor left a lot of money for the college, and I didn't think anymore about it.

We went across the street to the auditorium for the speeches. Frances Willard, national president of the WCTU, delivered the keynote address. It was thrilling to see in person a famous leader whom I had heard so much about. She is a handsome woman who commands attention when she walks into a room. When she began to speak, a deep hush fell over the crowd, and her clear ringing voice played on our heartstrings. Her descriptions of homes and families destroyed by the scourge of liquor brought tears to my eyes. She believes this is a war against a deadly drug, with women as the generals, since women are stronger than men morally and must be the guardians of the Christian home. Lizzie leaned forward in her seat, hanging on every word, her face rapt in attention. When Miss Willard finished, we all spontaneously jumped to our feet in a standing ovation. I had chills all over and wished that I could do something right then for the cause that is so much bigger than my own petty troubles.

"I wish I could move a crowd like that," Lizzie said.

Next we went to smaller groups and learned how to organize marches and approach saloon owners and write articles for the newspapers—practical things to do back home. At five o'clock we went to the hotel for tea, very elegant with tiny sandwiches and scones and a lovely English tea in a silver service, snowy white linen napkins and tablecloth, three pink roses in a crystal vase. Lizzie sighed and said, "I am really tired. We had to get up at five o'clock this morning to catch our train."

"Yes, I'm tired, too," Dean Powers said. "A full, rewarding day."

"In fact," Lizzie said, her eyes dancing with mischief, a hint of a dimple in her chin, "what I need is a good stiff drink. How about you, Dean?"

My heart stopped. I looked at the dean, but she continued pouring our tea, shaking her head slightly, one corner of her mouth tightened in a mock exasperated way. "Very funny, Elizabeth," she said. "Are you going to hoard the scones or will you pass them to Maude?"

I breathed again, and as we had our tea, we talked over the meeting. When we finished with the WCTU, the conversation turned to my prospects for employment. Thinking about that made me quite depressed. I told them how the Richmond superintendent had said I was first on the list if a place opened up, but that for now there were no vacancies. I had corresponded with other schools, too, but no luck. While I was telling this bad news and feeling worse and worse, the dean listened sympathetically, but Lizzie looked delighted.

"Will you starve?" she asked, smiles all over. I gave her a look, and she went on. "They need missionaries in China," she said. "How about that?" Lizzie is mischievous, but I had never known her to be deliberately cruel. My feelings were hurt, and I looked down at my plate without answering.

"Don't tease her," the dean said. "Maude, I don't want to stand in your way if you get a better offer in Richmond, but I have a proposal for you to think about. I can offer you a position at Hawthorne as part-time lecturer in the history department and assistant to the dean."

I couldn't say a word.

"You don't have to decide now," the dean went on. "Talk it over with your mother and let me know by the first of August."

"It's a miracle," I said and began to cry.

"I thought you'd be happy," Lizzie said in wonder.

"Sometimes," the dean said, "to gain your heart's desire is as painful as to lose it."

Ginkgo
1916

In my native land of China, far across the mountains and the waters, my brothers and sisters are gold and silver and their groves are sacred. In autumn millions of miniature fans fall suddenly in a rush of gold. The people of the East watch for this and say the golden fall is the work of the gods. In spring we bear the silver apricot, and in the East the people call the fruit sacred. They eat the fruit and are nourished.

Here where I stand my fruit is thrown away because the people do not like the smell. I am ornamental, though that is not Nature's true purpose for me. My brothers, equally as beautiful as I, are held in much higher esteem here because they bear no fruit. The fruit is a nuisance to people here, and as a result few females survive.

I stand alone beside the brick tower with the round face that chimes the hours because more than a century ago a man gathered plants from all over the Old World and created a sacred mountain for himself in the New. He placed my brother at a place of learning for men and me at one for women. This separation, which we could not understand, broke our spirits. The man intended us as symbols of the Old World reborn in the enlightened garden of the New.

In the New World we are not sacred. We are classified by botanists as "living fossils" because we are the only remaining species of a larger order of gymnosperms from the Triassic period. We are valued by horticulturalists for our tolerance for smoke, low temperatures, and drought. My brothers are often planted along avenues, of which there are many. The people of the New World are restless and are constantly moving from place to place searching for I know not what.

Another name for my breed is maidenhair tree. When I was young and newly planted in this place, a legend grew up around me and my brother, but it is forgotten now. It was said that if one of my fans fell on the head of a maiden at the same time one of my brother's fell on the head of a young man at his college forty miles away, then the two were touched by magic and would be united. I have never known if this were true, but young women dressed in blue and white used to come and stand solemnly under my branches while my leaves rained down on their bowed heads. I was grateful for their company because the fall is a time of suffering and death for my kind. But no maidens have stood with me for so long that I can hardly remember when they did.

As I wait golden in the full moon, I know my fall is near once again, and I hope, as I do each year, that it will be my last. For us the suffering is more intense than for other trees, whose leaves drift gently down over a span of autumn. Our leaves desert us quickly, sever themselves all at once, with a pain like thousands of razor blades, leave us bleeding and naked. In the East our suffering, too, was sacred, and the people understood it, making the pain easier to bear. Here it is a solitary dying. I have no living connections. No one even notices but the gardener, who rakes my fruit in disgust in the spring, never leaving even one to grow into a child for me. In the fall he curses me and burns my leaves.

The pain is beginning, it is building in my roots and radiating up through my trunk and out into each branch and twig and luminous leaf. The crescendo builds, and if I had a voice I would scream to the moon, I would cry for relief from this birth-agony that ends in death. Then in the moment of still before the leaving, the white spirit of a girl runs across the lawn toward me and stops beneath my branches. She lifts her arms toward me and says, "I saw you from my window in the moonlight, and I had to come and tell you. You are the best tree in the world. You are silver and gold." Then the spirit begins to dance slowly around my trunk, her face lifted toward me with an expression that may be reverence.

She dances faster and faster, spinning, whirling, in harmony with a million golden fans who dance with her, my fans, my leaves, and I am dancing, too, though I have stood in one place for a hundred years. The pain has become something else now, it is changed by the dance into something I have no words for.

Then I bless this spirit in the only way I can. I rain a shower of gold upon this spirit, who leaps and sings for joy.

Dean Powers
1916

A big frost is certain tonight from the feel of the air. I hate to see the winter coming. Cold, influenza, pneumonia, constant worry over the health of the girls. I get up from my desk and walk to the window and look out at the cold moon. I shiver and draw my shawl closer around me. A flash of white under the ginkgo tree catches my eye, and looking closely I see a girl down there. She is in her nightgown, dancing like a pagan beneath the pale moon. Lizzie! Of course. As I throw up the window to call her in, she flutters to the cold wet ground as if it were midsummer and the world a safe warm place.

Registrar
1916

Forever young, forever fair, but now alive, too. No Cold Pastoral but an ecstasy of life, whirling in a shower of gold. I am a marble man watching from the shadows of the tower. She dances to unheard melodies, to spirit tunes. Her movements are smooth as a bird in flight. She is Danaë embracing Zeus in a shower of gold. She is the dryad who inhabits the ginkgo tree. She is the sacrificial maiden, chosen to appease the gods.

When the clock strikes midnight above me, I, too, am a part of the dance. My heart, buried for thirty years under paper and schedules and records of others' achievements, stirs and yearns. The poem unwritten, the love unclaimed, the child unborn.

As the clock strikes, the dancer folds like a dying swan and the last leaf falls. A window flies up in the hall above, and a sharp voice calls, "Elizabeth Dunbar! Come in this minute. You'll catch your death!"

I sigh. No poetic flights with the dean around. No "marble men" or "maidens overwrought." I am the errant registrar wandering toward a cold room, a colder supper. And Lizzie Dunbar is a wayward schoolgirl again.

Douglas
1916

I leave the law school late, and when I turn the corner, a huge gold tree lights up the walk. Light, moonlight reflected, seems to come from within the tree. I stop for a minute to take it in. For some reason I think of the Dunbar girl. I felt responsible, but my friends said I would make it worse for her if I said anything. I try to dismiss her now, but the image of her coming to me through the water will not go away.

Suddenly a wind whips up and rings with a sound like Lizzie's laughter, and all the leaves from the tree seem to fall at once. They cover my head and shoulders in a blanket of gold. I laugh and throw my books down and race back and forth through the leaves like a schoolboy. I feel alive again until the clock strikes midnight, and I remember I am a married man with a wife waiting for me. I pick up my books and start for home.

Cynthia rocks and cries in the parlor. "You couldn't be studying all this time."

"Ask Hogarth. It's the midterm."

Her face is puffed and swollen. She is not beautiful anymore. "You go off and have fun while I'm left here to rot."

"Fun? Law school?"

"You don't need a law degree anyway. With your family's money we could go to Italy for the winter. If you loved me, you would."

She comes at me then and I think she will slap me, but she

reaches up and pulls a golden leaf from my hair. "Studying?" she says sarcastically.

Furious, I turn toward the stairs. "Tonight I was with a girl under a tree, and I was closer to her than I will ever in a lifetime be to you." Then I'm sorry I spoke because she will whimper and make me embarrassed for her, and I will wish we both were dead.

Lizzie
1917

Today I had a sad letter from Kate. Three of her brothers have joined the army and are going overseas. Even John. I can't imagine John in a war. I would like to see him in his uniform. Kate says she has decided she wants to be a lawyer and that she never wants to marry. I wish I knew what I wanted to be.

Maude thinks I am a clever writer, and she asked me to be on the yearbook staff. She is the faculty adviser. I asked her why in the world they call it *The Spinster*. I never liked that word.

"The original meaning is 'one who spins,'" she said. "Making a book is like spinning in a way, taking a lump of words and making it into something."

"But the motto—'Where singleness is bliss, 'tis folly to be wives.' What do you make of that?"

"You know where that comes from don't you, Lizzie? Thomas Gray. 'Where ignorance is bliss, 'tis folly to be wise.'"

"Oh."

"At Hawthorne we're all single, and it *is* bliss. We run everything, and there are no men to distract us and boss us around."

Sometimes I wish I thought that way, too. I wish I didn't think about boys so much, and I wish I loved Hawthorne as much as Maude does.

I asked Maude why she had on purpose set out to be an old maid, and she said she hadn't, that there just aren't any men around. Of course they're not around Hawthorne, except the teachers. Even if they were, Maude reads so much that she's bound to know more than any of them, and that's a disadvantage. Cynthia said no boy is going to like a girl who knows more than he does.

I told Maude this yesterday when we were working on the magnolia chain out by the Old Maid's gate. Seniors carry the chain at graduation and sing a song about it, like they've done for the past million years. "You're twenty-one years old," I said to Maude. "I'll bet you don't even walk backward through the gate to keep from being an old maid."

"That's just a superstition. Here, hold this bloom steady while I twist the wire."

"You need to find someone to love," I said.

"I love Hawthorne, and my students, and—"

"You know what I mean, silly."

"You need to get it out of your head that you have to marry to be happy," she said. "Who told you that, anyway?"

"Nobody told me. That's one of those things everybody knows . . . isn't it?"

"I don't know it. O.K., hand me another bunch of leaves. If you marry a man, he's liable to drink or die or go to war. Then where will you be? Home with a lot of children, probably starving."

"You're that way because your daddy died young. Not every man dies young. Do you think Dean Powers had a tragic romance?"

"I've never thought of the dean in connection with romance."

"I think she was in love with a poet who was sickly, probably TB, like John Keats, and before they could marry, he died in her arms, in Greece, and she vowed never to love another."

"Oh, my goodness," Maude said. "What have you been reading, Lizzie?" She laughed and looked over at me. She was holding one of the blooms close to her face and she looked like a blossom in the sun, too, fresh like that, and the breeze ruffled her brown hair, and she looked almost pretty, and I thought that it's a shame she's burying herself alive at Hawthorne.

"Lately I feel like I'd like to kiss and hug a boy," I said. "It's a little like the way I used to feel about my dolls or cat, but not exactly. Don't you ever want to be with one?"

"Even if I did, it wouldn't make any difference," she said, "because I'm not pretty. Hold that one tighter. What kind of boy do you want to find?"

"One just like daddy, only younger. I hope he'll love me better than Daddy does, though. I hope he won't send me away."

"I should think your father loves you very much to want a good education for you."

"I think if you love somebody you want them around."

"Birds throw their babies out of the nest. That's only natural." We finished that section of the chain and stood up to move down farther.

"I'm not a bird, thank you."

"You'd do better to develop your own talent than to worry about the boys."

"You sound exactly like the dean, just exactly."

"The dean thinks you are very talented, Lizzie. She says you could do anything you set your mind to." I was surprised by this because the dean fusses at me a lot. She seems to think I'm stupid.

"What talent?"

"She says you could be a political leader or a writer or a teacher or an actress, most anything—if you took yourself seriously."

"Be a stick-in-the-mud like she is?"

"Elizabeth Dunbar! How can you talk like that about the dean?"

"She's nice and I like her, but I don't want to be like that, so serious. I don't want to be sitting alone in some dormitory with a bunch of papers when I'm her age. Oh, come on, you know what I mean."

"Yes, I'm afraid I do," said Maude sadly, sinking to her knees by the next length of chain. "I guess you're too young to see. The dean lives a fulfilled life. She chose her life, and she does a lot of good."

"I know that. But her life is *dull*. I want to travel and have adventures." I picked up a magnolia in each hand and pretended they were fans and began to dance.

"Hand me those, you crazy thing," Maude said, "before you knock the petals off. I thought you wanted to find Governor Dunbar, Jr."

"Maybe I'll find him riding an elephant through India or in the rain forests of Brazil. Oh, I don't know. Life is too confusing."

"You're just barely going to make it out of the secondary form this spring because you haven't been going to classes. Why, Lizzie?" I hung my head like a guilty child and then felt angry that Maude can have that effect on me.

"If you don't graduate you'll have to repeat. You won't be able to go on to the college courses in the fall."

"So?"

"Don't you want your degree so you can leave?"

"I want to get out, but I don't care about a degree. A degree is not the point of being here, is it?"

"If you want to be practical."

"I was never practical."

Maude shook her head. "You don't want to be classified 'irregular' forever, do you?"

I almost told her then about what happens to me in classes, how I feel like I'm going to blow up like a bomb and shatter all over the class, but I'm afraid of what she will think. Instead I said, "All I want to do is read and write, and I can do that without classes. I can do that just fine all by myself."

So I've decided. I'm going out in the real world where I belong. My friend Olive is from New York, and she's a Socialist. She knows what's happening all over the world, things we never talk about here. She says this is an ivory tower, and that we're all living in a dream of the past. She's here because her daddy made her, just like me, but she's not going to stay here much longer.

Now that our country has gotten into the war in Europe, sitting around in classes seems more useless than ever. Daddy said in a letter that the way Mississippi's young men have responded to the draft makes him proud to be governor. He's not sad at all about the war like Kate is. He says President Wilson is exactly right that this war will end all wars and make the world safe for democracy. German submarines have been sinking merchant ships, and we can't tolerate that kind of blow to freedom on the high seas. What's even scarier is to think that Germans might decide to attack here if they get away with it at sea.

In New York we can really find out what's going on, Olive says. She says she has no intention of sitting out a war in this backwater place and that one night soon she's running away. When Olive runs, I'm running with her.

The Antique Shop

Mr. Cavanaugh heard Booker yell, "Jesus" from back in the clearinghouse, and he hurried to find him. Maybe a water moccasin had come up from the bayou, he thought. They did occasionally, and Booker would threaten to quit. But he had to laugh when he got back there and saw Booker holding a box of curly brown hair at bay with his broom.

"Lord have mercy," Booker said. "Some varmint after these papers. See, I told you not to drag that old piece of junk up in here."

"At ease, Booker. Let me show you. This box was in the back of that top file drawer, and it's addressed to Governor and Mrs. Dunbar at the mansion in Jackson and postmarked Virginia. Now the way I figure, this is Lizzie's hair."

"Lord," said Booker. "Reckon was she scalped?"

"No scalping that I know of going on in Virginia in 1917. No, what we've got here is a haircut." Mr. Cavanaugh beamed with satisfaction at his deduction, but Booker was not impressed.

"Never heard of nobody mailing their hair. And if you don't mind rats gonna be nesting up in here. You better let me throw this out."

"Not yet, Booker. But damn, don't you wish that hair could talk? Don't you know there's a story there?"

A Virginia Barber
1917

Eh, Lord, she tickled me. She come in here just as bold. Didn't
seem to make her a bit of difference that it was just men in the
shop. I knew she was from out at the college just by the look of
her, expensive like. Sat down in my chair without a howdy do
and let her hair down clean to her waist. Dark auburn color, I'd
call it, thick and shiny, seem like it was alive.

"Cut it," she said to me, couldn't a been more than fifteen
if she's a day.

"Well, now, Missy," I said. "I'm going to need to know more
than that. Cut it how much?"

"Bob it," she said.

"That's right drastic, ain't it? Pretty hair like this? Woman's
hair is her crowning glory."

"Are you a barber or a preacher?" she said. Sassy little ole
thing.

"I'm the best barber around and don't you forget it. But I
want my customers to be satisfied, and time you get back out
to that college with no hair, ain't nobody going to be satisfied."

"That's my problem, now isn't it?" she said. "Cut."

"O.K., sister," I said. "But you know what they say about
women with bobbed hair, don't you?"

"I don't much care," she said.

"Say they're fast, is what. So don't say I didn't warn you."

"Not that it's any of your business," she said, "but I am
going to serve my country."

"Oh, you are, are you?"

"I'm going to watch for enemy ships off the Jersey shore and sleep among the sand dunes."

"That sounds right crazy," I said. "Your folks know it?"

"They'll know it soon enough."

"If you was my daughter, you wouldn't be going nowhere. Leave this war to the men."

"I can contribute, too," she said, squaring her shoulders up. "Now are you going to cut my hair or not?"

So I done it up good and proper. Bobbed it right off, them thick curls piling up ankle deep on the floor. "You look like a flapper now for certain," I said, holding up a mirror so she could see the back.

"Convenient," she said, tossing around what little she had left. "I'll be too busy to fool with hair."

"Just what you propose to do, should you see a enemy ship, Missy?" I asked her.

"Cry out to the nation."

"So I can rest easier, can I? Now what you want to do with this hair?"

"I hadn't thought to do anything with it," she said, but then she got a big grin on her face. "Do you have a box?"

So I found a box that some bottles of oil come in, and I swept that hair into it. She said she wanted to send it home to her daddy and asked if I'd mail it for her next day if she left a label. I promised I would, and after she left I near fell out when I read what she wrote. That hair was going to the governor of Mississippi.

Right quick I made me a sign for the window.

HAIR BOBBINGS HERE.
WE JUST BOBBED THE DAUGHTER
OF THE GOVERNOR OF MISSISSIPPI!

Business has been steady ever since.

The President
1917

I first think enemy attack. Germans! Goddamn! The explosion rocks Main and shocks me awake clear across the street. I leap to the window and expect to see German troops marching into Main and dragging girls out by the hair, raping and pillaging. All I see, though, is the same thing I see anytime I look out this window: an old four-story brick building that dates from 1842, towers and turrets ugly as the day it was built. There is a full moon, bright as day.

"Sarah," I say, "what in the hell was that explosion?" She keeps snoring. Was I dreaming? I look back out at my fiefdom. Lights go on in the windows. Girls are screaming. I pull on pants over my pajamas and run for the stairs. I stop by the hall phone and call Daily to get over to Main with somebody from maintenance.

The power plant, I'm thinking now. Some boiler. Damn! I hate it when the machines break down, and I'm at the mercy of the clowns who understand them. That crew in maintenance is so afraid of hard work, it's a wonder the whole place doesn't blow up. I'm the president, for God's sake. I ought not to have to fool with this kind of thing.

I hurry across the street and through the gates of the campus. Girls are streaming out of Main in their nightgowns, some of them crying. The dean is trying to calm them down. She wears a pink-flowered robe, and her hair is down to her waist. She doesn't have her glasses. She looks almost like a woman. I stand staring, wondering what's under the robe, wondering what she would do if I put my hand inside the front of it. I am grinning at the perverse possibilities of lust with the dean when she stumbles onto me, squinting up at me in her nearsightedness.

"Oh, it's you," she says. "I suppose you don't know what the noise was?"

"Hell, yes," I say, annoyed that she's still herself. Takes more than disarray and moonlight to transform the dean. "A boiler at the power plant."

"No need to swear," she says. Bitch, I'm thinking, I could show you swear.

"The noise didn't come from the power plant," she went on. "I'm sure it came from inside the building. Why don't you run call Mr. Giles?" So I'm the errand boy now? She has to be right about everything. She moves on through the crowd of girls, who quiet down the minute they see her. Scared not to. Her sidekick follows in her wake with a list of the girls' names, checking them off as she sees them.

A truck clatters to a stop outside the gate, and Daily and Mr. Giles jump out and run toward me. Mr. Giles will be in his element. He likes nothing better than to lord his knowledge of machinery over me. He regards me always with a sardonic half-smile, as one hardly worthy of the label *man*, and unfit to do anything but sit in an office. He believes I got to be president because I can't do anything else. The wart at the end of his nose quivers.

"Big explosion," I say. "Sounds like a boiler at the power plant."

"Warn't that," he says gleefully, spitting an accurate stream of tobacco juice to the right of my foot. "We just come from there. I'd say we start checking in the basement." His foxy little eyes scan the crowd. "Whar's Mrs. Dean?"

"Thank goodness you're here, Mr. Giles," the dean says, coming up behind him. "It sounded like a cannon discharged down those metal tube fire escapes." The girls slide down the tubes during fire drills. They think this is great sport.

The dean's shadow comes from the other direction with the list. "Everyone is here except Lizzie and Olive. They must have slept through it."

"We must check their room at once, then," says the dean. "I want everybody out of that building until we get to the bottom of this. Maude, keep the girls out here. Mr. Giles and I are going back in."

The dean takes Mr. Giles's arm as if they are going to a cotillion, and they start toward the front door of Main, leaving Daily and me standing with 150 hysterical girls milling around us. I wonder if I can slip across the street without being noticed and go back to bed. I wonder if Mr. Giles and the dean—no. That defies even my imagination. "I'm going to the office, Daily. Report there when this is solved."

I hurry to the administration building, unlock my office, and pour myself a drink. I am just getting comfortable when Daily and the dean burst in. The dean holds what looks like the burned casings of large firecrackers.

"Someone has thrown explosives down the fire escapes," she says. "Lizzie Dunbar and Olive Smith are gone."

Olive Smith
1917

At the time it seemed like a good idea. I had brought the fireworks from New York but had not used them. "You can't leave those here," Lizzie said. "They're too good."

"Remember we're running away," I said.

"Let's go out in style," Lizzie said. So we did. We stood by the fire escape on the fourth floor, lit the firecrackers, and threw them down the metal chute. The noise was terrific. Childish thing to do, but exhilarating, an appropriate statement for two stifled at Hawthorne. Lizzie was beside herself with excitement, so much so that I had trouble persuading her to go, and we almost got caught. She pushed it just as far as she possibly could, almost like she wanted to be stopped. As she threw the last firecracker, I heard footsteps coming, someone about to round the corner and stumble onto us, and I threw both our suitcases down the tube, then pushed Lizzie ahead of me. We zipped to the ground faster than we could think.

We untangled ourselves, giggling hysterically, and ran as fast as we could with suitcases, out the gate and down the sidewalk toward the train station. Lizzie ducked behind a tree to look back. "Come on," I hissed.

"Damn," she said, "I forgot to walk backward through the Old Maid's gate."

"Good grief," I said, "will you come on?"

"We caused a commotion," she said. "Listen to them scream."

"If we get caught now, we'll be campused the rest of our lives. HURRY UP!"

"The president is running, about to lose his britches. Isn't this the funniest thing?"

"I'm going," I said, and started running. I half expected her to wait around until someone saw her, but she caught up with me in the next block, and in half an hour, we were on the last train for D.C., Philadelphia, and New York. Thank God for New York.

Lizzie is the oddest girl. She is smart, I think, remarkable in terms of natural intelligence, but she surprises me with the things she does not know. Her father's only opponent in the governor's race was a Socialist, but she knows nothing about socialism. As for the Bolsheviks in Russia, that whole thing could be happening on the moon. Though she says she likes politics, she does not follow it, at least anywhere outside of Governor Dunbar's range of influence. She would probably be as agreeable at a meeting of Republicans as of Socialists and might not even know the difference. She would have to ask daddy before she knew what to believe, yet she has jumped off the shelf where he left her.

I sometimes wonder if her desire to take part in the war effort is not a bid for his approval, or, at the least, his attention. She would certainly have his attention if he knew where she was.

Stephen
1917

Political suicide if it gets out that my daughter is a runaway. How can I govern if I can't manage my own home? Miranda's indifference has changed now that Lizzie has run away. She stares at me with real hatred as if this loss is my fault. "Go find her," she says, whenever she says anything at all. I have been to Hawthorne and to New York City twice, searching, creating public excuses for the trips.

"You go look," I told Miranda today. "I can't see that you have anything else to do."

"I will," she said.

"Don't be ridiculous. You couldn't get to Holly Springs by yourself."

"You'll see," she said and looked so determined that I put an aide to guarding her. All I need is for my lunatic wife to wander off looking for her lunatic daughter. The detective I've hired will find her soon, I'm confident. They are probably holed up in Greenwich Village. All it will take is time and money to flush them out—if she's alive. But I have to assume that; I can't entertain any other possibility.

Olive
1917

We are about as far from a conservative Virginia girls' school as it is possible to get. We are hiding out with two of my friends who are students at Columbia in a Greenwich Village apartment—a "hotbed of radicalism." Artists, writers, Socialists, Wobbles, intellectuals—the bohemian fringes drink wine and debate endlessly.

Lizzie takes it in, agreeing with whomever she's talking to at the time. One minute she will be nodding in agreement with a Socialist antiwar advocate that this is a war for empire, an economic necessity. The next she will be supporting the Espionage Act, whose real purpose, I believe, is locking up Americans who speak out against the war.

She is something of a curiosity with her Southern accent and manners. I have noticed, and she has, too, that people here make assumptions about her when they learn where she is from and hear her speak. They assume that she is ignorant and provincial, but at the same time they are charmed. The mixed signals keep her confused. She is torn between captivating them as belle or surprising them with her mind. She has taken to reading the *Times* for hours. She has discarded her fine clothes and dresses like a gypsy. She makes an effort, most of the time, not to say "y'all" and to put "ings" on the end of her words.

Men like her, not for her mind, either. I believe Southern women are trained in strategies for flattering a man, boosting his ego, manipulating him. Or maybe those methods are innate by now, maybe women have practiced them so long from their pedestals that belle genes are passed down to baby girls. Evolution at work, survival of the fittest.

"I don't know what you're talking about," Lizzie said when I commented. "I want everybody to like me."

"Just be careful," I said. "Not every man understands that. I can think of three who are in love with you."

"Who?" she said, simultaneously indignant and delighted. I forget sometimes that she is, after all, just sixteen.

"That Southern boy, Ben, is smitten, no doubt about that. The funny photographer with the eyepatch and the anarchist who wears black—those for sure, and probably more."

"Really?" Lizzie said. "Silly things." She beamed at me, the dimple dancing in her chin, her bobbed hair like a curly cap on her head. Maybe I was wrong to let her come with me. She is more naive than I thought and more lost. I have tried to persuade her to stay here with us to work in the antiwar effort so that I can keep an eye on her. She is prowar, though, probably thanks to her father's views. At least she is learning how to support an argument. She pointed out to me yesterday how some of our most prominent Socialists—Jack London, Upton Sinclair, Clarence Darrow—have become prowar now that the United States is in it. If only we had more women in the Congress, more who could have joined with Jeannette Rankin in voting no to war.

Despite my advice, Lizzie clings to the idea that the only way she can serve her country is to patrol the coast. "The sea calls," she said dramatically, sweeping her shawl about her and raising her wine class in the direction of New Jersey.

So next week Lizzie Dunbar, with help from some of our contacts, will go to work for the Coast Guard in Sandy Hook, New Jersey. She will look for enemy ships along our shores.

Lizzie
1917

The sea is mine tonight. I sit on a dune and look out at the dark water. A beam from the lighthouse a mile down the shore cuts the mist and makes a shining path. The waves almost reach my feet. They splash and pour white shells like an offering. They invite me, but behind the gentle waves a deep roar sings "Danger."

The moon hangs on the horizon like a crystal ball, or is it rising from the water? I wish it could tell me my future. What is it I want when I look at the moon so wishfully? The same moon shines on Holly Springs and Jackson and Hawthorne and the dead boys at Verdun and the Germans in their ships.

I am sure that I have seen German ships many times. They are terrifying, foreign, and dark. They loom suddenly from the water, tall as a ten-story building. Three times I raised my lantern in the signal for the Coast Guard men. They went on alert, their ships combing the shore, but no one else ever saw the Germans. Now they are suspicious of me. I can see it in their faces when I check in and out. I will not signal again until the Germans are close enough so that I can see their uniforms and their faces. Maybe I will like one of them, and he will kidnap me and take me with him to his castle on the Rhine. The war will end, and we will have half-German babies. Then I will emerge from seclusion and write a book about my experiences. I will become famous in this country. Daddy will read about me in the *Times* and will come to visit his grandchildren in Germany.

I wonder if Daddy would be proud of me if he knew what I am doing now. I think he would, but he is probably so angry because I left Hawthorne that he never wants to see me again. I miss him. I wonder if he is looking for me. And poor Mama. Mississippi seems as far away as Germany. I try not to think about the past.

When I sit by the sea, none of my problems seem so bad. The water draws me like a magnet. I can sit for hours and watch the tides ebb and flow and the moon rise and fall. I am alone, but I belong. I am doing something important.

On a clear day I can see New York from Sandy Hook. It shimmers in the distance like an enchanted city and calls me back. Though most of the time I am not lonely, I do miss the talk and the news. Next weekend I will visit Olive and the others in the radical apartment.

Miranda
1918

Stephen has promised to find her, but he has failed and so I resolved to do it myself. Last night I had a terrible premonition that she was in danger. I was up before the day to go and find her. I had no luggage, no tickets, no money, but I trusted in a higher power to take me to her. I am her mother; we are like magnetic poles, and if we are both set free we will find each other.

I dressed in the dark, and, trembling all over from fear and cold, I walked out the door of my suite into the upstairs hall. I was startled to see a man with a huge potbelly in a cane-bottomed chair right outside my door. He was leaning back against the wall and had his hat pulled down over his face. He wore a gun in a holster over his heart. He looked vaguely familiar, but I could not imagine what he was doing outside my room. As I started down the stairs, he woke up and jumped to his feet and grabbed my arm. When I tried to pull away, he took my other arm, swung me around facing him, and said, "Hold on now, ma'am, now don't you get excited."

"Let go of me. Who are you?"

"One of the governor's detectives, ma'am, just here for your protection is all."

"Detective? Take your hands off me, I say." I was struggling to get away from him, but the more I struggled, the tighter he held until he had my arms pinned behind my back and was holding me pressed against his stomach, his despicable little eyes leering in my face, last night's beer breathing in my face.

"Now you just be a good girl and get back in your room where the governor wants you to be. Don't give us no trouble."

"My daughter is in danger, and I have to find her."

"We gonna find that little girl, don't you worry," he said.

"I'm her mother, and I know something bad is about to happen to her. Please, please let me go." I began to struggle again, but he tightened his grip. The gun was so hard against my breast I felt as though it would burst.

"For a woman supposed to be a invalid you got a lot of fight in you, don't you? I got a theory about you being a invalid. I watch you a lot, you know."

"You're hurting me," I said.

"Where? Where does it hurt?" Something in his face scared me, like he could find pleasure in the pain of others.

"What's it worth to you to break out?" he said in a whisper, his mouth against my ear. "We might work a deal."

"I don't have any money."

"I ain't talking money. This here won't cost you nothing but a little of your time." He looked toward my bedroom door. "You might like it, too, you can't tell. Then you go on to hunt your daughter and by the time they miss you, I'm off duty."

When I realized what he was saying, I began to scream. He was so surprised he relaxed his grip, and I began to claw and kick and bite and then it was bedlam. Stephen ran out of his room. "She's hysterical. Get the doctor." Then he and the wretched detective and two or three aides held me in the bed until the doctor came and gave me a strong sedative.

My head is throbbing, and my confidence that I can find Lizzie has evaporated. I will be watched more closely than ever; the nasty little man will be lurking outside my door every night.

What kind of people has Stephen surrounded himself with? What is he up to that he has to deal with men of that caliber? Is this necessary in politics? I don't understand. Oh, how I want to go back home. I should have been a pioneer woman and lived with my husband and children in a cabin on the prairie with only the sky and earth for company. I could have been happy with that life.

Last year at a governor's meeting in Washington, Stephen found a young woman to be his secretary, and she takes care of everything. Her name is Gwin McCurdy, and she is from Iowa. She is crisp and businesslike and efficient. She is everything I am not. She arranges all the parties and organizes everything, and I am left alone, thank God. I had rather be lonely any day than tortured by trying to impress strangers.

I have a heavy foreboding whenever I think of Lizzie, which is all the time. I am sure that I will never see her again.

Dorothy Day
1918

The bitterest cold. Our breath freezes and falls like shards of glass in our path. Not enough heat anywhere in New York, and so we huddle together like animals trying to draw warmth from each other. Ideas at least can still comfort, though nothing has been the same for me since the Occoquan. Our crime—standing before the White House and saying excuse me is this the land of the free and saying we are citizens, too. Please let us vote. When *The Masses* was shut down in November the loss was of more than a job and a voice of hope and new possibility. It was as if our youth ended with that golden summer in the Village with Rayna and Mike and Maurice and the others, endless talk, endless singing, when a better world seemed possible, war far away, and change within our reach.

Now I despair of political change. I believe I will have to work out my salvation in a way other than political causes. I've felt that from the moment the attendant brought me a Bible in the Occoquan and reading it gave me comfort. I can't think a crutch like religion is the way any more than politics, but something I'm supposed to find I haven't found yet. Meanwhile all I try to do is keep warm. I am with Gene most of the time. Sometimes we spend the whole night walking from bar to bar, talking. He is not writing much and his Provincetown friends are worried. They need new plays. Poor death-haunted Gene is not the jolliest companion for the depths of winter, but certainly the most interesting. Last night we sat around a table in the back room of Jimmy Wallace's saloon at Fourth and

Sixth—the Hell Hole his crowd calls it—and he recited Thompson's "Hound of Heaven" from memory, the whole thing, all 180 and some-odd lines. His voice is monotonous, and he hangs his head while he recites, but the performance is impressive, it haunts me, and I ask him to do it again and again.

Last night a funny girl that Olive brought with her, Lizzie—Lizzie—Dunbar, I believe the last name is, listened rapt and then when he finished burst into applause. The rest of us followed, though usually the end of Gene's recitations are marked by sighs and gloomy silences. "You should be an actor," she said brightly in an unmistakable Southern accent. "How do you remember all that?" We smiled indulgently at her youth and naiveté—until she began to ask questions and talk about the poem in an unexpected kind of way. "What a strange mind Thompson must have had," she said, "to make God a dog."

"Well, yes," Gene said, undecided between annoyance and amusement, looking at her with his dark, sunken eyes, registering her fresh good looks despite his melancholy. "A relentless hound, though, not a lapdog."

"Jealous, too," she said. "He takes away everything the speaker loves, just so he will love God best. And then calls the speaker a dingy clot unworthy of love at all. Do you think God is like that?"

"I think God is not at all," he said. "But Death, now, we know that's real."

"Why did you go to the trouble of learning that poem," she asked, "if you don't believe God exists?"

"Maybe I still hope, but I know better."

"Know my favorite line?" she asked. "That one about fleeing 'down the labyrinthine ways of my own mind.' I feel like I'm doing that most of the time."

"You don't look as though there's anything so complicated behind those pretty eyes," he said. "What are you fleeing?"

"Who knows?" she said. "Aren't we all fleeing something?"

"Death," he said.

"You keep coming back to that. Dean Powers says only the young can afford to wallow around in fears of death."

"Oh she does?"

"It's not death that bothers me," she said. "It's how to live. In my fantasies I can swing 'the earth a trinket at my wrist,' but in reality knowing what to do is lots harder."

"Not for me," he said. "I've known I would be a playwright since 1912."

"You're lucky."

"When I throw myself into writing, everything else falls away. Guilt, uncertainty, insecurity, the rest of the world. I'm protected."

"I'm that way with my diaries," she said, "but if I were writing something other people would see, I wouldn't feel protected. I'd feel exposed."

If she wanted to get his undivided attention, she couldn't have said anything better. Gene loves "teaching" pretty young women, counseling them about what they ought to do. I suppose that's the one reason women are attracted to him—his sensitivity and attentiveness plus his air of tragic sadness. At first meeting he seems quiet and shy, the darker side of his nature not apparent.

I moved on to another table with a sigh, Gene and Lizzie talking writing in a world of their own. Gene is always in love after a fashion, sometimes with two or three women at once, but I believe him when he says he'll never truly love again after Louise. Later in the evening I drifted back that way, and he was writing a poem to Lizzie on his napkin.

When the Hell Hole closed, Olive went back to the Village, but Lizzie, Gene, and I and a few others went down to the waterfront, stopping at saloons all along the way, for the rest of the night. As the sun came up, we split off to go our separate ways. Nobody knows where Gene lives—his only address is the Hell Hole—but I wondered if he would follow Lizzie back to the Village or on to Jersey. I think he would have, but she seemed to sense the strange bond between Gene and me and said, "Could I go with you, Dorothy?"

I was surprised, but I told her sure, and we stopped for coffee first. We reached St. Joseph's on Sixth about the time of their early morning Mass. I often stop in there, why I can't say. The service is foreign to me, but appealing somehow. I would never admit to any of my bohemian friends that I do this, but on an impulse this morning, I said to Lizzie, "Want to stop in here for the Mass?"

"Is it warm?" she said. She was blue with cold, her hands deep in her pockets, her head with the furry cap held down against the wind. At least it was that, I could promise her. Two huge cedar wreaths on the doors of the church reminded me of the season.

"You aren't going south for Christmas?" I asked her.

"I can't leave my job," she said, "and besides, I've run away."

"Your family doesn't know where you are?"

"They don't really care," she said. "Not much." We walked into the church wincing as the warmth began to revive our fingers and toes.

"Explain it to me," she whispered, after we were seated in the back of the dim church, and the Mass had begun. "At home we're Presbyterian and speak English."

"I'm not Catholic either," I whispered back. "But something about it makes me feel peaceful. Maybe the candles and the incense."

We watched the rituals in silence then, listened to the Advent readings and were strangely warmed. Lizzie sat with her hands clasped in her lap like a child. Her eyes reflected the candlelight. Her face was expectant, like one who waits.

The Antique Shop

Mr. Cavanaugh is moving alphabetically through Lizzie Dunbar's files. He still can't believe that she kept files at all, much less this many. His memory of her is that of town character, a flashy red-haired woman that people whispered about. But these papers suggest something else. He has just picked up a folder labeled "Goldman, Emma." Wonder if that's some of the Goldmans down around Greenville? But as he reads through he decides not. This was evidently some Yankee woman, radical as she could be. The news clippings and articles with her name are shocking.

Because of the dust, he has taken to wearing a white mask over his nose and mouth, and soft cotton gloves. He takes off his mask and gloves and walks to the front of the shop where Booker is polishing some of the silver. "Not too busy today, are we?"

"No sir. But it'll pick up, long toward the end of the week."

"How about going down to the library for me?"

Booker used to like to go to the library and look up Mr. Cavanaugh's research questions, but ever since they got the new computer system in he's avoided it. Then in a move that outraged both him and Mr. Cavanaugh, the librarians threw away the card catalog. Mr. Cavanaugh cancelled his Friends of the Library membership.

"Last time I tried to mess with that computer, it squawked and carried on."

"You need to learn it, Book. Looks like there'll be lots to look up with these Dunbar papers."

Booker wonders why Mr. Cavanaugh doesn't learn it

himself if he wants to know stuff so bad, but he knows it won't do any good to say so. He can hardly do his own cash register that he's had for thirty years.

"Write it down," Booker says. "Whatever it is I got to look up."

Mr. Cavanaugh writes out "Emma Goldman" in his best hand and hands the piece of paper to Booker. Booker gets his St. Louis Cardinals cap from out behind the counter and starts out. He'll look around himself for awhile, and then if he doesn't find anything, he'll throw himself on the mercy of the first idle librarian he sees.

Olive
1918

Strange that Lizzie's father has not found her yet, though we try to be secretive. My parents have not found me either, but I suspect they have not looked. I am working for Emma Goldman on the staff of *Mother Earth*, the opportunity of a lifetime.

Each time Lizzie comes in to New York, she wants to go down to the office and help—proofread galleys, open the mail. Emma is in and out of jail, but several times she has been there; Lizzie is enthralled with her. Emma's charisma is powerful; she has convinced more decisive minds than Lizzie's to her anarchist point of view. Lizzie loves to get into discussions with her, and she knows quite a bit about reform movements, suffrage and temperance mainly. Emma thinks these measures are useless in getting at the real ills of society, that we must wipe out what we have and start with a clean slate. Emma thinks that the modern educated woman has freed herself from some bonds, but that she is making new ones for herself. She is neglecting her nature—"life's greatest treasure, love for a man, or her most glorious privilege, the right to give birth to a child."

Lizzie, who likes men, is delighted with this point of view. She told Emma about the dean at Hawthorne and about Maude. She thinks they fit perfectly into Emma's category of smart women who feel that true emancipation lies in making their way without a man. But then she mentioned another woman from her childhood, a woman who had five children and a husband she loved, but was also an active suffragist. Emma's reply was that she wished we had that woman with us, that she was on the right track, but misdirecting her energies. Suffragists are naive to think that woman's vote can purify a corrupt system, she says.

Lizzie persists in her support of President Wilson and his contention that this war will "make the world safe for democracy."

"Democracy?" Emma said. "Then why did I go to jail for opposing the draft? Why did Eugene Debs? Why was the professor over at Columbia fired for opposing the war? Why was Kate O'Hare sentenced to five years for saying American women are brood sows who raise sons to get into the army and be made into fertilizer? Why do we have such a thing as the Espionage Act that forbids criticism of the government, if this is a democracy? This is a capitalist war with the sole purpose of opening new markets and taking the workers' minds off their exploitation." Emma thrives on controversy, and Lizzie is no match for her, but Lizzie can set her off; I suspect she does it on purpose.

"All this is so confusing," Lizzie will say later to me, "but exciting, isn't it?"

I am not much of a talker myself, and I enjoy hearing them. Emma is impressed with Lizzie's native intelligence, not her ideas. She believes that Southerners in general are afflicted with congenital conservatism, but that with time she might be able to make something out of Lizzie.

In a way, Emma's influence over Lizzie, particularly as concerns love and men, may have come at a bad time in Lizzie's development. I'm afraid these ideas may encourage Lizzie in a reckless path.

She is becoming quite close to one of our organizers whom I do not trust. His reputation with women I distrust, not his politics, if that is a valid distinction. To be fair to him, he may not intend to be exploitive. He has an enormous amount of energy, sexual and otherwise, and women are drawn to him. His liaisons are always devastating to the woman and have caused dissension and heartache in our circle. His name is Kaev Random. He is just back from Russia, full of news from the revolution. He comes and goes mysteriously. He is never expected, but we treat him like the conquering hero when he appears. No one knows where he was born or who his people are, not that it matters. He is probably ten years older than Lizzie and handsome in a disreputable way, a black beard, large white teeth, a scar on his cheek.

When I spoke to Lizzie about him this afternoon, she said, "You sound just like Dean Powers, Olive. " We had been to the delicatessen on the corner and were packing food for her to take back to Sandy Hook.

"Seriously," I said, "women are disposable to him."

"You have experience?"

"If you mean has he rejected me and am I jealous, no," I said.

"We're just friends," she said. "He treats me like a little sister. He tells such interesting stories, and he's been everywhere."

"All the more reason he's dangerous," I said.

"He'd never like me anyway," she said. "Somebody sophisticated like that."

"Lizzie, I've watched him with you. He likes you."

"Really?" Her face glowed.

"He likes women in general, but his only allegiance is to revolution. You do not want a man in love with an idea."

"Better than being in love with himself, like most of them."

"It's the same thing. Anyway, please be careful."

"Why are you always warning me? Don't you think I can take care of myself?"

"I want you to read this," I said. "Emma was arrested a couple of years ago for distributing this." I handed her a tract on contraception. She looked at it and flushed and handed it back quickly as if it were a hot kettle.

"I don't need that. I'm surprised you think I'm like that,

Olive." So she left for New Jersey, looking like a little immigrant with her bag of food and books, off to keep the shores and Daddy safe from the Germans. I was relieved to see her go, and I hope the next time she comes Kaev Random will be on his way back to Russia. Sometimes when my conscience hurts me about her, I consider tipping off Governor Dunbar. I don't know if that would make her life better or worse.

Lizzie
1918

Alone in the dark I see a shadow move down the beach. At first I think it is an illusion, but then the shadow comes closer and takes a human form. The enemy. A submarine has come to shore and sent a spy. I will not raise my lantern or run toward the lighthouse. I will prove that I am brave. I crouch in my nest of sea oats. My hands tremble, and my breath comes fast. He must not hear me.

He wears a dark overcoat and walks quickly. Now he turns from the water and comes toward me. He will stumble over me in a few more steps. I am trapped, like an animal. He will gut me with his knife, like the hunters do to deer in Holly Springs. I shrink away from his path, trying not to move the grass, trying to make myself invisible. He stops, his boot inches away from me. Then a miracle.

"Lizzie!" The word rings across the night. Kaev. He said he would come if he could. I am sobbing, saying his name, and he is beside me, comforting me. His arms are warm and safe. He holds me like a child. My head is on his chest, and the beat of his heart, strong and steady, washes through my body like the tide. He turns me toward him and holds my heart against his, and our hearts beat together, the most amazing thing. He holds me that way and looks into my eyes, and then he bends his face to mine and kisses me for the first time. His kiss is gentle as tears on my mouth. I kiss him back.

Genesis
1918

War over, praise Jesus. People in the streets, happy, singing, dancing. Fireworks down to the monument. Them boys be back home soon, what's left. Malachi he won't be back. Armistice too late for Malachi, Mama's youngest, dead on foreign soil. I the oldest, Malachi youngest, first and last Mama called us. Draft black boys same as white. Don't be no difference when it come to fighting over the waters, just when they gets home. Black boy have to stand back then. Malachi sweet little ole boy, tenderhearted. Used to cry when the cat catched a bird, mouse even, couldn't put no worm on a hook. "Them worms mean?"

"Worms ain't mean or not," I say. "Just worms."

"How come you go stick a hook in 'em then?" he say. "Them still live and wiggling. How do you think that feel?"

"I don't think nothing about being no worm," I say. "You want a fish for supper or not?"

Never made trouble, Malachi didn't. Ain't asked much out of life. Didn't get nothing.

Armistice outside, war inside the house. Man with a gun by Miranda's door. Where Stephen think she going, can't hardly get out the bed. "My little girl, lost," she say over and over. "How can it be?" If he put a gun on his wife, what will he do to Lizzie when he catch up with her? If he do. Ain't gonna make nothing off Lizzie, though. She bout as bad as he is.

Sissy and Little Earl home in Holly Springs with Lula. Miss my babies bad. Be grown by time I get back home. Won't know they own mama.

Stephen
1919

Spring in Paris could resurrect the dead. I am twenty years younger and more alive. How much is Paris, how much Gwin, I don't know. Paris was Gwin's idea. She said Paris was a fool-proof way to make peace with an errant daughter. Gwin's indispensable.

In Greenwich Village when I found Elizabeth, she was pale and thin, but now she's beginning to look more like my daughter. Had she been forced to live in that bohemian way, how deprived she would have felt. As it was, the romance of it all, the drama of her role, seemed to blind her entirely to the squalor. She put up no great fight when I came for her; she's learned that she needs me.

She loves clothes. I guess that's the most feminine characteristic she has, the thing that gives me hope of making her a lady. She's tried on twenty dresses in every boutique in Paris, modeling them for Gwin and me. She enjoys our admiration. I suppose she hasn't had a new dress since Hawthorne. She's like a starving person in the shops.

When she starts babbling her socialist junk, I remind her of clothes. "So you want us all in gray sweaters and baggy pants, digging potatoes?" She flushes. She knows her own appetites. "No more dancing all night, no more late dinners at Chez Louie?"

I'm sure a man was involved in her running away, but she denies it. When women take off that way, there's a man in it somewhere. Women will follow men anywhere, across the sea in a tub, over the Rocky Mountains in a covered wagon, but I've never known one to strike out alone.

When she told Olive good-bye, Elizabeth whispered: "Tell me if you hear from him. Please. I'm so worried." She is learning how it feels for someone you love to disappear.

My daughter has outgrown her tomboy qualities, despite not having a mother to help her. I have Hawthorne to thank for that, or maybe the inevitable result of years. That ungirlish freedom of movement that used to worry me when she was younger has largely disappeared. She walks with decorum now, no longer strides along swinging her arms like a boy and whistling. The combined effects of father, school, and time have composed her.

Lizzie
1919

So sick. *Morbus Gallicus* the French doctor smiling as if it were
an honor. Then leering his face closer larger closer hot bright
eyes close to mine the words rolling in waves and I drowning
sweating burning straining to catch the meaning holding out
my hands to catch the words pull the words from the stream
belching from his furious mouth what the hell is he saying
daddy says what the hell this is the nastiest language how I
hate this goddamned language like throwing up words like
retching sounds why can't he speak English quack quacks
words like a duck quacks. My mind all crowding to my brain
beating crashing breaking to my brain until my head splits with
hurting from all the words splits in half my brain like jelly
quivering as the doctor shoots words. Monsieur Louis at the
podium Mademoiselle Dunbar listen listen Mademoiselle and
you will hear you are not listening Mademoiselle repeat after
me like this the words struggle in my nose gargle in my throat
tears join sounds then tears and syllables mixed up together.

One word if I could catch one word then I could know if it
were the right word it could be the key might be the key and
then I would know if I will die or what or get back home or
what I would like to know it doesn't really matter really but I
would like to know I set a net inside my ears a net with small
holes and I listen for two words I know I looked them up I
know these I will catch these if they come I will hold them in
my heart I did not plan the words but I will keep them Kaev
would come back then and stay with me he would hold me

and stay and we would live here I could speak if we lived here I could learn and so I watch the net and listen for *grosse* or *enceinte* I will catch a baby in my net fat and sweet my own I will wait until it swims to me wet and slick as any fish slippery with Kaev's eyes shining full of love.

D'une manière susceptible catches I pull the net up heavy net pull the net up and look not a baby at all no no burning sweating sick *avoir la fièvre* I know I know fever I know but which which fever will it kill kill which fever malaria? what kind of doctor Daddy is saying what kind of doctor is this what is he saying Elizabeth you studied didn't you didn't I pay for French didn't I what is he saying Elizabeth what are you hiding tell me you know I can see you know why won't you say Elizabeth—

Rouquer yes yes a rash red rash yes itching scratching yes*strychnisme* yes sssss coil and hiss and spit a poison isn't it good I will take yes I will take I will take it all *avoir soin de* take care of me yes I am sure take care of me yes*syphilis* dark hideous snake bloody dark and hideous coiled and hissing coiled in the nest fangs sucking life life my life and life of my babies not to be nothing death death.

Gwin McCurdy
1919

I can't imagine growing up with the kinds of privileges she had and then running away from them. In Iowa, we work for what we get. Women there are stronger and more independent than anywhere else. Southern women are pampered and soft. If somebody had offered to pay even a part of my way through college, wouldn't I have jumped at the chance? Instead, I had to go to Washington and work my way up.

In the middle of Stephen's trying to buy her back with clothes and attention, she up and got the malaria. I guess that's what it is. The doctor can't speak English. So now the trip's ruined, and we're going home as soon as Princess Elizabeth is able.

Lizzie
1919

Kaev doesn't know. I am sure he doesn't know. Syphilis affects different people in different ways, the doctor says. You are *d'une manière susceptible*. I try to think up ways to get word to Kaev. He should be seeing a doctor. He could die without knowing.

Daddy and Gwin say I have been out of my head with fever. Raving with malaria. We have taken an apartment near the hospital. I have fevers and skin rash. I wake up at night with sweat. Then the next minute I am freezing.

The treatment is, you take a little poison each day. The idea is to kill the disease and not yourself, but you wish you could die. You look at the medicine and think how easy to take a lot at once. The pills look so innocent. I need to talk to somebody, but there is no one. "What is wrong with me?" I ask. "Malaria," they say. "You will be all right. We will take care of you." But they don't know what the French doctor said, what I'm almost sure he said.

Daddy chomps at the bit to go home, but the doctor says we must stay longer. I told Daddy to go ahead, Gwin too, but they won't do that. I am an outsider with them. They talk to each other as if they've been together since time began. The tone is familiar or something, like the words aren't really important because they know the meaning already, before the words are said. I do not know their language.

"Do you think Mama would come if we wired?" I asked.

"Absolutely not," Daddy said. "She mustn't know you're

sick. That would finish her."

"*N'enfant jamais*," the doctor said yesterday. I think he meant I must never have children.

"What's he saying, dammit?" Daddy was getting frustrated.

"Don't forget the medicine," I said. "Get plenty of rest."

"I'll bet he knows English," Daddy said. "A medical doctor. Damn perverse French."

The doctor laughed ho ho ho and twirled his mustaches.

So much has happened.

The Antique Shop

A black-and-white photograph of a splendid house floated loose between two file folders in the Lizzie papers. Though the photograph was faded, the image was clear enough to stir Mr. Cavanaugh's memory. In his childhood and youth this had been the Dunbar house, the grandest house in Bolivar Landing, not far down the block from his own. He remembered watching the company come and go from it, the laughter of the parties that made its way from the terraces and into the bedroom window of a small boy. Mostly he remembered the fire, though, the delicious terror as it torched the night, striking ever so close to his own hearth. Losing the house and its evocative power was personally painful to him, who even as a young man preferred the glories of the past.

He was filled with gratitude that this filing cabinet had been somewhere else the night of that fire. Probably in Lizzie Dunbar's dress shop, which she ran in a building across the street from Mr. Cavanaugh's store and where Delta Do-Nut now bakes and sells.

Mrs. Davis
1920

Carpenters and contractors from Jackson are over building the Dunbar house, which is all right I guess, if that's what they want. Personally I'd rather see the business go to some of our people here in Bolivar Landing, but everybody's got their own ideas.

Miss Halle says our property values will skyrocket when the house is finished. I hope she's right about that, not that it'll do me any good since I aim to stay right here until I die. I lost Mr. Davis in this house, and had the babies here, too, and wouldn't leave under any circumstances. My old house must not know what to think coming face to face with the grandest house ever built in the Delta. They say it's a replica of Thomas Jefferson's place up in Virginia, though I wouldn't know about that. Sounds like something Stephen Dunbar would do. He has money's grandmother, and so he's going to just retire and see after it. Made it all out of Delta land and Delta cotton, but still Mississippi is not quite good enough for him. Had to copy something from up in Virginia.

Mrs. Dunbar's the one I want to see, but people say I won't. She's been in the bed for twenty years, they say, and is not likely to get up when they move to Bolivar Landing. The daughter's been out to the house some with her daddy, making sure they get the ballroom right, I reckon. She's a pretty one, wild too, they say. I guess I'll see some things once they get moved in.

Another woman comes out every day and talks to the carpenters. First I thought she was the daughter, she's so young.

But they say she's the secretary from up north and sees to things for Governor Dunbar. People say they wouldn't be surprised if there weren't more to it than that, but then people will say anything. I'll give them the benefit of the doubt. Prominent man has to have a good secretary the way I look at it.

I do love to watch a house being built, and I've watched this one from the ground up. Only the best materials, Delta pine and cypress and oak, bird's eye maple, mahogany, and walnut, marble imported from Italy for the entrance hall and fireplaces, slate from somewhere overseas for the roof, copper flashings, brick from Greenville. I go out and walk through when none of the Dunbar bunch is around. The carpenters are nice and friendly, explain whatever stage they're in at the time. From what I pick up, the Mr. and Mrs. have separate suites of rooms, which I guess is understandable, her being an invalid. Servants' quarters out back are bigger than my house.

One drawback is the traffic. People come from all over the county to see the Dunbar house. Biggest local attraction outside the docking of the showboat. Our street had been a quiet one even though it is just a block from the courthouse. Now there's a steady stream of wagons and buggies and automobiles full of people come to gawk. The price of fame, I reckon.

Lizzie
1920

Some days I wake up and I can't remember for a few seconds what has happened to me. Kaev and the love, because that's what it was, and Paris and the fever are like a distant dream, too far back to claim as my own. I have not seen Kaev again since those days we were together on the beach. Olive writes that she has not seen him either, that he has apparently disappeared into Russia for good. She says I must forget about him and go on with my life, but I can never do that. I don't want to do that.

I need to talk to somebody about my health. I don't believe I can be sick because I feel strong, except for the sadness inside. I watch my body for signs. Each time I take a bath, I stand before the mirror naked and look, but I am smooth and clear as marble in the Louvre. Occasionally I will see a bump and then I am terrified because I have read about the stages, and I know what can happen. Usually the bump turns out to be a mosquito bite or a chigger, but I agonize for days.

Sometimes I think I could talk to Kate. She is so sensible, enrolled in the law school now and sure about her future. I imagine telling Kate, but I couldn't bear for her to think of me as immoral and foolish. That she think well of me is much more important than the relief of telling her my secret.

If only I could talk to Mama, but that is out of the question. She cried and cried when I came home. She said now she could die because she had seen my face again. But she does not die, and she does not get any better. She was not that way in Holly

Springs, was she? Or does my memory transform our lives there?

At times I can almost convince myself that I imagined all that has happened since Hawthorne (how happy I was there and too much a fool to know it) and that I am starting over. A new house, a new set to run with. They know how to have a good time; I can say that for them.

The Delta is a lot different from the hills. People are more serious in the hills, more frugal, more religious, more conservative, more inclined to think about the hereafter than the now. Here people live for the day. "They're gamblers," Daddy says. "Farmers are the biggest gamblers, the more land, the deeper in debt, the bigger the gamble, the bigger the thrill." They don't live like people in debt; they live like kings. You'd think they didn't have a care. And I like that in a way because why not? Any minute disaster may strike.

The boys who have been away to college are all home for the summer. The girls have been away to finishing school and are back home with no purpose other than to make a good match so far as I can see. Parties and dances all the time, road trips and train trips to Memphis and New Orleans. I think the flat land is the reason for all the sociability. The land is so relentlessly flat in every direction that people have to get together to keep from going mad. I'm drawn into it in spite of myself and can think about new clothes and parties for hours at a time.

Most of the time we're one big group with no pairing off, and that's fine because I don't want to be with anyone. Vassar Lamar is the girl I like the best—high spirited and fun and frank—but she is nothing like Kate. She is known as a "belle" around the Delta, but she has no sense of direction like Kate does. She can drink as much as a man, then get up the next morning and be ready to go again. All her mother talks about is "prospects," as if marriage were on the stock exchange.

I like the boys in this group well enough, but none as well

as Kaev. How could any local boy possibly measure up to a man as mysterious and passionate as Kaev, who could speak five languages, who could move a crowd to follow him in Paris as easily as in New York, who was willing to die to fight tyranny and oppression? With my head I know I won't hear from him again, but with my heart I will never give him up.

Avent Easley is the nicest of the boys; he's smart and easy to talk to. He doesn't laugh when I talk about socialism and feminism, the ideas we talked about in New York. He was in the war and seems more mature than most of the other boys. He doesn't boast about how much he can drink or how many birds he can kill with one shot, like so many of them do. He has the bluest eyes and a reddish mustache. Walker Dubard is the wildest and most reckless, and though I know the truth is not in him, I like to be around him. He can make a day interesting. A man like Walker is so self-centered he is impossible to hurt, so you don't have to feel responsible for him. He will take care of himself; he will always put himself first no matter what. I think he and Vassar would be a good match, but she says not. She would like a man a little richer while she is at it, she says, since marriage is a lifetime deal.

If I were a man, my life sure would be easier. Vassar says that's nonsense, that men have the harder life. They have to make the money and support the family—so they have more responsibility. All women have to do, according to Vassar, is be smart enough to find a man to take care of them. Then they have to have the children, but after that the servants take over, and the women can play bridge and plan parties and do good works in the community if they want to. The women have more freedom, Vassar says, to do as they please. They have more control over their time, until the man gets home, that is. But for me, there's something wrong with that picture.

If I were a man, I know exactly what I would do. I would go over to the university law school and get a degree, then come back and go into practice with Daddy. He would be proud of me and would introduce me as his son, the attorney. I could be a real help to him at the office.

I told Daddy this idea, and he said if I were a man that's exactly what he would want me to do. Then I said, "Some women are enrolled at the law school now."

He said, "Yes, but not our kind. Men at the university don't think very highly of those girls, Elizabeth. I wouldn't want that for you."

"What do you want for me, Daddy?"

He looked startled at the question. "Happiness, of course," he said. "A home, a good husband and children, fulfillment."

Daddy often says that all his sons turned out to be one little girl. He says it in a teasing way, as a joke, but I know his family is a disappointment to him. Vassar says that all men want sons, sons who look just like them, named for them with a "junior" at the end.

Once I asked him why he and Mama didn't have more children. He said because of Mama's health. He said she didn't want any more, that I was enough of a handful.

That sounds silly to me, a woman with a house full of servants, but just like Mama. She has no spirit. I could shake her sometimes. She's off in another world somewhere, not paying attention to this one. If she had paid attention to me and been stronger, maybe I wouldn't have run off and gotten in this mess. If I had been Daddy's wife, I would have had as many children as he wanted. I would have had a dozen sons and not blinked an eye.

Sissy
1920

Sissy bout halfway scared of her. Miss Lizzie she get something on her mind, won't let up. Won't let you be. She come down to the kitchen, Sissy trying to make biscuits. Mama be still at our house with Little Earl, him sick. "You gots to make the governor 'em biscuits for they breakfast," Mama say. "Get on up there, don't they be down here hollin' at me."

So I get on up here, start in. Pull out the big wooden bowl, scoop in the flour, be working in the lard and here Miss Lizzie come. Don't never sleep look like. Ain't even sleep 5:30 in the morning.

"Sissy," she say, eyes boring through me, make me sweat. "Sissy, listen. Put down that spoon."

"Can't. Mama say make y'all biscuits."

She take hold Sissy's arm. Squeeze it tight. Dig in nails. Sissy stop stirring. Look down at the floor.

"How old are you, Sissy?"

"Fourteen."

"What does this say?" She hold up a newspaper, point at big words cross the top.

"Don't know'm." Sissy shamed. Face hot.

"I'm going to teach you to read, Sissy."

Sissy don't answer. Sissy don't want to know. Went to school one year, hate it. Like it outside. Like trees and sky and skipping rocks cross the river. Rather pick cotton than be in school.

"Look at me, Sissy."

Sissy look at her face. Skin like cream when it rise off the milk. Eyes gray-blue, ring of black lashes. Eyes latch onto Sissy's eyes, won't let go. She talking big words Sissy don't know. Suffer something. Nineteenth something. "Never forget this day," she say. "Women have got the vote."

"Did?" Sissy say.

"Do you know what that means?"

"Yes'm." Naw, Sissy don't and don't care. Just hope me and Mama don't get it.

"It means women are free. It means the country will change."

"Yes'm." Sissy don't know what she talking about. She all time talking, talking. She go on and on about votes and duty and women educating theirselves. Biscuits won't be fit to eat. Dough like glue.

"I'm starting at home," she say. "I'm starting with little Sissy. I'm teaching her to read."

Sissy trapped. Don't see no way out.

"Come up to my room at ten o'clock," she say. "We'll have our first reading lesson." Then she turn and walk out the swinging door to the dining room, sweet smell of her all that's left in the kitchen.

Bill Falkner
1920

Today I met a confusing girl from the Delta, ex-governor Dunbar's daughter. She was visiting Kate, who brought her to the Tea Hound for a meeting of the Marionettes. Usually I don't go to the meetings. I told them I will help with the plays, work on the sets, whatever they need, but I can't sit through the meetings. Tonight they were reading my play, though, and trying to decide if they should produce it.

Lizzie Dunbar is her name, and she calls herself one of the "New Women." I don't see what's wrong with the old ones. She professes to be intensely political, though it's hard to gauge her sincerity. Kate is political, too, the only woman in the law school, but she acts on it instead of talking about it, at least to me. Kate and I talk about books, she publishes my reviews in her column, and I pass on new books to her that Stone lends me.

My first impression of this Lizzie was typical Delta debutante. She sat at a table smoking a cigarette in a long holder and nursing a glass of bootleg white mule. Her fine white-stockinged legs were crossed, her short skirt pulled up to her thigh. Her mouth was painted bright red, her hair short and shiny. She was telling Ella and Ben about Paris, what the women were wearing over there this year, what the chefs were serving, what the best wines are, and how the Louvre is too quaint for words. She has just returned from a grand tour with her father. She thinks she may go back and get into the fashion industry because she does love clothes better than anything, and Daddy thinks she has a real flair.

I slipped in quietly and sat at a table in the shadows listening. I was thinking what a waste Paris had been on her. Then I began to sketch her on a napkin. Nobody noticed me, or if they did they didn't say anything. One reason I can tolerate this crowd is that they let me be. I was just about finished, pencilling in her full mouth, when she sensed me, turned in her circle of light toward the shadows, her eyes cutting through them like a cat's to find mine. She said in her best drawl, vowels rolling out of her like a blues song, "Well, who are you, and what are you doing back there in the dark?" I felt guilty like I was caught in an illicit act.

"Oh, that's just Bill," Kate said. "Come over here, Bill, and meet Lizzie." I got up and started for their table, stumbling over a chair on the way.

"Lizzie, this is Bill Falkner, " Kate said. "He's an artist and he writes, too. Bill, my friend Lizzie Dunbar."

"Pull up a chair, Bill," Lizzie said, moving hers over to make room. I sat down to be polite, not really wanting to get into a conversation. "Cigarette?" she asked, opening an expensive gold case and passing it to me. I took one, and then she struck a match and lighted it for me as if lighting a man's cigarette were the most natural thing in the world for her to do.

I had forgotten that I was still holding the paper napkin with her sketch. Kate noticed and asked to see, and since it was too late to try to hide it, I handed it to her. "Oh, it's you, Liz," Kate said. "Look how good."

Lizzie took the drawing and examined it so long and hard that I was more uncomfortable than ever. Usually women are flattered when I sketch them, and anyway it's just for fun. I don't mean to show their souls in what I draw.

The others went on talking and finally she looked at me with ambiguous eyes and said, "This is a pretty sketch, you're very good, but it's not the real me." She took a deep draw from her cigarette, and threw her head back to exhale, her red mouth an O.

"Who are you then?"

"God," she said, her eyes narrowing slightly, "I wish I knew."

"If you don't know, how do you know I've missed?"

She held the napkin up in both her hands and stared hard at it. "This woman is confident, I am not. She is happy, I am not. She is pretty, and I don't feel so."

"Then appearances deceived me," I said, surprised she was saying these things to a stranger.

"You're sweet," she said, smiling. Her introspective mood passed, and she turned the intensity of her attention on me. She put both her arms on the table and leaned toward me, staring me in the face. "Who are you, Bill Falkner?"

"Nobody much, if you ask people around here."

"But I'm not asking them; I'm asking you."

"I draw. I write."

"I write, too," she said. "Writing courses were all I ever took in college."

"I flunked freshman English," I said.

"So what?" she said. "Are you any good?"

"As a writer?"

"Wasn't that the topic?"

"I'm good," I said. "I aim to get better. Are you?"

"I don't know," she said. "Probably not, but I wish I were. I admire writers."

"Such as . . . ?"

"Such as Charlotte Gilman Perkins. Have you read *Women and Economics*?

"God, no. I wouldn't touch a book named that."

"It's wonderful," she said. "She lays it all out. How women can stop being economic parasites and be full participants in the society. Men and women will both have the work that fulfills them, people will live in cluster communities, cooking will be done in one central area by those who like to do it, the children will be cared for by those temperamentally suited for it. Nobody will be a drudge. Everybody will have a choice."

"Goddamn," I said. "What does the governor say about that?"

She laughed and took a long slug of her drink. "You don't have any whiskey, Bill. We better get you some before it's gone." She turned to Ben, who had the bottle, and said, "Pour Bill some of that stuff, Ben." She had brought it with her from home. Stole it from Daddy. Authentic Perry Martin. Dunbar probably has a private pipeline from the still to his house.

"Is there marriage in this utopia?" I asked her.

"Oh, if people want to," she said. "But it won't really matter. A woman won't sign herself over like now. She won't have to for economic security."

"What about sex?" I asked. The New Woman actually blushed a little, a faint pink tint on her face and neck.

"Oh, silly. We're not talking about the end of the human race here."

"No, I mean how would it work? If you yourself were in Mrs. Gilman's compound, would you choose a mate for his genes, or for his ideas, or his disposition, or would you have a different man each night or what?"

"Since you put it on such a personal level," she said, her blush deepening, "I'd have to say I would choose for love."

"So love is a necessary prerequisite for sex?"

"Of course."

"I agree with that. In fact, with sex as one's most intimate act, I'd say it should definitely be done the first time with someone loved deeply and known for a lifetime, in one's own family—a father, mother, brother, sister. Not for reproduction, of course, just initiation. The system you describe might expedite that."

She drew back from me, her spine stiffened, and the fashionable flapper slouch disappeared. "That's disgusting," she said. "You surely don't believe it."

"I believe it," I said.

"A FATHER?" she said, with a stricken look. "What made you think such a thing?"

I'll admit I throw these notions out sometimes just to see what people will do, but her reaction was extreme. Kate interrupted and said, "Hey, you two, break it up. We're ready to do the reading." Then she looked at Lizzie and said, "What's the matter?"

"Bill Falkner is outrageous," she said.

"I thought you liked to talk about ideas," I said.

"Is he talking about incest again?" Kate said. "You just love incest, don't you, Bill?" Then turning to Lizzie she said, "Don't pay him any attention. That's just Bill for you." Looking back at me, she said, "Bill, do you want to assign parts?"

I didn't. I couldn't sit there any longer. I escaped out the back door and tramped through the woods before I went home to bed. I was tired of them all, especially Lizzie Dunbar, just back from Paris, with all her money and freedom and basic provinciality. A woman like that can wear you out in no time.

Sissy
1920

Mama say it a waste of time, my time her time too. Say she need Sissy at the house with Little Earl, in the fields chopping cotton. Say Miss Miranda teach her to read too, but why? Ain't never done her no good. No time for reading, Mama say. Got too much work. Folks to feed, clothes to wash, houses to clean.

Every morning Sissy sit in Miss Lizzie's room, trying to learn. Pretty room. Big tall bed with a white tent over it. Pink roses on the wallpaper. White ruffles on the bed. Thick rug soft on Sissy feet. Shiny bottles smelling sweet all over the dresser. Sissy want to put some of that behind her ears, paint up her nails.

Sissy stare at the page. Scratches all over it, like a hen set loose.

"This is *A*," Miss Lizzie say, pointing to a little tepee with a line through it.

"What it mean?" Sissy ask.

"Means *A*. First letter of the alphabet."

"What it do?"

"Goes with other letters to make words."

"Which words?"

"Lots. *Apple. Alligator.*"

"Who thought them letters up?" Sissy ask.

Miss Lizzie frown. "Don't worry about that," she say. "Just learn the letter. This one is *B*."

"How many letters there be?"

"Twenty-six."

Mama taught Sissy to count. She know twenty-six. Two dozen eggs and two more. Looks at them books on Miss Lizzie's shelves, a million pages covered up with words.

"Mean to tell me all them books made from twenty-six letters?" Sissy ask. "Sissy don't believe that."

Miss Lizzie laugh and laugh. "You have a funny mind, Sissy," she say. "All the books in the English language from twenty-six letters. It's true, trust me."

So Sissy learn the letters but still can't read. Sissy disappointed. Be a lot more to reading than Miss Lizzie let on. "Words next," she say, show Sissy the dictionary. Millions of words. Now Sissy know it hopeless.

"S-i-s-s-y," she say and write it out. "Crooked letter *i*, crooked letter, crooked letter, *y*. Like in Mississippi. Know what word that is?"

Sissy can't make it out. Shake her head. "No'm," she say.

"That's you," she say. "That word is *Sissy*."

Make Sissy feel funny to see it on the page, feel trapped. She don't like Miss Lizzie writing her down.

Today Miss Lizzie make a string of letters on a page. "Read it," she say, put the paper in Sissy's face.

Sissy stare at the words. She get *cat* and *cotton*, then letters swim like tadpoles in the creek. Sissy start to sweat. "Jesus," she say.

"No need to bother him on this one," Miss Lizzie say. "Sissy can learn this on her own."

Kate
1921

I'm lucky because I know what I want to do. Mama's influence had a lot to do with my choosing the law, I know, but I like to think I could have found my calling on my own. When people tell me that I am asking for trouble by trying to break into a man's world, or that I am rejecting my womanhood and no man will ever want me for a wife, my resolution is stronger than ever. Whenever I see Lizzie, I worry that she has not found her niche yet. She's at loose ends as far as I can tell, biding her time for who knows what.

Her father is fond of saying, in a joking way, but I think he means it, that he will rest much easier when Lizzie is married. But she's never mentioned being in love to me. What she talks about are plans that involve herself alone—going to New York to write or studying fashion design in Paris or coming with me to law school. Every time I see her there's a new scheme, but I can't dismiss them. She could take any of those roads and make a good race.

Instead she stays on at Bolivar Landing, spinning her wheels, dabbling around with the gentry, center of the social scene. She complains about the purposelessness of the high living, but it's as if she's in thrall to it, under the spell of the mystique of money and power. She tells herself and me that Governor Dunbar needs her. She says that since her mother has nervous trouble, she has to be the lady of the house, but from what I've observed Gwin manages that office quite well.

What goes on in other families is a mystery, after all, even those families you've loved since childhood. Governor Dunbar has always been a gentleman around me—he has perfect manners and great charm—but rumors fly about him and his business deals and shady connections. That tends to be true of any public person, I suppose. Actually as governor he was more progressive than we would have predicted, even getting through some child-labor reform and money for a new asylum.

Once on the way to Moon Lake with Lizzie for the weekend—she was driving the little Ford her daddy gave her for her birthday—we passed a Negro cabin with a big car parked in front of it. This was so unusual that I looked closely, and I'm sure the car was Governor Dunbar's. If Lizzie saw she didn't let on, and I didn't either. Of course, there are many reasons why he might have been there, but most of the time white men visit the Negro quarters for one purpose only. Even if Lizzie suspects that he is not the straight-laced church man he purports to be, she can never admit it. I guess that's something you're slow to admit about your own father. She adores her father, and even if she stumbled on his feet of clay, I don't think it would matter to her.

Mama says Lizzie would be better off if she had fewer talents, fewer possibilities. Then she would have to focus on one thing. Every time she comes to the university to visit me, I almost persuade her to stay. She's stimulated by the people, and she sees that she would have a place there. But something blocks her.

"If I could just know for sure," she says. "If God would just write it on the sky in big letters, I would do it, no matter what it was."

"That's not how people find their work. Unless you're Paul on the Damascus road or somebody like that."

"Life is too hard," she says. "About the time I think I have myself and life figured out, something comes up that changes my mind."

"Such as . . . ?"

"Such as being sure last week that I should come to law school and that I would like a public life. I want to do some good in the world, be a champion of women's causes, maybe run for an office someday."

"Sounds reasonable."

"But then Daddy pointed out that I left Hawthorne without a degree, and I would have to start over and that I'm basically more a private person than a public one. He says I would make a better writer than a lawyer. And he says women lawyers, well, never mind."

"No, tell me."

"Nothing. Really."

I know what he said, though, as surely as if I had been a fly on the wall. The slightest look of disapproval from him is enough to derail her. I can see him with his smile of complete self-assurance, feeding the ambivalence in her that he has nurtured all along, making her feel that public office for a woman is tainted and unnatural and at the same time training her to think with a man's mind, his mind, to be exact. And he probably doesn't even see what he is doing.

Lizzie
1922

The worst thing has happened, unbelievable really. I have fallen in love with Avent Easley. I have refused for months to accept this, but it is becoming increasingly clear. I thought after Kaev I would never, but it's the same feeling. I live to see him, the time I am with him flies by, everything that happens during a day has meaning only in relationship to him—how I will tell him about it, what he will say. I've always believed that destiny intends one person in the world as your mate and that Kaev was that one for me and that since he is gone, I will never feel that way again, but here it is like a terrible sickness. I can't stop myself; I know it is wrong and not fair to Avent, but I am only at peace when we are together.

We see eye to eye on politics and religion and women's issues, and I had fooled myself into thinking that we could go on and on this way forever, riding our horses and sharing books and ideas, but then tonight he asked me to marry him. He had kissed me at the door and gone to his car, and I was watching so I could wave good-bye, and all of a sudden he bounded back up the walk and steps and blurted, "Marry me, Lizzie." My first proposal, but instead of joy, I staggered against the door like he had pounded me in the stomach.

"My God, Liz," he said, taking my face between his hands. "Is it such a bad idea? I thought you liked me."

I began to cry, and he didn't say anymore. He held me a long time until I stopped, and then he kissed me good-night and said he would see me tomorrow. He will never ask me to explain; he has too much pride for that, and so I guess he will assume I don't love him—oh, I don't know what he thinks, if only I were brave I could tell him the truth, or at least what may be the truth, I don't really know, but I can imagine his eyes grow cold and his body stiff and see him lose respect for me, see it drain from his face and see a shadow of contempt eclipse the look of love. Maybe he doesn't want children, but yes, I have heard him say, "I will teach my children someday . . ." yes, he wants them. Or sex, maybe he does not want, he has never asked, Vassar and Walker do, she says he is good for that at least, she says men must, but Avent has not tried—but that's crazy, of course he wants to. I have felt him want to when he kisses me he wants as much as I do except he does not know I do too so at least I have not done that yet I should get some credit for that, but I should have stopped the whole thing sooner, if I had had courage, I would have stopped the whole thing sooner, if I had any courage I would have stopped before he loved me, I should have turned cold early on, I could have stopped.

I will ask God for an answer, I will kneel by the bed like I did as a child and ask God if he is there to answer and say why he has let this thing happen to me why has he made me want Avent so much if it is wrong and why must I try to live so flawed, so poisoned. I am death and poison to any man who puts his seed inside me, any child I bear, and if I am to live how must I do it? The river, there is the river, the current is swift, swift to the Gulf, and drowning is quick and clean and bodies are never found.

But no, that is weak. I will not, no, I will tell the truth. I will tell Avent the truth, and he will hate me, but I will do it, I will for once do a strong thing.

The Antique Shop

In a file of correspondence, Mr. Cavanaugh found this letter:

April 5, 1922

Dear Liz,

Guatemala is a marvelous country, perpetually spring. The days are warm and sunny, the nights cool enough for a blanket woven on a hand loom by an Indian woman in a nearby village of the *los altos*. I am writing from the front porch of my house. It is a white wooden house with a wide central hall through the middle. A dogtrot house, we would call it at home. It has a tin roof that during the rainy season will make music for me. Except for the view and the weather I could think I was back in Mississippi. From the porch I can see the snowy top of our local volcano, which is still active and could any minute pour a wash of fiery lava out onto the icy cone. Nearer on the horizon is the cornfield, which Mayan descendants will plant during days of feasting, dancing, and ceremony. Their costumes are of the colors of corn—red, yellow, white, and black—and their dances recreate the Mayan legend that the earth's first four men were created from corn paste. (And no, they don't specify what the first women were made of.) My own yard is a riotous blaze of color, an exotic tangle of vegetation where bright birds dart and sing among the cedars.

What a setting this would be for you. A wild country we could explore together, with mules, boats, trucks, trains, or on foot if you like—from the banana plantations of both coasts where the humidity and malaria are like the Delta and Negroes work the land because the Indians cannot bear the heat, to the remote mountain Indian villages where life has not changed since the Spanish conquest. Ruined walls and courtyards of the Jesuit monasteries and the cloisters of Las Capuchinas. Open-air markets where women make tortillas on charcoal fires and weigh out grain, black beans, and fruits to sell. Some of the women carry their wares to the market in baskets on their heads—a live turkey, or a pot of honey, or calla lilies. Another will have a baby in a sling on her back with its little head covered to protect it from the evil eye.

Managing a coffee *fincas* turns out not to be as different from running a cotton plantation as I first thought. Our laborers are *ladinos* of mixed white and Indian blood. Most of them live in quarters here on the plantation. I have three servants who come with the house—a cook, a houseboy, and a yardman. They are afraid I am lonely. "Have party," Maria, the old *ladino* cook, urges me. "Beautiful women in Antigua will come to your house, and I will make a feast to win their hearts." I am lonely, it is true, but not for the society of Antigua.

Antigua must be the most romantic city on the continent. Until an earthquake in 1773 it was the Spanish capital and reportedly the richest city between Mexico and Peru. It is still a proud city, with many of the lovely Moorish palaces restored and an Old World charm that you would like, I know. Coffee *fincas*, ours among them, have sprung up around the town and mingle in the ruins of the monasteries.

I look at this strange new world with a single idea—how I would love to show it to you. I stare in the direction of Mississippi and try to figure out what happened between us. Why don't you write me, Lizzie? Did I misunderstand that you love me? Didn't you imply you would join me in Guatemala? Is my love for you so strong that it blinded me and made me imagine you felt the same way? I wish you would just say.

Give my best to Governor Dunbar and your mother. And Lizzie, do write me a letter. I would like nothing better than to hear from you.

> Until then I remain, truly yours,
> Avent

I declare, thought Mr. Cavanaugh, feeling a bit like he was intruding into someone's secret heart, what a sad love letter. I had forgotten one of the Easleys went off to Guatemala.

Buck Allen
1922

Sweet smell first, then light, walks lightly, calls lightly, "Buck? Ready to run, Buck Allen?" Head over stall and she rubbing my nose, eyes to mouth. "I love your nose. You got such a soft nose." Nuzzle her, bite softly.

"You just want sugar, like all the men." Sugar lump between teeth then, good, sweet juice melt. Soft hand touch quick pain shoots front hooves high cry.

"Whoa, whoa, O.K. O.K. Hurts?" Pats neck softly softly. "They've had that twist on your nose again, haven't they? I told them not to. Damn." Walks to door. "James!"

"Yes'm."

"Come look at this raw place on Buck's lip."

"Yes'm."

"I told you not to use that twist."

"Yes'm."

"Why then?"

"He too wild."

"He is not. I've ridden him a year."

"Blacksmith come, couldn't get near him."

"Why didn't you call me?"

"Mr. Stephen, he say don't."

"Why would he say that?"

"Don't know'm. Say we got to break this horse."

"That's ridiculous. Get me the twist."

He brings metal rod and chain. I shy kick.

"Whoa, Buck, whoa boy. It's O.K. We're not going to use it. See?"

She hold it up to James. "How'd you like for me to catch your lip in a chain and twist it until the blood comes?"

"Ain't gonna catch up my lip."

"I might if you do that to Buck again."

"You better get away from me with that thing. I ain't no horse."

"You think Buck's lips don't feel, just like yours and mine?"

"I ain't studying no horse's lips. I got work to do."

"Anybody looks for this torture instrument, it's in the river."

"Better give me back that thing. Mr. Stephen be looking for it, mad."

"He won't be as mad as I am."

"He say he gonna ride Buck today. Say for you to ride Molly."

Bridle over ears lightly, bit between teeth. "He can't ride Buck."

"No'm."

Blanket, saddle, girth tight. "He'll break his neck."

"Yes'm."

"I'll take Buck. Save Daddy's life."

James laugh laugh laugh. "Lord have mercy."

She's up. Reins flick, knees light in my ribs. Into bright sun dazzle, through the lot, the gate, around the house, down the road, sky, trees, ditch, thicket, cotton cotton cotton white white white then up the levee, nose to north.

"Now." She leans, reins slack, I run faster faster faster legs stretch mane tail fly air rushes ribbons of river willows cattle white egrets blackbirds red wings green levee. Feel her breath, heart beat, soft hands but then faster faster faster then horse rider river levee air sky all one rush one flesh one joy.

James Harris
1922

Standin' round here talking to me about horse's lips, all the work I got to do. Act like she think these animals is people. Like to have a fit when Mr. Stephen told me drown them kittens in a tow sack, cats about to take over the place. Animals is animals and people people, but these here animals get treated better than some people I know.

Mr. Stephen he be coming in here looking to ride Buck Allen, or try. And who have to tell him she gone again? Ole James. Who get hollered at and cussed? Ole James. How come he think I can stop her if he can't? Say he paid a lot for that horse. Say Buck Allen bred to be a racehorse. "Won't be fit to kill when she get through," he say. "Might as well feed him to the crows."

I done warned him when he traded for Buck, a coal black colt with four white socks. "One sock buy him, two sock try him, three sock shy him, and four sock feed him to the crows."

"Superstition," he say. "Old wives' tale. I don't put stock in that." He wish he had now, I bet.

Don't look like to me it'd hurt a horse to be rode. I figure he mad because she can ride him and he can't. "Never saw a horse I couldn't break," he say. Maybe he ain't, but he looking at one now. That horse hate him. All he have to do is walk in the door and ole Buck's eyes roll up in his head, mouth pull back from them teeth, and he start in neighin', buckin', kickin', like he gonna tear down the stall.

"Goddamn bastard," he say. "I'll ride you if it kills you."

Kill him be more like it. Any killin' done, I'd lay odds on ole Buck.

"What she do to him?" He all time askin' me. "Feeding him dope? Doping my fine horse?" I has to laugh at that.

"I'm holding you personally responsible, James," he say. "Don't let her ride this horse again."

How come he don't tell her to her face, stop her if he can? How I get dragged into this? What I look like, some kind of telephone?

Buck Allen
1922

Six men close in, long knives and buckets, ropes, towel strong smell over my nose, no air strong smell struggle struggle and then fall, knees first, hard, then down down down far down and the dark for a long time.

Now I stand again different, pain, white cloths wrapped around, she stands with arms around my neck, head against mine, water from her eyes run down my nose.

"If only I had been here," she says. "How could they?" James in the door.

"Don't take on. He just a horse."

"Why did you let them?"

"Ain't my horse."

"Leave us alone," she says. "Go away."

He walks away. She stands and holds my head until the pain is bigger than I am and I fall again.

Stephen
1922

I try to be calm. I deliberately don't answer her for a full minute. I concentrate on my steak. I slice it carefully. It is bloody in the center like I like. It quivers under my knife, and the juices gush onto my plate. I put down my knife and fork and look at Lizzie. Her face is swollen and ugly. She wears pants, though I have asked her to dress for dinner. She sits, not eating, and turns her steak knife round and round in her hand.

"If you're looking for someone to blame, you can blame yourself," I say in an even tone. "I had asked you repeatedly to stay off him. Stallions are not to be trusted, especially with women riders."

"He was gentle with me. He would never hurt me."

"That's naive. They're unpredictable. They'll turn on you. Did you ever see how he behaved to me? He has a mean streak. Wait until you have children. You'll see how I feel."

"His spirit is broken. He'll never be the same."

"That's good. Geldings make wonderful saddle horses. Now I won't have to worry when you ride."

"I thought you wanted to race him. He won't be any good for that now."

"Your safety is more important. The foreman at Alligator saw you riding on the levee clear up there."

"So?"

My face flashes, iron twists my gut. I take a deep breath.

"This is not Holly Springs. Bolivar Landing is a wide-open town."

"What has that got to do with where I ride?"

Heat flares in my throat. My voice is louder than I intend. "You want some nigger to rape you? I believe you do, running wild through the county like a bitch in heat." I regret the words the minute they are out. Gwin puts her hand on my knee under the table. She shakes her head at me.

Lizzie draws back as if I have struck her. My eyes cloud and I remember Holly Springs, Lizzie a little girl in pinafore and braids. She lives to please me. I can protect her then. I can take care of her. I reach for my child, but she is a sullen, angry woman. She stands abruptly and knocks her chair over. "I would never have believed how I hate you," she says and runs from the room.

Gwin
1922

In Iowa women work hard, not like here. Mrs. Dunbar lies in the bed all day, and Lizzie does exactly what she pleases. Reads and rides her horse and plays the piano sometimes and goes to parties. The black women do all the work, the black women and me.

Lizzie gets more difficult every day. She keeps Stephen torn up and angry. She knows just what to do to get at him. I'm sure she does it on purpose. It's all I can do to hold things together.

What she needs is to get married and get out from under her father's roof. She strung Avent along for fun, but when it came time for commitment, she wanted no part of it. She knows when she has it easy. No sooner was Avent out the door than she took up with Walker Dubard. He's a rounder you can tell, nice looking, roving eye. He flirts with me until it's ridiculous, just like a lot of these Southern men do, but I don't pay him any attention. I have more sense than that. He'd be a good match for Lizzie, actually. He's as wild and restless as she is. Stephen doesn't know it, but they stay out all night sometimes. I certainly won't tell him. Maybe she'll be forced into marrying him. I believe that's about the only way she'll do it.

She's getting ready to go on some trip now, something about women voting. If those women had to work for a living like I do, they couldn't pick up and go for a week to Baltimore to talk about women's rights. But I'm glad for her to go. Every hour she's out of the house is a blessed one for me. Stephen is afraid she won't come back, but she will. I couldn't be that lucky.

Vassar Lamar
1922

I was upstairs in my room experimenting with a new lipstick when I heard the doorbell ring and heard Roberta let Lizzie in the front door. "Where is she?" Lizzie said, out of breath. I glanced out my window and saw her horse wandering around the front yard, not even tied up.

"Ain't seen her since dinner," Roberta said, "but she around here somewhere. Primping probably." Before she finished, I heard Lizzie's boots on the stair, thump, thump fast on the carpet, heading this way. She flung open the door and burst into the room like a March wind, not knocking or anything. She wore riding pants as usual. The tie to her blouse was twisted around her neck and hanging down her back. Her face was flushed and her eyes shining. She looked like a girl in love.

"What?" I said. "Let me guess. You've relented and are going to Avent in Guatemala."

She stopped dead and gave me such a look. "Oh, God, Vassar," she said. "Are men all you think about?" She flung herself across my bed and caught her breath.

"I admit it," I said, turning back to the mirror, "I'm fond of men. If that ole horse gets in Mama's tulips there'll be hell to pay. Do you think my hair looks better parted on this side or on the right?"

"Does it bother you that we're parasites?"

"You speak for yourself, Lizzie Dunbar," I said, putting on a little more lipstick. "I think this new shade is right becoming."

"Our fathers spent money on years and years of education

for us, and we're useless. We don't contribute anything to the economy."

"Anytime I go to Memphis shopping, I contribute plenty to the economy and so do you."

"But it's our fathers' money."

"Of course it is. And it's their duty to give it to us. They've got plenty. If we didn't fix up and look nice, it would reflect on them. Should I wear this skirt or this one Saturday?"

"I mean we don't produce anything ourselves."

"So what do you want to do about it? Pick cotton? Set up a loom in the front hall?"

"All we do is go to parties and act silly." Lizzie was lying on her back on the bed now, gazing up at the ceiling.

"Well, what on earth else would you want to do?" I asked. "I'm having fun myself. Don't worry. Time enough to be a drudge after we marry. Mama says we're eating our white bread now, and we better enjoy it."

"Don't you ever feel like there's got to be more to it?"

"To what?"

"Life." She jumped up and began to pace up and down the room.

"Oh, honestly," I said, turning from the mirror to look at her. "You make me tired when you start that up. It's those dreadful books you read. Surely you didn't ride all the way out from town to talk about the meaning of life."

"No," she said. "I want you to go to Baltimore with me. Next week."

"Baltimore? And miss the biggest dance of the year in the Delta?"

"You know the League of Women Voters?"

"I won't do it," I said.

"Just listen. They're having a national meeting in Baltimore, and all the old suffrage leaders will be there, like Mrs. Catt. They're going to talk about real things, child welfare and women in industry and what women can do now that we've got the vote. Kate and Miss Meems are going. If you came it would be perfect."

I looked at her. "We could also shop," she said, "and maybe go down to Washington. We could have fun."

"Sit down," I said, taking her hands and sitting beside her on the window seat. "If you weren't my friend, I wouldn't say this to you, but people are talking, Lizzie."

"What people?" she said.

"I'm not calling names. But they're saying you're odd. You know, with those ideas about women taking over."

"What do I care?" she said, pulling her hands away and looking out the window. "I never paid much attention to what people say."

"Don't be mad," I said. "I just don't want to see you hurt, or see you ruin your chances with Walker."

"Walker," she said. "Oh, Lord."

"Why are you so mean to him?" I said. "He's crazy about you, any fool can tell, and he's rich somewhat and good looking. I can't understand you, Liz, I really can't."

"I'm not mean to him. I'm not a bit mean to him. *You* wouldn't marry him either, remember."

"He didn't ask me. Besides I don't love him."

"I don't either, and I don't want to marry anybody.

"You don't mean that," I said.

"You won't go with me?"

"And miss the fun here? You must be crazy."

With that, she left the room, not even saying good-bye. Out the window I watched her whistle for the horse, who was munching Mama's tulips. She climbed on and rode down the lane toward the river, never once looking back my way.

The Antique Shop

Mr. Cavanaugh is meticulously reading his way through the file drawers. His dust mask and gloves make him look like a surgeon or a man operating a cotton picker.

Booker sticks his head in the door and shakes it at the familiar scene. "Got to make a deposit fore the bank close," he says. "Can you mind the store?"

"Now?" Mr. Cavanaugh mutters through the mask, not taking his eyes off the file labeled "Baltimore, 1922."

"Ain't got but ten minutes," Booker says crossly. "You needs to get out this back room anyhow. Breathe."

"Listen to this," says Mr. Cavanaugh and begins to read from page 12, torn from a magazine called the *Woman Citizen*:

A Pledge for Conscientious Citizens
by Maud Wood Park, President
National League of Women Voters

BELIEVING IN GOVERNMENT BY THE PEOPLE, FOR THE PEOPLE, I WILL DO MY BEST—

First   To inform myself about public questions, the principles and policies of political parties, and the qualifications of candidates for public offices.

Second   To vote according to my conscience in every election, primary or final, at which I am entitled to vote.

Third   To obey the law even when I am not in sympathy with all its provisions.

Fourth   To support by all fair means the policies
           that I approve of.

Fifth   To respect the right of others to uphold
           convictions that may differ from my own.

Sixth   To regard my citizenship as a public trust.

This is a simple pledge, but if it were taken—and kept—by a majority of the voters of this country, we should be much nearer the Kingdom of Heaven upon earth than we find ourselves today.

After a pause, Mr. Cavanaugh looks over his glasses at Booker and says, "What do you think?"

"Think must not of been many signed. You want me to take this here money to the bank or don't you?"

Mr. Cavanaugh sighs deeply, takes off his mask, and follows Booker to the front. He takes his place at the desk while Booker walks across the street to the bank. If a customer were to come in and demand that he operate in the present tense, he's not sure how he will respond.

Lizzie
1922

Baltimore to Bolivar Landing. Ideas are "transferring like ants" in my head, as Genesis would say. One for every click of the train's wheels. The pale green Shenandoah Valley flies by on my right, and Kate sleeps on my left. For the first time since the Coast Guard I know what I want to do. I want to start a newspaper for women in Mississippi. I want to educate women on how to use their vote for the most good, so they won't just vote however their husbands say.

The idea came to me on the second day of the conference. I was standing at the publications table looking at all the newspapers and magazines and pamphlets that women are publishing for women. A delegate from New York was talking to one from Philadelphia, and both of them worked on women's newspapers. New York said, "Women have no political tradition. Most don't know what the issues are, much less what to do with this new political power. And those who do know find it hard to speak up."

"Yes," Philadelphia agreed. "We must start where we are and find our voices."

I stood there for a long time, not hearing or seeing what went on around me, but with "start where we are" and "find our voices" echoing. Mississippi is a most unlikely place, but a Mississippi woman has one vote same as a woman in New York. I have political connections, and I can write. Next year at this table, Mississippi can have a paper. Kate came up and touched me on the shoulder. I jumped a mile, and she said, "Isn't this a strange place for a reverie?" I told her what I was thinking and, thank God, she didn't laugh.

Kate and Miss Meems encouraged me, but I could see doubt on their faces. I am full of good ideas, Kate hints, but I don't follow up. This idea feels right in a way that others haven't. Writing and politics—what I like best.

"A newspaper will take a lot of money," Kate said.

"Make Stephen cough it up," Miss Meems said. I think he might, though lately he complains about the cotton market. Last night in our room in the Belvedere, such an elegant hotel, I practiced asking him. Miss Meems played Daddy. She is really good. She had Daddy down to a T.

"Daddy, I have found my life's work."

"About time!" Miss Meems booms.

"Your influence has led me to this. Now all I need is some start-up money for a woman's political newspaper."

"Elizabeth, you don't want to waste your time and my money on busybody club women."

That's what will stop me. It won't be the money. It will be the way he says "club women," the tone of voice that makes a thing seem slight and insignificant and makes me lose interest in it in spite of myself.

Even Daddy would have been affected at Wednesday's general session when a smiling gray-haired woman stood suddenly in front of the platform covered with flowers from the gardens of Baltimore women. A shock of recognition, then thunderous applause from the thousand women in the Century Theatre. Emmeline Pankhurst. No one had known she was there. To be a leader like that, having a chance to go to jail for what you believe, and then to live to see your goal reached. What could be better?

Suffrage. The word sounds brave. The most significant political movement of the century, and I missed it. When you're young you don't know. At Hawthorne it was as if I were asleep to the world around me, tangled in my personal unhappiness and blind to the larger picture. What was I doing, thinking during all those interminable hours there?

Jane Addams made a surprise appearance, too. Daddy would say she showed her true colors when she went against the war and became such a pacifist, but I think she may have been right. She thinks that women can never be equal in a society that sanctions violence because they can't match men in physical strength. Kate and I remembered when Miss Meems gave us a copy of *Twenty Years at Hull House* back at Holly Springs, and for weeks afterward we lived in the slums of Chicago and took turns being Jane Addams.

Women are here to stay as a political force, there's no doubt about it. When women got the vote, everybody said that with the loss of that goal, the suffrage women would go back home to the kitchen. They said the League wouldn't last because it didn't have as clear a cause as the Suffrage Association. But this year, the League's second convention, 150 reporters came to cover it. This is no dead organization.

The thing I liked best about this conference was that it included all the Americas, from pole to pole practically, Canada to Chile and Argentina, twenty-two countries in all. The Pan-American Conference they called it, come together to discuss not war or boundary disputes or commerce but problems of women and children. Lively, charming Spanish-speaking women, many of whom spoke English and made me wish I had taken Spanish at Hawthorne since most of our hemisphere speaks that language.

One evening we had "Great Women of the Americas" and the delegates told about famous women from their countries. The story that moved me most was of Princess Isabel of Braganza, the daughter of the last emperor of Brazil. She was acting as regent when her father was in Europe for his health, and she signed a decree freeing all the children of slaves. Then later when her father was gone again, she prepared a decree freeing all the slaves. One of her councilors asked her if she knew what that meant. She said it meant the end of slavery. He replied that it meant the end of the empire. "Even so I will sign it," she said. She did and soon the empire fell and a republic was established. She relinquished a throne to free the slaves.

I was so taken with this story that I went to the public library one afternoon to find out more. The princess wasn't mentioned anywhere, though. The history books talked about a "bloodless revolt" and how the emperor then went into exile. If I had lived and owned slaves in Mississippi before the Civil War, would I have had the kind of courage the princess had? I like to think so. I wish I could do one brave thing.

I learned some other surprising facts this week. The United States is not necessarily top dog in everything. Peru had the first university in the hemisphere. Costa Rica spends more money on education than on war or any other government department. Most of those countries give factory women several weeks off with full pay to have babies. Latin American women have property rights laws that are more favorable than ours because their law comes from the Spanish which comes from the Romans. A remarkable woman named Mrs. Mabel Walker Willebrandt, the new assistant U.S. attorney general, explained all this. I would never have believed such a subject could be made interesting. The Roman property law said that when a man and woman married, their property went into a joint partnership for the home and the children. But the English common law that our law is based on has the wife losing her property and her personal identity to the man when she marries. Another good reason not to.

The most amazing coincidence at the final session. If I read this in a novel, I would never believe it. Sitting to my right was Señorita Graciela Vitale from Guatemala, an exotic young woman with flashing black eyes. "And where is your home?" she asked me in her wonderful accent after we introduced ourselves. When I said Bolivar Landing, Mississippi, she looked surprised and said, "It is a very large place?" I said no, very small, and she said, "How strange." When I asked why, she said, "I know a man from your town." She smiled and her eyes grew tender. "He is most charming," she said. "Last week I went to a lovely dinner in his home. Do you know him? Avent Easley?"

A cloud fell on me and colored the rest of the evening. It took me until the next morning to shake it off. Any number of conversations with myself were required. What did you expect, Elizabeth? That he would live his life like a monk in Guatemala, true to you forever, writing love letters? You had your chance.

Not really, Lizzie answers through tears. I never had a chance at all.

The Antique Shop

All of Mr. Cavanaugh's discoveries pale by the side of the one he just made. Two of the file drawers were stuffed with old newspapers, and Mr. Cavanaugh had delayed looking at them, thinking they were simply saved copies of the Memphis *Commercial* or some such as that. He pulled one out this afternoon, though, and gasped when he read the masthead.

The Woman's Voice
Bolivar Landing, Mississippi   *Editor, Elizabeth Dunbar*
A Newspaper for Mississippi's Women

Carefully he lifted the papers out of the drawers, afraid they would turn to dust before he could read them. They were dated from 1922 to 1928.

The idea of a newspaper for women in Mississippi in the twenties was incredible to Mr. Cavanaugh. How had he missed this? Lizzie Dunbar started *The Woman's Voice* only seventy years ago, yet it could have been 2,000 for all people know about it. Even historian-type people in her own hometown. "Dern shame." His only memory of Elizabeth Dunbar was as town character, a red-haired woman people whispered about. But an earlier image was surfacing in his memory like a photograph in the developing tray. A tiny office with a ceiling fan, a young black woman at a typewriter, a young white woman laughing and holding a telephone receiver to her ear. Were the filing cabinet and the newspaper part of his scene? Had its impression been lurking sixty years in his brain cells, waiting for fate to bring the actual objects back around to his eyes? Mr. Cavanaugh thought undoubtedly so.

Sissy
1922

He sho a bad little ole boy. Sitting up there at Sissy's typewriter, ice cream drippin' on the keys. Sissy come in from the post office, say, "Get away from my typewriter with that ice cream cone."

He say, "Show me how it works, please, please."

"I show you something all right," Sissy say. "Something you don't want to see, you don't move out the way."

"You grouchy," he say, climbing down out Sissy's chair. "I had a typewriter, I'd show you."

"You ain't, though, and look like you trying to ruin mine."

Phoebe curl up sleep in the window. He squat down by her, hold his ice cream to her nose. "Want a lick, kitty, kitty, kitty." She lift her head, look at him, yawn, go back to sleep.

"Dumb ole cat," he say.

Sissy start in typing, click, click, click. He run over jumping up and down, "Let me, let me, let me."

"Can't," Sissy say. "Gots a deadline."

"I'll get one too," he say. "Then you let me?"

"Don't let nobody pound my typewriter," Sissy say.

"Mama!" He set in hollin'. "Mama, that mean lady won't let me type."

"Hush, Clovis," Mrs. Cavanaugh say, walking out the back with Miss Lizzie. "Oh," she say, surprised like, when she see Sissy at the typewriter. Clovis grab up a galley proof, wad it, pitch it up at the ceiling fan. "Behave, Clovis," his mama say.

"This is my secretary, Sissy," Miss Lizzie say. "Sissy, this is

Mrs. Cavanaugh." Mrs. Cavanaugh stare at Sissy, don't say nothing.

"We couldn't run the paper without Sissy," Miss Lizzie say.

"Can she type?" Mrs. Cavanaugh ask, like Sissy ain't there.

"Excellently," Miss Lizzie say.

"Read?"

Miss Lizzie laugh. "Certainly."

"How . . . nice," Mrs. Cavanaugh say.

Now he holding the telephone receiver up to the ice cream. "Hallow," he shout. "I scream for ice cream." He *bad*. Seem like he everwhere you look.

"I didn't know niggers could type, Mama. You said they's all dumb."

"Clovis, hush!" Mrs. Cavanaugh hiss out the words, grab him by the arm. "Put that phone down this minute." Face red and splotchedy.

Miss Lizzie jump in, change subject. "We'll run your DAR story next week," she say. "Don't worry." Clovis he shake loose and climb up the new file cabinet like it a ladder with his ole sticky self.

"Get down from there, you bad boy," say his mama, grab him by the arm, pull him back, start for the door. He turn around, stick his tongue out at Sissy. Phone ring, Miss Lizzie answer, "Woman's Voice." Hold receiver way out, try not to get chocolate ice cream in her hair. Mrs. Cavanaugh give Clovis a shake, drag him out the door, short fat legs kickin', hollin', "Make that nigger let me type, Mama, make her, hear."

Miss Lizzie hang up, flop in her chair. "Thank God they're gone," she say. "Don't pay any attention to that brat, Sissy. Children just repeat words they hear at home."

Somehow that don't make Sissy feel no better, but in a few minutes she don't care. She go down to that safe spot inside where hurt words can't get to. She type and type and type away, strong black words on a page white as new cotton.

Mrs. Sallie George Anderson
1922

I was driving through town in my electric car when Lizzie Dunbar crossed the street in front of me, not looking right nor left, up nor down, and not bothering to speak. That we should have a person of her reputation speaking for the women of Mississippi is one of Fate's ironies. A whisper of scandal or the mere appearance of impropriety are enough to destroy the credibility that women are struggling for, now that we have the vote. But it was not her personal reputation that infuriated me then, her wild crowd with their smoking and drinking, but the latest issue of the *Woman's Voice*. I pulled over to the curb, got out of the car, and followed her into the newspaper office.

"Here come Mrs. Sallie George," I heard the Negro girl call to Lizzie, who had disappeared.

"Where is she?" I asked.

"She making the coffee," the girl said, swiveling around from the typewriter. "You want to sit down?" The two cane-bottomed chairs against the wall held stacks of newspapers.

"I am too angry to sit," I said, "fortunately, since every chair is piled high with that scandalous paper."

The girl looked alarmed at this and jumped up and ran through a swinging door to the back. "Elizabeth Dunbar," I called in that direction, "Come out here at once." I took off my gloves, opened the latest issue to the offending page, and spread it on the desk. When Lizzie burst through the door flanked by her Negro, I rapped smartly on the fleshy face of James K. Vardaman staring up at me like a country ham. "Have you gone quite mad?" I asked.

"Sit down, Mrs. Sallie," she said, swooping an armload of papers off a chair. "Let me get you coffee."

"Don't try to deter me, girl. I want to know why you have an endorsement of this scoundrel in what purports to be a League newspaper. No decent woman would vote for this hillbilly, this white trash, nor decent man either, for that matter."

"That's a paid political announcement, Mrs. Sallie. It's not my opinion or the position of the newspaper."

"Fiddle. What do the women of the state think when they open the paper and see a life-sized Vardaman and an exhortation to vote for him? And where does it say 'Paid Political Advertisement?' Show me." She couldn't, of course, because it wasn't there, and to her credit she looked worried.

"I should have put that, shouldn't I?"

"No, you shouldn't have accepted an ad from Vardaman in the first place. The demagogue."

"I have to sell ads. The paper needs the money."

"Nobody needs money enough to promote Vardaman. You should know that a petition is circulating to sever the name of the League from this paper, and the issue will be brought up at the convention in November."

"Oh," was all she said.

"Furthermore, people are saying the reason you ran that ad is Vardaman's handsome, if unsavory, son."

She flushed angrily at this. "People will say anything. You surely know that."

"I also know that public figures must be careful not to fuel the rumor mongers."

"Am I not to have a social life?"

"I will not presume to instruct you how to live your life," I said, pulling my gloves back on, "but I will say you are watched. You are a reflection on your sex."

I walked from the office without another word, leaving the editor, I trust, a great deal to think about.

Lizzie

1922

I wish I had never heard the name Vardaman. I knew what he was from long ago; anybody who has connections with Theodore Bilbo you have to look out for. And yet in politics nothing is clear-cut. A person may do good on the one hand but damage on the other, and so when you try and decide whom to support, half the time you go with the lesser evil, which is not particularly inspiring.

When he was in the Senate, he did vote for woman suffrage, and for the Child Labor Act, and he voted against the world war. Those votes were not popular in Mississippi, but they are with me. In fact, he was burned in effigy in Bolivar Landing because of the war vote, and a blacksmith from Leland sent him a huge iron cross to Washington. But when he started *The Issue*, one of his main themes was "Keep the U.S. out of the League of Nations," a position I can't tolerate.

Daddy calls him a redneck and a demagogue, and I know he's right. Yet if you look at Vardaman's record both in the Senate and as governor, you see he was often surprisingly progressive, siding with the common man. *If* the common man or woman is not black, or any color but white. Sissy and Franz Boas brought that to my attention.

It is a curious thing how an injustice you've grown up with seems perfectly natural and how hard it is to shake those ideas, even when you realize intellectually that they are false. Twenty years ago everybody I knew and probably the majority of the people in this country assumed the white race was superior to all others. This was accepted as fact. So Vardaman wasn't alone in that belief. He just capitalized on it for political advantage, cashed in on the fear and hate that simmered beneath the surface. The whole society is racist, but not in the raw, open, rabid way of Vardaman.

In New York I had friends in Franz Boas's anthropology classes at Columbia, and so I know that scientific evidence shows no superiority of any race. But back home the situation between white and black was the same as it has been for hundreds of years, except that slavery is outlawed. Lapsing into the old patterns seemed inevitable. Who is strong enough to go against their own culture, even if it dawns on them to do so? What happened to the first person who decided that human sacrifice was wrong or that women were human beings too or that the insane were not demon possessed?

When Jim Money brought Vardaman by the office on their campaign swing, I was shocked at how different he looked from my memory of him in a parade I had seen as a child when he was in his prime. Six feet fall, shoulder-length black hair, dressed in white, even to white leather boots—"The White Chief." I can see him still, pulled through town by a team of oxen, the crowd in a frenzy. I remember the excitement I felt when I saw him, the sheer animal magnetism of the man. His hair is white now, his frame bent. He tries to look the part of the aristocrat and at the same time plays the populist tune. I had often wondered if he is really as obsessed as his race-baiting indicates, or if he simply knows that appealing to the voters' basest prejudices and insecurities is the way to be elected.

I was on the phone when they walked through the door. Vardaman leaned on a white walking stick, and Jim Money held one of his arms. The old man wore a black Stetson hat, which he took off at the door. Sissy swiveled around to greet them.

"Hey, Jim Money," she said. "This your daddy?"

"Yeah," he said. "Why don't you sit down here, Daddy, and wait for Lizzie to get off the phone." The old man fell heavily into the chair and settled his walking cane and hat beside him.

"How you, Mr. Vardaman?" she said.

He didn't answer and looked at his cane as if it required his full attention.

"Y'all want some coffee?" she said. Jim Money shook his head no. Vardaman looked up from his cane and slowly around the room and then fixed his eyes on me. I hurried to get off the phone. Sissy turned back to her typing. I walked around the desk to his chair, and, weak and ill as he obviously is, he stood, took my hand, bowed, then sat back down abruptly.

"Young lady, you're as pretty as Jim Money said. And I want you to know I admire what you're doing here." As he talked, he kept one hand over his mouth. The excuse his campaign gives for his not speaking in public is that his false teeth do not fit.

"Thank you," I said.

"I've always believed women were better than men morally," he said. "I voted for suffrage because I believed the woman's vote could bring about change. I believed it could raise the quality of government."

"We'll soon see, won't we?" I said. I sat down beside him, and we talked pleasantly for a few minutes about politics in general, journalism in general. I waited for him to say something crude and shocking. I wanted him to live up to his reputation, but he was affable and courtly. He continued to hold his hand in front of his mouth in a pitiful gesture of vanity. I had heard rumors that he had lost his mind, but I saw no evidence of that. Jim Money said he had high blood pressure and sometimes on a bad day would lose the focus of a conversation, that was all. To his credit, Jim Money tried hard to persuade him not to run.

"When I heard you started a paper," Mr. Vardaman said, "I figured your daddy was behind it, but now I see you have a mind of your own."

"Daddy has supported me," I said.

"He made a pretty good governor, your daddy, but we don't see eye to eye."

"No."

"I'm a plain old country boy, a redneck. Your daddy's got a lot more polish than I do, and a lot more money. He always stood in with the society crowd."

I had to smile at his generalizations, and yet he had hit on an interesting question. Did Daddy hate Vardaman for his class, or the class he appealed to, or for his politics?

"You're no more a plain old country boy than I am, Mr. Vardaman," I said. He looked surprised and dropped his hand from before his mouth. "You're as shrewd a politician as they come." He smiled and his teeth rocked forward with such force that he barely caught them before they fell out of his mouth. When he spoke again he was not smiling.

"I want the support of the *Woman's Voice* in this election," he said.

"I'm glad you think our support is worth asking for," I said. "But the *Woman's Voice* is a nonpartisan paper."

"Nonsense," he said. "No such thing."

"Maybe not with you as editor," I said, "but my paper is." He had changed the name of *The Issue* to the *Vardaman Weekly* and frankly admitted to his subscribers that his paper was a tool for his reelection. He had returned part of their subscription money.

"You ought to run for something yourself," he said. "Why don't you?"

"I'm not qualified. I rather report from the sidelines."

"You're as qualified as anybody else," he said. "Look around at who runs."

"A well-qualified woman is one of your opponents right now. Why would a woman vote for you?"

"Most women are going to vote the way their husbands do. But, if a woman looks at the record and sees who's done the most for women, she'll have to vote for Vardaman. And another thing about this race, two men and a woman in it. The woman can't win, but she can split the vote. Now that may be good for me."

"You're assuming a lot," I said. "And I think you're wrong."

"At least run an ad for me," he said. "A paid political announcement."

"I can do that," I said. "That's nonpartisan enough."

Jim Money sat glumly through the whole conversation. He was unhappy at having to spend all his time driving the old man around and trying to cover up his illness. He handed me one of his father's political advertisements and wrote me a check. I was glad for the money because several of last month's bills were not paid yet. The old man picked up his walking cane, but instead of standing to go, he suddenly pointed the cane at Sissy, still typing, with a look of such pure hatred as I have seldom seen. "You're making a big mistake having that nigger in your office," he said. "No good can come of it." He had not seemed aware until now that she was even in the room, and so the suddenness of his attack almost took my breath. Sissy's back stiffened as if she could feel his walking cane boring into her spine.

"A little liberality, a lessening of standards, and first thing you know we're all back with the apes swinging through the trees."

Jim Money fidgeted, then stood up and tried to pull his father to his feet. Vardaman stood with great effort, but he was not ready to go. "You've studied history," he said to me, his lips curling above his dentures. "You know that the only significant progress on this earth has been made by the white race. Look at Haiti, look at all of Central and South American, for that matter. That's what mongrelization will get you. Is that what women want?"

"I don't know how we got from my secretary to the mixing of the races, " I said, "but I'll say this, the race mixing that's been done in the South has been initiated by white males."

"Yard chillun," he said, waving his arm as if to dismiss the argument. "Still niggers no matter who the daddy is. Men will be men. That's what I'm saying about the moral superiority of the women. No, young lady, the purity of the race depends on the women, and a prominent woman like you ought to be setting an example."

If I had had any courage, I would have thrown his ad in his face and shown him the door. But I did neither. I was "a lady." I deferred to age and gender. I politely shook his hand good-bye.

"He's not himself," Jim Money whispered apologetically as they left.

Sissy sat, head bowed, as if she had suffered blows from Vardaman's cane, staring at her hands clasped together in her lap.

"Oh, Sissy," I said when they had gone. "He's old and senile, Sissy. He doesn't speak for white people. You mustn't pay him any attention." I was babbling, and my face was burning. She looked up at me with that inscrutable look, the whole continent of Africa reflected in her face, the look that says you can never know what I'm feeling, what I'm thinking, you never ever will.

"See now why they calls him the White Chief," she said.

In my confusion and guilt and anger, I packed up his ad with some other copy and sent it off to the printer without the "Paid Political Advertisement" line. I wanted to get it out of the office. I told myself I was being a good journalist, that I was supporting the people's right to know who is running in a free election even though I disagree with the candidate. Now everybody is mad, except probably Vardaman. People are saying he "bought" the *Woman's Voice*. A petition signed by all the prominent women in the League was in the Memphis *Commercial Appeal* this morning, disclaiming the paper. They're going to cancel their subscriptions, too.

How does a good editor know when to be objective and impartial and when to take a stand? I am ill prepared for this job, really. I wish I had taken some courses in journalism.

The Antique Shop

"Book! Ah, Booker!"

Mr. Cavanaugh had just found some interesting documents in the *Woman's Voice* file that he wanted to tell Booker about. He pulled off his surgical mask and shouted toward the front of the shop. "Booker, you need to see this."

Meanwhile at the front, the phone was ringing, Mrs. Metcalf was quizzing Booker about the techniques of stripping old varnish off walnut and retaining the patina, Mrs. Avery was waiting for him to gift-wrap the biscuit box she had bought for Joyce Henry's wedding, and word about a wreck out on 61 had just come over the scanner, but with all the commotion Booker couldn't get the details. He felt like getting his hat and going home to dinner. This was not the kind of work Booker enjoyed.

What Booker liked was refinishing and delivery. He liked to take a battered old table, black with hundred-year-old varnish, douse it with Homer Formby's, and watch the grime bubble. He liked to wipe away the years and see the table come to life again, see the wood breathe and glow. Then when the table was changed into something beautiful, he liked to pack it carefully in the truck with quilts and blankets and take it to its home. He liked the looks of amazement on people's faces: "You don't mean that's Mama's old back-porch table? You're a regular magician, Booker." He liked to discuss with them the best place to put the new piece. "Should it go by the window, or in the front hall so everybody will see it first thing when they come in the door?" He usually wound up moving a good bit of furniture and spending a good bit of time, but he didn't mind. He had a sense of where his furniture should go, and he didn't like to leave it until the owners saw it his way, and it was in exactly the right place.

Mr. Cavanaugh couldn't understand why it took Booker so long to make deliveries. "Hell, Booker, you refinish them quicker than you deliver them. One day I'm going with you to see what in the world takes so long." He never did, though, because somebody had to keep the shop, but Booker knew that if he did, they would spend three times as long once Mr. Cavanaugh got to talking. Not only that, but they would never reach a decision about where to put the furniture. Something about Mr. Cavanaugh confused any issue.

Now in the middle of this chaos in the shop, Mr. Cavanaugh was hollering from the back like life or death. "Do he want to be in the antique business or the old paper business?" Booker said. "He need to decide."

"What's that, Booker?" asked Mrs. Avery.

"Can you decide on the ribbon?" said Booker. "Here the scissors and the tape if you can finish this up. I got to see what do he want." Then he turned to Mrs. Metcalf. "I'll come look at that old chair this afternoon. See can it be stripped." He answered the phone and assured Mrs. Cavanaugh he would make Mr. Cavanaugh come home to dinner. To the customer just walking in the door, he said he would be back in just a minute. He looked regretfully at the scanner and headed toward the storage area.

"What?" he asked Mr. Cavanaugh as he walked into the back room. Mr. Cavanaugh's cheeks were rosy with excitement. His white hair was standing straight up on his head where he had run his hand through it, and his surgeon's mask hung from around his neck.

"You won't believe this one, Book," he said. "Those women had a big state-wide meeting out at the college in 1925. Guess what about?"

"Charity ball," Booker said.

"No."

"Garden clubs."

"No."

"Books."

"No."

"Ain't got time for no games," Booker grumbled. "Madhouse up to the front. You got to go eat, too."

"Listen to this." Mr. Cavanaugh held up a folded program and read from the cover: "Mississippi Conference on the Cause and Cure of War."

Booker looked over Mr. Cavanaugh's shoulder to see if he was making that up. "Didn't mind taking on the big one, did they? What was they?"

"What was what?" asked Mr. Cavanaugh.

"Cause and cure of war? I'd like to know."

"God knows," said Mr. Cavanaugh. "Let's see. Hmmm, judging from the titles of the speeches, looks like hate and politics for causes, education and friendship between countries for cures."

"What was they going to do about it?"

"Well, they sent a high school boy from Clarksdale to Geneva."

"Why?"

"He won some contest about the League of Nations so he got to go see it. Came back and made speeches."

"They hung hopes for peace on one little ole high school boy?"

"Here's an editorial from the Jackson *Daily News* that says the 'pacifist nonsense' is 'seeking to undo the lesson of preparedness which the Great War taught.'"

As he turned through the folder Mr. Cavanaugh spoke to Booker as if he were delivering a lecture. "Oh, and here's a red scare one—clipped out of the *Woman Patriot*, January 15, 1927. Listen to this: 'As for the Communists they are logically letting the Gold Dust Twins, Feminism and Pacifism, do their work. . . . The pinks are all red sisters under the skin.'

"I don't think Lizzie Dunbar was a Communist," Mr.

Cavanaugh went on, "but maybe a Gold Dust Twin. Read this editorial and see what you think."

"You work with the public, you got a responsibility," said Booker sternly. "You got to see to it."

Mr. Cavanaugh looked baffled. Booker often spoke obscurely when he was upset. "Be direct, Booker," he said. "I don't know what in hell you're talking about."

"People standing all over the shop up there, wanting somebody to wait on 'em. I can't do everything. I'm feeling all this stress, I got too much stress."

"Damn the public anyway," said Mr. Cavanaugh, pulling his mask off and standing up. Booker had been with him twenty years, and he knew when his assistant had reached his limit. "Damn fool public will worry you to death. Can't get anything done for 'em. You stay here and take a break, and I'll cover the front." He started out the door at his fastest pace, a sort of brisk stroll, and then turned around with a calculated afterthought. "I'll call Irma to bring us dinner."

"Only man I know cuss his own customers," Booker mumbled, but he was cheered by the thought of Mrs. Cavanaugh's cooking. He decided not to quit Mr. Cavanaugh today. He looked with disgust at the file drawers of old papers. "Shoulda dumped these papers in Beulah Lake." He sat down, picked up the typescript from the top of the folder, and began to read:

> The *Woman's Voice* editor attended the recent Mississippi Conference on the Cause and Cure of War and believes more strongly than ever that our nation must become involved with the League of Nations. Women must demand it. They must work to ensure that World War I was the war to end all wars and must resolve that they will never again provide their sons for such barbarous sacrifice.
>
> Those who say that war is inevitable are forgetting that

once men regularly lost their lives in duels, but that as civilization progressed, they became more willing to settle their disputes in the courts. Who is to say that nations, too, may not make such progress, may not reach a level of civilization where international courts are arbiters for disputes?

The League of Nations is the most promising step ever made in the direction of sane and sensible world government. The *Voice* will inform you of its activities and of ways that you can make yourselves heard on this issue.

"Lord, Lord," said Booker, shaking his head. "If that woman and Mr. Cavanaugh had got together, they could have talked each other to death."

Tom Williams
1923

"Dinner at the Lamars," Grandfather says. "You can bring your book." The Lamars are rich. They have a big plantation house out in the country away from town. Their house is ten times bigger than the rectory. If Mr. Lamar doesn't tease me, I can have a good time. I can forget about school and how bad it is. I can forget that bully Brick, who beats me up and calls me sissy.

I sit in the front seat of the car between Grandmother and Grandfather Dakin. There are just the three of us now. Mother and Rose have gone to St. Louis to find Father.

Grandfather drives past St. George's Church, on through town and up the river road. The land is all flat here around Bolivar Landing, not like Columbus where it's hilly. The fields are brown and bare now, but they turn gold as the sun gets red and drops behind the levee. The only other color is red berry bushes in the thickets along the road. I lean my head back on the seat and count the hawks who sit in the tops of the trees. I pretend that I am flying over the levee and across the river into Arkansas.

It is dark when we get to Devonshire. That is the name of the Lamars' plantation. Grandfather turns the Ford into the long lane that leads to the house. "See in the East, the Star of Bethlehem," Grandfather says. A bright star hangs over the fields. I pretend we are wisemen following it. The road makes a big curve and then we see the house. The house is built of dark red brick. It has two stories and huge windows all over. Every light is on, and we can't see the stars anymore. A lot of cars are in the circle in front of the house. "Bigger party than I thought," Grandfather says. He pulls the car over and stops.

"Some of those are probably Vassar's friends," Grandmother says. "I imagine they're going to Moon Lake."

I hope Miss Vassar is there. She is very beautiful and laughs a lot. I pretend I am grown up and one of her gentleman callers. She does not talk to me, but I like to look at her across the table. Her hair is gold and glittery.

Jefferson stands on the porch in a white jacket. He shines like he's been polished with oil. He hurries down to the car as soon as we stop. He smiles real big and opens the door for Grandmother. "Evening, Miz Dakin," he says, then helps me climb out. "How you, Tom? Got a surprise for you!" Jefferson is nice. He gives me peppermints and sticks of gum. After I had the diphtheria and couldn't walk for so long, he would carry me to the barn to see the puppies or the kittens. He goes around the car and holds the door for Grandfather to get out. "How the Reverend this evening?"

"Fine, Jefferson. Big party?"

"Twenty be eatin'," he says. "But then Miss Vassar'n be going to a dance."

He walks beside me toward the house. "I open them doors, you better get ready, cause you gonna see something then." When we get up to the big double doors, he stands there for a minute with his hands on both doorknobs. "Shut yo eyes till I say 'when,'" he says to me. I am excited. I want to know what he's got in there. I put my hands over my eyes. Then I hear the big doors swing open. "Now!" he says.

I can't realize. I forget to breathe. Red, green, white, yellow, blue, orange lights reach to the ceiling, thousands of lights. "Oh, my," Grandmother whispers behind me. We stand there staring. Jefferson laughs and laughs.

"A sight, ain't it?" he says. "Took me and Roberta all day stringing them lights. You looking at the biggest electric cedar in the Delta."

Up through the colors an angel shines at the top of the tree and seems like to me I'm part of the light. I forget school and St. Louis and being sad. I make my eyes into little slits and all the beautiful colors blur like they are under water.

"He know he like that tree," Jefferson says. He puts his arm around me. He sounds glad. Then he takes our coats and goes away.

Mrs. Lamar runs out into the hall. She is very fat and talks a lot. She is not pretty like Vassar. She comes between me and the tree. "Darlings," she says and kisses us. "So glad you're here. Look how you've grown, Tommy, my goodness." She pinches my cheek. I really hate that—worse than the kissing. She herds us toward the library. "Come on in here, we've got a nice fire, dinner in a little while, any trouble on the road? We worried about you driving after dark. You'll say grace for us, won't you, Father, you know how Milo hates to say the blessing, he just won't hardly do it if you're here."

"I want to stay with the tree," I say. She looks down at me.

"Well, all right, honey," she says. "You look at that tree all you want to. Vassar and Lizzie and I went to Memphis shopping and had lunch at the Peabody and they had a beautiful tree in the lobby and Vassar said 'Mama, why can't we have one like that at home?' so after lunch Jefferson drove us down to Goldsmith's, and we got us enough lights to cover the Delta it seemed like, but it turned out to be just enough, and Milo is going to be disappointed if the tree doesn't burn the house down, but Vassar and I love it." She is still talking when they disappear into the library and close the door.

The bottom step of the staircase is a good place to lean back against the wall and look at the tree. I don't want to ever forget it. I am looking at the top of the tree when something moves and at first I think it's the angel and then I think the tree is falling. But then I see a girl all in white standing where the staircase curves and she is kind of mixed up with the tree. She starts down the stairs toward me. Her dress is shiny and reflects the lights. Her hair is shiny too but dark, and her mouth is red like Christmas ribbons. She smells sweet as spring. Brick would try to peep up her dress if he were here, but I don't. I look at her face, which is smiling.

"Hello," she says. She stops and sits down two steps above me. Her dress is short, and it comes up high when she sits down. Her stockings are shiny too, and her knees are pressed close together. "My name is Lizzie. What's yours?"

I have to think a minute to come up with my own name. Finally I say, "Tom. But I hate it."

She smiles. "Why?"

"Because everybody's named Tom."

"Everybody's named Elizabeth, too, but I always looked at that as an advantage, a connection."

"I'm going to change mine someday," I say.

"So what shall I call you?"

"Tom, I guess. For now."

"Tom. The tree is magic, isn't it?" she says, the pretty colors dancing in her eyes.

"Yes." I can't think of anything else to say, as much as I want her to stay here and talk to me. I stare at the tree.

"I could sit here and look at it all night," she says. "I wish we could."

"Yes," I say. We are both quiet, staring at the tree.

In a few minutes she says, "Do you know 'O Tannenbaum?'"

"No."

"I'll teach you," she says. "This tree deserves a song." She begins to sing very softly, strange words I never heard before. When she finished, she says, "Do you want the German or the English?"

"German."

"Good." Then she repeats the words slowly, and I repeat after her. Then I say the whole verse by myself.

"That's good," she says. "You're smart, aren't you?"

"Yes," I say. We sing the verse together, and I feel happy

singing and looking at the tree with Lizzie. Neither of us notice a man coming around the tree and walking up to us. He is very tall and his face is red. He holds a glass of something. He doesn't look at me at all. "My God, Lizzie," he says, "do you have to use that damn Kraut lingo?"

"Oh, come on, Walker," she says.

"If you had had to go over there fighting you'd never want to hear it again." He takes a long drink from his glass.

"Are you drinking already?" she asks.

He doesn't answer the question. "I read that editorial that came out in your little paper this week. Where do you get those ideas?"

Lizzie turns her head away from him, back toward the tree.

"You're a goddamned pacifist, aren't you?" He takes another long drink from his glass. "Why do you write about things you know nothing about?"

"You're drunk," she says.

He stares at her in a funny way. "Come here," he says, very loud. She doesn't move. "Come here, goddamn it," he shouts.

"Hush. Everybody will hear you." Her face is frowning, and she gets up and walks down the steps to him. She hardly comes up to his shoulder. He puts his arms around her all of a sudden, dropping his glass behind her. It breaks and whiskey spills all over the floor. I can hear his breathing. With his other hand, he pulls her head back and puts his mouth on hers like he's going to swallow her. She tries to get away. He puts his face in her neck. I start to cry. I don't know what to do. "No, Walker. Tom," she whispers, trying to move his arms from around her. "You're hurting me."

"Oh, baby, baby." He is moaning. His hands move around her breasts and her bottom. He gets handsful of her dress like he is going to tear it. I run for Grandfather, but then Miss Vassar and another man walk in. Lizzie breaks away from Walker.

"Here you are," Miss Vassar says. "Roy and I were looking everywhere." She looks at the broken glass and then at me.

"What a mess," she says.

"I didn't do it," I say.

"Go fix your lipstick, Lizzie. Have y'all been fighting again?" Lizzie wipes her lipstick on the back of her hand. Walker has a lot of it on his mouth.

"I hate you," she says to Walker. He leans against the wall breathing. Then Grandmother and Grandfather come through the door of the library into the hall. Behind them are some other men and women, two by two, and the last ones are Mr. and Mrs. Lamar.

"Gentlemen, find your ladies," Mrs. Lamar calls out. "Dinner."

Lizzie grabs my hand. "Come on, Tom," she says. "Be my partner." We fall in behind Grandmother and Grandfather and leave Walker to follow alone. His face is dark as night. At the table I sit in between Walker and Lizzie. He pouts. He doesn't eat much, and he doesn't drink his wine. Lizzie talks to me like I am a person. I tell her about diphtheria and school and Columbus and Rose. The candles from the table are in her eyes.

Mr. Lamar is a big grizzly bear. He sits at the head of the table, Papa Bear. He wolfs his food. If I ate that way, Grandfather would send me from the table. His voice booms. "They may have Prohibition in the hills, but they'll never prohibit the Delta." He drains his wine glass, and Jefferson fills it up again.

Mrs. Lamar giggles. "Milo loves his little drink after a hard day."

"Goddamn government foolishness," he says.

"Alcoholism is a problem, but Prohibition is not the answer," Grandfather says.

"Bunch of busybody church women with nothing else to do," Mr. Lamar says, his mouth full of ham and mashed potatoes, "thought up the damn Eighteenth Amendment just to make it hot for the men. Jealous because we have so much fun."

"Women have good reasons for wanting men to drink less," Lizzie says. Everybody stops talking and gets quiet.

Mr. Lamar stops chewing and stares down the table at her. Miss Vassar looks down at her plate. "You don't say, Miss Dunbar," Mr. Lamar said. "And how did you come by that information?"

"We all know men who can't control their drinking. It creates hardship." She looks at Walker as she says this.

"Any man worth his salt can hold his liquor," he says. "It's not just the men who enjoy drink either, ain't that right, Mama?" He winks at Mrs. Lamar, who giggles. He drains his glass again. "Not the government's business what people drink anyway, goddamn it." He fills up his mouth with food again. "But as long as Perry Martin keeps his still pumping and the boats keep running in from New Orleans, your daddy and me are O.K., Miss Lizzie.

"God help us, now they've got the vote," Mr. Lamar goes on. He snorts as he eats, and the hairs in his nose wave around. "Next thing the Carrie Nation types will be bustin' in folks' houses and smashing their liquor."

"Honey, don't get started on the voting business," Mrs. Lamar said. "You know Mississippi women don't want the ole vote. They'll still leave politics to the men. Not good for your digestion to get so worked up."

"I'll discuss whatever damn subject I want to, Mama," he hollers. "Why don't you stay out of it? You always have to put in."

Lizzie lays her fork down. I see Miss Vassar look at her from across the table and shake her head a little bit.

Lizzie looks at Mrs. Lamar. "I don't agree with you, Mrs. Lamar. I think Mississippi women are proud to have the vote. I think they'll get things done."

"You sounding like Miss Susan B. Anthony, now," Mr. Lamar says. "Got radical on us up north, did you? You better remember where you are, girl."

I can't tell if he is mad or teasing, but he makes me want to hide. Sometimes he teases me, but I don't think it's funny. I will die if he says anything to me with Lizzie here. I hang my head and stare at my plate.

"Hey, Tom," he says, noticing me. "What you got yo head in yo plate for? Trying to lap up yo gravy like a dog?" Then he laughs, har, har, har, har, real loud. "Look at me, son," he says. "You are pretty as a girl, you know it? Look at him blush, y'all."

"Leave him alone," Lizzie says. "You are a bully, sir." Then she gets up and leaves the table, and Walker follows her.

Mr. Lamar looks furious. "Goddamn. No sense of humor a'tall. Walker can't control his woman."

He doesn't say anything else to me. Nobody talks to me, and Lizzie and Walker do not come back. After dessert the old people and I go back in the library. In a few minutes, the young people come in to say good-bye before they leave for the dance. Lizzie has on a long fur coat. Walker has his arm around her like she belongs to him, but she doesn't seem to mind now. "Merry Christmas, Tom," she says to me and waves a little bit.

I feel sad and lonely when they leave. The room looks dull. I lie on the floor by the fire with my book. The grown-ups think I am reading, but I'm not. I'm not listening to them talk either like I usually do. I'm pretending I'm grown up, dancing with Lizzie Dunbar by the light of an electric Christmas tree.

Ruth Newcomb
1923

Before I met Kate and Lizzie I didn't know women like that, the New Women who think about business and politics rather than the home. Now that I've gone to work for Lizzie at the paper, my brothers tease me terribly. "You're not turning into one of those New Women are you, Baby Sister?" I don't think I'm smart enough to be one, but I do have a good head for figures and that's why I'm keeping the books.

I was in my senior year at Clarksdale High when Miss Jamieson asked Kate and Lizzie to come to our commercial class and talk about careers for women. They were wonderful speakers and not much older than we. All the girls wanted to be either lawyers or newspaper women after that.

The next week the state meeting of the League of Women Voters was held in town, and several of us went after school hoping for a glimpse of Kate and Lizzie. Turns out, the women were mad at Lizzie because they thought she was a Vardaman supporter. Kate made a speech to try and get them not to withdraw their endorsement of the *Woman's Voice* as their official newspaper, but they voted to do it anyway.

Lizzie was terribly angry, and later when we had Cokes with her and Kate at the drugstore, she threatened to blast them in the next issue of the paper. Kate told her she would have to be thicker skinned than that in political life. She said women needed to provide a united front, that any disagreement they had would be pictured in the newspapers as a "cat fight," and that the men would say, "See there, they can't get along among themselves. How do they expect to elect a candidate?"

Then Kate had the idea of hiring me to keep books for Lizzie. She said Lizzie had too many details to see about to keep accurate records. I jumped at the chance, and after graduation I moved in with my aunt at Bolivar Landing and went to work. I was a little bit shocked to see that the secretary was a Negro girl, but I just didn't mention it to Mama and Papa because they wouldn't have understood, but Lizzie acted like that was a natural thing to do, and Sissy was so nice that soon I didn't think a thing about it. Lizzie tells us we're making history. On a slow day, and we don't have many, Lizzie goes out, on purpose I do believe, to *make* something happen. She can, too. She's good at that. The election for governor is coming up in November, and Lizzie says she has no intention of being nonpartisan now that she doesn't have to worry about the League. If the women can get together, she says, they can show their political clout by electing their candidate. The candidates think so too because they're all leaning over backward to try and get the women's vote. They're wooing the *Woman's Voice*, but Lizzie says she hasn't decided yet whom to endorse.

The Antique Shop

Guilt has gotten the better of Mr. Cavanaugh, and he has decided he can no longer keep the *Woman's Voice* from his wife. She still has not found a topic that pleases her for her research paper and is becoming glummer by the day. On Sunday afternoon, he suggests they go to the shop.

"Clovis Cavanaugh, you dirty dog," she says when she sees them. "You've played these down on purpose, haven't you?"

In the interest of family harmony, Mr. Cavanaugh finds it necessary to stretch the truth a little bit, but not much. Like a true scholar, Mrs. Cavanaugh has soon made a remarkable discovery. She finds the subscriber list for the *Woman's Voice*. Accompanying the list is an article from the local paper about the success of the *Woman's Voice*. It says that Lizzie Dunbar's paper has 10,000 subscribers representing every county in Mississippi. With the article is a photograph of Kate Clark and Lizzie Dunbar in white dresses circulating among the crowd at the Bolivar Landing Fourth of July picnic and selling subscriptions.

"We had representatives in other towns selling subscriptions, too," Miss Dunbar is quoted as saying. "We stayed up all night in the office tabulating the sales as the girls called them in. We're extremely pleased with what this says about women's interest in participating in the political process."

Enthralled by this find, Mrs. Cavanaugh can hardly be persuaded to go home in time to cook supper.

"Write up whatever, but please don't let the MacAuley woman in on it until you have to," says Mr. Cavanaugh, pleadingly. "I need more time."

Kate
1924

Lizzie has found her niche with the paper in a way that's wonderful to see. Her editorials are strong, undertaking complicated issues like the League of Nations, labor laws, education. She even dared to defy Stephen Dunbar in endorsing Henry Whitfield for governor. Stephen thought he couldn't win, but Whitfield had been president of the woman's college, and women all over the state liked him.

I went to the *Woman's Voice* office to follow the election returns with Lizzie and her workers and friends. First one person would get to listen to the earphones and then another. When it became clear that Whitfield had won, Lizzie danced around the room kissing everybody, then she danced to her typewriter and didn't stop writing until she had an editorial about how the women turned out and elected Whitfield and that from now on women would be considered a powerful political force.

Somebody came in with champagne and the celebrating began. Lizzie jumped up from the typewriter and proposed a toast. "To a new day," she said, holding her glass high, "a day when women assume full rights and responsibilities of citizenship and become equal partners with the men."

"Here, here," we all said, touching each other's glasses before we drank, "to a new day."

Lizzie
1924

Finally I take a day off and go with Kate on the train to Holly Springs. I am apprehensive. Kate says Miss Meems has not been the same since John died. I should have gone then.

Mr. Henry meets us at the station. I am shocked at his white hair. He is an old man. I have not seen him since we left Holly Springs.

We drive to the house in his Ford. When we turn down our street, my eyes unexpectedly cloud. The houses and yards are as familiar as the palm of my hand, yet changed. They seem smaller, closer together, different from the Hollies of my childhood. I have walked these streets in my dreams for ten years, but they don't remember me. They are no longer home.

I ask about each neighbor as we go. Old Mrs. Burdine died, and all her pretty things were sold at auction. Now strangers live in her house. Mr. Thomas is in a nursing home; his house is rented out. Mrs. Walthall is still home, but feeble. The Shurfords sold their house and moved to Florida to be near their children.

We pull into the Clarks' driveway. I half expect the boys to bound out and wrestle around in the yard or to see Miss Meems in the roses, but the rose bed is scraggly and untended. The house is still and quiet. The front-porch swing is gone as if no one sits out there anymore. A big white cat suns at the edge of the porch. "Koca?" I say.

The cat does not know me. "One of her kittens," Mr. Henry says. "You girls used to love that ole cat. Dress her up in doll clothes and stroll her down the sidewalk." He chuckles and holds the front door open for us. My eyes adjust after the bright sun. The hall clock chimes noon as we step inside, and the smells of dinner—fried chicken, fresh vegetables, cornbread—hit my heart as the smells of home. I know I am back at the Clarks' now, though John is dead and Mr. Henry and Miss Meems are old, and Kate and I and the boys have grown up and moved away.

Minnie comes out to meet us. She is huge and fat and exactly the same, beautiful. I run to her and hug her in relief. "Look at you," she says, "just look at you growed up. Ain't you something." I feel the tears again as I bury my face on her shoulder. She begins to laugh and shake. "I done locked up the cake," she says. "You ain't skinning this one before dinner." We all laugh then and remember the cake. "You was a sight, honey," she says. "Sho was. Always into something." She holds me at arm's length and looks at me. "Kate say you off into a newspaper now. Mmmm. Mmmm." She shakes her head. "Y'all wash up now. Cornbread soon be out the oven."

We walk up the stairs behind Mr. Henry, who carries our suitcases. When we reach the top, Miss Meems walks out of her room. She walks with difficulty and holds a cane in her right hand. I am stunned by how she has altered since Baltimore, only two years ago. Kate and I try to embrace her at the same time, awkwardly, with the cane in the way. We make small talk about the train ride up here, but we are all thinking of John.

Later we sit around the long table in the dining room and seek comfort in the familiarity of Minnie's fresh corn and butter beans, sliced tomatoes, and chicken fried as only she can. Miss Meems congratulates me on the paper, and I try to persuade her to write an article for me. I tell them some of the problems, too, financial mainly, and how worried I am about that. They don't take that very seriously, I think, because of Daddy's money, but times are not what they once were.

As we finish our chocolate cake and Kate pours the coffee, Miss Meems says, "Six months Tuesday since John died." We stare down at our plates and don't know what to say.

"Yes, Mama," Kate says.

"I will never get over it," Miss Meems says. Then she laughs, horribly. "To think how happy we were that he lived through the war, how we celebrated when he came home."

We sit uneasily, and Mr. Henry clears his throat. "Life must go on, dear," he says.

"Why? Tell me if you can. Why live in a world where a few rich old men can order ten million young men to kill each other in a single war?"

Mr. Henry fidgets with his coffee cup. I am sure he has heard this many times.

"Sensitive young men like John who didn't die come home maimed, if not in body, in soul and spirit. The waste!"

The clock chimes one in the hall, and Minnie slips in with more coffee. The bright sun shines through the lace curtains and makes dappled shadows over the whole dining room. Miss Meems turns to me with a fierceness.

"Write this in your paper if you have the courage. Write that World War I had nothing to do with freedom and democracy. It was about imperialism and economics. Study the facts, not the rhetoric, and you will see that I am right."

"Yes," I say, my eyes on my plate. I feel guilty, as if I am an accomplice of the power brokers.

"All of you, remember this." Her eyes glitter, and she lowers her voice, though it is no less fierce. "Germany has been stripped of any vestige of self-respect, making it ripe for a despot to rally the most aggressive nationalism. The seeds have been planted in Europe for another war more devastating than the last. Mark my words and fear for your sons, Kate and Lizzie." The hairs on the back of my neck stand up and chill bumps cover my arms. It is though an oracle has delivered a prophecy impossible to escape. I see myself burying my sons who will never be born.

We sit in silence; the shadow of death hovers. "Do you know what he used, Lizzie?"

"Mama, please don't." Kate's voice breaks, and she reaches for her mother's hand, but Miss Meems draws away.

"The dueling pistols. Remember? In the orchard playing William Tell? Why didn't I throw them away?" She shivers and pulls her black shawl tight around her. Her face is pinched and drawn. "My God, the legacies we leave our children."

Mr. Henry pushes back from the table, goes to her and takes her arm. Minnie comes from the kitchen as if on cue and takes her other arm. "You need to rest, dear," Mr. Henry says gently.

"Every time I speak truth, they say I need to rest, Lizzie. The truth is tiresome, is it not?" But she stands obediently, and the three of them make their way slowly out of the dining room.

Kate is sobbing in her napkin. "Mama sees too much. She could be so much happier if she were more simple minded."

Kate
1924

Home has become an excruciating place to be. I am grateful
that Lizzie has come with me. This afternoon we walked over
to the Freeman place to see Cousin Kate. She's lived here since
her mother and grandmother died. She says New York is not
the same since the war.

As we walked down the sidewalk toward the Freeman
place, we passed Lizzie's childhood home, and as it is so near
town, it has changed for the worse. The pastures that
surrounded it are built up now with small bungalows. Mud
and old cars are in the yard where the green grass was. The
house has been divided into apartments, with a row of
mailboxes on the porch. The front porch sags and the paint is
peeling. "Oh," was all Lizzie said. She walked much faster and
turned her head away.

We remembered how Cousin Kate had been our glimpse
into an exciting world. We coveted her talent and her life. We
even took art lessons for awhile, from old Mrs. Springer who
painted a great deal before she got arthritis. But after about a
year of a robin on an apple bough, Lizzie and I decided that
painting was not our gift.

When Cousin Kate came to the door, we didn't recognize
her. We thought she was a neighbor come to visit. She is every
inch the genteel Southern lady now, bathed and powdered and
dressed to receive afternoon visitors, as familiar to us as our
own childhoods. Her face is sweet and bland and smiling and
her graying brown hair soft around her face. She wears a spring

dress, a string of pearls. All of the dash, the style that had marked her as "artist" for us is gone. Some of the change is mere aging, but not the heart of it. If she saw dismay on our faces, she didn't acknowledge it, of course. That might make us uncomfortable, and the comfort of everyone around her is the major concern of the lady.

"What a lovely surprise," she said as we greeted her and I reintroduced Lizzie. She showed us into her parlor of polished wood and velvet settees. Everything is exactly as I remembered it, as generations have remembered it. "I am so sorry about your brother. How is your mother, dear?"

"Mother's not well, Cousin Kate. I worry about her."

"I get out to church and the post office and Thursday club, but that's about all. I never see Meems. And you're practicing law now?"

"Yes, in the Delta."

"My, my." She shook her head. "I imagine Meems and Henry worry a great deal about you."

I was puzzled. "Worry?"

"Off alone over there without any of your people. And the law, don't you find it a rather . . . " she searched for a word that wouldn't offend but would express her reservations, "hard profession for a woman?"

"I love my work," I said. "It is what I am meant to do."

"I see." Her face registered exactly nothing. She turned to Lizzie then. "And you, Miss Dunbar?"

"I have a newspaper for women now."

"Oh." Now it was Cousin Kate's turn to look puzzled. "Club news, recipes, fashions?"

"Some of that," Lizzie said. "But the main purpose is political."

Cousin Kate visibly winced and repeated the word softly as if it were off color. "Political?"

"We try to keep the women informed on the issues so they can use their votes effectively."

"Oh, of course, the vote." Her tone was noncommittal. She looked at Lizzie as if she were a Martian. Then she laughed girlishly and said, "Well, that's enough serious talk. Let's go out and look at my garden, and then we'll have some tea, shall we?"

As we walked toward the French doors in the sunroom that opens into the garden, Lizzie stopped in front of two portraits hanging side by side over the wicker sofa. Both were Cousin Kate, but the difference is striking. One is a spirited, handsome young woman in a white dress, wind blowing her hair around her face, a full sensuous mouth. This was the woman Lizzie and I remembered. In the other portrait, the woman wears a hat with a feather and a lacy shawl. She holds a teacup, daintily. She looks exactly like the Old Maid in the deck of cards from my childhood.

"Who painted these?" Lizzie asked.

"Mr. Chase painted one before his death," Cousin Kate said, "and I painted the other."

"And which is a truer likeness?" Cousin Kate perceived the hook in the question. Neither is signed, and so we couldn't know who had painted which. My guess was that she had done the free-spirit one, and that the man who had wielded such influence over her, the man she called "The Master," had painted the constricted one. I was wrong.

"The Master flattered me," she said, "and though the quality of his painting is far superior to mine, yet the woman in the hat is I."

We walked on through the doors to the garden then, lovely with brick walks and a goldfish pond. The crocuses were blooming, white, yellow, and blue, and the first yellow jonquils were about to pop. The fact that the trees are still bare made the spring blooms more striking and welcome.

"You have a green thumb," Lizzie said.

"Oh, I didn't plant the bulbs myself," Cousin Kate said. "I can't stand to get my hands messy, but I planned the garden so as to have color in every season."

"Planned it with a painter's eye," Lizzie said. "You must have your easel out here often."

"I don't seem to find time to paint much anymore, though I'm sure I'll get back to it." She seemed to feel she owed us an explanation. "I've not gotten over the loss of the Master and Mama." Her eyes filled. "I have to recover from that."

"You must get back to it," Lizzie said. "You have such extraordinary talent."

"No, quite ordinary," she said. "And quite dated now." She laughed. "Since the Armory show, modernism is all the rage. Those who resisted it, like the Master and me, are shunned in the art world. Anything recognizable in a painting now is passé. Our day has passed, I'm afraid."

"Don't say that," Lizzie said. She reached out and squeezed Cousin Kate's arm. I know that Cousin does not like to be touched and that her reserve is extreme, but she did not pull away. She placed her hand over Lizzie's.

"It's all right," she said. "I have my dog, my cat, my embroidery. What practical good does painting do in the world anyway? What do you think of teaching?"

"Teaching is fine," I said. "But couldn't you paint and teach?"

"Perhaps," she said. "We'll have to see." She stared off into the orchard, then came back to us all hostess again. "Teatime," she sang gaily. "Follow me."

Her tea table was set in a bay window that looked out on the garden. Her Yorkshire terrier lay at our feet, and a calico cat was curled on the window seat. The white cloth on the table and the matching napkins were beautifully embroidered with pink flowers and light green stems. Her handiwork, we learned. We drank tea from china cups as fragile as egg shells. The cups were white with pink rosebuds, the cookies delicate as lace.

"Now," Cousin said conspiratorially when we were settled, "Tell me about your beaux. Such pretty girls, you must have lots of beaux."

Lizzie smiled weakly, and I said, "We work six days a week. We don't have much time to socialize."

"Oh, come," she said, winking. "I can't believe that. When I was a girl, we spent the social seasons in Washington. Lovely young men." She sighed. "That was before everything changed. Now the women smoke and drink and wear pants and play golf, just like the men." She smiled. "I guess I'm an anachronism in more ways than one."

We drank our tea and made small talk, with Lizzie falling more and more silent. When the clock struck five, she rose, her face flushed, hands shaking slightly, and said, "We must go, Kate," and before I could answer started toward the hall and the front door.

"Don't rush off," Cousin Kate said automatically, and I said the correct things about hating to leave, but mother would expect us back, et cetera. Both of us were at the same time trying to catch up with Lizzie.

At the front door, Lizzie turned and said to my cousin, "Don't bury your talent. That will kill you."

Cousin Kate's face turned cold. For a minute I thought she would cry or get angry, but she struggled and kept the mask of gentility in place. "You take things too seriously, dear," she said lightly. "I am perfectly fine."

Out on the sidewalk I could hardly keep pace with Lizzie. "I was smothering in there," she said. "I felt buried alive."

Knowing Lizzie's penchant for drama, and thinking she was overreacting, I didn't answer at once, just tried to keep up.

"It's sad she has no career now," I said finally.

"No, that's not it," Lizzie said. "That's not the worst. The worst is that she has no inspiration." We walked on through the dusk.

"Please God," Lizzie said as we reached our street. "Don't let us wind up like that."

Sissy
1924

Must of typed a hundred pages about women votin', women holdin' office, women cleanin' up the government, this, that, and the other. But Sissy ain't there. Sissy missing from them pages. Finally ask Miss Lizzie, say, "Is Sissy a woman?"

Miss Lizzie laugh. "You're eighteen, Sissy. Of course you're a woman now."

"Sissy a slave?"

"Why, Sissy!" she say, shocked. "I pay you, don't I? Don't I pay you a fair wage?"

"Sissy a citizen?"

"Well . . . " she begin to see what I'm gettin' at. "To me you are. As far as I'm concerned you're a very good citizen."

"Then why Sissy invisible? This here paper, this not about me."

Miss Lizzie get real serious then. She sit there at her desk looking solemn. She don't say nothing for a long time. Finally she say, "You've hit on a problem, Sissy, one I don't know the answer to. Race is a problem, just like sex is. The people who don't want women to vote, like the Mississippi legislature, don't want Negroes to vote either, men or women. Our legislature still hasn't ratified the Nineteenth Amendment."

"Look like Missippi not the place to be."

"But change is coming, Sissy. The survival of the *Woman's Voice* is a sign. So is the fact that Governor Whitfield won because of the women's support. And just think, in June I'll go to the Democratic National Convention as a delegate. That's progress!"

Sissy just look at her, wonder do she hear herself. Still ain't explain where Sissy fit.

"Takes time for justice to get done."

"How long you reckon?"

"Well, I can't predict. May be a while yet."

"You gonna write it up?"

"Write what?"

"That Negro women needs a vote, too."

"I can't write that, Sissy. The white people wouldn't buy the paper anymore, and they're the only ones who buy it."

"Only ones can read it, too," Sissy say. "Just about."

"That's true, so maybe education is where to start. I could write that all children should be educated equally."

So she done it. Wrote about the progress Missippi making in the field of education and ended up saying, "Chance has placed us here together—Negro and white—in our beloved South, and so we must work together to see that all our children are educated, that they are equipped to grow into full, responsible citizenship."

"Wasn't no chance to it," I tell her when I read it. "Was white men coming and dragging us out of Africa."

"I know it," she say, "but if you want us to stay in business, I can't write everything I know."

Sissy still not satisfied, but then she get another idea. Get to thinking about Mound Bayou, the all-Negro town. They got clubs and all like the white people. They always stirring around, Isaiah Montgomery and Benjamin Green and all them. Mr. Montgomery was a secretary too, they say, start out a slave but got to be the secretary for Jefferson Davis's brother and then got a land grant to start Mound Bayou, no white people in it. Mama and us, we go up to Mound Bayou to church, ain't far. James get a wagon and a team and we ride. So one Sunday I ask a woman, "Y'all got any politics up here?"

"See that woman over there?" she say, point out a pretty woman dressed to kill. "That's Mary Booze. She Isaiah

Montgomery's daughter. She a National Republican Committeewoman." That sound important, and so after church Sissy go up and shake her hand. Tell her Sissy secretary on the *Woman's Voice*. Educated woman you can tell.

"I've seen that paper," she say. She begin to ask questions, and we talk and talk and finally Sissy ask her to come in the office next time she in Bolivar Landing.

Sissy tell Miss Lizzie first thing Monday morning. She interested. Say she's heard of Mary Booze. Long about Thursday here she come in the door. She and Miss Lizzie sit and talk for the longest. Sissy serve coffee. They talk about social change and how it is up north and the new day for women. Sissy like to hear them talk. They talk good. Never heard a Negro woman talk so good.

After Mrs. Booze go, Miss Lizzie say, "Isn't that remarkable, Sissy? Two women, two different races, representing the two major parties on a national level, living ten miles apart in rural Mississippi? I'm going to write that up."

She write an editorial, Sissy type it. Talk about cooperation and change and women leading in it, sound real nice. But when it come out in the paper, all hell break loose.

First thing, big rock through the plate glass during the night, then a note say "Nigger lover get out of town." Phone ring all day, folks canceling they subscriptions. Governor storm in and call Miss Lizzie a fool. "If you intend to live and work in this town," he said, "you better remember what state it's in."

Mama upset, won't let me go to the office. "They won't do nothing to Lizzie cause she the governor's daughter," she say, "but you, girl, ain't nobody to save your black skin but your mama."

Miss Lizzie bring the typewriter home, and Sissy type there. "This will blow over, Sissy," she say, "but we do have our hands full, don't we?"

Stephen
1927

She has no judgment. She has a fine mind in some ways, but it's as if the compartment labeled *Judgment* has nothing in it. Always some crisis with the damn paper—Vardaman, race, Reds. She is full of ideas about "freedom of the press" without any understanding that a newspaper is a business like any other, dependent on advertisers and readers. She is also full of ideas about equality that no one will tolerate. My people tell me that more conservative factions around the state associate her with radicalism and the Reds.

I never thought the paper would last this long. I thought it would amuse her for a year or so during the first flush of woman suffrage, and then she would marry and lead a normal life. The nation is getting back to normal. None of the forecasts about women voting in a bloc have come about. Women are having children and taking care of their families and voting as their husbands do.

Elizabeth seems determined not to lead a normal life. Young men are always hanging around, but nothing ever comes of them. "What is it?" I asked her. "Who will be good enough?"

"That's not why," she said. "I have the newspaper. I don't have time."

"You're twenty-five years old. No spring chick. I don't know what you're thinking."

"Not about marriage," she said. "I can tell you that."

"Am I so wrong to want to know you'll be taken care of?"

"You've taken care of me quite well enough, Daddy," she

said, with a look that made me uneasy.

"I want a grandson, like any man does, an heir for all I've worked for."

"You'll never have one," she said, with a chilling decisiveness.

"Don't give up yet. The right man hasn't come along."

"Give up? How little you understand. Do you think I am biding my time for the right man to open my heart and womb?"

"Elizabeth!"

"Sorry," she said, absently.

I should never have let her start the damn newspaper. She's playing career, letting life pass her by. In flush times the money didn't matter, but now it matters more than I can make her understand. This household of women continues to live in the high style of the past. Even Gwin has grown soft and dependent.

"I need to talk to you, Daddy."

"How much this time?"

"The woman selling ads in Jackson didn't do very well this week, and we're a little behind with the printer in Memphis." She had her key ring in her hand and kept turning it over and over, her eyes glued to it.

"Elizabeth, I have told you . . . "

"Only $220. Not nearly so much as last time."

"But I've never been repaid for the other times. Not a penny."

"I know. But I'm going to. We'll get back on our feet in a few weeks."

"No."

"What?" She looked at me surprised.

"I can't do it."

"It's a pittance to you. I've seen you spend more on one evening in Memphis."

"You've seen that, but you won't any longer. I'm broke, Elizabeth, land poor. I'll be lucky to raise enough to pay the taxes and buy seed to plant."

"I don't believe it."

"You had better believe it."

"I have to have the money," she said. Her face was flushed, her body animated with anger. "You don't understand. If I don't pay the printer, he says he won't do another issue."

"No. Case closed."

"Don't use that tone on me. Don't talk down to me like I'm a child."

"If you understood anything about finances, I could explain to you."

"You never taught me," she said. "You 'protected' me from knowing a thing about your finances."

"So now your failure is my fault? Am I understanding that?"

"Don't ever call me a failure."

Then before I could finish, she jerked the bottom drawer out of my desk and threw it across the room. The drawer hit the wall on the other side of my study and splintered to the floor. I sat stunned while she stood there panting. I waited for her to apologize, but she didn't. "I'll print the paper without your help," she said finally, "you'll see."

But she didn't, of course, and the tension between us grows more acute every day.

Tonight men who still have money came to dinner. They were my last chance. I was counting on Genesis' cooking and Elizabeth's charm. "Dress for dinner," I said to Elizabeth, "and be nice to these men."

"Why?"

"So they'll believe in me as a good risk, a stable family man."

"How funny," she said, in a way that made me clench my fists. What is so goddamned funny about it? She's lived like a princess all her life. Her mother has done strictly as she pleases, which is to do nothing.

The dinner began pleasantly enough, with plenty of Perry Martin's liquor followed by a Genesis feast. Elizabeth and Gwin both looked well and chatted with the men, three of whom had brought their wives and two of whom had not. After dinner we were back in the library for more drinks, when Elizabeth, who was standing in front of the fireplace, said in a loud voice over the striking of the mantel clock, "Actually, I'm not his real daughter." She said it as if she were making an announcement to the whole party. Conversation stopped, and everyone looked her way. "We pretend that I am, but I'm someone else. I'm sure you find it confusing, since I'm called Elizabeth Dunbar, but the name means nothing."

The room had grown as quiet as death. I made my way through the guests to her and took her arm. Her eyes looked at me wildly, as if I were a stranger. "You're trying to ruin me," I said to her fiercely under my breath, but aloud to the guests I said, laughing, "Such a practical joker, this girl. She loves to tease me."

With that, she turned on me like a she-bear. She shook herself loose from me and screamed, "Get your hands off me. Don't ever touch me again, do you hear me?" Then shrieking, as if with genuine fear, she ran from the room.

A more effective way to disperse potential creditors can hardly be imagined. My lame explanations about "too much to drink" were met with embarrassed silence. Within minutes they had all cleared out sheepishly, none of them willing to look me in the eye. They took with them any chance I had of recovering my losses. Thanks to Elizabeth, it looks as though we'll all be out on the dole.

Kate
1928

Lizzie struggled so to keep the paper. She sold her Ford first, and then a lot her father had given her earlier. She put everything she had into it and every ounce of energy. It's not just that her father is no longer backing her, either. Sales are way down, too. Part of it is economic, I guess, but I'm afraid a large part of it is that women have lost interest.

I went to Bolivar Landing to be with her when she put out the last issue. She and Sissy and Ruth were all crying. "I know it's silly," Lizzie said to me apologetically, "but I feel like I'm losing a child."

"Of course you do," I said.

"To finally find your niche and then lose it is bitter. The paper was my first success, and I think it will be my last."

"Nonsense," I said. "You're young, smart. You'll have plenty more successes."

None of my efforts to cheer her up did any good. She was too depressed to eat, she said. I even tried to tempt her with going on a flight with the barnstormer who stops on the levee ever so often and was there today. Even that didn't get her attention.

I left Bolivar Landing with a foreboding that shadowed me for a week.

Lizzie
1934

I can't plan or make any decisions since I lost the paper. My will is gone. I think of how Mama lives and am terrified that that will happen to me. Aunt Nelda, Uncle Leroy's wife, asked me to go in with her on a dress shop. She'll put up the money if I'll work. I don't really want to. That seems so insignificant compared with newspaper work.

Words. They're all that help. I write in my diary each night, a safety valve. I wonder if many people have kept a diary since they were six. Women have always kept diaries. You can tell the truth in diaries like nowhere else because no one will read them until you're dead, and then what will it matter? I can't leave children or monuments or a newspaper or a business, but my diaries are wonderful, if I do say so myself.

They are in the secret shelf in the heart of Daddy's desk. He doesn't know they are there. Mama and I found that place to keep them long ago. They are in a neat row in red leather bindings, the sum of who I am.

Sometimes at night when I can't stop the thinking, I go in there and pick one out to read. I run my finger down the row, one book for each year in my literate life. I let my hand go, like on a Ouija board, and wherever it stops, that's the year I read. Elizabeth takes the book back upstairs to bed to look for messages from Lizzie.

Miranda
1934

A lifetime is not nearly long enough to do all we dream. I dreamed of home and love and a fruitful life, of children crowded around me at dusk while I lit the lamps, warm little bodies nesting in my lap while I read them stories that filled them with delicious imagining. In my dream I wrote the stories and poems, lovely words published in a book to be handed down. I am preparing for this work, but no one knows. I exhaust myself with reading as preparation for the future because it is all I know to do. I will not repeat anything that's ever been written.

Genesis says I am fifty-two, but that is not possible. Only yesterday we left the Hollies. The memory catches at my heart with fresh grief. Since then there have been only darkened rooms and shadows that come and go. Each day is interminable, but the whole life has flown. It has been an instant, a gleam of a single firefly in a dark field.

Lizzie is my immortality. She will succeed where I have failed. I have not failed yet, though. As slowly as a day goes, like centuries from the sun on my drawn curtains in the morning until the darkening of the window at night, surely there is still time for one small dream.

My cough is worse and the pain in my chest excruciating, but I do not complain. If I have accomplished nothing, at least they cannot say that I complained. I stayed out of their way, which was the best that I could do.

Genesis

1934

She been down so long, wouldn't nobody pay no mind when she got bad, wouldn't believe she sick. Mr. Stephen say, "She'll outlive us all. She's the only person I know who has managed to isolate herself from any possibility of stress. She folded her hands in death twenty years ago."

He one surprised man when she die. Look like he don't believe it till she in the ground.

She never let on she hurt, but I hear the coughing and I know. Last few days she scare me so bad, she talking out of her head. She thought her mammy and daddy was in the room, and they might of been, you can't tell, somebody about to die, you don't know who they see. She thought we was back at the Hollies. Then she want to set up at the desk. "Bring me my pen, Genesis, I must write a book."

Got Lizzie, made her come and see for herself. "Oh, poor Mama," she say, start in to cry. Should have thought poor Mama sooner. Should have been up here to see about her stead of fooling around with that dress shop, such as that. She run called the doctor, then sat by her mama's bed three days straight, wouldn't eat nor sleep. She always have to overdo on anything, underdo or overdo, that's her. "Genesis, I had no idea," she say. "Why didn't you tell me sooner?" I don't say nothing, just look at her.

Seem like a woman twice her age laid out. Must not of weighed eighty pounds. Graveside service, not even proper burial. He can't put on no funeral look like. Guess he think he don't have a funeral be like never was a life. Didn't make him and Gwin any difference, they went right ahead on with they business Miranda or not. God see him, though. God punish likes of him sooner or later. May not be in this life, but He'll get him.

Lord, Lord, a lot done happen in a short time. Flood like to washed us away and the depression come right on in behind that. Flood, famine, death. Guess fire be next.

Both my babies in Chicago now. Say they doing real good. Little Earl working regular in a meat plant. Sissy got a job in a office, married a plumber, got two babies herself now. Wants me to come up there. Writes me a letter ever now and then, but I ain't going off up there. What I do off up there?

No, Lord, my burden here. Promised Miranda I'd see to Lizzie, and I aim to try.

The Antique Shop

Mrs. Cavanaugh stopped by the shop after class, almost in tears. Dr. MacAuley had returned the draft for her research paper and said it was inadequate.

"What!" Mr. Cavanaugh was furious. "She didn't think the *Woman's Voice* was adequate?"

"She thought it was terribly exciting BUT, she said all I've written is a report about it."

"So, what's so wrong with that?"

Mrs. Cavanaugh wearily threw the paper down on a Queen Anne writing desk and sat on the tiny chair that went with it. "I shouldn't have tried to go back to school. I'm much too old." She put her head down on her manuscript, covered with MacAuley remarks in pencil. Dr. MacAuley said red ink was too discouraging.

"Isn't it enough to know the *Woman's Voice* WAS?"

"I need a thesis. Like what caused it or what its effects were. Here's one comment: 'You need to approach the subject critically; I want to see more analysis here.'"

"Hell's bells," shouted Mr. Cavanaugh. "Hogwash! Who could know causes and effects? Does the woman think you're clairvoyant?"

"I'm dropping the course."

"No!"

"It's no use, Clovis. My mind doesn't work like a historian's."

"Hold on now," said Mr. Cavanaugh, feeling responsible, "your mind works fine and so does mine. Let's go back there in those papers and see what else we can find. She wants thesis, we'll give her thesis."

"I rather be playing bridge," said Mrs. Cavanaugh as they walked toward the back. "This is all your fault."

Gwin
1935

"I'll tell her," I said to him. "I'm not afraid of her." Men are weak. What can she do but pitch a fit? So I went down to the dress shop, which is nothing but a joke, racks of dresses in among the filing cabinets in the old newspaper office, but at least it gets her out of the house. She may know about books and clothes, but not about business.

She was surrounded by a crowd of high school kids, young people love her for some reason, probably because she keeps Cokes on hand for them.

"Hello, Gwin," she said, as cold as if I were a perfect stranger.

"I need to speak to you."

"Well, speak."

"Alone." The kids scattered at that. One girl had a dress over one arm that I'm sure Elizabeth gave her. You can't expect to succeed in business when you hand out the merchandise to everybody with a hard-luck story.

"Stephen and I are going to be married," I said. "This afternoon." She stood there staring a hole through me.

"We'd like for you to be there." Still not a word, just staring. Finally she grabbed some tickets out from under the counter and began adding them on the adding machine. The only sign that my words had registered was the way her hands shook.

"Will you come?" I asked. Still nothing but click, click, those long red nails on the adding machine keys.

"You could be civil," I said. "He's your own father." Click,

click, click. She must have been adding up the price of every dress she ever sold.

I should have walked out, but I couldn't. She owed me at least a word of recognition.

"You know your problem?" I said. "You're spoiled rotten. Nothing bad has ever happened to you." That hit close to the bone. All the color drained from her face and the clicking stopped.

"All those years?" she said, hoarsely. "You and Daddy?"

"Your father and I have had a long, intimate relationship," I said. "I make him happy." For a grown woman to be so naive is incredible. People see what they want to and no more.

"Get out," she said. I wanted her to attack me, really, and then maybe Stephen would see how she is and would do something about her. But she didn't. She went back to her adding, and I went home to marry her father. I left her there clicking away, as if adding those pitiful tickets was the most important work in the world.

Mrs. Davis
1935

I hate to see a place go down like the Dunbars' has. "Pride goes before a fall," Mrs. Purvis says, but I don't take any pleasure in watching the fall from my front room like some do. I prefer a place painted and spruced up with the windows washed and the yard cut and the walks swept no matter how prideful the owner might be.

The present owner could use some pride if you ask me. Seems like there ought to be a law to protect a neighborhood against people opening their homes to anything drifting around. Who would have thought fifteen years ago that the showplace of the Delta would become a boardinghouse, and such a boardinghouse, too. Yankee laborers mostly, here to build the levee. Rough, loud men who sing, and I'm sure drink, over there until all hours. I'm thankful to have the levee, of course, we all are since the flood of '27 tried to wash the whole state away. Only good thing I can think that the federal government's done around here is see about the levee. Took them a hundred years to get started, but that's about average for them.

I can't see why Governor Dunbar doesn't put a stop to the carrying on over there, but he may not know about it. Upped and moved to Jackson with his secretary, married her, not to my surprise because I always thought there was more to that than met the eye. Some blame him for marrying so quick, but not me. A man needs a woman to take care of him. He turned the whole place over to the Dunbar girl, and we haven't seen his face since.

Regular as clockwork, every morning at nine, Miss Lizzie comes out of the house and walks to town to the dress shop. She's put on weight in fifteen years, just like the rest of us, and she's dyed her hair a bright red. That in itself is a bad sign. Her eyes are still real pretty, though, I've always said she had the prettiest eyes I ever saw in a human, different some way from anybody else's. Pretty hands too, soft looking but strong at the same time. A pity about her, that's all I can think, a pity. Born with a silver spoon, she couldn't be expected to know how to make her way. Sometimes I think this depression is worse on them that were rich than on the rest of us because they don't know how to get along and make do. On the other hand, anybody can behave themselves, no matter how hard times get.

She stays at the dress shop all day, though heaven knows who's got money for a dress. I haven't been in there myself, but they say after school is out the place fills up with young folks who love to joke and talk with Lizzie. Not my idea of a wholesome influence, and if I had a young'un she or he would not be hanging around there.

Long about five o'clock she comes back over to the house and I guess helps the Negro with the supper. Genesis they call the old Negro, she does the cooking for the ten- or fifteen-odd levee men that live over there now. They start piling in around sundown, mud from head to toe; I hate to think how it must look in that house. Then about eight the commotion starts, ragtime music on the piano, which I am sure Miss Dunbar is playing, and loud singing.

Mrs. Purvis says the racket doesn't bother her, but then she lives farther down the block and is also deaf. I told her that the noise does bother me but that I try not to let anything get the best of me. I continue to read Psalm 23 every night before I go to sleep the same as if there wasn't a honky-tonk across the street.

"I know Psalm 23 by heart," Mrs. Purvis said.

Well, I know it too, for goodness sake. Who doesn't? But I

like to see the words. They're reassuring. Mrs. Purvis is getting spiteful in her old age.

If I were Governor Dunbar, I'd sell the house and make that girl come to Jackson and do something normal. Surely with all her education she could get a job. She could work in his law office if nothing else.

She's a scandal, really. She keeps the whole town talking.

Meems
1937

I did not know her. She walked here from the train station. She was standing at the end of our sidewalk gazing at the house when I noticed her from the window. She stood there staring a good ten minutes. She was strangely out of place and yet somehow familiar. She wore a black dress that had been fine in its day but now strained to hold itself around her waist. A hat of black feathers fit closely to her head behind a frame of red curls around her face. Pearl earrings dangled almost to her shoulders. Finally I stepped out on the porch to ask if I could give her directions or something to eat. The depression has brought stranger hardship cases than this to my door.

"Miss Meems," she called gaily, jumping up and down and waving like a little girl. "My, you look old." She walked up on the porch and hugged me fiercely. I felt strangely disoriented as I struggled to place this woman.

"I've come to see Kate," she said. Then I knew who she was. The realization was disturbing, shocking even. I could see a glimpse of Lizzie buried there, but the slightest glimpse. It was as though I were looking at an actress made up for a play, aged and disguised purposefully with dye and makeup and padding around the middle. But the physical changes were minor compared to the sense I had that the person before me was not the Lizzie I had known. This actress, for this is how I perceived her, had altered herself so convincingly for her role that even those who had known her best could no longer recognize her.

"Oh, dear, I thought you knew," I said. I was sure she knew that Kate had left the Delta.

"My God, she's dead." Her face flushed and tears swam in her eyes, still beautiful.

"No, no. She went to take a job in Washington."

"Then I've missed her. I do so need to see her. She could help me. Kate is so smart, you know."

"Come in so we can talk," I said. We walked through the hall and into the sitting room and sat facing each other on the love seat where she and Katie used to play "Ford."

"She'll be back soon, then?"

"She has a job, Lizzie. She works for the government. And she's married a nice young man who works at the Pentagon. They may be back for Christmas." I found myself speaking slowly and distinctly as if to a child or to someone deaf.

"But what will I do? They're trying to get my business. The flood ruined the dresses. We had to go to town in a boat and the dresses were already floating out in the street. Silk dresses from France and flowery Easter bonnets and pearl necklaces were floating on waves of muddy water. Pastel pinks and yellows and blues. We put what we could up on the counters, but already . . . snakes, too. Black water moccasins swimming all through the pretty clothes." She grew increasingly agitated as she talked. She could not sit still, but paced up and down the room.

"I didn't know, Lizzie. I am so sorry." I was sorry, but more about her state of mind than about the dress shop. The flood was ten years ago when she still had the newspaper.

"So I tried to rebuild, but the crash came, and the building had a musty, underground smell, and we didn't have much money for dresses, and nobody came in anymore. I tried everything I could think of. I would sit in the window so that when women came by I could wave and invite them in, but they would pretend not to see me and hurry on by."

"Many people lost their businesses during this depression,

Lizzie. That is nothing to be ashamed of."

"My case is different, though. People don't like me. I see it on their faces. I started the boardinghouse, but they didn't want me to have it, either. I work as hard as I can. I work awfully hard, but there's never enough money. If I knew about bookkeeping, that would be good, wouldn't it? Do you think I should go out to the college and take bookkeeping?"

"What does your father think?"

She looked at me amazed as friends will do whom you have not seen in a long time but who assume you automatically know what has happened to them in the interim.

"He's gone, of course."

"Gone?"

"He and Gwin after Mama died. Gwin despises me, and they moved to Jackson so Daddy could practice law." I knew Miranda had died. I had written Lizzie at the time but never heard from her.

"Gwin?"

"His secretary. She turned him against me."

"They married?"

"You didn't know? A month after we buried Mama."

"I see."

"But that doesn't bother me. Really. I want him to be happy. He's a wonderful man, Miss Meems. He's given me every opportunity." Every opportunity to conform to his ideas, I wanted to say, every opportunity except the one you needed.

"Did you know Bill Falkner is publishing books? 'Count No-Count,' they called him when he and Kate were together at the university, and yet he . . . " She stopped pacing and sat down beside me again.

"Why am I such a failure?" This was the Lizzie I knew. The directness of the question, the clear pain on her face caught me off guard, and I murmured something meaningless to try and comfort her. I am old and ill. I was overwhelmed at the depth of her despair, not strong enough to face it with her. Why some are survivors, some not, why some can triumph over adversity and some cannot, why some find their work and others wander like shades in the underworld—these are mysteries we cannot know. I had no answer to give her. She read my hesitancy, my unwillingness to undertake her question, and the veil fell back on. She smiled a gay, false smile.

"Just to show you how much Daddy cares about me—when the crash came and Mama died and times were at their worst, he put the house and the farmland that was left in my name. I've kept it, too. That hasn't been easy, but I've held on, but now they're after it."

"'They?'"

"My enemies. I make the mortgage payments except they've started sending me letters and saying I haven't or the payments are not enough and they will have to take the property."

"Wait. What do your records say? Your canceled checks, your mortgage agreement? You should be able to prove easily that you're current with your payments."

"I don't keep up with that. I have too many other things to do, but I send a check every month. You could ask them at the bank."

"You must keep up with such things, Lizzie."

"I thought Kate could help me. She's so good at sorting out details and organizing."

"Isn't there anyone in Bolivar Landing?"

"No one I trust."

"Couldn't you go to Jackson and get Stephen to help you get your records in order?"

"He hates me, I tell you," she said impatiently. "Haven't you been listening? When will Kate be back?" It was that hopeless moment when you realize you are mired into a conversation with someone not quite rational—not completely detached from reality, but not capable or desirous of reasoning in the usual ways. My head was splitting, and I didn't know how to respond. But she stood up suddenly and said, "I should have known this wouldn't work." She started for the door, and I fumbled with my cane to follow her.

"Lizzie, don't go. You must spend the night. We'll have supper, and you'll feel better. Lizzie . . . "

But she was out the door, down the steps, and gone. She turned around several times at the end of the walk, as if she didn't quite know where she was. Then she started in the opposite direction of the train station, but I had no one to send after her. I watched her disappear down the sidewalk, her hat bouncing angrily on her head like a bird of prey.

Avent
1939

Seventeen years since I left Bolivar Landing. In some ways it is no different—the cotton fields stretching to infinity in any direction, the dusty roads, the mules, the swamps, the Negro baptizings on Sunday afternoons, the town itself like a green button on a huge cotton shirt. The biggest change, not surprisingly, is in the people, for whom seventeen years is a much longer time than it is for the land.

Tonight Grace and I left the children in the country with Mama, and we drove into town to the picture show. *Gone With the Wind* is playing, and news of it has even reached Guatemala. We stood in line for our tickets at the old Lyric Theatre where our crowd used to go every Saturday night to see the silent movies. I was remembering those times, when a couple walked down the sidewalk together and fell in line behind us. I scrutinize everyone I see for a possible old acquaintance.

The man was short and stocky and dressed in khaki pants and shirt. His hair was thick and black and curling slightly at the neck, his skin dark. He was smoking and coughing in between draws on his cigarette. His teeth were his most distinctive feature. They were perfectly even and straight and remarkably white for a smoker. His hands were calloused and his nails short and black, and I surmised that he was a levee man, one who had come here in the last few years to build the new levee along the Mississippi that was to end all floods. I was satisfied that he was no one I knew.

The woman with him seemed overdressed for a picture

show in Bolivar Landing. She had on a blue silk dress with a white lace collar. She wore too much rouge and her hair was an artificial red. We could smell her perfume. She was fleshy like the man; they appeared to be a couple who enjoyed good food and drink. I could picture them with their sleeves rolled up, tearing into a barbecued chicken, and downing it with bottles of cold beer. Probably she was a woman who followed him from town to town. I did not think she was local.

I turned back to Grace, and we wondered what the children were doing. We leave them so seldom; four-year-old Armando has never been left by both of us at the same time. I glanced over my shoulder then to see if anyone else might have joined the line, and I caught the eye of the red-haired woman behind us. They were familiar eyes, beautiful smoky-blue eyes rimmed with black lashes. I stared because my brain refused to make the connection between Lizzie Dunbar and this woman. I turned around quickly and faced the front of the line until we had bought our tickets. Soon we were sitting with our popcorn in the dark theatre and were back in time to the Civil War, though not so far back in the minds of Southerners as it is to the rest of the world. I thought no more about the couple until we walked out of the theatre, still in that spell that follows a good picture. I didn't even notice as the red-haired woman walked up to us on the sidewalk outside the Lyric.

"You don't know me, do you, Avent?" the woman said as I jumped and then stared like an idiot. She laughed, a high, false laugh and put out her hand. "I'm Lizzie Dunbar."

I put out my hand dumbly.

"And this must be your wife."

"Graciela," my wife said and offered her hand.

"And this is my friend, Roy Stubbs," Lizzie said, and the man flashed his teeth, his black eyes taking us in suspiciously, and shook our hands.

"Well," I said, finally finding my voice, "it's been a long time."

"Your mustache is almost white, isn't it?" she said to me in surprise, as if I should look exactly the same.

"And how do you like this country, Graciela?" she said, turning to my wife and pronouncing her name perfectly.

"Very, how would you say, modern?"

"More industrialized than Guatemala?"

"Oh, yes, and more daily conveniences."

I was not ready to let go of *Gone With the Wind* for a comparative discussion of Guatemala and the United States. "Tremendous picture show, wasn't it?" I said. "A real epic quality about it."

"I hated it," Lizzie said with a vehemence that startled me. "That picture show will set us back a hundred years." At least she had not lost the quality of unpredictability that I remembered so well.

"How?" I said.

"Glorifying that war," she said. "We'd do better to forget it."

"Can't we learn from the past?"

"We learn the wrong lessons."

"Isn't Scarlett a woman you can admire, the strength and spirit?"

"She was manipulative," Lizzie said, "and a fool. She didn't understand herself at all."

Roy took a deep breath and took her arm. "Honey, I gotta git up at five," he said. He was like a child tugging at her skirt. So we stood there a few more minutes, strangers making talk, catching up. Names and ages of children, marriages of friends, deaths of parents and other relatives. None of the questions I really wanted to ask a woman who had once been the center of my life. Did you ever love me? Why wouldn't you marry me? What has happened to you? Why are you with this man? What are you thinking?

"I would ask you home for a drink, but I run a boarding-house now," she said.

"We have to go back out home, anyway," I said. "See how Mama made it with the children."

"Good luck," Lizzie said, "and stop in the shop if you get a chance before you go home." I knew I wouldn't do that, and she knew it, too, but it was a thing to say to keep the good-bye from seeming final, a thing that Southerners do, a reluctance to let go of a moment. I couldn't be sure, the neon light from the Lyric cast strange shadows, but I think her eyes clouded as she said good-bye.

As they walked off down the sidewalk, I heard Roy say, "Is his wife a nigger? She's awful dark." Grace didn't seem to hear. She smiled, my beautiful Latin wife, and took my hand as we walked to the car.

"Is she the one I met in Baltimore?" she asked. "She is not the same woman."

When the children were in bed, Mama and Grace and I sat on the screen porch under the ceiling fan with a nightcap of bourbon whiskey and water, and I brought up the subject of Lizzie Dunbar. "God was good to you, Avent," Mama said. "Wouldn't you have been a pretty looking thing married to Lizzie Dunbar?"

"What is her life like?" I asked. "I mean really like?"

"Oh, she has a good time," Mama said. "Don't you worry about that. She flashes around town, laughing and talking, always has some man in tow, dancing at Moon Lake and what not. She has fun for an old maid supposed to be on her way to the poor house."

"The governor lost his money?"

"Nobody could ever tell what the governor had, but yes, he lost a lot. He married the live-in and moved to Jackson for a more lucrative law practice they say, and left Lizzie here on her own. She started up that dress shop, Elizabeth's, moved it right into the newspaper office. It's the funniest little place you ever saw. Racks of dresses in among the filing cabinets, real fancy things. And she has the boardinghouse in the mansion. She's enterprising all right, but how successful I don't know. Of course, nobody has any money now."

"I wouldn't have known her," I said. "She seemed so . . . "

"Common?" Mama said. "Yes, time has coarsened her. Time has not been kind to Lizzie Dunbar. She's a survivor, though, if there ever were one."

Lizzie

A Diary Entry

1939

I am by nature divided. Half of me is contemplative, values privacy, likes quiet to think and write, but the other half loves people and sociability. Reading the poetry of Matthew Arnold the other night, I saw that he had the same problem, the tension in the public and the private. Finally he gave up writing poetry because it turned out to be so depressing, he thought the world would be better if he left it off. I think he was right. Imagine the state of mind of a man who wrote "Dover Beach" on his honeymoon. Imagine the effect on his wife.

The newspaper was the closest I ever came to synthesis. That work required both thinking and writing, as well as getting out and stirring with the crowd. But I could not keep it. The temper of the times for women changed as the twenties ended, and they forgot justice for their gender to concentrate on bread for their children. Looking back, I wish I had been more tenacious in holding on to the paper. If only I could have found someone to finance it. If Sissy hadn't gone to Chicago, and Ruth hadn't married. If, if, if.

At other times I think my big mistake was not moving to another place. Why couldn't I make the break from home? Why didn't I go back to the university when I was younger and prepare to do something to support myself? I could have been a lawyer, or gotten a degree in English and taught. But by the time the paper went under and the crash came, I thought I was too old and thought we couldn't afford it. And like a fool, I thought I could turn my love for pretty clothes into a profitable business. I saw myself a successful businesswoman, going to New York to buy clothes. My trouble may have always been an overactive imagination.

I should have moved to a city, like Washington. With Daddy's connections I could probably have gotten a job there. Or New York. Somewhere out of the South. Where I could find people, women especially, who think like I do, whom I could talk to and feel at home with. In Bolivar Landing you don't count as a real person unless you're married; you are a shadow in the social scene, an embarrassment. Surely there are places where a woman is not defined by marital status, where her ideas and her work count for something.

People in Bolivar Landing do not understand or approve of me. I know this. I can see it in their faces; I can hear it in the whispers as I pass. They think that I have "let myself go" and am helpless in the face of circumstances. They think I am a whore. They may not use the word, but if a woman is not married and has relationships with men, then *whore* is the only possible category they can put her in. A woman's identity is determined by her sexual function—married, old maid, whore—while a man is more apt to be identified by his work.

The truth is, my direction was taken consciously. When I accepted the fact that I could not have children and when the paper failed, I told myself: I will have *something*. If not husband and children and rewarding work and spiritual enlightenment, I will have something. I am not a martyr. Whatever life offers me I will take. So I looked around to see what was there. And there was good food and Genesis to cook it, and so I decided, I will eat all I want as long as the garden produces and I can pay the grocery bill. And there was enough money when I sold my Ford to set up a dress shop. So I said I will wear rouge and fancy clothes and act the part of a successful shop owner and if I believe it, it will happen. And Walker was also there, and so I thought why not? I did not have the courage to tell Avent the truth about myself, so I told Walker because I didn't care what he thought. He said that made no difference to him, that probably the disease was in my imagination, but that there are ways to stay healthy and he knew them.

The other boarders have been just that, except Roy—an unlikely attraction. I would never have thought a man like that would interest me, rough and uneducated. It is as if we grew up on different planets, and I like to hear the stories and imagine his life. His father was a bootlegger, and he spent his growing-up years running whiskey and dodging the law. His body has a gravitational force that draws me like the moon does the tides. His teeth are beautiful and white even when he smiles and his hair thick and curly.

Some days I am sick with guilt about my appetites. I remember Dean Powers and Maude and other strong, wonderful women and wish I could be self-sufficient like them. If I were more religious, I think, or if I had a cause— Then other days I am consumed with anger about my life, the random unfairness of it, how all the universe seems to have conspired against me, and God, if he is there, pays me no attention at all.

Daddy has never denied himself a thing, I think, and he has never suffered a minute of isolation, a word of condemnation from the community. He is happily married and into a new life. Yet I am stuck here and judged loose and degenerate.

Most days I can manage not to dwell on the past and my circumstances, but there are mornings when I wake up panic-stricken, my heart racing so that I can hardly breathe. I am getting old, my hair gray before my time, and what have I accomplished? What will I leave behind?

Mrs. Davis
1939

Awfullest fire you ever saw, lit up this part of town like it was day and rained ash and sparks over here on me. The heat melted down my lamppost on the front, and I thought sure my little house would go up in a puff of smoke any minute.

August dog days anyway, so hot you could fry an egg on any street in Bolivar Landing if you had a mind to do it. I had had me some ice water before I went to bed and had the fan blowing right on me. I don't generally have it blowing right on me because I'm liable to take a headache, but last night was that hot.

First thing I knew, sparks came flying in at the window, and a hot red light was shining in on me. I got up quick as I could and looked out. Seemed liked the whole world was on fire, the last judgment. "Oh, Lord," I said. "Oh, Lord God." I fumbled around until I found my glasses, and then I could tell more about it. The Dunbar mansion going up, flames so high they were way above the old oaks, it looked like. The fire engine was clamoring down the street and them boarders were running out like rats from a sinking ship. Well, I hope you're all out, I thought, because if you're not you're fried for sure.

Then here comes Lizzie Dunbar out from the side door. She had on a black shiny gown of a thing, not decent really, and one of the swarthy boarders was right behind her in his drawers. Then she wheeled around and headed right back in, though any sane person could see that nothing could live a minute in that fiery furnace. Now what could she be after is what I wondered at the time. But the man, he quick grabbed her and had to all but wrestle her down to keep her out of there. She was screaming at the top of her voice; it fairly chilled my blood.

Didn't make any sense, really. A child, or some other family member, or maybe even a pet dog or cat might drive a woman back into a hopeless fire, but she didn't have any of that. I wouldn't have thought after this depression that there would be any family jewelry left, but it was something valuable that she was willing to risk her neck going back after. I wondered could it have been deeds to some of that Dunbar land.

I dressed as fast as I could and went on out, grabbing up mine and Mr. Davis's wedding picture as I went, and the family Bible.

That Dunbar girl was pitiful, I can tell you. She was running back and forth distraught like, and nobody knew what to do for her. The boarders had all they could do to keep her from going back in. I went back in my house and brought out a robe to put around her. She was right indecent as it was.

Amazing how fast it burned, and it brick, too. Everything's just so dry; the whole county is a powder keg.

When the old Negro came up from her little house at the back, she stood there in the shadows and watched the ceiling caving in on the marble ballroom and the firemen squirting a little water on it, though any nitwit could of told it wouldn't do no good. She stood there looking and shook her head. I walked over to her and told her I was sorry. "Was a misery house," she said, "right from the beginning. Maybe it be over now." Then she made her way over to where the girl was wringing her hands and crying. "You come on home with Genesis now," she said. And the girl went with her then, obedient as a child.

The Antique Shop

Mrs. Cavanaugh has finally found a topic that suits Dr. MacAuley. A good thing, too, or Mr. Cavanaugh thought she would lose her mind or leave home one. What she's going to do, as she explained to Booker and Mr. Cavanaugh this afternoon, is to analyze the demise of the *Woman's Voice* in terms of the "feminist crash" that happened nationwide at the end of the twenties.

"In the first place," she lectured, "after suffrage was won, the women lost their focus on one cause, and they couldn't get the younger generation fired up. And people kept stereotyping them as humorless battleaxes and such. Then the child labor and equal rights amendments failed, and that was a giant setback."

"That the same as the ERA?" Mr. Cavanaugh questioned suspiciously.

"The very same. And did y'all know a Mississippi woman helped draft it? Sure did. Young lawyer from Copiah County named Burnita Shelton Matthews.

"Well I be dog," Mr. Cavanaugh said.

"Then the depression came along. So the *Woman's Voice* wasn't all that went bust."

Booker said he didn't see how in the world Dr. MacAuley could find a thing wrong with that. Mr. Cavanaugh asked if that meant she would start cooking supper again.

"Clovis, I am not cooking a bite until this paper is done. Breakfast, dinner, AND supper, you're in charge."

Mr. Cavanaugh could have sworn Booker snickered, but when he glared over at him, he was solemn as a judge.

Vassar Lamar Dubard
1939

Somebody is going to have to do something about Lizzie Dunbar sooner or later, but it won't be me. She had all those grand ideas about women becoming a "third force" in politics and on and on. Just goes to show. She would have been better off to live an ordinary life like the rest of us. Being married to Walker Dubard is not easy by any means, but at least I have the children and a good living.

People say she's been crazy since the fire. I don't know about that. I do know she's always had a peculiar streak and that one day when I drove down the street where the Dunbar house had been, she was out in the ruins, pawing through the ashes. I drove on by quickly and pretended I didn't see. I was embarrassed for her. She's living with the Negroes in the shotgun house at the back of the property now. I can't imagine a white woman of her background sinking that low, but that's what has happened.

She's been going down for years, though. She wears all that rouge and dyes her hair and seems not to know that she's a middle-aged woman instead of a girl. She's sure mixed up. When she was young, she had the ideas of an old person, and now she's in reverse.

We keep thinking surely the governor will come up here and get her, but he may not know. Somebody needs to step in. You stay out of it, Walker says. She's not our problem. We don't need to get involved. And I know he's right about that.

Ruth Newcomb Malone
1939

Last Tuesday a week ago Mattie and the baby were taking their naps, and I had started peeling some apples for a pie for supper when Lizzie came to the back door. I had taken her some things after the fire and had thought she seemed vague and not like herself, but nothing like she was that day. I was very surprised to see her because while we got along well when I worked at the paper, we were never close. She is so smart, and I never knew what to say to her. "They finally did it, Ruth," she said. "They've ruined me."

"Who?"

"My enemies," she said, extremely agitated and raising her voice so that I knew she would wake the children. "For years they've tried, and now I have nothing left. You surely can't think that all of this is coincidence, the flood, the fire, the depression?"

"Who are they?" I asked, but she didn't answer.

"I must close the dress shop, they say."

"Have you paid the rent?"

She didn't answer this question either. She dismissed it as irrelevant with a downward sweep of her hand. We sat down together at the kitchen table, and I asked her if she wanted a Coca-Cola, which she refused.

"If I had had a stronger mother, I'd be different, don't you think?"

I didn't know what to say to her, but that didn't seem to matter because she didn't listen to what little I did say. The longer she talked, the more frantic she became. She talked steadily for an hour, a long painful hour that was heartbreaking to me. She dredged up a lifetime of slights, some undoubtedly real and some imaginary, and she relived the hard blows suffered in the last few years. I gathered from what she said that not only had she lost her businesses and her home, but also a man she cared about who had followed the levee work on out of town without a word.

I realized how lonely she must have been in Bolivar Landing and felt terrible that I had not ever invited her to our home. No one in Bolivar Landing is interested in what she's interested in, and everyone her age is married and spends all their time with their families. "As hard as I try, I can't figure it out," she said to me finally, "why everything I touch turns out so badly."

Little Mattie woke up then and stumbled into the kitchen, her blue eyes dazed with sleep and her golden curls tumbling in her face. Lizzie stopped talking and drew her breath in sharply. "What a beautiful child," she said. Mattie climbed into my lap and Lizzie smiled at her, almost shyly. "You are very lucky, Ruth," she said.

"Please stay for supper," I said. "Tip will be in from the fields after while, and we're having pork chops and apple pie."

"Oh, no, I can't drop in on you that way," she said, but she made no move to go. She talked on and on, some of it not making much sense to me. Finally Mattie whispered in my ear, "Who is she, Mama?"

"What did she say about me?" Lizzie said sharply, standing up. "I'm sorry I've worn out my welcome."

"Oh, don't go. Mattie just wanted to know your name."

"How cruel children are," she said.

Embarrassed and upset, I did my best to persuade her to stay, though actually I was relieved to see her go. I have never been so exhausted as I was when she walked out my kitchen door. Whatever will become of her, I wondered, and how on earth can I help her?

Two days later I heard that the sheriff had taken her to her father in Jackson. "For her own protection," Mrs. Davis said when I saw her in the store, tapping her temple and nodding at me. I went home sick with guilt.

"Don't blame yourself," Tip said. "You have all you can do with your own family."

"I could have been her friend," I said. "She gave me my first job. I ought to have done better."

"Her father will take good care of her in Jackson," he said. "Be glad she has some family left."

Genesis
1940

No need in the world to take her off like that. Mr. Trapp, he come to the door early one morning say, "Genesis, I feel responsible for Elizabeth with her daddy gone."

"I'm taking care of her," I say. "Don't worry about her."

"People are talking," he say. "Way she's acting."

"What she do?"

"It's not normal for a woman to dig through the ashes of a burned house and to rant to everybody on the street about imagined enemies."

"That against the law or something?" He one of the enemies, Miss Lizzie think. Think he trying to get her property, but I doubt it. He got too much already to fool with hers. The fire chief he say the fire caused by a boarder smoking in the bed, but none of them gonna own up to that. Lizzie think somebody set it a purpose, think now they after the shop.

"Woman alone that way," he say, "my old partner's daughter, I feel like she's my duty." He don't say it, but I know what he thinking. Thinking she living in a nigger house must be crazy.

"I promised her mama to look after her," I say, "and I aim to."

"You've done your best, but we need to think about what's best for Lizzie." Then he go on off toward town.

Next morning, before Miss Lizzie leave for the dress shop, here come the sheriff. Say Mr. Stephen need her in Jackson, need her real bad. Told her to bring a few things, come on. She quick got together a gown and toothbrush, a change of clothes, and went right on off, worried to death about her daddy. Think he must be low sick to send the law after her.

Last I seen of Lizzie. Mr. Stephen he sent word long about April that she at Whitfield now, say she getting good care.

Then the next thing I know, Mr. Trapp come by, say he done bought this place, and I gots to fine me another house. Sissy and Little Earl bout to have a fit for me to come up to Chicago, but I ain't going to no Chicago. So they send me a little money along, and I rented a house over close to the church. Mr. Trapp, looks like he's seeing to everything, he brought over the filing cabinet and typewriter from the shop. Sissy and Lizzie don't neither one need them now, and I sure don't, but I'll let them sit. They don't bother me.

I'm a mother of the church now. Got the respect of people. Do a little cleaning for a few white women to buy the groceries, but it don't take much for me to live.

This here is home now. Lord done brought me home.

Gwin
1940

I am not living out the rest of my life with a crazy person, I told him. She was determined to get his attention one way or the other, even if she had to go out of her mind to do it. She hasn't slept a wink the four months she's been here, nor has Stephen. She keeps him up, talking, talking, talking, pointing out where he went wrong as a father. Instead of writing it off as the talk of a madwoman, he keeps trying to reason with her and persuade her to another point of view. He's wasting his time and making himself sick in the bargain.

She's spoiled and selfish is her trouble. I have no doubt she could snap out of it if she wanted to. She said terrible things to Stephen about how he had made her like she was, how she could have done something worthwhile with help from him, how he had held her back all along the way. Held her back! The money he spent on her would amount to a small fortune, especially now.

"I want to hurt you," she said to him. "I want to figure out how to get you back."

This kind of talk scared me to death, but Stephen was heartbroken. "I love you, Lizzie," he kept saying until it made me sick. "Don't you know I love you?"

During the day he went off to the office and left me here with her, but she didn't badger me. She didn't say a word to me, which was fine. She sat around in her gown, smoking cigarettes, staring off into space. She wouldn't eat anything I cooked. She said it tasted funny, implying that I had poisoned her. Then after I had cleaned up the kitchen, she would go back in and get ice cream, but she wouldn't eat but a bite or two and would leave the counter sticky and a bowl of melting ice cream calling to every ant in Jackson. She lost weight and had dark circles under her eyes. Her roots were showing because that red dye job was growing out.

"She's turning into her mother," Stephen said, "except for the anger." We had to talk in whispers, and then if she came in and caught us at it, she accused us of talking about her behind her back, which we were. "She's going to take to her bed pretty soon and be her mother."

"Not in my house she's not," I said. "You can forget about that."

Along about the first of March when Stephen was gone, I asked her, "What are your plans, Lizzie?"

"What are your plans?" she said.

"This is my home, mine and Stephen's."

"It's mine too, now," she said. "You know the house burned down."

"But you can't stay here indefinitely," I told her.

"I only just got here," she said. "I need some time to figure things out."

"You've been here four months."

"That's a lie," she said.

That made me angry, and I said some things I probably shouldn't have, but they were all true. And by the time Stephen got home, she was raving.

"You've upset her," he said to me. "You have to be careful what you say."

I let him know then that it was Lizzie or me. I couldn't live tiptoeing around a madwoman.

He checked around at some of the private mental hospitals and found out what it would cost to send her to one. So I had to put my foot down again and let him know we weren't sinking everything into Lizzie. She's already been enough of a drain to last a lifetime. "It's unthinkable," he said, "for a governor's daughter to go to Whitfield."

"You helped establish it, didn't you?" I said. "What's so bad about it?" Before long he got used to the idea. He knows one of the doctors out there, a Dr. Lowry, and he got him to agree to come by here and see Lizzie. She was as sane as you ever saw around Dr. Lowry. Sat and talked to him about some book. That's one reason I don't think she's really crazy. That performance slowed the process considerably because Dr. Lowry couldn't see how she really was. This dragged on until I packed up and got a room at the King Edward Hotel. With that, Stephen came to his senses and got Dr. Lowry to take her in for observation.

On the day he took her out there, he came back and cried like somebody had died. I have never seen a man cry like that. I wonder if that's love or wounded pride?

Lizzie
1940

"Elizabeth," he said to me that Sunday. "Come, let's take a ride in the country. Maybe you'll feel better." And so I went. We drove out away from the city and into the open countryside where the roads weren't paved but were gravel and dusty. The April day was cool and sunny and the pale green woods were full of dogwood in bloom. The birds were singing in the trees, and yellow butterflies fluttered around the car. The day reminded me of childhood Sundays in Holly Springs. I did feel better, and I thought this is probably what I need, some time in the country. I have always known about myself that I am at peace in the natural world, but I forget it in the business of life.

We passed fields where cows grazed and a pond where two boys sat with fishing poles, and forests of pine trees with a smell pungent enough to reach us in the car. White houses with tin roofs and red barns were washed in the new light of spring.

Then suddenly, unnaturally, an enormous old brick building with thick white columns loomed ahead. The institution, for I knew at once it was an institution, sat on a high hill and towered over the countryside. It was alien to the rural surroundings, threatening, and the sight of it frightened me. It looked like an orphanage from a Dickens novel where Gothic horrors were inflicted on children.

Without a word Daddy turned the car into the long lane that led up the hill to a nightmare, and I knew. He kept his eyes straight ahead and drove fast. He would not answer my questions. "Don't scream," he kept saying, "Nobody is going to hurt you. Don't scream."

But I wasn't screaming. I was just asking where we were going. I wasn't screaming at all.

Dr. Lowry
1940

When I come across a case like Lizzie Dunbar, I understand the severe limitations of our science, and I am disheartened. We don't know enough yet, and we may never.

Miss Dunbar has a fine mind, one of the most interesting I've come across. When she is lucid, she is astonishing. She can discuss abstractions, ideas, with amazing clarity. But if the conversation turns to her family, particularly her father, or to her business, she becomes completely irrational. A deep anger and paranoid gloom take over, and the sessions leave me depleted and depressed. Clearly the best thing for her is rest and a severing of all the old ties. Then maybe gradually she will be able to deal with the past. I have ordered all mail and visits to stop.

Stephen has trouble with this. He thinks he's deserting her if he stops his visits, but each time he is here, she is much worse for days after. First, she wants him to take her home, and from there they go to other grievances, real and imagined. I finally told him I would work with her no longer if he didn't stay away. We have four thousand patients here with only three doctors. I work sixteen hours a day, some weeks without a day off. The work is exhausting, heartbreaking, and I don't have time for patients who won't follow my directions.

The complexity and mystery of the human mind. Why wasn't I satisfied with general practice where I could set a bone, lance a boil, deliver a baby, ease suffering, heal? With the mind, you're never sure if you've done any good or not.

Gwin
1943

My conscience is clear in regard to Elizabeth Dunbar. When Stephen and I sold her property in Bolivar Landing, he put aside part of it in a trust for her, and I didn't cross him on that. The money means she can live better than the rest of them at Whitfield. Once again, she gets special treatment.

When Stephen died, I packed up some old things that had come from Holly Springs—photographs, dishes, even Miranda's silver—though I had every right to it. I took them out to Dr. Lowry and told him he could give them to her or not as he saw fit. And with that I washed my hands.

She never liked me, and I'll admit the feeling was mutual. She had some bad breaks, but haven't we all? I see no reason she couldn't pull herself together and go on like the rest of us.

I will always believe that grieving over Elizabeth was what killed Stephen. We were happy before she came down here and camped in our spare room with her misery. Stephen was never the same. It's a wonder I was able to get him to commit her before he died. Thank God I stood firm on that, or I would have been stuck with her. Wouldn't that have been a life?

Mrs. Sallie George
1943

If it weren't so pitiful, it would be funny, I guess. I was in Jackson for the Federated Women's Clubs meeting, and some of them said Lizzie Dunbar had been trying to organize the inmates at the asylum, get them to demand better living conditions. That sounds just like something she would do. Can't organize herself, but set out to organize the madhouse.

Once right after they sent her down there, I tried to go out and see her. I always liked Lizzie, exasperating and fast as she was. High-spirited girl, I remember that from the '24 Convention. But that doctor, Lowry I believe his name was, he wasn't allowing any visitors or mail. He said it was important not to upset her and that anybody from home did.

Stephen Dunbar's dead, and I'll bet Lizzie doesn't even know it. The wife got everything he had and has already married somebody else, some young lawyer in the firm. Millard Trapp bought the Dunbar property in the Delta and built himself a fine house in town where the Dunbars' had been. Trapp probably beat Stephen out of it, but I didn't trust either one of them. Tit for tat as to who was crookeder.

Poor girl, not much for her on the outside either. I wonder if she knows a war's going on. I guess the less she knows, the better.

The Antique Shop

Faithfully, Mr. Cavanaugh has read his way through the Lizzie papers until he has reached the bottom drawer. An assortment of clippings had been stashed there, obviously by some other hand than Lizzie's. Booker thought the file cabinet must have been at Genesis's and that probably before she died, she added things that seemed to belong.

A long obituary of Governor Dunbar from the Jackson paper was there, along with a big picture. "Remember him well," Mr. Cavanaugh said, "offices right across the street there where Jimbo Norris is now."

An article that almost made Mr. Cavanaugh jump out of his skin was an editorial from the *Delta Democrat* down in Greenville. The editor had gotten a letter and a petition from Whitfield about the conditions there. He printed them in their entirety. The letter said the sickest patients were confined like animals in squalor in one large room. Food was slid under the door to them and occasionally the room was hosed down. Violent patients were beaten and locked in cages until they were docile. The three doctors were "well intentioned" but overwhelmed by the needs of four thousand patients. Many of the orderlies were ignorant, brutal, and unprepared to handle mental patients. As for food, there was never enough. A thin bowl of grits for breakfast, turnip greens with a small piece of cornbread for dinner, and watery potato soup for supper.

"Many people are here for no other reason," the letter said, "than that they were an inconvenience or an embarrassment to their families. I am smuggling this letter out by a janitor because I am not allowed to write letters. I know your reputation as an editor concerned with justice and the rights of human beings. An editorial from you could make a difference."

The letter was signed by Lizzie Dunbar.

Dr. Lowry
1947

Damn newspapers, sensationalize everything and always get it wrong. If you know the facts and then see a newspaper account, it's always a little off, even if it's not completely inaccurate. The wire service picked up an editorial by a Delta bleeding heart based on a letter to him from Lizzie Dunbar and a petition signed by three hundred of our patients. All about inhumane conditions here. Not a word about those of us killing ourselves in service for a lot less pay than we would get in the private sector. Nothing more intriguing to the public than a scandal, especially one from a place they are as afraid of and misinformed about as the asylum.

Lizzie had brought up the subject of patient care many times, and I tried to explain that we are a poor state and we do the best we can with the appropriations we have. I still can't believe she has betrayed me. I have tried in every way to help her, and I thought she trusted me. I arranged for her to have a cottage across the lake and free run of the place. I bring her books and we talk about them during her sessions. "Bring me the work of a woman psychiatrist," she said, and I assured her that when one appeared of the stature of Freud and Jung, I would. She is better under my care, much less depression and fewer lapses into irrationality, and I am writing an article based on my experience with her that should be helpful for the doctors of other women with nervous problems.

Furious about her letter, I left my office and walked down the path that leads around the lake and to her cottage, the newspaper under my arm. It was a late summer afternoon, and the grounds were peaceful. The ducks were floating lazily on the lake and the sun was sinking behind the woods. If you didn't know better and were put down here suddenly, you would think you were on a college campus or in a summer resort where roads meander in and out among brick cottages and trees. This is not a bad place, I thought angrily. Beauty is here, and the possibility of healing. I am investing my life and getting no credit—worse, I am being attacked.

Lizzie sat with a book on her front-porch swing. Her long dark hair, streaked with gray, was pulled back loosely. She wore a white cotton smock and leather sandals. Her figure is trim now, her skin clear and unmade-up. I don't know why I noticed these details in my anger, except that she looked like Sappho on a Greek Isle, not like a woman suffering deprivation.

"What's the matter?" she said, putting her feet down out of the swing and motioning for me to sit. She knew something was wrong. I threw my hat and the newspaper on the small wicker table and sat down.

"I hope you're happy," I said. "You've probably gotten me fired."

"How interesting," she said. "I didn't know the doctor could feel anger."

"Why did you make up those lies and send them to the newspaper?"

"My letter was published?" She looked delighted.

"Along with an editorial calling for a legislative investigation. I thought you liked me, Miss Dunbar."

"The letter didn't have to do with liking you or not. The letter was about conditions here that you never see."

"I'm here all my waking hours. How can you say that?"

She started the swing in motion as if this were some ludicrous lovers' quarrel.

"Yes," she said softly, "but you're the doctor, and that's quite a different point of view. Social strata exist here just like anywhere else, and I'm among the privileged. You never see the hopeless, the ones in straitjackets living in their own filth on the wards."

Fine, I thought, swinging, now I'm lectured on hospital administration by a madwoman.

"I don't want to hear it," I said. "You don't understand the realities of running a place like this. It's not a resort hotel, but nobody is hungry or mistreated. You're fantasizing, projecting your own fear—"

"How dare you say that to me," she said, stopping the swing with her foot. "Do you think I sit in this cottage and read all day? I know what goes on around me, sir, and you would be a better doctor if you did."

We sat glaring at each other, the doctor-patient relationship dangerously out of kilter. I wanted her to apologize to me. I wanted her to say she didn't mean me when she wrote the letter. Why, I don't know, but my attention focused on the tiny beads of sweat on her upper lip and the way her dark lashes tangled around her blue-gray eyes. Then a tiredness came over me, so profound that I didn't think I could get up and walk back to the office. She, whose mind I should know perfectly, is a complete and utter mystery.

Without a word, I walked down the steps and back to the office. I never thought once about my hat and the newspaper.

Lizzie
1947

I have come through the valley of the shadow, through fire and flood, I am melted, molded, tested, a hammered gold ring whole eternal encircling all the globe all lakes marshes rivers oaks cypress holly goldenrod butterflies cattle robins egrets doves. I am a gold ring enfolding creation for eternity Creator God my heart will burst for joy the warm sun flowing over me Daddy and me blood and spirit floating in the pine-scented air through the country air peacefully free and out of time breathing free I am breathing again tight iron bands turn to gold rings and I am free—NO inexplicably the landscape torn a shape huge ominous threatening looms, draws the car like a magnet, pulls it out of the air to its brick towers to its prison horrors please stop please please rushing faster faster toward the dark "Quit screaming" but I am not I am not I am drowning silently I am making no sound in my drowning.

Dr. Lowry
1947

"The late Governor Dunbar," one article began in the paper I carelessly left with her. Good news is all she's known since she came here, according to my orders. She hasn't known about Pearl Harbor, the war, or her father's death. Now she has pulled her curtains and taken to her bed in her darkest depression yet. The attendant who came for me said she hasn't eaten in a week.

"I'll have to put you on the ward if you won't eat," I tell her, standing by the bed in the dark cottage. No response. The covers are over her head, and so I can't see her face. "Now do you see why I don't want you to read newspapers?" Nothing. I sit on the edge of the bed and put my hand on her thin shoulder. The muscles are hard and taut. Even as sick as she is, I can feel the life beneath the skin.

Since her first anger at being brought here, she has been cooperative. She has agreed to be interviewed by groups of psychiatrists at professional meetings here many times and even edited articles I've written for journals. "I'll bet not many patients edit their doctors' work," she joked. Sometimes I have surprised the doctors—bringing her into a discussion group and not telling them her status until later. "Where did you find her?" they will ask and never quite believe she is a patient. We have read and studied together, everything from the mystics of India to the latest scientific research in psychology, and I have become nationally recognized as something of an authority on the nervous problems of middle-aged women.

I want her back now. I am panicked that she is gone for good. "Please, Lizzie," I say. "Don't do this to me." I pull the covers back. She wears the same white smock of a week ago. I run my hand down her back. Her spine is rigid as an iron poker. I knead her stiff neck muscles. I am trying to revive a corpse, a drowned woman on whom rigor mortis has set in. I take the dress off. Her body is still beautiful, the skin smooth and elastic. I begin to massage her, remembering a Chinese teacher from medical school, the pressure points, the healing touch. I know her spirit is still there, and I am determined to reach it, to bring it back.

I am outside time. I am in a trance when I hear a sound, a low moaning sound, so terrible that I freeze, my hands limp around her neck. I am doing her no favors. The sound intensifies. It is primal and despairing, subhuman, like no sound I have ever heard.

"Lizzie!" I call her name, and she opens her eyes, luminous, glowing in the lamplight, then black with the pain of realization.

"The paper was wrong," she says. "I would have felt something if he had died. We are going back to the Hollies. He promised. I will take care of him and read to him when he is old."

I feel her grief in my gut in a way that I never allow myself with patients.

"Yes," I say. "Yes, of course."

Florence Alabama McVay
1947

Dr. Lowry come knocking on my door about 4:00 A.M. "Florence," I hear him whispering. "Get up." Somebody gone wild in the ward, I'm thinking, and I got to quiet 'em down. I'm good at that. "You're better than drugs," Dr. Lowry told me once, and it's the truth. I can take the worst by the hand, and they'll get just as calm. Pa says I'm casting out demons, and says I can do it because I'm washed in the blood. Dr. Lowry, though, he don't have no truck with demons. All he talks about is nerves.

I quick jump in my uniform, twist up my hair, and open the door. Dr. Lowry standing there, looking like he been beat all night with a stick. Dark circles under his eyes, whiskers shadowing under his chin, tie undone, hair tousled all over his head. Usually he looks like he stepped out of a bandbox.

"What happened to you?" I ask him.

"I need you to stay with Miss Dunbar," he says. "She's in a crisis, but I've got to get home. My wife's probably frantic now." Everybody knows he's partial to Lizzie Dunbar. Studying her, I reckon. She pretty well takes care of herself, but if she needs anything he calls a nurse usually, not an orderly like me.

People don't know what in the world Lizzie Dunbar's doing out here anyway, her a governor's daughter and all. Looks like she'd be in a private sanitarium.

"If she asks about her father," Dr. Lowry says, "just say she can see him when I say so."

"You mean lie?"

"I mean have compassion. She can't deal with his death right now."

"He's been gone since I was a child. How long it's going to take?"

"Don't be difficult, Florence," he snaps. "Just do as I say. And when she wakes up, get her to eat."

I set off down the path not knowing what kind of shape I'd find Miss Dunbar in. She's sleeping peaceful, though, a little lamp by her bed and her long hair spread out on the pillow. I sit down in the rocking chair and look things over.

Her cottage puts me in the mind of a dollhouse. It's fixed up real nice. She's got a porch, a little kitchen, a sitting room with easy chairs, a writing desk with pen and paper, lots of books, and a pretty white bedroom with lace curtains, an oval mirror, white bedspread, and now and then some color—a blue vase, a honey-colored hardwood floor. I can tell that here's a woman can take almost anything and make it pretty. Now me I could put that piece of blue cotton over that bedside table and put that lamp on it and it wouldn't look like nothing, but she does it and it looks like a magazine.

On the table by the bed sits an old picture in a heavy silver frame. Three people are in it, looks like a daddy, a mama, and a little girl. The man is holding the little girl, and there's a big space between him and the woman. She's pale and thin and looks like she's about to disappear off the edge of the picture. My eyes naturally fall on the little girl. She has a dark braid hanging over each shoulder, round little cheeks that look like they're pink even though the picture is black and white, eyes that look like they're laughing at a big joke. The girl is Miss Dunbar, no doubt about it. Funny how some people got such a definite look they don't change much when they grow up. That photograph looks old as Ma's that was taken when she was a little girl. Ma seems a lot older than Miss Dunbar, but then Ma had ten children. Miss Dunbar hadn't had no cakewalk either, though, so they say.

After while the sun shines through them curtains, making a lacy pattern on Miss Dunbar's face. She groans and stirs around and opens her big eyes and looks over at me. She don't seem surprised.

"Who are you?" she asks me.

"Florence Alabama. Dr. Lowry asked me to come."

"Oh."

"I'm hungry," I say. "I'm about to cook us some breakfast."

"Nothing for me," she says. "I intend to starve." She's not joking I can tell.

"Why?"

"Why not?"

"God knows that," I say. "Not me."

"Then he is strangely silent," she says. "And I don't intend to wait on him any longer."

"Starving is a hard way to go," I say. "I'd pick a quicker one."

She looks at me real funny. "What way?"

"You could drown in the lake. Or hang yourself."

"No," she says, sitting up in the bed, her hair falling all around her. "I'm a coward for violence. But starving I can do. I don't remember when I've eaten, and the thought of food sickens me." She looks thin all right.

"Suit yourself," I say, getting up and going toward the kitchen. "I'm hungry." So I'm in there mixing up some biscuits and getting ready to fry bacon when a knock comes at the front door. I figure it's Dr. Lowry, and I'm glad because I don't like that starving talk. I go to the door and a young man in a gray suit is standing there holding a tablet and a pencil.

"Good morning," he says. "I'm Blair Hawks, an investigator sent by the legislature. I'm here to see Miss Dunbar."

"She can't see you now," I say loud. "She's killing herself."

He jumps back, drops his pencil. While he's scrambling around for it, here comes Miss Dunbar, wrapping herself in a long flowerdy robe, hair pulled back, looking sane as anybody.

"Hello," she says to the man, sticking out her hand. "I'm

Lizzie Dunbar. Won't you come in?" He's flustered as he can be. Drops his tablet, shakes her hand, picks up the tablet, stumbles in the door. I go back to the kitchen and keep an ear toward the living room.

I pretty well know why he's here. Everybody's talking about the letter and petition Miss Dunbar smuggled out. We figured the legislature would poke around, and they ought to. We do the best we can, but there ain't enough of us. She tells him good. Tells just how it is. Lets him know she's one of the lucky ones. Most of them don't live near this good. She's awful clear for a crazy woman.

By the time he leaves, I've got the biscuit out of the oven, the coffee made, the bacon and eggs fried up. I set two places at the table with some pretty little dishes with pink roses on them and real silver. She comes and stands at the kitchen door. "There's plum jelly in the refrigerator," she says. "Kenneth brought me some plums, and I made it myself." Well, now, I'm thinking. So Dr. Lowry is Kenneth to her, is he?

She sits down at the table without another word. I say the blessing and then we start in. Good thing I fixed a lot because that woman can eat. We talk about conditions around Whitfield, and we're sitting there with the second cup of coffee when she says, "I want to see how this investigation turns out. Then I'll starve."

"Makes sense," I say.

"You interest me, Florence Alabama," she says. "Tell me about yourself."

"Not much to tell. I'm nineteen years old, oldest of ten, come here from the farm to get work and help them out at home."

"What are your plans for the future?" That's a funny thing to ask somebody. We're too busy finding the next meal to worry about the future.

"That's the Lord's business. I don't have time to think about it."

"You better think," she says. "When I was your age, I didn't plan ahead either, and look what's happened to me."

That made me sad, like she thinks she's to blame for being here. Set me thinking, though.

"I'd planned to marry Clyde Junior, but he went off and got killed in the war. So what's the use of planning?"

"That's true," she says with a sigh. "I didn't know about World War II until just lately. They had said the first world war would be the last."

"Always gonna have war. Bible says so."

"Still it's essential to find the work you're meant to do, stick with it."

"Woman's work is pretty clear," I say. "That's in the Bible, too. I'll do like Ma, have some kids, raise them best I can to be good Christians, and then die."

"What if you can't have children?" That thought hadn't never come up. All our folks have plenty of kids. The trouble's always too many instead of not enough.

"I don't know," I say.

"Women shouldn't let biology determine everything," she says. "Men don't. Can you imagine a man not knowing what else in the world to do if he couldn't sire children?"

Of course I couldn't. That was too strange an idea.

"Take you," she went on. "You're young, attractive, smart. You must be good at what you do here."

"I am," I say. "I've got a knack for it."

"Well, then. There you go."

"What, do this for life?"

"Not exactly the same job, but in the field of psychology. Make progress."

"I'd love to be a nurse, but that would take more money than we'll ever see."

"Why not a doctor?" she says. That's getting crazy there. I stand up, start clearing the table.

"I guess I'll let Dr. Lowry keep his job awhile longer," I say, laughing. She's not laughing. Her eyes are deep and serious.

"Listen to me," she says, "you must make an effort to realize yourself. Just because I made a mess doesn't mean I don't know better."

Something in her voice makes me tremble. I know I'm not going to forget what she says, as bad as I may want to, as much trouble as it's probably gonna cause me.

Lizzie
1947

"Are you in love with your own suffering?" Kenneth asked me. "Walter Freeman is the most eminent in the field, Lizzie. Think what it would mean to have him here, the father of American lobotomy."

"I know who he is," I said. "But he doesn't know me. Who is he to alter my brain structure?"

"Hundreds of women, all over the country, have been restored by this man. And we could get him here. I'm sure we could."

"And you could get another article out of it."

"That's cruel, Lizzie."

"I'm sorry. You're dedicated to your work, but you don't know what's best for me. You're the doctor, but you don't know everything."

Florence
1948

It's been a year since I've been checking in regular on Miss Dunbar. Dr. Lowry says I do her good. Did her good when the legislature investigated after her letter, too. The upshot was, the governor called a special session and made a lot of changes. "A clear-cut case of the influence the press can have on social conditions," Miss Dunbar said.

She helps me out in a night course I started at the med center. I wouldn't of stayed in if she hadn't helped me because I was never much on school. She is one smart woman.

Pa says all she needs is some old-time religion. "Witness to her," Pa says. When I get done with them witnessing talks, though, I don't know who's witnessed to who or what's what. One day I asked her, I come right out with it, "Are you saved?"

She looked thoughtful. "I'm not sure what that means," she says.

That stopped me. How could anybody, even in the asylum, raised in a Christian nation, not know what being saved meant?

"I like to think of a God-seed in everybody," she says. "And if it doesn't grow in this life, it'll get a chance in another. We may have to be planted in lots of gardens, lots of lives, to grow like God intends."

"Even them that don't know Jesus as their Lord and Savior?"

"Everybody. I believe there's more than one way to grow toward God."

When I told Pa that, he said, "Heathernish. No wonder she's locked up."

Tennessee Williams
A Radio Interview
1954

We are in the New Orleans apartment of playwright Tennessee Williams talking to him about his new hit play A Streetcar Named Desire. *Mr. Williams, I'd like to start the interview with a question about sources. You've lived in both New Orleans and Mississippi, where Stella and Blanche DuBois grew up.*

T.W.: Yes, I was born in Columbus, Mississippi, in the Episcopal rectory. My grandfather, who is here with me now, was the priest there, and my mother and I lived with him until I was nine years old. Then we moved with my father, a salesman, to Saint Louis. When I was four or five, my grandfather moved to Bolivar Landing to be priest there, and so we lived for several years in the Delta region of Mississippi, the richest land this side of the valley Nile.

Interviewer: Blanche talks about Moon Lake, which I believe is in the Delta.

T.W.: That's right. The wealthy planters had cottages there in the first quarter of the century. There was a lodge with a dance floor and a casino. Bands came down from Memphis. I was too young to go, but I heard the grown people talk about it.

Int.: You listened to them talk then?

T.W.: Oh, yes. You see, they thought I wasn't paying attention. My grandfather, as priest, and my grandmother were often invited to dinners in the mansions of the planters, the parishioners. They would take me along and I would lie on the floor with a book after dinner, pretending to read. But I would listen to the stories, wonderful stories about life there.

Int.: Do any of those stories appear in your work?

T.W.: Transformed by the power of the imagination, but yes, you could say that some of those stories are in the plays; they influenced me.

Int.: What about characters? Are there any characters in *Street Car* that have definite living sources? Take Blanche, for instance, to me the most fascinating character in the play. Were there women like Blanche in Bolivar Landing?

T.W.: As a matter of fact, I was in love with a woman in Bolivar Landing a bit like Blanche and yet not Blanche at all. Blanche is something like my sister Rose and like Laura in *Glass Menagerie*, but this woman, Lizzie Dunbar was her name, wanted something more than the approval of men. I don't believe I could capture this woman in a play. I believe she was beyond her time and mine, beyond my capacity to understand and write about. I was only nine, but I was obsessed with this woman, then and for years after, not for just her looks, which were unique, hard to describe, but her mind. Her mind was poetic and political at the same time, an odd combination. She was the daughter of a former governor of the state, and when he left office and came back to Bolivar Landing, he built a house that was the exact replica of Jefferson's Monticello. She was sometimes at the dinners we were invited to, there with one of her gentleman callers. She would talk to me as if I were a person. She seemed to take me seriously.

Int.: She was a belle, you might say, and in that was like Blanche?

T.W.: Yes, part of her was a belle, at any rate. She never married, and when the depression came and her father lost his money, she ran a boardinghouse in the mansion. Except that people said it was more than a boardinghouse. I don't know anything about that, though. I had been gone from Bolivar Landing a long time, and I only heard rumors. Later she went quite mad they said, quite mad and was sent away.

The Antique Shop

Among the clippings in the last drawer was one that Mr. Cavanaugh couldn't figure at all. It did have the dateline "Holly Springs," though, and he knew the Dunbars had come from there. Must of been somebody they knew way back when, somebody Genesis remembered. She's probably the one who handwrote "1957" in the margin.

HOLLY SPRINGS, MS (AP) —Residents of this small north Mississippi town were stunned this week to find themselves beneficiaries in the will of a deceased Holly Springs native.

Over 1,000 works of art and a fund for a gallery to house them are a bequest to Holly Springs from Kate Freeman Clark. Most of the works of art were original paintings by Ms. Clark and had been stored in New York City since 1922.

"I never knew her to paint," said a neighbor. "She was quiet and retiring and so far as I knew spent her time reading and gardening with her dog and cat for company. Sometimes she went with me to the Thursday Club, but she never mentioned art."

Ms. Clark studied painting in New York City with artist William Merritt Chase from 1895 until his death in 1916. Her paintings were exhibited widely in the early part of the century under the name Freeman Clark. When her mother died in 1922, Ms. Clark returned to Holly Springs and lived the last thirty years of her life alone in her ancestral home, Freeman Place.

"Kate never painted again after she came back home," said a cousin, Meems Clark. "That fact is sad to me, but Kate did not talk about it. Perhaps to give up painting was the only way she could reconcile the conflict she felt between the 'place' of the Southern lady and that of the professional artist. But she's left her town a marvelous legacy, and I'm glad Mississippi will at last know of her talent."

At its completion, the gallery will house not only Ms. Clark's paintings but also Clark family papers, books, and other collections.

Whereas in the hands of an average person this article would be just another fishwrapper, to Mr. Cavanaugh it was the signpost of a trail he knew must lead to something delicious and interesting.

Sissy
1963

That woman know she old, old as she can be. And stubborn as she be old. "Mama, why you so obstinate?" I ask her. "Why won't you come on back home with me and Connie?"

"Ain't none of my home," she say. "My home right here." Little ole shotgun rent house not big as my front room. She look around satisfied like it the White House.

"Home ought to be where your family at," I tell her.

"Home ought to be where your mama at," she say, "but go ahead on back to Chicago. Nobody trying to stop you."

"Nothing but trouble ahead for black folks in Bolivar Landing," I say.

"Always been trouble for black people," she say. "Won't be nothing new in that."

"Connie say the revolution coming." Mama proud of my girl Connie. She come to Mississippi a lot, civil rights lawyer. Always come by to see her grandma.

"Humph. What Connie know?" Mama say.

"Know a good bit. Always have been smart since she a little ole girl."

"Smart ain't all of it," Mama say. "Look what happen to Lizzie."

"Something bad wrong with what happen to Lizzie," I say. "Lizzie different, but that don't mean she crazy."

"Wonder is she dead?" Mama ask. "Lord have mercy."

I got to thinking about Lizzie then, them days when we had the paper. That girl was a sight. If there wasn't any news, she'd get out and make it. Go stir up Bilbo or Vardaman or some of them. She took it hard when the paper shut down, too. The paper was her identity. She cry when I told her I was moving to Chicago. "The South needs women like you, Sissy," she say. "Your roots are here."

"Roots got to have some fertilize, don't the plant starve."

"Oh, God, Sissy. If only I had money."

Last night I dream Mama setting under a mimosa tree in a chair, family pinning money on her dress for her birthday, but nobody know how old she be. Mama herself don't know, say what difference it make, live till you die. Lizzie she come up to Mama crying, hug her, say, "Genesis I don't have a gift."

Next morning I wake up, say, "All right, Mama. It's Fourth of July. Let's get in the car, go find Lizzie."

Mama grumble around. She don't like to ride in the car with me. Think I can't drive a car when I drive all over Chicago. Finally she take a bouquet of sunflowers out the yard and some teacakes and we load up and drive down 61 to Freedom Village where Connie registering voters. "Get in," I say. "We're going to Jackson." Connie look nice, dressed up in a white suit, high-heel shoes. She smile real big, think we're going to shop and eat and shoot off firecrackers at Farish Street, I guess.

"I'm due a day off," she say. "Let me tell Jack."

In a few minutes she come back with a briefcase, get in the back seat, looking important. Make me proud. We go off down the road, laughing and talking. When we get to Jackson, hit Woodrow Wilson, I say, "Reckon where is Whitfield?"

"What?" Connie say, sharp.

"East of town?"

"Mama, what are you talking about?"

"We going to find Lizzie Dunbar."

Connie she outdone. Fuss and fuss, but she tell me how to get there. She registers and marches all over Mississippi, know where everything at.

"They're strict about visitors," she say. "What makes you think they'll let you in?"

"You the lawyer," I say. "Make up a story."

"Mama!" She hopping mad. "I've been kidnapped," she say.

Her grandma think that real funny. She laugh and laugh, big red flower on her hat bobbing all around. We see signs then, and I turn off the road, head up toward a big old house with columns, look like a plantation. Gatekeeper come up to the car. I say, "We come to see my sister, bring her some flowers."

He nod and say, "Stop by the office, sign in."

"Your sister, my foot," Connie say as I drive on. "What are you going to do when they ask her name?" Figured I'd think of something but was saved the trouble because soon as I parked the car, I see Lizzie Dunbar walking up the path from a little lake. I'd know her anywhere.

"Can you imagine?" I say. "There she come right now."

"Don't startle her," Connie say. "You don't know her frame of mind." So I get out the car real slow and walk down to meet her. She a handsome woman still, hair white now. She look up from the path, see me, blink her eyes still blue as scraps of sky. I don't know if Lizzie in there or not. I stop. Feel like I can't breathe. Wish I hadn't of come. Wish I's home in Chicago.

"Sissy?" she say, like I a ghost.

I run down the path to her then, catch her up in a hug. We both crying. "I never thought I'd see you again," she say. "It's a miracle."

"Mama here too."

"Genesis? She's still alive?"

"And my girl Connie."

So we go back to the car and have a reunion. She never do ask how we found her. She invite us to her house, nice little brick house across the lake. She act like the flowers pure gold, put them in a vase in the middle of the table and keep touching them. "I'll put them out this winter for the birds," she say. Then she mix up some lemonade and serve Mama's teacakes. She take up one reverent-like, like it's the sacrament in church, take a bite, close her eyes and say, "My, Genesis, if this doesn't take me back!"

We talk a long time about the old days. Lizzie don't seem crazy to me. Seem about like she always was, sadder maybe, but who wouldn't be after all done happen to her? Connie like all the talk. She ask questions about how it was. We feel like we safe if we can keep the talk on the old days.

Lizzie turn the talk to Connie finally. Can't get over she my baby and a lawyer. Say it sure must be a new day for women, but she ain't allowed a newspaper. Don't know nothing about civil rights, but she interested. Specially want to know what the women doing.

Finally come time to go. "Oh, baby," Mama say, hugging Lizzie, start in to crying. "Wish you could come home with me."

"I tried to leave once, Genesis," she say. "Dr. Lowry helped me get an apartment on North State Street and a job in a state office, but everything was so loud and confusing. I couldn't keep up. They've got new medicine now. They're trying to clear everybody out of here, but I don't think I can. Isn't it funny? For years I spent all my energy thinking how to get out, but once I did. . . ."

Then she see how we looking like a funeral, and she start in trying to cheer us up. She the one locked up, I'm thinking, and she trying to make us feel better. "In a way I'm freer than anybody," she say. "What else could happen? I've got all I need, even some work. Lots of people here can't read or write, and I help them if they ask me. That's one thing I can do."

"Yeah," I say. "You do that real good. You don't never let up once you start in on somebody about reading."

We set in laughing then, telling Connie about how she taught me. We start walking back to the car, and she walk alongside us. Hug me and Genesis again, shake hands with Connie.

"Lord gonna take care of you," Mama say.

"And you too," Lizzie say.

We drive off waving, and she still standing in the road like a statue, one hand raised up good-bye.

The Antique Shop

Booker found Mr. Cavanaugh in the clearinghouse, crying. He tried to straighten up when Booker walked in, but Booker knew and was alarmed. What had happened? Mrs. Cavanaugh? One of the grandchildren?

Then Mr. Cavanaugh shoved a clipping across the desk at him. "This, is all."

BOLIVAR LANDING — Graveside services were held at Memorial Cemetery today for Elizabeth Marshall Dunbar, 66. She was a resident of Whitfield.

Born in Holly Springs, MS, in 1902, Dunbar lived in Bolivar Landing from 1920 to 1939. From 1922 to 1928, she edited and published a newspaper for women.

Dunbar was preceded in death by her father, former governor Stephen A. Dunbar, and her mother, Miranda Marshall Dunbar. She leaves no survivors.

Florence
1968

Kenneth Lowry just called to say that Lizzie Dunbar is dead. Heart failure. He couldn't be more upset if it had been his wife. To be a good doctor in some ways, he's an idiot in others. I really don't think he knew he was in love with her.

The last time I was out to see her I had a premonition that we were saying a last good-bye, and I had to thank her. Neither one of us is much on sentiment.

"If you hadn't egged me on," I said, "no telling where I'd be today."

"I can't take much credit," she said, "but I'd like to. Kenneth says you're the best psychiatric nurse he knows. He says you could be director of the state mental health someday."

"You put it in my head—that life had more possibility than I had imagined."

"Isn't that odd? When my own life was reduced to the lowest common denominator, I could see the possibilities clearly for the first time."

I left her on her porch swing in the late afternoon, the evening sun glowing on her white hair and blue eyes.

The Antique Shop

Mrs. Cavanaugh has invited Jane MacAuley and her husband Charles Able to Sunday dinner. She didn't want to do this until after the grades were in because she didn't want Dr. MacAuley to think she was trying to influence her, but she wanted to let her know how much the course had meant to her. She made an A, just as Mr. Cavanaugh had predicted all along, but she would have had them to dinner no matter what.

She has outdone herself with a crown pork roast, squash casserole, fresh green beans and tomatoes from the garden, mashed potatoes, homemade rolls, and a chocolate cream pie to die for. Mr. Cavanaugh has had a better time than he expected. The young couple is appreciative of the dinner and his stories. In the course of the meal he has grown almost fond of Ms. Dr. Jane (as he calls her, but not to her face), even if Charles did say he cooked every other night and ironed his own shirts.

In fact, Mr. Cavanaugh has become so mellow that he decides the time has come to show Dr. MacAuley the extent of the Lizzie papers. He offers to, after the pie and coffee, and the couple jumps at the chance. They all load up in the Falcon and drive down to the shop.

Mr. Cavanaugh notes with satisfaction that Dr. Jane's cheeks are flushed, her eyes shine, and she scarcely breathes as he opens the filing cabinet and begins showing her things and telling her what he's learned. Then he hands her the first issue of the *Woman's Voice*.

"Incredible," she says softly, as she spreads it with great care on Mr. Cavanaugh's huge oak table and winces as an inch of yellowed newsprint sloughs off the bottom edge. She studies the page as if it were the Gospel. After a long time she says, "Irma, what a find."

Mr. Cavanaugh clears his throat. "She tell you how I came upon 'em?"

"At the pawn shop, wasn't it? Amazing. How good of you to understand their value, Mr. Cavanaugh." She and Charles and Irma turn through the first issue, pointing out ads that seem funny now, reading bits that catch their eyes. "Put the newspapers and these files together with the diaries I have, we'd have a book, wouldn't we? As Grace Paley would put it, we might save Lizzie Dunbar's life."

Mr. Cavanaugh can't imagine such a collaboration, but stranger things have happened, he knows.

"Isn't it miraculous," Dr. Jane says finally, "that they survived at all? Didn't you say this file came through the flood? They're deteriorating badly though, aren't they?"

Mr. Cavanaugh has to admit that they are.

"We must get them microfilmed. And the originals should be in the Archives."

Mr. Cavanaugh knows this, too, but just hearing the words makes his heart fall. He looks sadly at his treasure.

"We'll get a microfilm of the whole thing for the college, and you can come read anytime." Mr. Cavanaugh nods, but he knows it won't be the same, the delicious secrecy, the sense of discovery as he holds the papers themselves in his hands.

"The Mississippi Historical Society meets in Jackson next month," Dr. Jane says. "We could all go down, and Mr. Cavanaugh could present this wonderful gift to the Archives, and then we could celebrate. You'll be giving Lizzie Dunbar back to the world."

Put that way, his loss doesn't seem quite so bad.

"Irma," Dr. Jane goes on, "I want to talk to you about a few revisions on your paper. I don't think you realize how good it is. With some work, I'm sure you can get it published."

Mr. Cavanaugh, to his credit, feels no pangs of jealousy but beams with pride.

Kate
1968

A brief obituary from the Jackson paper, no more than three inches of type, falls out of a letter from my oldest daughter. Nothing in the article about a passion for life that animated every cell of her, about the enormity of her hopes and dreams, about her capacity for love and loyalty. Pitifully insufficient to sum up the life of Lizzie Dunbar. But could I write it any better, could I find words to explain her?

"Such a waste," I sobbed to Mama on the telephone when she called to tell me of Lizzie's breakdown a lifetime ago. "She has so much to offer."

We persisted in believing she would soon be well, though we had no basis for thinking so, other than our memories of Lizzie. We wrote her letters, which I later learned were never delivered, and once in Jackson I tried to go and see her but got no further than her kindly but adamant doctor in the administration building. "If you are her friend," he said, "I'm sure you would not want to set her back."

Then there were my children, career, the war, Mama's death, Cliff's death, the strenuous business of living day to day. The friend of my childhood and youth faded, and if I thought of her at all it was guiltily and with a hope that she had found peace.

I have often remembered a conversation I had with Mama about Lizzie once on a visit back to the Hollies. What went wrong? What was the matter with her? Could we have helped her? Everyone who knew Lizzie's story had different answers.

Mama had deep regrets concerning Lizzie, as if she had personally failed her.

"You know, Kate," she said this day as we sat at the kitchen table shelling peas for supper. "I was remembering Lizzie Dunbar the other day, and it occurred to me that we do her a disservice by dwelling on her failure. We should instead remember what she did."

"Yes, I suppose," I said absently, as the peas fell through my fingers into the pan.

"We can't judge the worth of a life. That's God's job. A life is like a current in the river. Who can know what other lives it touches and how it contributes to the flow?"

"Some currents are dammed almost at the source, though," I said, "by one obstacle or another."

"So it seems to us," she said, "but I believe in a larger picture." She smiled as she said this.

I remember her smile now, and her words, as I hold this clipping that fits into the palm of my hand.